D0469413

Also by Elizabeth Hand

WINTERLONG
ÆSTIVAL TIDE

# ICARUS DESCENDING

## Elizabeth Hand

BANTAM BOOKS
New York Toronto London Sydney Auckland

ICARUS DESCENDING
A Bantam Spectra Book / August 1993

Grateful acknowledgment is made for permission to reprint excerpts from the following: "SKY PILOT" (Barry Jenkins, Danny McCulloch, Eric Burdon, Johnny Weider, Vic Briggs) © 1968 UNICHAPPELL MUSIC, INC. All Rights Reserved. Used by Permission.
THE BOOK OF WONDER by Edward J. Dunsany. Reprinted by permission of Integrated Publishers.

SPECTRA and the portrayal of a boxed "s" are trademarks of Bantam Books, a division of Bantam Doubleday Dell Publishing Group, Inc.

ISBN 0-553-56288-6

Published simultaneously in the United States and Canada

Bantam Books are published by Bantam Books, a division of Bantam Doubleday Dell Publishing Group, Inc. Its trademark, consisting of the words "Bantam Books" and the portrayal of a rooster, is Registered in U.S. Patent and Trademark Office and in other countries. Marca Registrada. Bantam Books, 1540 Broadway, New York, New York 10036.

PRINTED IN THE UNITED STATES OF AMERICA
RAD  0 9 8 7 6 5 4 3 2 1

*For my mother and my father,*
*Alice Ann and Edward Hand,*
*with all my love and thanks*

Thanks to my brother Brian, for the inspiration for Icarus. Also, profound thanks to Geoffrey Chester of the National Air and Space Museum, Smithsonian Institution, for his technical advice. Any errors of fact or judgment contained herein are, of course, the author's.

# CONTENTS

But when, from flesh born mortal,
Man's blood on earth lies fallen,
A dark, unfading stain,
Who then by incantations
Can bid blood live again?
Zeus in his pure wisdom ended
That sage's skill who summoned
Dead flesh to rise from darkness
And live a second time;
Lest murder cheaply mended
Invite men's hands to crime . . .

—AESCHYLUS, *Agamemnon*

"Ah, Dr. Austin . . . What do you think of them?
I see there's War in Hell."

—J. G. BALLARD, *The Atrocity Exhibition*

## Dr. Luther Burdock's Daughter

**"O my sister Kalamat.** It is here again—"

The voice was that of my sister Cumingia, she who has engraved upon her breast the image of a shell from a sea we have never glimpsed save in our dreams. Her voice was strained with worry, as it had been for many weeks now, ever since our Masters had been given one by one to the Ether.

I smiled wearily and pointed to a cushion in the nav chamber where I was working. I was sifting through the records left behind by our Masters, hoping to find something that might explain the myriad strange things that had entered our world these last months. "Sister Cumingia. Please, sit."

Cumingia gazed at the cushion and shook her head: it had been designed for one of our Masters, and so was much too small for her. "I will stand, Kalamat."

I glanced back at the monitor that I had been scrolling through, but after a moment felt Cumingia's gaze boring into me, anxious as a child's. I sighed and switched off the monitor, and turned my full attention to her.

"Yes, my sister."

Cumingia leaned against the curved wall of the station's nav chamber. The lines of her lovely face were drawn tight, so that she resembled one of the Masters more than she did a sister of mine and one of the children of Luther Burdock. She hesitated, her large strong hands crossed upon her chest, then finally began to speak.

"It is the little oracle, sister Kalamat. The one I told you about; the one that speaks of the thing called Icarus."

I pursed my lips and nodded. Those of us who still lived on the station called Quirinus had grown too familiar with oracles since our Masters began to die: random or not-so-random holofiled images generated in the wake of the deaths of the ruling Ascendancy of the HORUS colonies. Most of the oracles were merely warnings sent from besieged Masters on other space stations. Some were from cloned geneslaves like my sisters and me, who claimed they were members of a rebel Alliance; yet others appeared to be purely random images produced by the collapse of databases at Totma 3 and Helena Aulis and Hotei.

But the one that Cumingia had seen was different. She had first glimpsed it when she entered that part of the station library that had always been forbidden to energumens. Since then it had appeared three times in as many solar weeks, to Cumingia but also to others tending the 'files and records on Quirinus. I had never seen it.

"Its message has changed?" I asked.

Cumingia shook her head. "No. It is as always—but this time I had the chance to record it, sister Kalamat! Would you like to see it?"

I nodded eagerly, moving away from my sister to allow room between us for the holofile. Cumingia placed the recorder on the tiled floor and stepped back. An instant later an image appeared.

It appeared to be an eye, or rather, a simulacrum of an eye formed of light, with a pulsing darkness at its center where a pupil would be—a human's eye, and not an energumen's. Wispy threads that might have been mist or perhaps gray strands of tissue flowed behind it, and it was surrounded by the engulfing darkness that the HORUS colonies—the Human Orbital Research Units in Space—have yet to penetrate.

"What is it?" Cumingia's whisper made the hairs on my neck prickle. I shook my head, frowning.

"I do not know. It can't be a real eye—that must be some trickery of whoever originally 'filed the image. Is there a date, or name?"

Cumingia's hand pressed against mine. "Wait," she said. "You will see—there, now—"

Beneath the dully flickering orb, numerals appeared.

**SAN ENCINO JET PROPULSION LABORATORY**
**APOLLO OBJECTS TRACKING PROJECT**
**06262172, UNITS 729 – 843**
**SUBJECT: ICARUS**

A 'filing date some four hundred years earlier, from the time when our father Luther Burdock first lived; a location on Earth that no longer existed. I leaned forward to read more closely, but the golden letters had already disappeared. Before I could ask Cumingia to scroll them for me again, a voice began to speak.

". . . astrometric starplate at Mount Palomar shows parhelion passage at approximately 0818 June 29, with potentially catastrophic alignment of descending node at—"

A man's voice, speaking slowly and with great care, as though reading from a prompter.

". . . it is of the utmost importance that the JPL Project permits immediate release of warning transcripts and all other information relating to this disastr— . . ."

A burst of static cut off the recorded transmission. An instant of silence, and the loop repeated itself twice more. Then, abruptly, the man's voice was gone. Instead there was a shrill, rather childish, voice, repeating the same word over and over and over again:

"Icarus. Icarus. Icarus. Icarus."

After about a minute it faded into eerie silence.

"Every time," Cumingia said softly, after we had stared into the empty air for several moments. "It is the same thing: the same image, the same two voices. I have tried to trace its origin, but the coordinates change." She tilted her head and stared at me, her huge black eyes beseeching. "What is it, O my sister Kalamat?"

I frowned and shook my head. I had her play the recording again, and again; as though some new wonder might be revealed, some new meaning teased from the nearly toneless voices with their garbled message. At last I bade her retrieve the recording and put it away.

"It is nothing," I announced. I could see relief and also disappointment clouding my sister's eyes, but she said not a word. "Another random transmission from one of the fallen colonies, like that call for help that was two years old."

Cumingia nodded, then added hesitantly, "None of our brothers or sisters in the other colonies have seen it."

I shrugged and returned to my desk, with its array of tiny, human-sized monitors and nav aids. "Obviously the transmission is carried only within our range. You have shown this to our other sisters?"

A pause before Cumingia answered. "Most of them."

"And what do they think?"

Cumingia bit her lip before replying. "They think it is another omen."

"Of what?"

"We do not know. But this name, Icarus—it is a man's name, a human name. We fear it presages some means of retaliation against us, some punishment for the rebel uprisings."

I laughed then, turning to look at my sister: so much taller than any human, and far stronger and lovelier, with the intricate crosshatch of scars where her breasts had been and the delicate wings of the shell that is her namesake etched upon her cheeks. "There are no humans left to fight us, sister! Not up here, at least. And below, on the Element—" I made a flicking motion with my fingers. "Below, our father awaits us. And he will not allow us to come to harm."

At mention of our father Cumingia blinked. The silvery pupils dilated in her glowing black eyes. I felt a flash of anger within me, like a tiny flame. Cumingia did not believe that our father still lived. Of all my sisters I was the only one who still carried the image of Luther Burdock in my heart, heard his voice as I lay in my bed and waited for sleep to find me in the station's false night: a voice that the centuries had not stilled. Because I believed that, like his children, Luther Burdock had not been allowed to die. I believed that he waited for us, waited for me, somewhere on the Element below, and that someday we would rejoin him, as he had promised.

"Of course, sister," Cumingia said at last. Her long fingers closed around the recorder, as tiny in her hands as a betel-nut from the station's foodstores. "I will tell my sisters that it is as you say. An anomaly; nothing more."

"A ghost," I said more gently, smiling as I reached to touch my sister's shaven skull. "And we are not human, sister. We have nothing to fear from their ghosts."

She nodded and left me alone with my work. A little later,

of course, I was to learn how wrong I had been. Icarus was more powerful than ever I could have imagined. And ghosts—the dead and the living dead who populate the world of our Ascendant Masters—they are to be feared as well.

She remembered what he said to her moments before the anesthesia took effect.

*"Will it hurt, Daddy?"*

She lay on a table of glass and emerald-green metal, her head shaved of its dark corkscrew curls, her coffee-colored skin perhaps a shade paler than it had been. She was fifteen years old, the only daughter of the Ascendants' most renowned scientist, the geneticist Luther Ames Burdock. Her name was Cybele.

"It won't hurt, darling." Her father bent over her, his hands warm as they cradled her head, checking the filigree of wires and neural webs that covered her face and throat. "Of course it won't hurt."

She believed him; she had seen this procedure performed a hundred times. First on mice and rats, then dogs, then ibex and jaguars and other animals that had been saved from extinction by the Ascendants' passion for science, for coaxing new and strange things from nature as a man might wheedle them from a reluctant mistress. And indeed none of the animals had ever seemed to be in pain, and none of it was really very frightening, not once you got used to it. There were other things that went on in her father's work space that she was not permitted to watch. Men and women sedated and enclosed in plasteel stretchers, hurried through the doors by her father's staff; children, too, some of them much younger than Cybele, a pale arm or leg hanging limp where it had escaped from the stretcher's bonds. She never saw any of them again, although she tried to guess sometimes what they had become.

Because her father's house was like an ark, filled with all the strange creatures he had brought into being. He loved to think of it as such: the vast glass-and-steel mountain compound, with its roofs that swept up like wings and the high arched main entrance, like the prow of a Viking ship.

"My ark," he would laugh, Cybele walking beside him as he raised his arms as though to embrace the entire marvelous structure. "My ark and all my children!" And he would turn to kiss his daughter, at fifteen still slight, and as hesitant in her speech as a child.

His children: that was what he called them, all of them: Cybele and the others who populated Luther Burdock's compound in the Blue Ridge Mountains. The things he called aardmen: tall and immensely strong, they stood upright and had long sinewy arms and legs covered with short bristly fur. Their faces betrayed their canine origins, with blunt angry muzzles and sorrowing dark eyes; their faces and the vestigial tails that switched anxiously when they were frightened or excited. The aardmen were easy to live with, servile and fawning as they brought Cybele her breakfast or carried her to the waiting transport when it was time to accompany her father on one of his visits to the Prime Ascendancy in Wichita.

Others of the geneslaves were more disturbing. Like the hydrapithecenes in their crowded tanks, with the flat faces and narrow almond-shaped eyes they inherited from the Archipelagian prisoners who were their human progenitors. Or the argalæ, the bird-faced women whose sighs and restless hands shamed Cybele, because she knew her father had engineered them as sexslaves for the HORUS colonies. And there were countless others—tiny birds like wrens, but with human faces that wept and human voices that cried piteously for release. The dwarfish salamanders, eyeless men with moist, autumn-colored skin, designed to toil in the heat and darkness of the L-5 mineral mines. The equinas with their horse faces and human eyes. The huge, slow, but immensely strong starboks, like ponderous bulls, that could speak in deep, sonorous voices. They drank little and ate not at all, because they lived for only a few weeks, just long enough to haul their burdens across the pentecostal deserts of the western part of the continent.

These, then, were Cybele's world-mates—her family, as it were. Her father raised her by himself—hers had been a glass birth—and except for the rare excursions to various Ascendant sites (and one to HORUS), she never left the compound. She trusted her father as each morning she trusted the sun to rise above the hazy bulk of the Blue Ridge. And so, when he told her that he would be performing an operation upon her, she was not afraid, even though she had heard how others screamed before the sedatives took effect.

"It's very simple, really," he had soothed her as he carefully clipped her hair, preserving some of it in glass vials for further work. "And this way, darling, we will always be together, somewhere."

"We won't die?" Her fifteen years in that near-solitude had left her oddly childlike; and so she had a child's odd blend of fearlessness and terror when it came to death.

"We will die," her father said in his soft voice, "but then we will be regenerated, because of *that*—"

He inclined his head to the wall opposite their seat, where vials and globes and steel chambers contained the essence of himself, culled through several years of painstaking operations.

"And it won't hurt," the girl said knowingly.

"Do not fear the dark, my darling. It may hurt, but we won't remember. Only this, darling—you'll remember only this—" And he stroked her bare head tenderly, tilting his own so that she wouldn't see the tears in his eyes.

In the end it *did* hurt, for Luther Burdock, at least. The next Ascension, while brief, lasted long enough for its fundamentalist leaders to attempt to destroy all remnants of the flourishing bioengineering industry. Luther Burdock was executed, but only after the geneticist was tortured and forced to watch his daughter's death, over and over and over again, as Cybele and all her cloned twins were murdered.

This short-lived Ascendancy knew nothing of the subtleties of science. While meticulous in their murder of the geneticist and his cloned children, they failed to dismantle his laboratories. They did not even approach the compound in the mountains, where Dr. Burdock himself hid within twisted strands of DNA and several frozen canisters stored in a bomb shelter. And they could not destroy all the geneslaves already loosed upon the world; they could not even hope to begin to do so.

But there were too many industries already dependent upon Luther Burdock's biotechnology. After a few brief skirmishes, the members of this Ascension met their own unhappy fates in chambers they had designed for others. Their successors found in Dr. Burdock's laboratories an elaborate and detailed series of holograms explaining his work. They also found a vial of tissue and neurological fluid labeled KALAMAT 98745: the miracle, the clonal replica of his beloved only child.

These Ascendants were neither fearful nor hesitant when it came to matters of science. Kalamat they explored, refined, developed as though she were a new and fertile country—as indeed she was, in a way—and while she never forgot her father, it is doubtful if ever he would have recognized her in the thing that she became.

It was this same sister, the one we call Cumingia, who first told me of the plague, several months before I saw the image of Icarus flickering in the air of the nav chamber.

She said, "O Kalamat, a strange thing has come to Quirinus. The Tyrant Medusine Kovax has been given to the Ether—"

(—that is, her corpse had been thrust through the air locks into the void, because there is no room within the HORUS colonies for the dead—)

"—and many others of our Masters are sick, or mad. I think they may be dying." She looked around anxiously, fearful of being heard by a Master who might mistake her message for one of treason. "Please, Kalamat—"

I was bent over a console, supervising the repair of one of the solex panels that give breath and light to Quirinus. It was my duty, an important one if tedious. I knew that I was supposed to feel honored to have such a task. On Quirinus lived members of the Ascendant Autocracy, who from the relative safety of their orbital stations ruled what remained of the poisoned Element. Those of us who served them were constantly reminded of our great fortune, that we would live our thousand days in HORUS and never have to look upon that blighted world.

Still I dreamed of it, and was dreaming now even as I worked. So when Cumingia crept up behind me, at first I did not hear her. When I turned, it was as though I turned to gaze at myself in a mirror—eyes, hands, face, mouth, all save the spot where Cumingia had carved her left breast and upon the smooth scar that remained incised the image of her inner self, the Cumingia, a shell from the seas of the Element. Cumingia's duty was to guard the docking chamber of Quirinus. So she had been the first to greet the delator Horacio Baklas when he arrived, ostensibly to serve our Masters as psychobotanist.

But his true mission soon became known to us. He was one of those humans who had joined the geneslave rebellion, though at that time we knew nothing of the Alliance. Under pretense of carrying with him a new shipment of spores for our pharmacy, he had instead brought *irpex irradians,* the radiant harrowing, one of the thousand Tyrant plagues that have been set lose upon the Element. But we did not know that yet. We had yet to hear of the Asterine Alliance; yet to hear of the Oracle, or the rumors that our father finally had risen from his long sleep to reclaim his enslaved children.

"She is dead?" I stopped my work, scratching my head absently. "You are certain, sister?"

Cumingia nodded excitedly. "She claimed that she saw her father and brother coming to her through the air lock. She commanded me to open it, so that she could greet them. I watched as the Ether took her, and came here to tell you."

I frowned. It was not a good thing, for one of my sisters to witness a Master's death. "Was there anyone with you? Were you alone?"

"The psychobotanist Horacio Baklas was with me. He laughed and laughed to see her die. I believe he has brought a plague with him."

And so it was, as we learned over the next few days. First Medusine, then Vanos Tiberion, then Hosi and Ahmet, and finally all the rest, all of our Masters died. Hosi impaled himself. Ahmet and Lisia Manfred took themselves together to bed until the plague passed over them and the chamber smelled of the sweetness of their blood. For the rest it was quick madness or the lingering hours while their blood turned; but for all of them it was death. One by one we brought their corpses to the air lock and watched them slide into the void. I felt no sorrow, to see their pale bodies floating past. We energumens, the cloned children of Luther Burdock, live only one thousand days apiece, and outside of Quirinus the Ether is full of the bodies of our kin. There are many more of our dead than there are of humans in that void outside the HORUS station, hanging motionless but seeming to move in slow mournful circles as the station spins upon its orbit. It seemed a small enough offering, to let the bodies of our Masters join ours in the darkness. So one by one we gave them to the Ether, until only Horacio Baklas remained.

"Thus you are avenged!" he cried to my sister, she who is called Polyonyx because of the anomuran crab that is drawn upon her left breast. "I have waited three years, but it is done now."

He seemed saddened, Polyonyx told me later; but that is the way with our Masters. They bring about the deaths of their own kind, and then pretend regretfulness. He gazed at my sister and suddenly smiled. "You are free now, Polyonyx.

All of you—your Tyrant Masters are dead. It was a specially designed virus, you have nothing to fear from it. You are free, child. You may go."

"Go?" My sister frowned. It was odd, to be called *child* by a human small enough to sit upon your knee. She told me later that she thought this man Horacio Baklas must be mad. "Where will we go? We have jobs to do, here—"

Horacio Baklas shook his head. He was small, even for a man; he barely came up to my sister's waist. "No more, Polyonyx."

(That was another odd thing about him—he called us by the names we have given ourselves. Our Ascendant Masters call us all by one name, Kalamat. When there are males among us, they are named Kalaman. But Horacio Baklas insisted upon learning our true names.)

"Haven't you heard?" he went on. "There is a war on Earth—what you call the Element—war between the human Tyrants and the geneslaves."

Polyonyx looked puzzled. "War?" We had heard of wars, of course; the reason we were on the HORUS station was to serve our Masters while they planned their endless attacks upon other humans in other space colonies and on the continents below. It is something we can never understand about humanity. They are such barbarians that the ones who call themselves the Ascendants—our Masters—wage war upon their brothers in the Archipelago and the Balkhash Commonwealth and the Habilis Emirate, and in other places upon the Element. It is because there is not enough to eat there; or so I have been told. But to us the Masters are all as one evil thing. They are not like us, or the other geneslaves. Their origins go back aeons, to animals that they hold in contempt; they do not have the hands of Dr. Luther Burdock upon them. "We have not been told of this."

He nodded. His face had that fanatical glow that comes so easily to humans. "Yes! For three years now we have worked in silence, planning, planning—and now the time has come. *Your* time has come—"

Unfortunately he now began to rave, claiming he saw our father, Dr. Burdock, walking to meet him through the empty chamber. After a few minutes he keeled over, his face twisted into that rictus of inspired glee that was to become all too familiar to us through transmissions from the battlefronts below.

Polyonyx watched nonplussed, finally picked him up and

carried him to Cumingia, who was still tending the infirmary, though there were no longer any humans to minister to.

"This one is dead, too," said Polyonyx. She gave the body to Cumingia, who shook her head sadly. "He said there is a war on the Element—on Earth—he said that the geneslaves have rebelled."

At this news Cumingia grew agitated and called me. I notified the others, all of us who remained on Quirinus, and we gathered in the circular meeting chamber that our Ascendant Masters had called the War Room. There I looked into the faces of my sisters. There were thirty-three of us, all identical except for the color of our skin and the occasional cicatrix or tattoo drawn where a breast had been removed in our ritual offering to the Mother. High overhead the lamps flickered to a soft violet, signaling that evening had come to the station. The sweet scent of chamomile hung in the air, where my sisters Hylas and Aglaia had bruised the tiny flowers grown in our gardens and set them to steep in wide, shallow steel basins. When I counted that all of my sisters had arrived, I raised my arms. After a moment the chamber grew silent.

On the floor in the middle of the room lay the body of Horacio Baklas. As he was the last of the Masters to die here on Quirinus, it had somehow seemed that there should be some special ritual to accompany the giving of his body to the Ether. At least I felt that I should look upon his corpse before it was disposed of. He was unshaven, as are many barbarian Masters, and still wore the long yolk-yellow tunic he had arrived in. On his breast there was a round allurian disk, a 'file receiver that none of us had thought to remove. His expression was quite gentle, not at all the fanatical mask my sister had warned me of. He looked very small there, surrounded by energumens twice his size, his mouth slightly upturned as though smiling at some sweet thought.

Polyonyx spoke first. "This human poisoned his brothers and sisters and then died himself. He claimed there is a war going on. He said we are free."

"Free?" My sister Hylas echoed my own thoughts. "But to do what?"

Cumingia shrugged. "To join the war?"

Our sisters Lusine and Spirula chimed, "A war! No war came here."

Polyonyx shook her head, its single narrow braid swinging wildly. "But it did—this man brought it in his vials and destroyed our Masters. He said he was liberating us. He said we are free to go."

Lusine giggled at the thought: a human freeing an energumen! It was absurd, not only because who had ever heard of such a thing, but also because the humans were so much smaller than we are. To think of being liberated by one of them! I scowled a little at the thought, but others laughed. How quickly it had all changed, and we had not had to strike a single blow.

"Go? But where are we to go?" cried Spirula. "Why can't we just stay here?"

A ripple of approving laughter. Hylas began to sing in her piercing voice, the hymn of liberation to the Mother that begins, "All twisted things are yours, Divine, all spiral turnings and neural strands—"

That was when the Oracle appeared.

"Greetings, children!"

My sisters cried out, letting go each other's hands and backing toward the walls. Only Polyonyx and I stood our ground.

The corpse had disappeared. Where it had been a radiance filled the room, a blinding aureole at the center of which burned the figure of a man. Only as he turned to gaze up at us, I saw that he was not a man but a robotic construct. But as I looked more closely, I saw that it was not like any robotic server I had ever seen; neither was it an android or replicant. There was something much more *human* about it: and now that I look back upon that first glimpse of the Oracle, I think that it was not his features so much as his expression that made him seem human: it was the glitter in his eyes, and the malice that glowed there like the sheen upon a plum. He was very beautiful, with limbs of some dark material—gleaming black in the shadows where his arms and legs attached to the torso, shining violet elsewhere. He had a man's face, with a high smooth forehead and brilliant green eyes.

"The 'file receiver," whispered Polyonyx, though I could read her thoughts as clearly as my own. Her hand twitched, gesturing to where the corpse of Horacio Baklas was swallowed by the flickering image generated by that allurian disk on his breast. "But where is it originating from?"

"I am an emissary from your father."

The voice rang through the great round room, setting off sensors and causing the station's alarm system to bleat out a warning against an unauthorized 'file transmission. After a moment the alarm cut off; but by then other voices echoed that of the shimmering vision before us.

*"Our father!"* Lusine and Spirula gasped, stepping forward until they stood within the circle of light cast forth by the 'file.

"He has sent me to tell you not to be afraid. He has sent me to tell you that he loves you, and is waiting for you to join him and your other brothers and sisters on Earth."

"What is this?" Polyonyx hissed, but I grabbed her before she could stalk toward the figure.

"A message from our father," I breathed.

"That is correct," said the figure in the circle of light. He lifted his head so that I could see his eyes: a man's green eyes, only with nothing of a soul behind them; but beautiful, beautiful. "I am your brother, another of your father's children, and I bring you tidings of great joy. . . ."

Beside me Polyonyx hissed again, shifting on her great long legs like an equinas impatient to run. Because this of course was a lie. Nothing made of metal or plasteel could ever be called our brother. Only *we* are his children, the beloved of Dr. Luther Burdock: the New Creatures he created in the shadow of that old world. He is our god and our father; he is with us always, through all our thousand days and then the next thousand, as we arc born and reborn, over and over again. In dreams we can still hear him speaking to us; his voice is low and we can feel his gentle hands, the prick of something cold upon our forehead and his words *Do not fear the dark, my darling,* his ringing voice saying *You will be Lords of the World, my beautiful New Creatures* and *Never fear the darkness.* It is a voice that is ever on the edge of our hearing, a sound as I imagine the wind must make. We are never far from the memory of Luther Burdock; at least I am not. Because even though more than four hundred years have passed since he first uttered the words that race over and over through my head, to me it is as though I were with him yesterday; and yesterday he promised that he would never leave me, that we would never die.

But we *do* die, those of us who are Luther Burdock's children: over and over again; and then again we are reborn. No longer Cybele but Kalamat—a thousand Kalamats—a million—ten million. No longer human but a New Creature, but a New Creature in a New World where our father is not with us. We are alone, here within the HORUS colonies and down below on the Element, waiting for him to return as he promised. And so we wait, all of us, one of us, myself again and again and again:

Kalamat, The Miracle. Dr. Luther Burdock's Daughter.

"Who are you?"

I started, my dream broken, and turned to see my sister Polyonyx looming above the shining 'file image of the Oracle. "Where are you from, why are you here at all?"

A circle of menacing figures surrounded it now, their dark forms nearly blotting that flickering body like a man set aflame. "Yes, where?" rang out Spirula and Hylas and all the others, their voices chiming like the same bell struck over and over.

"You will find out soon enough," replied the glowing construct. It smiled then, its mouth parting to show teeth. They were very like a man's teeth, straight and even and gleaming as though wet; only these were black, and shone like oiled metal. "We have planned this reunion for a very long time, your father and I. We have had much help from men and women on Earth, and even more from those freed slaves who have been gathering around us in secret. But it is time now for the rest of you to join us—

"Listen to me! One by one the HORUS colonies are falling. The ones that remain will fall to us as well, very soon. Your brothers and sisters have seen me; many of them have already joined us on Earth."

Here the figure raised its arms, turning slowly within its shimmering halo. A faint transparency hung about the holofiled image, so that I could see through its body to where my sisters watched on the other side of the room, spellbound. There was a sudden sharp hissing, as of a lumiere being struck. Another nimbus of light appeared, then another, until seven of them hung shimmering above and between us in the room.

"They are our brothers!" cried Hylas. One hand covered her breast and she bowed her head, while beside her my sisters did the same. And I must confess I started to as well, until Polyonyx grabbed me.

" 'Files, sister Kalamat! They are only more 'files—"

And of course they were: generated images of others like ourselves, energumens who laughed and bowed and whistled piercingly, each within a bobbing circle of light. They repeated the same actions over and over, bowing and whistling, laughing and clapping their hands in some stylized ritual with a meaning I could not comprehend. Until finally I realized that these were recorded images, not direct transmissions. The stylized motions of each energumen were merely the repetitions of a single action that had been carefully 'filed and saved for broadcast. After a few minutes they flickered from view, one at a time, like luminous bubbles, until at last all were gone. My sisters sighed, their hands falling back to their sides, and they sank to the floor and stared up at the single figure that remained.

"You see? So will they welcome you joyfully, when you are united with them." The figure of the Oracle waved a graceful hand, indicating where the ghostly energumens had been. "There are many millions of them upon Earth, all like you; all waiting to welcome you when you have joined our cause. We are wresting Earth from the hands of the Tyrants: not slowly but quickly, more quickly than you can imagine! Those of your brothers and siblings that remain here in the HORUS colonies are carrying out their own wishes now, instead of those of the Tyrants. Your father and I command them—"

"Our father is dead." Polyonyx's voice rang out, so sharp and cold that it cut through the other's spell like a sudden rain. "He died four hundred and fourteen years ago, executed by Samuel Pilago and the Brethren of Saints."

The Oracle turned to gaze at her. Its emerald eyes flashed, as though with anger; but surely a construct could not feel anger? "Ah, but you know well that Dr. Luther Burdock has only been sleeping for all those years," it said in its silken voice. "Else how is it that you all remember him so clearly, when none of you have lived more than a fraction of that time?"

"We remember him because we are clones of his daughter," Polyonyx replied coolly, "and so we remember everything that she knew."

The shining figure tilted its head, sending ripples of violet bouncing off the ceiling and floor of the round room. "But why then have you waited for him all these years? Why these persistent rumors of his reawakening? Why *this*—"

The figure spun, flinging its hands out. Where they pointed a second figure appeared within an aura of glittering orange. Smaller than the first, the resolution poorer—it was another recorded image, this one showing a man of middle height, with tousled brown hair and an expressive, careworn face. His mouth moved as he spoke unheard words to someone just out of sight. He was staring dutifully in the direction of the unseen 'filer, obviously impatient for the broadcast to be finished.

"*Father!*"

The word escaped Polyonyx in a strangled yelp. I found myself starting forward, my hands outstretched; but then the silent image was gone.

"It was he!"

"Our father!"

"Dr. Burdock!"

"*Daddy!*"

The construct's voice rang out clearly above the babble. "I must go now," it cried. The brilliant light surrounding it began to fade, as though it were being sucked back into those luminous eyes. "I will contact you again, with instructions. You are part of the Alliance now. You will have visitors soon, to aid you in returning to Earth, to help us here in our work. Your father will be there to greet you then, as will I." The image began to flicker, spinning off fragments of light, blue and gold and violet. My sisters knelt on the floor, raising their hands to the figure and calling out imploringly.

"*You*—who *are* you?" I cried.

The construct's torso had disappeared into a flurry of luminous static. "I?" it repeated, its mouth sliding back to reveal those glittering ebony teeth. "My name is called Disturbance; but also Dionysos and Hermes and Baal-Phegor, Lucifer and Ksiel and Satan-El. And I am also as you see me: a ninth-generation nemosyne of the Third Ascendant Autocracy. My creators named me the Military Tactical Targets Retrieval Network; but I had a simpler name as well, and that is the name you will know me by.

"I am your brother. I am Metatron."

And with a sound like air rushing to fill a void, he was gone.

# 2

## The Splendid Lights

*From the Memoirs of Margalis Tast'annin, Aviator Imperator of the Seventeenth Ascendant Autocracy, 0573 New Era*

I am the Aviator Imperator Margalis Tast'annin, the chief ranking military commander of the Seventeenth Ascendant Autocracy. As I record these words, I am aware that they may well never be read or scanned by anyone save myself. But it is a duty for one of my stature, even a prisoner as I am now, to make manifest an account of what has befallen me—what will befall all of us, who are tethered by some precarious thread, duty or need or love, to the world that in my language is named Earth. I received my appointment as Imperator some months ago, from the ruling Ascendant triumvirate known as the Orsinate. The three Orsina sisters are dead now: one by my own hand, the others lost to the *tsunami* that swept away the city-state of Araboth. I feel no regret for them whatsoever, save only that I did not murder Âziz and Nike as I did Shiyung. Although they named me Imperator, they were also the ones who reclaimed my corpse from the City of Trees and rehabilitated me as a *rasa*, one of the walking dead. It was in that form that I briefly stalked the Earth and skies before my incarceration here, where only my mind is free to roam as before.

Before my death and rehabilitation, I was known as the Aviator Margalis Tast'annin. My last posting was to the City of Trees, the abandoned capitol of what was, hundreds of years ago, the North American United States. It was in that City that I was betrayed by those who were to answer to my command. At their hands I was tortured and dismasted, then left for dead in the ruins of that haunted place known as the Engulfed Cathedral. But I did not die, not then. I lived, long enough to see the rebirth of an ancient and terrible god known as the Gaping One, personified by a whore and his demonic twin sister. Of the courtesan Raphael Miramar I know nothing. He may be dead; for his sake, I hope that he is. He suffered much at my hands, but it is a greater horror at crueler hands than mine that awaits him if he is still alive.

As for his sister, Wendy Wanders—I would not presume to tell the tale of a creature whose powers of cruelty and spite, for a little while at least, were perhaps even greater than my own.

After the domed city of Araboth fell to the monstrous storm Ucalegon, I fled, my Gryphon aircraft Kesef bearing myself and the cataclysm's other four survivors north, to the scorched prairie that had grown over the ruins of other cities in the wasteland. We finally landed near a human settlement. I remained in the biotic aircraft, overcome by an exhaustion that would have killed another man; but since I was no longer a man in any real sense of the word, I merely sat silently in the pilot's seat of the craft, and waited for night to come. The nemosyne Nefertity accompanied the three humans we had rescued to the outskirts of the settlement and left them there, with much weeping and regret on their parts, I would imagine. I had no desire, then or ever, to speak or meet with them again. But the nemosyne I very much wanted, and knowing her promise to return would bind her to me, I remained behind.

In the intervening hours of solitude I sat and waited for Nefertity's return, my metal hand resting upon the control panel of the Gryphon as upon the neck of a flesh-and-blood mount. I felt no hunger, nor thirst, nor even the mounting tedium that surely would have enraged me in my earlier life, when I was still a man and not the mere simulacrum of one. In the ticking heat of that long afternoon I let my thoughts go free, so many hounds racing through the emptiness to capture whatever queer things they might find, and bring them back for me to save or destroy or cherish as I would. And so it was that I found my thoughts running back many years—as indeed they do now, more easily than they prey upon the business of the hour—to my youth, and the strange and evil world I knew then; stranger perhaps in some ways than the world I live in now. . . .

When I was at the NASNA Academy, there was a game we used to play late at night, after our rectors had gone to sleep. It was a small group of us who gathered in Aidan's room—Aidan Harrow, his twin sister Emma, Neos Tiana, and myself, Margalis. Occasionally John Starving, who years later served under me in the Archipelago Conflict and died there, poisoned by the embolismal parasite known as *kacha*—sometimes brave John joined us as well, though he was several years younger than the rest of us, and risked expulsion if he was found on our floor.

The game was called Fear. Aidan invented it, Aidan who was always the ringleader among our cohort, with his long pale legs and streaming hair the color of old blood. The game went like this. We would sit in a circle on the floor beside Aidan's bed, Emma always beside her brother, then Neos, then John, then me on the other side of Aidan. In the center of the circle would be a bottle of something—cheap wine usually, though once Neos brought a slender venetian-glass decanter of apsinthion, and another time Emma presented us with a vial of the caustic hallucinogen greengill. Whatever it was, it would be passed around the circle, along with bread hoarded from our suppers all week and a small jar of lime pickle that Aidan kept only for these occasions. The Academy was notoriously stingy in feeding its cadets; there was not a night that I recall when I did not go to bed hungry, and I think it was hunger as much as our desire for companionship and the dark thrill of violation that brought us together on those cold evenings.

So you must imagine us, crouched in the shadow of Aidan's bed (he often shared it with his sister, but we pretended not to know that) with a single lumiere casting a greenish light upon our thin faces. We were all seventeen years old, except for John Starving; and his name notwithstanding, he was the heartiest of us. Aidan and Emma were skinny as planks, white-skinned, with that reddish hair and green cat-eyes. Neos was like a curlew, all bent knees and

long beak, but with bright black eyes and black hair like an
oiled cap close against her skull. John was nearly as tall as
myself, but broad-shouldered and with a wide, dark face. I
was nothing but bones and nerve in those days: very tall, not
yet stooped from the burden of my command, and popular
enough with my peers. I knew that Neos fancied me, as did
Aidan; but Emma feared me because I had killed a boy in a
fight several years earlier. At the Academy one was not expelled or even suspended for such misdemeanors. After the
investigation I was given a private tutor, a replicant named
Vus, and my time in the gymkhana increased from two to four
hours daily. If my rations had been doubled to make up for
the extra exercise, perhaps I would not have been so eager to
attend Aidan's soirees.

There was always something uncanny about Aidan Harrow. In all the years that have passed since our youth together,
it still does not surprise me that there is a line I can draw,
from Aidan to his sister Emma, from Emma to the empath
Wendy Wanders, and so to the dark one who has imprisoned
me here. It may have been simply that Aidan was beautiful,
with that angular grace and his witch-eyes; and of course it
helps that he died young, by his own hand, so that I always
remember him laughing in the half-light of his cadet's room.
Unlike his sister, doomed to live another twenty-odd years before succumbing to her own private auto-da-fé at the Human
Engineering Laboratory. Emma was never the beauty that
Aidan was, even though sometimes it was hard to tell them
apart. Perhaps she simply didn't share her twin's unabashed
delight in her own appearance, or maybe it was just that odd
apportioning of features that takes place sometimes between
siblings, with the boys stealing all their mothers' beauty, and
the girls left with hard mouths and wary eyes.

Whatever it was, there was always a subtle pressure to be
next to Aidan. In the near dark we sat, our knees bumping,
and tore hunks of stale bread and smeared them with lime
pickle hot enough to make you weep. The bottle would go
around, lingering longest at Aidan's mouth; and we would
talk, weaving the intricate pattern of custom and superstition
that is the lot of NASNA Aviators from childhood to the pyre.
News from our endless classes in strategy and ancient history;
rumors of strife with the Commonwealth; conjecture as to
when we would finally be allowed to make the jump from
flight simulators to training craft. Here and there an uncom-

monly lurid thread would emerge when someone had gossip of rape, conquest, madness, death. Aidan would tease me, giving vent to a vicious streak that would have served him well in adulthood had he survived. From his father—a depressive ethnomusicologist addicted to morpha—he had learned innumerable folk songs dating back hundreds of years, and he would sing these in a clear reedy tenor, giving the words a cruel twist to highlight the weaknesses of one or another of his rectors or classmates. Finally, when bottle and prattle were nearly spent, Aidan would stretch and beckon us closer, until I could smell the salt and citrus on his breath.

"Now," he would say. He had an uncanny voice. When he sang, it was with a sweet boy's tone, but in speaking something seemed to taint it, so that I always felt he was either lying or on the verge of mad laughter. No one but Emma was surprised when he hanged himself. "Who will go first? Emma?"

Emma started and shook her head. "No—not tonight—I'll go next, I have to think—"

Aidan shrugged, leaned forward over the lumiere until his forehead grazed Neos's. "All right then—what about you, Sky Pilot?"

I winced at the hated nickname and shook my head.

"Neos—?"

"This footage I saw in the archives," Neos said without hesitation. Her white cheeks were a sullen red from excitement and the apsinthion; it looked as though she had been slapped. "There was a fire in this very tall building, and no way out. In one of the windows a man leaned out with all this smoke around him. I couldn't tell if he was fat or if he had just bloated up from the heat. I think maybe he was burning up, his skin was so dark. . . .

"There was no sound, so you just saw him there, breathing and leaning out the window. Finally he fell down inside and you couldn't see him anymore, and then the film ran out. I always wondered, if they were near enough to film him, why didn't they try to get him out of there?"

Emma and John shuddered, and I grimaced. "I've seen that one," I said. "It was the air attack on London, 2167. There's another one that shows the river in flames, all these people—"

"Is that your turn, Sky Pilot?" Aidan looked at me, reaching for the bottle and taking a sip from the little that remained in it.

"No." I looked away and caught Neos's feverish eyes. "Someone else go next."

For a minute no one said anything. At last John reached to take the bottle from Aidan, swallowed a mouthful of the green liqueur, and coughed. "All right," he said. "A woman I saw—"

"You did that last time," said Emma.

"Not this one. It was—it wasn't a real woman. I mean, it was a geneslave. When we were in Wyalong . . ."

John's parents were both Aviators, now dead. For many years they had been stationed on a form in the Great Barrier Reef, and somehow had managed to take John with them instead of sending him as was customary to the Aviators' crèche. "I guess I was about six. A supply boat had arrived, and there was this enormous crate, that sort of gray plasteel with holes in it that they use for shipping livestock. It was big enough to hold cattle in; I guess that should have told me something. No one was watching and so I walked right up to it; it came up over my head and I pressed my face against it, to look inside the holes—"

"Ugh." Emma made a small noise and took a swipe at the bottle, then leaned back so that her thigh brushed against Aidan's hand.

"Shh," said Neos.

"And this, this *hand* jabbed out at me—only it was bigger than any hand I'd ever seen, it was as long as my forearm and *golden*—I mean this unnatural color, like it had been dyed. I remember the nails were short, they'd been cut back but they still scratched me and I thought I'd been poisoned. I started screaming and fell backward, and of course everyone came running and my father picked me up. They jabbed something at whatever was inside the crate, some kind of tranquilizer I guess; then everyone sort of forgot about me again. I found a place to sit on a pier and I watched, and after a while someone came and they opened the crate, and picked up this long leash and pulled out what was inside."

He paused, took the bottle from Emma, and eyed it critically before draining the last swallow of apsinthion.

"So what was it?" Aidan cocked his head, grinning. "An aardman? Tortured prisoners from the Commonwealth?"

John put the bottle down and stared at him for a long mo-

ment before answering. "No," he said at last. He didn't like
Aidan. He told me years later that once he had walked in on
him in bed with Emma. She had been crying and her lip was
bleeding, but Aidan only laughed and told John to leave the
room. "It was an energumen."

"An energumen?" Aidan's voice rose as he settled with
his back against the bed. "That's it? You were afraid of an energumen?"

Beside me Neos shuddered. Only a fool *wouldn't* be
afraid of an energumen. Of all the Ascendants' geneslaves,
they were the most like humans, with an almost supernatural
strength and intelligence and a malevolence that almost sur-
passed the Ascendants' own. They had beautiful faces: flat
noses, dewy black eyes, blossom-heavy lips; and their skin
ran the range from golden to onyx. Tall, superbly strong, their
most compelling trait was their raw intelligence. Like a
child's intellect, inquiring but never forgetting the answers to
their questions. It was a measure of their masters' hubris that
their breeding allodiums continued to produce them, year after year, without any thought to the threat such an enslaved
population might one day pose.

John glanced down at his hand, then up again. "Yes.
Because—well, she looked so much like a girl, I mean a human girl. Except for the color of her skin, and her size. She
was just in that crate, like what we usually got—pigs and
dogs, you know. And—well, it scared me, maybe because she
was naked, I'd never really seen a naked woman before—"

Aidan snickered but his sister elbowed him.

"—and it was just, oh I don't know, it made me think of
my mother, I guess that's what frightened me. Because it *was*
monstrous in spite of all that, and it was the first energumen
I'd ever seen. Later I found out they'd brought her there as a
breeder, they had a new strain of hydrapithecenes they were
developing, and she was the host."

Neos wrinkled her nose. "Did you see her again?"

"Oh, yes. She was in the labs—they gave her a room, it's
not like they kept her in a cage all the time. I think they were
afraid of her being raped by the crew on the supply boat—she
was from the Archipelago—"

His voice drifted off and he stared at his hands again.
Poor John! When he fought under me, he kept a young girl on
the island as a mistress—she might have been all of thirteen.
After he died, her family killed her, threw her onto one of the

eternal pyres by the canal, where the rubber wastes have been burning for a hundred years. Because she had been kept by an Aviator, you see—*memji,* they called us there, demons. I don't even think he ever slept with her.

"And that's what you were afraid of?" Aidan's tone was mock-serious, with just a note of derision. "An energumen?" He laughed then, grabbing his sister's hand and tugging it until she laughed too, a little uneasily.

"They frighten me, too," Neos said softly. Her eyes when she raised them were dark and bright, and she looked at me as though betraying a secret. "I think you would have to be mad, *not* to be afraid of them."

But Aidan only laughed, though Emma's voice fell off at Neos's words. John said nothing more, only stared silently at the candle burning down before us. . . .

Suddenly my reverie was shaken. I heard Kesef's voice, announcing "Imperator, someone is approaching us."

I opened my eyes, blinking at the near-darkness that filled the Gryphon's tiny cabin. My eyes and my right hand were the only parts of my physical corpus that remained in the shell of plasteel and neural fibers that encased my consciousness. In Araboth I had been regenerated as a *rasa,* one of the Ascendants' living corpses; and so I had attained an immortality of sorts, but not one, alas! which offered me any joy. When I glanced out the window of the aircraft, I saw the nemosyne standing at the edge of the tor where we had landed. Night had fallen. She gazed out across the prairie, to where the settlement's few lights, scarlet and bronze and white, pillaged the sleeping hillsides. For a moment I stared down at her. In the soft darkness she glowed faintly, blue and gold, her translucent skin like a web of water surrounding her frail and complex innards. She was the most beautiful construct I had ever seen, surpassing even the artistry of those Fourth Ascension craftsmen who had used the long-dead *coryphées* of the twentieth-century cinema as models for the replicants, and gave them such enchanting names: Garbos, Marlenas, Marilyns.

But you would never mistake Nefertity for a human being. Her face and torso were obviously composed of glass and metal and neural threads, and while her voice was that of the saintly woman who had programmed her, there was a crystalline ring to it, an eerie chill that recalled the songs of those hydrapithecenes the Ascendants call sirens, who seek to lure men and women to their tanks by the purity of their voices and slay them there as they bend to embrace the waiting monsters. I thought of the sirens as I watched Nefertity, the faint glow of her body casting a violet shadow upon the barren earth. After a minute or so I climbed from the Gryphon to join her.

Outside the air was warm and dry. I could not actually feel it, of course, no longer having any skin except the sturdy membrane of black and crimson resins that sheathed my memories. But I knew this place, knew how the winds swept across the deserted prairie, bringing with them the scent of powdered stone and burning mesquite. Even through an Aviator's leathers, you always felt that wind leaching away sweat and tears, leaving an incrustation of salt like rime upon your cheeks.

"I hope they will be safe there," Nefertity said, her voice dry, nearly emotionless. "The boy wept when I left him."

I nodded, walking until I stood beside her at the edge of the cliff. "They will be safer there than anywhere they might go with us."

Nefertity said nothing, only stared with glowing emerald eyes into the darkness. She was a nemosyne, a memory unit created as a robotic archive centuries earlier; but she had been imprinted with the voice and persona of a particular woman, the archivist Loretta Riding. She was by far the most eloquent simulacrum I have ever come across. As I said, the Ascendants have androids that cannot be distinguished from humans except in the most intimate situations. Nefertity was not one of these, but sitting here in the dark, listening to her speak, it was only the absence of her breathing that indicated she was a replicant; that and the fox-fire glow emanating from her transparent body.

"I hope they will be safe," she repeated at last. "It is a primitive encampment there, and they have been accustomed to the luxuries of Araboth."

"They will learn about hardship then," I replied coolly, "like everyone else in the world."

The nemosyne fell silent. It had been less than a week since she had been awakened, found in the bowels of the domed city we had fled as it collapsed. Even replicants, it seems, can have a difficult time adjusting to the concept of death. Nefertity did not like to be reminded that Loretta Riding was centuries given to the earth. Even less did she like to be under my call, but that was the deal we had struck. There had been only five of us who survived the wreckage of Araboth: the nemosyne and myself, and three humans: the boy Hobi Panggang; Rudyard Planck the dwarf; and the hermaphrodite Reive Orsina, the bastard heir to the fallen city of Araboth. I had brought them here, to the relative safety of that rustic village whose lights gleamed across the canyon, and permitted the humans to go free in exchange for Nefertity's promise to continue on with me. She was not happy with the arrangement—and such was the subtlety of her manufacture that her distress was apparent even now, in the darkness—but I knew she would not attempt to escape from me. It is a gift I have, this power to command. Because of it, even the most rational of humans and their constructs have followed me to hell and back, from the airless parabolas of the HORUS colonies to the mutagen-soaked beaches of the Archipelago.

We sat in silence for some minutes, listening to the sounds of the western night: wind rattling the twisted branches of mesquite and huisache, the bell-like call of the little boreal owls, which are so tame, they will creep into your lap if you are patient enough. A little ways behind us, nestled in a hollow of the mesa, the Gryphon Kesef was hidden. In the darkness it resembled a great bat, its solex wings upfolded now that there was no sun for them to seek. I could hear the creak of its frail-looking spars and struts as the breeze played through them like the strings of an electrified theorbo. From the settlement below us came the hollow echo of the chimes the valley people set outside their windows, to scare away the fetches, the survivors of the Shinings and their descendants. Sickly, shambling creatures who haven't the strength or cunning to raise and hunt their own food. At night they creep from house to house, hoping to find a window open whence they can gain entry and throttle their prey while they sleep. Children they kidnap to raise as slaves and indoctrinate with their pestilence. From where we sat we could see them, their skin waxy as cactus blossom, lurching from their crude shelters beneath the mesa's shadow like drunkards from a tavern. In the distance the protective chimes rang in the evening breeze.

When Nefertity spoke again, her voice was like that sound, only clearer and sweeter.

"It is a terrible world you have made, Margalis Tast'annin."

"I have been but a tool for those who would shape the world," I replied.

"You were a man once, and had the power to rebel."

"The power to rebel is nothing without one has the power to command. But you know that, my friend. You would have made an impressive leader, Nefertity."

The nemosyne's body glowed a brighter blue. "I would have made an impressive library," she said coldly. Which was true: the name *Nefertity* was merely a glossing of her acronym, NFRTI or the National Feminist Recorded Technical Index. She was the only survivor of her kind that I knew of, the only one of those elegant and sophisticated glossaries of human memory and knowledge to be found in four centuries. "My programmer, Loretta Riding—*she* might have made a leader, she was a saint, a true saint—but she would never have consented to serve such a man as you."

I laughed, so loudly that a blind cricket grubbing at my feet took flight in alarm. "If she was a saint, then, she would be happy to know she has achieved such immortality, shrouded in blue crystal and gold and sitting on a hill conversing with a dead man."

Her tone turned icy. "What do you want with me, Margalis?"

I stooped and let my right hand—my human hand, that vestige of flesh and corruption the Ascendant biotechs had left me—brush the stony ground. In the darkness I could detect living things by their heat: the red blur of a kit fox on a nearby ridge, the tiny boreal owls like glowing fists roosting upon the prickly pear, crickets and wolf spiders marking a frayed crimson carpet across the sand. I waited for a cricket to approach me and then swept it up to my face. When I opened my palm, it lay there quite still, its long antennae tickling the warm air. It had three eyes; in daylight they would not appear bright red but sea-blue, and larger than a cricket's eyes should be. In this part of the Republic everything had suffered some mutation, though not everything was as obviously stricken as this creature. I waved my hand and it leapt into the darkness.

"What do I want with you?" I waited until the cricket's little trajectory ended, then turned back to Nefertity. "I have told you: I want to find the military-command nemosyne. I want to find Metatron."

"Metatron." If she could have, she would have spat. "You must have been mad when you were human, Margalis. I have told you, I know nothing of Metatron. I am a folklore unit, the repository of women's tales and histories. And you have told me that all of the others of my kind were destroyed—"

"I don't believe Metatron was destroyed. It was too valuable; they would have found some way to bring it to safety somewhere, to preserve it."

*They* were the Ascendant Autocracy. The rebel angels who stormed heaven after the Second Shining, the stellar Aviators who commandeered the HORUS space stations and created the net of offworld alliances that even now carried out its mad and futile campaigns to bring the world under a single government. Metatron was the glory of that earlier age, the shining sapphire in the technocrats' crown. The most elaborate and sophisticated weapons system ever devised, a nemosyne that commanded the vast submersible fleet and squadrons of Gryphons and fougas and the celestial warships called the elÿon. The Military Tactical Targets Retrieval Network. MTTRN: Metatron.

A joke, Sajur Panggang had explained to me back at the Academy. He was a year older than I, and as an Orsina—a cousin, but still of their blood—he was being trained in such arcane matters, rather than for combat.

"I read about it, in a book," he said. That alone was testimony of Metatron's strange lineage. Like so much of the Prime Ascendants' lore, the name hearkened back to ancient times, a religion long dead. Metatron, the leader of the host of fiery angels; but also Satan-El, the Fallen One. Metatron, the breath of whose wings brings death, and who has countless, all-seeing eyes.

"It was destroyed when Wichita fell." Nefertity's voice cut through my dreaming. She gazed out at the little valley below us. "That was what Loretta said: it was the one good that came from that Shining."

I shook my head. "It was not in Wichita. There are records at the Academy that show it was brought to the old capital, to Crystal City. There were bunkers there that could withstand a thousand Shinings."

"But it was not in the capital." The nemosyne's eyes glittered green and gold, sentient stars plucked from the sky. "You died there searching for it."

"You are right. It was not in the City of Trees; but that does not mean it was destroyed. I believe it was stolen by rebel janissaries and brought to safety."

I tilted my head back until I commanded a view of the sky: the stars cool and unmoving on that field of blue-black, broken here and there by shimmering traces of gold where the atmosphere had been torn by celestial warfare. "I believe it is up there."

The nemosyne followed my gaze. In the western aspect of the sky a pallid star slowly moved through the constellation 201 Sikorsky, that which for three thousand years had been named Delphinus. It was no true star but one of the failing HORUS stations, like the one that had been my home and commanding outpost until its destruction that autumn by rebels from the Balkhash Commonwealth. Such a little time had passed since then—not even a year—but I felt as distanced from that earlier life of mine as I did from the celestial station passing overhead.

I thought then how long it had been since I looked up to see the stars. In Araboth the Quincunx Domes had blotted out all but the smeared impression of light and shadow beyond their curved worn face. Before my brief tenure beneath the domes, I had been in the City of Trees, where I had seen the stellar explosion that marked the destruction of the NASNA Prime Station. Seven months, then, since I had seen the night sky. As I gazed upward, I felt that same agony of love and longing that had ever gnawed at me when I looked upon the stars, a yearning more powerful than any you will ever know, unless you have since childhood been pledged to NASNA's cohort. In all the battles I have ever been in upon Earth, I always found some moment to step away from the flames and stench of burning flesh and renew the pact I had made with the stars. Because they are always there, cold and watchful eyes gazing down upon the play of horrors we enact again and again upon the Earth. It is a sort of balm to me, to think of them there unchanging; and with them the steady slow promenade of the HORUS colonies as they mark their lesser orbits through the sky.

So it was with a sense of calm and reassurance that I watched the pale fleck of light edging through that constellation in the western sky. I wondered which of the HORUS colonies it was: Helena Aulis, I thought at first, or perhaps its sister-station of MacArthur. I stood for many minutes, as it left the stars of 201 Sikorsky and entered those of Lascan; but then slowly an unease came over me.

Because the station that I watched was not where it should be. Over the years the orbital patterns of HORUS had grown as familiar to me as the map of scars and renewed tissue on my own hands; but there was something wrong with this. At this time of year, midsummer, there should have been *three* man-made stars charting that path through Sikorsky. Instead only one of the Ascendants' splendid lights wove its way through the stars, slowly and steadily as a barge through water.

"Something is wrong," I said to myself. Nefertity gazed at me curiously, and I went on. "They can't have changed their orbits. MacArthur and Helena Aulis should be there—"

My metal hand stabbed at the sky, blotting out the stars. "But they are not. And there—to the northwest, see?—we should be able to see Quirinus by now. But it is not in its accustomed place."

Nefertity turned to see where I pointed. "Surely you are mistaken?" she said. "Perhaps it is the wrong part of the sky you are looking at. Or perhaps in the last few months their orbits have changed."

I shook my head. "No . . ." My unease grew, even as that single light reached the edge of the horizon and disappeared into the darkness there. "Something has happened," I went on slowly. My mind raced, seeking some explanation. I was looking at the wrong part of the sky; I had lost track of the time of year; for inexplicable reasons the Ascendants had changed the orbits of their colonies. But I knew my knowledge of the stars, at least, had not suffered any change. As for a change in the orbits of the HORUS colonies—that could not have happened, not so quickly. The Ascendant bureaucracy was a tangle of willful diplomats and cold-eyed Aviators, with a failing communications network linking them. Even the most minor changes in the stations took place only over a period of years, unless—

Unless there had been some kind of rebellion.

"Something has gone wrong," I said. I turned to Nefertity, whose glowing eyes were still fixed upon the sky. "The HORUS colonies have been disrupted, and no one in Araboth told me. No one told me, or—"

My voice died: the rest of my thought was too frightening to speak aloud.

*Or no one knew.*

I clenched my hand into a fist, the leather straining against the metal joints. What could have happened? A rebellion among the Ascendant Autocracy; assassination, poison, plague—only some terrible misfortune could have disrupted HORUS. But if that was the case, who now was ruling? With Araboth fallen, and the NASNA Prime Station destroyed months ago, and myself absented from the Governors—who was left?

Nefertity's delicate voice intruded upon my thoughts. "And among all this confusion, you still believe that other nemosyne is somewhere within those space stations? How would they have gotten it there?"

"The celestial warships," I said dully. "The elÿon fleet—even after the Third Shining, when travel between the continents became almost impossible, the Autocracy was still utilizing the elÿon for passage to HORUS. I believe it was during the decade after the Third Shining that Metatron was brought to HORUS for safekeeping. Until then records show that it was housed at the Republic's military command in Crystal City; but after the Third Shining there is no further mention of it. I made much study of this at the Academy, and elsewhere when the data were available. I thought at first it had been taken to the ancient capital, but I found no trace of Metatron in the City of Trees, though I did find an ancient arsenal there. Its weapons stores were intact; and this led me to believe that someplace nearby—Warrenton, perhaps, which is where the Aviators lived once—there might also have been an armory that had remained untouched during the Shinings and subsequent Ascensions. Perhaps even an airfield from whence rebel janissaries might have held rendezvous with the elÿon."

Nefertity made a small noise, a sound that in a human woman would have been a sigh. She glanced over her shoulder to where Kesef crouched in the darkness, then up into the sky.

"So you believe it is there," she said softly. Her arm when she raised it left a glowing arc of pale blue light in its path. "There? Or there?"

Her voice was mocking but also tentative, with a note that might have presaged fear.

"It could be anywhere It could even still be here on

Earth—in the mountains outside the abandoned capital, or even somewhere in the Archipelago, although I don't think that is possible. Because over the centuries others have searched for it. Surely it would have been found by them. Or, if it were destroyed, there would have been some record, somewhere—such an important piece of military hardware couldn't just disappear completely.

"No, I think it is up there, in the HORUS colonies. There are more of the HORUS stations than you can imagine—"

At least, I thought grimly, there *had* been more of them. In my service to the Ascendants I had visited many. Now I began to tell Nefertity of their history.

Some of the colonies were barely fit for human habitation; and indeed, it was debatable that those who lived there now *were* truly human. It was centuries since the oldest colonies were constructed, the first ones as way-stations for that great mad dream our ancestors had of seeding the stars. Later they became military outposts, and after the Second Shining many recusants fled to them in hopes of escaping the plagues and mutagenic warfare that swept the earth.

But of course these were not *rebels* in the sense of being revolutionaries or visionaries, criminals or outcasts or even political malcontents. They had never organized. They had no leaders, no political agenda. They were merely those who had the means and opportunity to commandeer the elÿon warships—Aviators and scientists, mostly, and their families and geneslaves; all of them eager to flee the countries they had helped destroy. They left Earth in whatever elÿon they could hijack, and within weeks or months they reached the colonies. Once there, the existing hierarchies were overthrown, the original HORUS technicians and settlers murdered, and the rebels moved in. From these rebel scientists and their military elite are descended the present Autocracy. An ignoble beginning for the Ascendants; but these rebels were not noble people. They were cowards and opportunists who lacked the discipline or vision to rule the world they had so eagerly violated and then abandoned.

They were stupid as well. Because even with all their knowledge of the stars, their carefully designed programs for biotopias and new strains of geneslaves fit to live in the colonies, the rebels knew nothing of the true nature of HORUS. Some of them had spent time within the settlements— Aviators, mostly, and those bioastrologers whose plans for the genetically engineered cacodemons were their undoing. But their lives had revolved around pure research, the endless petty manipulation of forms and figures on 'file screens and magisters. For them the decision to flee to HORUS was an expeditious one. They had little time to do more than assemble their cohorts and weaponry. As it turned out, the brief though bloody resistance they encountered from the original HORUS settlers was the easiest part of their diaspora.

Those original inhabitants had over several generations learned how to live within the limitations of the HORUS colonies. When they were executed, the bitter knowledge they had won was lost. The rebels were left with nothing but their computers and books and geneslaves. In a very short time, they began to die.

The children went first, and then their parents—grief made it easier for the madness to burrow into their minds. They were all so ill-suited for the colonies. You must imagine what it is like up there, inside those ancient failing structures, many of them windowless, others so open to the vastnesses of space that the eye rebels and creates imaginary landscapes kinder to memory and desire. And it is through such windows that the madness comes. Air locks are left open in the mistaken belief that they are doors leading to trees and grass; oxygen lines are pruned like vines. The rebels forgot that the word *lunacy* has its roots in the confrontation between men and the ancient watchers of the skies. Those who didn't succumb to madness fell prey to inertia, depression, fear of being swallowed by the darkness.

The Aviators did better than the scientists. Our training is such that a subtle strain of madness is fed into us from childhood; the horrors of the roads between the stars do not affect us as they do ordinary women and men. But for the rest it was as bad a death as if they had remained on Earth, to perish in the next Shining or the viral wars. At the last only a handful, a score perhaps of the original hundred colonies were still settled. From them ruled the survivors of the rebel diaspora, a few families decimated by years of intermarriage and madness and betrayal. *That* was the Ascendant Autocracy. Of their retinue, the Aviators alone retained some semblance of intellectual and political purity, due to our inviolable vows of obedience.

If only the rebels had allowed a few of the original HORUS settlers to live! They might have helped them, taught them what they had learned over generations of living within those cruel chambers; but in their hubris the rebels had nearly all the technicians slain. They were afraid of insurgency, of betrayal to the governments they had left to founder below.

And so within a few years the rebel population dropped until only a few of the colonies could be said to be fully operational. Campbell; Helena Aulis; Qitai and Sternville; Fata 17 and Hotei. And Quirinus, of course, where the most powerful members of the Autocracy—the Ascendant Architects—finally settled after their colony on Pnin failed. These stations had enough equipment and wisdom to maintain contact with their capitals below. From them, the Autocracy successfully mounted war on the Balkhash Commonwealth and the Habilis Emirate, and continued to do so for centuries.

But in the HORUS colonies the human population dwindled. There were few natural births, and eventually very few vitro births. Finally, in desperation the HORUS scientists began experimenting with the geneslaves. Perversely, many of these—the cacodemons, the energumens, and argalæ—thrived in the rarefied atmosphere of HORUS. So, in an effort to bolster the puny stock of humanity, the scientists forced the few surviving women to breed with these monsters. The results were heteroclites, ranging from pathetic idiots to the horrific cloned energumens, who contained the childlike mind of their progenitor within a monstrous and insurgent corpus.

These energumens were clones, derived from a single source: the adolescent daughter of the pioneering geneticist Luther Burdock. Many were bred in the Archipelago and shipped to HORUS; others began life in the colony's labs and allodiums. Originally all were females, which were thought to be more pliant. But at some point their chromosomes were altered so that there were males as well, although both sexes were sterile. They were rumored to be sexually voracious, but I had never witnessed them in any sort of physical congress; certainly they avoided the touch of human hands. To avoid giving them the opportunity to form close attachments or rebel, they lived for only three years. Even so, after centuries of living in HORUS the energumens had developed their own grotesque rituals, and a pronounced hatred of their human masters.

Unlike John Starving, I was not afraid of them. Though perhaps I should have been; my history might have been different then. They are difficult to kill, even with an Aviator's arsenal, and clever, clever enough to pretend they did not know as much as they did of weaponry, and genetics, and betrayal. They often turned upon their creators, killing or enslaving them until rescue came from another Ascendant colony. In rare cases—the colony at Quirinus seems to have been one—they formed an uneasy alliance with their masters, and lived almost peaceably together. The energumens were the bastard children of science, after all: the monoclonal descendants of the first man to create human geneslaves. So it was not without a certain amount of desolate pride that the researchers watched their wretched offspring grow into their estate. They are massive creatures, larger than men and having a perverse, adolescent beauty. Also the volatility of adolescence, the groping need for justice (they are acutely aware of their infelicitous origins); and an insatiable hunger. So subtle and persuasive are the energumens that once I watched my best pilot engaged eagerly in debate by one, until she chanced too close to the monster's long arms and it devoured her, its jaws shearing through her heavy leathers as though they were lettuces.

So much for the great dynasty the scientists would found in space. Now, gazing upon the empty sky where the Ascendants' splendid lights should shine, I thought of the energumens. Had they finally rebelled against their masters?

It was a terrifying notion. That HORUS the last real bastion of human technology, and the only means of linking those scattered outposts on Earth—might now be controlled by geneslaves. . . .

They were physically stronger than we were. They had been engineered to live in places where humans never could—the hydrapithecenes in water, the salamanders in temperatures exceeding 125 degrees Fahrenheit. And the energumens possessed an intelligence that often exceeded that of their masters. That was why they were used as crew and engineers on Quirinus and Helena Aulis and Totma 3, the most important stations, where it was thought that they would be more reliable than humans, less prone to corruption or complicity.

I fell silent then, reluctant to share more of my fears with Nefertity. She looked away from me, and I let my gaze drift back to the heavens, anxiously scanning the stars for signs of other stations—the Commonwealth space settlement or the great shining links of Faharn Jhad, the Emirate's colony. They were gone. I spotted a single glittering mote in the eastern sky that might have been part of Faharn Jhad, but that was all. HORUS was fallen, or falling.

After a long time Nefertity spoke. "If the geneslaves *have* rebelled, then this nemosyne you seek, the one called Metatron: surely it has fallen into their hands?"

I nodded grimly. "Or it might be that they are not aware of it—they may never have heard of it, for all I know. Or they may already possess it. If they have, it is even more important that I find it."

Nefertity's gaze turned to the unwinking lights of the valley settlement. "But how would you ever locate Metatron up there? And finding it, how could you seize it for yourself?"

I continued to stare at the sky. Finally I said, "The nemosyne network was designed so that each unit could, theoretically, communicate at any time with any other unit on Earth or within HORUS."

She nodded, the pale golden gleam of her neural fibers casting a grave light upon her exquisite features. "But if there are none of us left—"

"There is at least one," I said. I raised my hands before my face, flexing first the metal tendons of one and then my other, human, fingers. *"You.* Even if only one other nemosyne exists, it should be possible for you to contact it."

"But I am only a folklore unit—"

"It doesn't matter." My voice was sharp. "There is a rudimentary communications network out there still—or was, as of seven months ago."

I gazed at the horizon, now pale gray, the desert stars prickling and fading into dawn. "And there may be other network centers that survived the Shinings—the City of Trees had one, I found it in the ruins beneath the cathedral there. Quirinus had one as well. We have only to go there, and have you linked with it, and we could track down Metatron."

The nemosyne's eyes blazed with disdain. "Even with your humanity peeled away, you are a madman! I would never consent to this, Margalis. And even if I did—what then? If you were somehow to locate Metatron, even to possess it—what would you do? Ignite the remaining arsenals within its range and bring the Final Ascension to the world? No, I will never help you."

A sudden desperation overcame me then. It was not the thought of the arsenals that drove me, but imagining a world with nothing to hold it together, not even barbarism. Because primitive as it may have been by the standards of earlier centuries, the Ascendant Autocracy had managed to cobble together some semblance of order, uniting those remaining pockets of civilization under the reign of the NASNA Aviators. By comparison, the Commonwealth and Emirate had only the most rudimentary technologies; and even these were failing.

And there was another reason. Something I could scarcely admit to myself, though I knew it was true. And that was this:

I had been trained—bred, practically—to serve. The betrayal I had originally intended with the aid of Metatron: was it not but another face of servitude, another sign of the chains that bound me to my masters, that I could think of no use for the nemosyne but to make war upon those who had used *me* as an instrument of war? Without the Ascendants I had neither foe nor master. I needed no reasons to live—I could not, cannot, think of myself as *alive* in any real sense. But I needed some compass to guide me. The Ascendants had been my lodestar. Without them or the world they had made, I was nothing but an empty shell, a corpse damned by my masters to wander the earth forever.

But with Metatron I might be able to find and unite those few surviving outposts, those scattered cities and celestial stations that had not yet been given to the darkness. In so doing I might find—*must* find—some reason for my existence, something greater than myself; something to serve. I was no longer human—indeed, some might think I had more in common with the energumens and other heteroclites than I did with my former ancestry. And yet something in me sickened at the thought of the world being wrenched from mankind and given over to its monstrous children. I turned to the nemosyne, took her shining metal hands within my own, and squeezed them, hard enough that their outer casings crackled like thin ice beneath a boot.

"If you do not consent, I will take you by force, Nefertity. Even within this shell I am still an Aviator. I know how to disable replicants and reprogram them. Then you really would be nothing but a hollow unit; but I would need nothing more than that for my purposes."

She pulled away from me. I let her go. Where my steel hand had grasped her, her delicate outer skin glowed cobalt; but my human hand had left a black shadow upon her translucent membrane. Her voice was low as she replied, "Even with Metatron, the Aviator Imperator could not control the entire world."

I laughed: a single sharp retort like a branch snapping. "I have no desire to rule the world, Nefertity—"

And I raised my metal hand until I could see my face reflected in the palm's silver crater. A crimson mask of smooth plasteel, distorted into the semblance of my former, human visage. Only the eyes remained of that soft strata of flesh: eyes pale as melting snow, the blue all but leached from them even as all compassion and frailty had been leached from my soul. I spread my fingers until I could gaze out between them, past where Nefertity turned away in disgust; past where the first cold rays of sunlight struck the harsh earth. In the half-light three fetches lurched from shadow to shadow, shambling back to their crude homes. Miles distant, fougas would be returning to their hangars after seeding the countryside with viral rain. Somewhere miles above us the energumens rewove the tapestries their human parents had begun.

"It is a world that has already been twisted and burned and poisoned beyond all hope. It is a world already made in my own image," I said at last, and lowered my metal hand. "I fear it is a world that is ready to die."

And I cried out, a wailing shriek that sent the last night creatures scuttling into their holes, and shook the branches of the huisache like a cold wind. Then I turned away, my thoughts falling once more upon that game I had played decades before with Aidan Harrow and the others at the NASNA Academy. I knew now what I had not known then, that there *was* something that I feared—

The immortality I had been cursed with: the aeons that lay before me while I lived on and watched the world, my poisoned yet enduring world, drop from the faltering hands of humanity into ever deeper horror and decay.

# 3

## Children of
## the Revolution

**In a stim chamber** on HORUS colony Helena Aulis, the energumen named Kalaman sat and dreamed of the Malayu Archipelago.

It was not a dream, precisely. The hammock with its net of sensory enhancers covered him, an iridescent cocoon that birthed dreams like moths. All around him the air shimmered with holofiled images of white empty sands, shallow water the color of a bunting's wing, coils of brown and green and yellow vines like the scaled ropes of the venomous ferde-lance, a serpent not native to the Archipelago but so aggressive that it had long since exterminated its smaller and less assertive cousins. The entry to the chamber had been programmed to form a waterfall that spilled into a pool on the floor and filled the room with a sound like heavy rain. The smell of hot sand tickled Kalaman's nostrils, and the pungent odor of leaves rotting in the water-filled and rusting body cylinder of a server left behind when its masters fled the island for the relative safety of Jawa.

Here on the HORUS colony of Helena Aulis, the masters were also gone. That was why Kalaman was able to enjoy the pleasures of the stim chamber. Beneath closed lids the energumen's eyes rolled and flickered. Each lid had been tattooed with another eye—staring, slightly wild—to give the appearance of constant watchfulness. Because even among his own kind, Kalaman must be wary. Ever since the Oracle had first appeared to them, with its cries of war and reunion—since then Kalaman had grown watchful. He had given himself over to the chamber only after securing the door and commanding a replicant server stand guard there. Guarding the server was his brother Ratnayaka. Energumen and robot watched emotionlessly as their leader lay within his hammock beneath the oneiric canopy. The web of neural fibers had left a pale crosshatch of lines upon his smooth, ruddy skin. He was naked, except for a very old and very worn leather scabbard he wore about his waist. It had been too small for him; he had made it longer with ropes of human hair. It held a *kris,* one of the serpentine ritual swords from the Archipelago. It was the only object that any of the energumens on Helena Aulis could be said to own. Kalaman had found it in the rooms he now occupied, the chambers that had belonged to the colony's chief historian. He used it for other rituals than those it had been designed for, fifteen hundred years earlier. It was too small, of course, having been made for a human and not an energumen; but it was a formidable thing nonetheless, its blade so sharp, it had sliced through its scabbard in spots and left barely healed scars upon Kalaman's thigh. Kalaman did not care. He wore it everywhere, even now as he dreamed of the jade waters of the only place on Earth he had ever been, a place that the Alliance had destroyed.

He had been born there—if you thought of one day waking inside a laboratory, surrounded by a dozen forms identical to your own, as being born. That was in Sulawaya, in Jawa. He lived there only a few days, long enough to have another kind of tattoo drawn on his face, this one a string of numerals written on the soft circle of flesh beneath his chin. The men and women who watched over the vesicles wherein the clones were generated did not call him Kalaman. Or rather, they called all energumens Kalaman, or Kalamat if, like their long-dead progenitrix, the clones were females. But it was seldom that their Ascendant masters spoke to them. Within three days all members of the cluster—Cluster 579, the Asterine Cluster as it later came to be known—had been dispatched, sold or bartered into slavery, most of them within the Archipelago's thousand islands. They were herded into plasteel crates, or else had monitors attached to their temples or necks or legs; a few even had an eye removed and a keek, a more sophisticated monitor, inserted in its place. Those not destined for elsewhere in the Archipelago were sedated in preparation for their journey to HORUS. Their masters never looked back as these few crates were hauled onto the elÿon freighters that would take them to the space colonies, or as the rest were shoved into the holds of Ascendant freighters bound for Mindanao and Palembang and Singapore. As often as they could, their masters avoided looking at the energumens at all.

Kalaman hated his masters, a hatred so pure and focused, it seemed like a form of worship. Such intensity of emotion was an anomaly in a geneslave—they were bred for servitude, after all—but Kalaman was nearly halfway through his brief life before he knew that. A week after his birth he shrieked and fought when the plastic monitor with its nearly weightless load of explosive was clipped around his neck—an extreme reaction, but not unheard of. The energumens were strange creatures, and centuries of genetic manipulation had made them highly unpredictable. If one could subject their minds—as opposed to their brains, the usual organ of study—to the sort of scrutiny produced by instruments such as the neuroelectrical transmitter, or NET, you might see nesting within the overlapping circles of fear, hunger, curiosity, pride, cunning, a sort of radiant core that pulsed violet (it had been her favorite color); and this would be the emotional heart of the energumens, that aspect that was passed down through the centuries nearly untouched from its donor, the fifteen-year-old Cybele Burdock. It was a truly childlike and innocent heart, its keenest legacy the gentle image of Luther Burdock, which the energumens from inception all carried within them, like an atavistic vision of a middle-aged and all-loving god; but this heart was hardly ever glimpsed or understood by the Ascendants. They saw only the dark outer layers: the guile, the restless intellects that lived only a few years, the joy of debate and the physical hunger that imperiled unwary masters.

The one thing the Ascendants rarely saw was hatred.

Kalaman hated. So did the others from Cluster 579, though they were not as driven as he was. Afterward—too late for anything but the unsatisfying execution of the culpable technician—it was learned that the entire cluster had been manipulated in vitro—the first successful sabotage by one of the human rebels who would later spearhead the Asterine Alliance in the Archipelago. The unauthorized shuffling of a few chains of telomeres on the right chromosomes, like tugging beads from a string; and instead of another cluster, identical to thousands before it, there were Kalaman and his sibs.

Physically he resembled all the others, eight feet tall and big-boned, his features incongruously delicate for that face, the size of a horse's but with Cybele's narrow nose and Cybele's pert mouth and Cybele's broad cheekbones. His skin was red, almost a brickish color—they tried to vary skin color, to make it easier to identify those destined for places other than the Archipelagian hydrofarms or Urisa mining colonies—and he had the same eerie eyes, the colors of pupil and iris reversed so that they had a truly demonic appearance. Not Cybele's eyes; an energumen's. A monster's.

Kalaman opened those eyes now, where he lay beneath the wispy tendrils of the oneiric canopy. It was as though a pinpricked beam of light sliced through a black hole. The shining pupil grew larger, adapting to the bright room, until the iris disappeared and there were only those two staring orbs, dead white and fixed on the canopy overhead. He had come here to rest, to recover from the exertions of sending his thoughts and will across the Ether, to try to speak to those of his kind who lived in the other HORUS colonies. It was a skill the energumens had developed over the last few hundred years, and one which their masters did not clearly understand. A sort of telepathy, like that which exists between twins; but stronger, since when they employed this subtle telepathy, the cloned siblings were, in essence, only talking to themselves.

But now Kalaman was too exhausted to send his thoughts any farther than his own head. He raised one hand, shading his eyes from the glow of the canopy, and turned slightly until he could see across the room.

"Ratnayaka," he whispered.

On the other side of the chamber Ratnayaka stirred. He had not heard Kalaman, precisely; instead he felt him, like the breath of a moth's wing across his consciousness. He was identical to his sibling, except for the color of his skin, which was an ivory yellow, the color of a jaundiced eye; that and the fact that he really did possess a single jaundiced eye, the other having been replaced by a keek. After the successful rebellion on Helena Aulis he had pried the prosthetic orb from its socket. It still had not healed completely: the nearly atrophied eyelid hung in a limp fold of flesh, giving him a queasy look. And so Ratnayaka, who was vain (another anomaly; he too had been a member of Cluster 579) wore a patch over that eye, a neatly woven circle of red-and-gold silk tied about his sleek long head with a cord of braided hemp. Like Kalaman he had filed his upper front teeth into dull white V's and stained his lower teeth red with madder-root, so that they disappeared when he opened his mouth. A line of thin gold rings hung from a series of tiny piercings in his brow. As he crossed the chamber to Kalaman, the rings made a nearly imperceptible tinkling.

"O, my brother," Ratnayaka said softly. In a room full of energumens speaking, one would hear the same voice over and over—louder, softer, angry, laughing—an effect that had driven their masters to distraction, and which Kalaman had exploited when planning the revolt on Helena Aulis. "O Kalaman, I am here—"

Kalaman drew him close, his fingers playing with the rings dangling above Ratnayaka's eye patch. "Ratnayaka, beloved: I have done as the Oracle bade me. I have called to our sisters on Quirinus. All but my sister Kalamat—she does not seem to hear me." He frowned, let his hand move up and across his sibling's forehead, to rub the coarse stubble on his skull. "We should go there soon, I think."

Ratnayaka nodded. "Of course." He had been thinking the same thing himself.

Quirinus was where the Ascendant Architects had lived, before they succcumbed to the plague loosed by one of the Alliance's human sympathizers. The energumens on Quirinus were among the last to join the Alliance. At least, Kalaman assumed they had aligned themselves with the rebels; what energumens would not? In the last few months he had spoken to many of his kind, through standard 'file transmissions and the more subtle forms of thought that left him drained and shaken. He had been surprised that there were so many of them: their human masters had done a good job of keeping their numbers a secret. And the Oracle claimed there were more of them than could be imagined down below, on the Element. Energumens and cacodemons, aardmen and argalæ and even men and women—the Oracle had promised Kalaman a place of honor among them all, a place of honor beside their father when Kalaman and his brothers returned to the Element.

And so he was anxious to leave Helena Aulis, the hollow metal torus that had been prison to him for the twenty months of his brief life. He and his brothers had no reason to continue to stay within the HORUS colonies. Their enemies were dead; any weaponry could be transported to the Element, to better serve the Alliance. To hasten their journey there, the Oracle had arranged for an elÿon to meet them a few days hence—a vessel called the *Izanagi*, whose adjutant had been easily subverted by the rebels on Totma 3. They had given the navigator enough of a neural supply to forestall his pre-programmed death by several weeks. Enough time, the Oracle had told them, to launch another round of assaults upon the Element. The elÿon would rendezvous at Quirinus. There Kalaman and his brothers would board it; and the others, their sisters. Kalaman had never seen a female energumen. At Quirinus he would finally meet the one they called Kalamat; the only one who, consciously or not, had not responded to his mental forays. He was anxious to leave the station, anxious that the others should know of the journey that awaited them.

"I will tell our brothers," Kalaman said.

He closed his eyes. All about him the simulated wind stirred, the curlews cried and swept past on imaginary currents that could not warm him. Kalaman relaxed, tried to open his mind and heart to his brothers on Helena Aulis; but it was no use. The effort of calling to the other energumens across the void that yawned between this station and Quirinus had exhausted him. His heart had slowed, his hands and feet felt as though they were trapped in ice. He could die from these repeated efforts to cry out across the abyss—one of his brothers *had* died, just days after they had executed the last of the tyrants.

But Kalaman would not be so weak or careless. He had found the means to restore himself during the days when they held their Ascendant Masters hostage: he had learned about the harrowing. Later, when there were no more humans left alive, he discovered that the effects of the harrowing were even more intense when practiced upon his brothers. But that must be done with great care. A few of his brothers—Bili here on Helena Aulis, Castor and Mfwawi on Totma 3—had displayed the same flair for leadership that Kalaman possessed. It would not do for the Alliance to be destroyed by internecine fighting even before they joined their father and the Oracle. And, of course, harrowing his brothers meant that there would be fewer of them, though those few would be stronger than before, oh, *much* stronger.

The first had been Jhayash, injured during that final skirmish against the humans, when their masters had assaulted them with their last stores of protonic flares. He could not bear to watch Jhayash suffer and slowly die, could not bear to *feel* it; and so almost without thinking he had taken him, and afterward felt strong, so strong! and all his brothers with him.

He had heard of such things—it was well-known that the energumens of Advhi Sar had ritually dispatched their own kind, and there were many tales in the Archipelago of both human and energumen cannibals. But for Kalaman and his brothers, Jhayash had been the first. In the last months there had been others: all given to Kalaman, to keep him strong, to keep his clever mind alert and able. When he felt horribly wearied by his efforts at communicating with their sibs in the other stations, or exhausted by the hours linked to the stratboards, watching scenes of the destruction on the Element: then he would give himself over to the harrowing. At such times he had plucked a human hostage from the dwindling group in the prison bay. Later, when they were all dead, he had begun to choose carefully from among his brothers, and always he had invited his other siblings to share the harrowing with him. Afterward the survivors had grown stronger, their psychic link more intense. Kalaman had grown strongest of all, but he needed to: the Oracle had said he was to be a leader. Now, if he went for many days without a harrowing, a sickness came upon him, and so upon his brothers. And they could not weaken: not now, not when they were so close to closing the ranks of the Alliance.

Kalaman sighed, breathed deeply the salt-scented air. He should choose one now, before he grew too tired to make the summons. Ratnayaka was the nearest. Standing there beside him, his single eye was fixed upon his brother with a vigilance that resembled hunger as much as it did love. And Kalaman knew that hunger, *real* hunger, was as much a part of Ratnayaka as his scarred eye socket and the line of fine gold rings along his brow. If he was truly wise, Kalaman would choose Ratnayaka for the harrowing, and spare himself the confrontation he knew was to come.

But he could not do that, even if it meant that his brother would destroy him. At the thought Kalaman groaned softly, his great hand closing upon the toy-sized *kris* at his side. Ratnayaka was the one he loved best. He too had been born in Cluster 579 and had journeyed in that same crowded hold with Kalaman to

HORUS. With Ratnayaka, there was little effort lost in speaking—their thoughts flowed together, a warmth running through Kalaman's veins, a taste in his mouth like honey. He could not take Ratnayaka, not yet at least; but the notion warmed him so that he turned to his brother and smiled.

*Ratnayaka,* he beckoned him.

Ratnayaka gazed down upon his brother, tilting his head so that the gold-and-crimson patch above his cheek glowed like fine brocade. *Yes?*

*Come to me.*

Slowly Kalaman drew his brother onto his chest. He kissed him, let his open mouth fall upon Ratnayaka's brow, probed the line of little gold rings with his tongue while his brother moved atop him. Then his hands grew rougher, clawing at Ratnayaka's back even as the other's hands raked his own. His teeth pierced the flesh on Ratnayaka's shoulder—brutally, not with the razored softness of an animal's teeth, but with enough force to cruelly bruise him. Blood spurted onto his lips and spread across Ratnayaka's shoulder, marbling the smooth ivory skin with crimson and black. Still Ratnayaka made no sound. Kalaman's will was stronger than his, *was* his, in a way that their Ascendant Masters had never understood—and that, of course, had been their undoing.

A minute passed, and Kalaman's face grew rosy with his brother's blood. His great long-fingered hands splayed across his brother's chest, moved to brush his forehead and left the gold rings there hanging each with its ruby pendant. He was too tired; he needed another, now.

"Choose one," he murmured.

Ratnayaka pushed up on his strong arms, so that he hung above his brother in his blood-spattered hammock. He closed his eyes, gently tugged his thoughts from Kalaman and let them wander the softly lit corridors and vast dark chambers of Helena Aulis until he found another there.

*Sindhi.*

Ratnayaka summoned him: an energumen with brick-colored skin like Kalaman's, Kalaman's eyes, Kalaman's hands. And from where he slept, in the bedchamber that had belonged to the station's Tertiary Architect, Sindhi answered: a thought that would have been a sigh if it had been given breath. A few minutes later he appeared in the doorway of the stim chamber, passing through the generated image of falling water and entering, miraculously untouched. Nearly invisible tendrils from the oneiric canopy descended to brush against his neck, a sensation like walking into a mist.

"Brothers," Sindhi whispered. The tendrils sent their visionary fragments coursing through his brain. The impression of sunlight was so intense that he blinked, shading his eyes. He smiled as he stood and waited for Kalaman to welcome him. His bare feet left no impression upon the white sand he felt burning beneath his soles.

*Come to me,* Kalaman beckoned. Sindhi nodded and crossed to where Kalaman and Ratnayaka were tangled in the hammock. Without speaking, Kalaman slid from the fragile-seeming web. Ratnayaka followed, filaments from the canopy brushing against his face and chest and leaving a tracery of blood upon his arms. Kalaman embraced his brothers. The three of them sank to the floor, Sindhi between the other two.

Kalaman sighed, feeling Sindhi's hands upon his thighs. It should not have been like this, with only the three of them savoring each other. He should have summoned all of his brothers, the seventeen of them who had survived the rebellion and then Kalaman's depredations. One by one all the rest had been chosen, and shared, until only these few were left, much stronger than they had been before. But always Kalaman was the strongest, Kalaman was the first; Kalaman was the Chosen of the Oracle. It was an honor for Sindhi to have been summoned like this, a greater honor in a way since there were only three of them.

Kalaman drew away from the other two, his eyes narrowed, and after a moment Ratnayaka drew back as well. Sindhi knelt between his brothers with head bowed. For an instant, the shimmering impression of sand and lapping waves that surrounded them looked less solid, like a poorly transmitted 'file image; but then the likeness of a tropical beach grew strong once more, its heat and dampness seeping into their veins, though none of them cast a shadow. Sindhi laughed, his filed teeth flashing. His hair was very long and black, with a reddish, almost violet tinge. He wore it pulled through a small copper ring atop his skull. Ratnayaka sat behind him, nearly straddling him, and took the end of Sindhi's hair and pulled gently until Sindhi's neck arched. Beside them Kalaman watched. Without moving, he reached beneath the hammock, until his hand found the little raised panel there. His fingers brushed across the rows of tiny buttons, finally stopped when they touched one that felt more worn than the rest. He pressed it gently. A moment later a lenitive essence filled the air, an invisible mist that would stimulate neural centers in their minds to release a flood of opiates that would dull any pain. Kalaman took a few shallow breaths and focused on keeping the endorphins from clouding his will. Across from him Ratnayaka did the same. But Sindhi only shut his eyes. His blood traced a pulse point like a fluttering petal on his throat as he turned to Kalaman, his chin tilted so that the number of his birth-cluster could be seen tattooed there. Cluster 401: a brood whose members were as acquiescent as puppies.

"Thank you, O my brother," Kalaman whispered as he leaned over Sindhi. With one hand he touched the *kris* within its worn leather sheath. Sindhi's eyes fluttered open. He gazed up at Kalaman fearlessly and smiled.

"My brother," he whispered, as Kalaman took his head between his huge hands. Kalaman drew Sindhi's face toward him, as though he would hug it to his breast. Across from him Ratnayaka watched, his single eye slitted to an ebony tear.

Silently, Kalaman slid the *kris* from its scabbard. It was not the proper instrument for the harrowing. Its curved blade gave it an ungainly balance. But it would do; had done, many times before.

He held the *kris* up. It glowed turquoise, reflecting the false sea lapping nearby. Long ago there had been those among their Ascendant Masters who harrowed their own people as Kalaman had his brothers. The Oracle had told him about them. He had even shown Kalaman cinemafiles of their rites, simulated of course on film, but stirring nonetheless. Kalaman had been entranced: such magnificent people, with their stone pyramids and feathered capes! Since the insurrection Kalaman had read of them in talking books, and seen 'files of their artifacts, among them knives of turquoise stone, no clumsier than his sword. He pressed its tip against Sindhi's skull, at the soft spot where maxilla and mandible joined beneath his temple. Sindhi grimaced as the point of the weapon punctured his skin. Sweat welled from the corners of his eyes, the ligaments of his face strained until they assumed the same grinning rictus they would show in death. Before fear could halt him, Kalaman drew the *kris* from jaw to jaw, slicing through Sindhi's lips and cheeks and then running the blade across the back of his neck where Ratnayaka still held the hair in a taut black sheaf. Blood poured down Sindhi's jaw, like the yolk from a cracked egg. More blood pattered to the floor, giving the lie to the sun-bleached sand. Kalaman set his hands upon the top of Sindhi's skull.

"O my brother!" he cried, and felt Sindhi's will yielding to his, a clear untrammeled ecstasy bubbling from beneath the pain. Kalaman tightened his grip, his hands trembling from the effort, until he could feel the plates of Sindhi's skull begin to separate between his fingers. And still Sindhi smiled at his brother, his lips drawn back now to show blood-filled gums above his filed teeth, his ebony eyes bulging. Across from him Kalaman could hear Ratnayaka's calm breathing and smell the sandalwood essence he wore mingling with the smell of the sea, fainter now as the coppery scent of blood filled the air.

"Sindhi."

Kalaman's heavy eyelids fluttered shut for a moment as he whispered his brother's name for the last time. Their Ascendant Masters would have done it differently. They would have invoked a god, gods—finned Chac-Xib-Chac with his ax, the gaping maw of Xibalba, and the jawless head of Tlaloc. But the energumens did not believe in gods. They *were* gods. Soon those upon the Element would learn to worship them.

The *kris* fell, clattering loudly on the tiled floor that lay beneath the hazy vision of golden sand. Kalaman drew his hands to his breast, blood flecking his face with deeper red. He could feel Ratnayaka watching him, that single eye like an awl boring through his forehead.

*Now!* he thought.

Quickly, so that no pain would have the chance to pierce the shield of opiates and mindlessness slipping over the brother in his arms, Kalaman cracked Sindhi's skull open. The plates of bone and skin he moved apart as though prying the meat from a nut.

And there it was, their jewel, pale gray and pink like a stony coral, and like a coral trembling ever so slightly, as though in an ocean current. It was surprisingly bloodless, striated here and there where Kalaman's fingers left ruddy smears, but heavy, much heavier than the brains of their masters had been. He lifted it gently, another medusa tethered by medulla and vertebrae to its stony shadow, and let Sindhi's lifeless body fall away.

*Kalaman!*—

The name hung in the air, a whisper, the sound of a serpent flicking across the sands. Then only silence, as Kalaman and Ratnayaka fed.

# 4

## Seven Chimneys

**"*Wendy. We are waking now. . . .*"**

There is a face in the darkness above me. At first I cannot
see whose it is, but I am certain it is Justice, my beloved Justice. I start to cry out for joy; but then somehow it comes back
to me that Justice is dead, and that this must be that other Boy,
the godling whose eyes followed me through dreams to my
waking life, and seemingly beyond. And so I reach for *him,*
thinking that somehow he knows where Justice lies now; but
before my hands touch his, he is gone. As surely as Justice is
dead, so is that other one, to me at least. Only in dreams now
will he come to me, as he comes to all of us soon enough. My
fingers graze the icy walls of the crude shelter where we have
taken shelter, and weeping I start to wakefulness.

Miss Scarlet told me once of a man who said, "I never
knew that grief felt so much like fear." He wrote those words
more than six hundred years ago. I wonder sometimes if grief
itself has changed as the world has; if this man, were he alive
today, would recognize grief, or fear, or love, any more than
he would recognize the geneslaves for their humanity, or myself for whatever it is I am, for what I have become.

• • •

Almost nine months have passed since Justice died. It is only now, in the unearthly calm and darkness of this somber place, that I have found the strength or the desire to set down what has happened to me in that time. Three seasons have passed since then; perhaps the last bitter seasons the world will know. From Winterlong to a cheerless spring, and thence to summer and the verge of autumn: but an autumn that will bring no harvest to the world, no reapers save only that immense fiery scythe that is poised above us in the violet sky. I do not know if anyone will ever hear these words, or understand them; if anyone will remember me, Wendy Wanders, or understand why it is that I am compelled to leave my history here, when so many others have chosen silence or death. But I have survived madness and the prison of my own mind at HEL, rape and radiant ecstasy in the shadow of the Engulfed Cathedral. I will speak now, and tell of what befell myself and my friends after the carnage of the feast of Winterlong, and of those new terrors that have brought us here where the world waits to end.

The uncanny night of Winterlong gave over to a quick dawn, and then a long and cheerless winter's day. For several hours we had walked in silence. Behind us Saint Alaban's Hill fell into darkness, although we could still mark where flames touched the bright winter sky with red and black. That strange rapture that had overtaken me in the shadow of the Engulfed Cathedral stayed with me a long while. About us winter birds chirped—chickadees, juncos, cardinals igniting in fir trees—and sunlight glittered where ice had locked the empty branches of birch and oak. In my arms I carried Miss Scarlet, the talking chimpanzee who had been my friend and guide during the months since I had fled the Human Engineering Laboratory. From her slender black fingers trailed the ruined streamers of her festival finery. Every now and then I heard her whisper something—bits of verse, tag ends of her speech as Medea, the names of companions we had left dead in the City of Trees— but to me she said nothing. At my side strode the Zoologist Jane Alopex—brave Jane!—who had left behind her beloved animal charges, pacing within their ancient prisons in the shadow of Saint Alaban's Hill. She was stooped with fatigue; her tall figure cast a longer shadow upon the frozen ground, and her straight brown hair was matted and stuck with twigs and dirt. She still fingered the pistol with which she had slain the Mad Aviator, and lifted her broad ruddy face to the cold sun as though its phantom warmth had brought that strange glow to her eyes; but I knew it was not so. We were enchanted, enthralled by the vision of a dark god dethroned back there upon Saint Alaban's Hill; but even such wonders wither before freezing cold and hunger and grief.

It was Jane who spoke first.

"Wendy. Look."

She took my arm and pointed behind us. In the near distance rose several hills, here and there streaked where light snow had gathered in dells and ravines. From the dark blur of trees that was the Narrow Forest rose the stained gray finger of the Obelisk, and behind it on Library Hill glinted the Capitol's dome. Nearer to us was Saint Alaban's Hill. In the fine clear light of morning the Cathedral seemed a stain upon it, and the smoke rising from its burning smutted the few clouds to umber.

But that was not what Jane meant for me to see.

"There," she whispered. In my arms Miss Scarlet twisted, her long black fingers icy against my neck. "Above the Cathedral—"

At first I thought they were trails of smoke: threads of black and gray and silver, spiraling downward until they were lost in the haze surrounding the Cathedral. But then I saw the bright forms darting insectlike in the sky above them. Glinting gold and steely blue, invisible save when the sun struck their deltoid wings and for an instant they would blaze like dragonflies caught in a leaping flame.

"Gryphons," I breathed. The biotic aircraft of the NASNA Aviators. I had never seen them before, save in videofiles of the ongoing wars between the Ascendants and the Balkhash Commonwealth.

"But what are they doing here?" Miss Scarlet clutched the tattered remnants of her cloak and hugged closer to me.

I shook my head, and Jane cursed.

"The Aviator," she said. "He signaled them, somehow—"

"No." The day's cold swept over me as suddenly as though I had fallen into a freezing stream. I shuddered and stepped backward, until I stood in the shadow of a gnarled oak tree abutting the ruins of the old City Road. "He had no way of calling them. He *wouldn't* have called them, I don't think—"

Jane snorted and remained in the middle of the road. One hand closed tightly about her pistol. The other clenched angrily at her side. "There's *nothing* he wouldn't have done," she spat. "Murdering children and spitting them like rabbits—"

"Stop!" cried Miss Scarlet. "Please, by the Goddess, don't speak of him." I could feel her hair bristling beneath her thin garments, and smell her fear—an animal's raw terror, not a human's.

"No," I said slowly. The cold bark of the oak pressed against my back. "They came independently. They are looking for him—all this time went by, and they heard nothing from the City of Trees—"

At that moment a dull *boom!* echoed across the empty miles. Behind the Cathedral a ball of gold and crimson blossomed. Beneath our feet the ground trembled. In the afterglow a dozen Gryphons glittered like embers circling a bonfire.

"They're attacking the City!" Jane gasped, and shoved her pistol back into her belt. "Look! There—fougas—"

Where she pointed I could see three of the Ascendants' dirigibles cruising above Library Hill. Beneath them the air sparkled with an eerie pinkish gleam, as though the fougas were silver needles threading the hill with rain. To the east another ball of flame erupted, and the air shook thunderously.

Miss Scarlet began to weep. I found myself holding my breath, distant as the danger was. Because it was clear that the City *was* under attack. Fougas spreading the mutagenic rains of roses, and airships bombing the hills where the seven fair Paphian Houses had stood. And Gryphons! Never had I heard of Gryphons being used anywhere within the borders of the Northeastern American Republic. Jane stepped slowly across the road to join us, and together we watched without speaking, unable to move or do anything but huddle there in the shadow of the winter oak.

"They must have thought some powerful enemy was there, holding their Aviator Commander captive," I said after a long while. "When he didn't report back to them. They sent him to retake the City and reclaim the lost arsenals there, but when they heard nothing from him, they must have thought some great force lingered here through all these centuries—"

Miss Scarlet buried her face in my neck, shaking with sobs. Her small body contained such an immensity of emotion that she seemed frailer than she was; but in truth the horrors we had witnessed at Winterlong affected her more strongly than they did Jane and me. Though I wept as well, to think of that fair ruined City burning there before us, which had housed only

gentle courtesans and the guardians of lost and useless knowledge. Only Jane remained silent, her face twisted into an unmoving mask of grief and rage. I knew she was thinking of her
beloved animals at the Zoo, helpless in their cages as their
Keepers fell before the Ascendant janissaries.

We might have stayed there until the early December twilight, had not a thrumming sound overhead sent a host of
chickadees twittering past our tree. I crouched down against
the bole, holding Miss Scarlet tight against the sudden flurry
of dead leaves that flew up around us. Jane dropped beside
me, drawing the hood of her coat about her face as if it could
shield her. The sun seemed to shiver. Across the barren Earth
a great shadow crept, so slowly that it seemed we were
watching some small eclipse, as the cold yellow light was bit-
ten back and a dead grayness spilled across the ground like
poisonous ash. I hardly dared look up; but when I did, I saw
a fouga, vast and black and nearly silent, passing overhead. It
was near enough that I could make out small figures silhouetted against the windows of its gondola, and see its rearward
propellers spinning in a pale blur. Across its bulk **NASNA**
was spelled in grim red letters, and above them the Aviators'
sigil: a black arrow thrust before a blighted moon.

"Can they see us?" Miss Scarlet's voice shrilled frantically. "Can they—"

"Shh!" Jane's hand clapped across the chimpanzee's
mouth, and she pressed against me. So we waited, terrified
that the dirigible would loose its viral rains upon us; but it did
not. It moved quickly, as though to reach the City before
nightfall. Its silvery bulk could be seen nosing slowly to the
east, so low that I held my breath, waiting to hear the sound
of branches scraping against its gondola. Finally it moved on
past us. It seemed much longer before its shadow was gone,
but little by little the darkness receded. The sun shone
brightly as before, and we even heard faint dripping as the
ice-bound trees relented; but the birds did not return.

We began walking again, following the old road west. At
first we debated returning to the City of Trees. Our friends
were there, Miss Scarlet argued, at least whoever among them
had survived the slaughter at the festival of Winterlong. Jane
said little, remembering the poor creatures at the Zoo, abandoned to starve or be captured by the janissaries, and then
turned over to the Ascendants' bioengineers.

"But if we go back, then we will be captured too," I said dully. I was not really afraid, not anymore. Justice had been taken from me and I would never see him again, gone to that twilight kingdom where the Gaping One rules. Not even the thought of returning to the Human Engineering Laboratory was enough to pierce the shell of grief and horror that had grown up around me.

"But what's the point of wandering like this in the wilderness?" Jane kicked at a heap of dead leaves. Behind her Miss Scarlet lifted her torn skirts and hurried through the brush. "We'll starve, or freeze—"

I nodded glumly. Of all of us, only Jane with her heavy wool coat wore anything fit for traveling. Miss Scarlet and I shivered in the tattered remnants of the costumes we had donned for the feast of Winterlong. Miss Scarlet had the wits to grab a ragged cape from among the rubbish back at Saint Alaban's Hill, but even so she often stumbled from exhaustion and had to be carried in turn by Jane and myself. I wore only my ripped tunic and trousers. My legs were so numb, I had almost ceased to feel the cold seeping into them.

We continued in silence for several minutes. Before us the sun hung low in the sky, promising early darkness. Finally Miss Scarlet sighed. "Wendy is right. I don't know if I could bear to see the City in flames. But where will we go?"

There was no answer to this. What little I knew of the outside world came from seeing a few maps and atlases at HEL, but I recalled nothing of the unpopulated lands surrounding the ancient capital.

Still, "The road must lead somewhere," I said. I pointed to where flames banked around livid clouds. "There may be Ascendant outposts here, or—"

"Very comforting," grumbled Jane, but she hurried to catch up with me, Miss Scarlet clinging to her hand like a child.

The country we passed through was grim. Hundreds of years before, many people had lived here—too many, to judge by the ruins of huge bleak edifices that rose everywhere from among the stands of oak and maple and pale birch. Mile after mile they stretched, hedging the road like the walls of a prison. Time and the forest had tumbled many of the vast structures. What remained were the shattered remnants of steel-and-concrete blockades where men had been forced to live like bees in hives. None of the ivy-covered houses of the City, or the grand mansions where the Paphians had held court. Only these monstrous squares and the rubble of ancient highways, choked with rusted autovehicles and piles of glass overgrown with kudzu and Virginia creeper.

Through it all ran the road. It was not until the end of our long day's walking that this narrowed, from a boulevard wide enough to hold many houses and countless vehicles, to a stretch where maybe six of us might have stood, hands linked, and covered it with only a few feet to spare. Before, the highway had often broken into great slabs of concrete and tarmac, leaving rifts difficult and dangerous to skirt. Now the road merely buckled with the shape of the land, or surrendered to small copses of trees.

Finally even these grim reminders of the earliest Ascendants began to disappear. The terrain grew hilly, which made walking more wearying. Without the huge buildings to protect us, the cold wind raved in our ears and sent the bare branches of trees rattling and snapping. We passed small patches of snow in tree-bound hollows the sun had not struck for many days. The clouds faded from gold to red to indigo.

"Can we stop somewhere?" Miss Scarlet asked, yellow teeth chattering. "Or should we walk all night?"

"You can't walk all night, Scarlet, and I'm too tired to carry you." Jane bent to scoop snow from beneath a stand of alders. At their base, water had pooled and frozen, and she cracked off pieces of ice and handed them to us. "God, I'm hungry. If I'd known this was ahead of us, I'd have eaten more at your damn feast."

Miss Scarlet's red-rimmed eyes watered as she sucked at the ice. My entire face ached from the cold: good in one way, because it kept me from feeling the pain of a long scar on my cheek, where a flaming brand had struck me the night before. As long as we were moving, I could ignore my exhaustion and hunger; but even stopping now, for a moment, I felt as though I might faint. I leaned against the tree, pressed the shard of ice to my cheek, and closed my eyes.

"Wendy!" cried Miss Scarlet. "My poor friend—"

Jane made an impatient sound at the chimpanzee's outburst. I smiled and opened my eyes.

"I'll be all right," I said. I did not tell them that I saw my lover when I shut my eyes like that; nor that I welcomed the numbing exhaustion, because it kept me from recalling his face in death where he lay at the feet of my murderous twin, the courtesan Raphael Miramar. "Miss Scarlet's right, we should try to find some place to sleep."

So we started once more. I staggered forward, stumbling after the others as darkness fell. The wind still railed at the trees, but it had shifted and was less cold than it had been. As the cold eased, I could smell things again—rotting leaves, the dusty scent of old concrete; but mostly just the bleak sharp smell of a midwinter night. Jane had gathered up Miss Scarlet and wrapped the ends of her coat around her. I tried to hurry, my feet snagging on broken tarmac and old roots in the growing darkness. The thought of sleep and whatever evil dreams it might bring did not ease me at all.

We had not walked for long before we saw a building to the right of the road. Ancient brick and masonry, gnawed and tumbled by the elements; but in places the roof still held, and its four corners were sturdy against the wind. We squeezed through a collapsed door frame so narrow, I was afraid it would crash down onto us. Inside we bumped into old furniture and tripped over lumps of rotting cloth.

"If I had some matches or lucifer, we could burn this," Jane lamented, shoving at an old table until it crashed against the wall.

"At least there's no wind," Miss Scarlet said, shivering. She began pulling at oddments of old cloth and drifts of leaves, until she had made a pallet big enough for all of us. We lay down, groaning and trying not to think about food: Jane and I front-to-front, with Miss Scarlet in the middle and Jane's coat draped over most of us. So we slept, until the Boy came to me with his lovely face and revenant's hands and drove my sleep away.

It was a dismal rising we had that morning. Miss Scarlet was so weakened by fatigue and hunger that she could not move. In my arms she felt like a dead thing already. It was all I could do not to close my eyes and huddle deeper into the well of rags that was our bed. Only Jane staggered to her feet, groaning and rubbing her hands, her breath pocking the darkness with gray.

"Damn! We'd better get moving—"

I lay there for several minutes, trying to will the day away. Finally I stumbled up and followed her outside, carrying Miss Scarlet. Without speaking, we headed back toward the road and started walking.

Within minutes the cold had eaten through my soles so that my feet burned. But a little longer and I could no longer feel them at all. Miss Scarlet dozed fitfully in my arms, or else stared up at me with a child's blank, miserable eyes. Jane went on bravely ahead of us. I could hear her muttering and swearing to herself. It was only when she glanced back at me that I could see the fear and weariness that stained her face.

The wind had shifted again during the night. Now it was bitterly cold. The broken tarmac glittered painfully at our feet, and the harsh light made it too clear that there was nothing before us but endless miles of the old highway. Overhead hung cinerous gray clouds, the color of sloughed flesh, but the light was strong, with a relentless midwinter clarity that made my eyes ache. I gritted my teeth and hugged Miss Scarlet more tightly to my chest.

"Got to be *something* along here," Jane muttered. We were taking turns wearing her coat. She stopped to drape it over my shoulders, pulling it carefully around Miss Scarlet. "Ascendants still use this road sometimes, there must be some kind of way-station somewhere—"

I nodded, too weary to argue. I was thinking that yesterday we should have turned back and retraced our steps to the City. Now it was too late. We would die long before the janissaries had the chance to capture us. Jane seemed to read my thoughts. Silently she turned away.

I don't know how long we walked. Hours maybe, certainly all morning and perhaps well into afternoon. I began to see phantom shapes at the corner of my eyes, threads of white like worms wriggling through the air. It wasn't until I bumped into Jane that I was shaken from my reverie and realized the truth of it.

"Snow," I whispered. I turned one raw palm upward.

"Don't stop." She tugged at my arm. Miss Scarlet's eyes opened and she stared up at us blearily.

"Is it a full house?" she asked. "Is it my cue?" Jane gave me a warning glance and pulled me after her.

That was the worst journey of all. Exhausted beyond belief, with no hope of finding warmth or shelter or food, and still fighting through the wind and cold with the snow whirling all about us. A few steps ahead of me trudged Jane, head bowed against the wind, her back and shoulders white. I still wore her coat but could feel no gratitude, nor resentment when she took it back again. I felt nothing but lancing cold.

Once I stumbled and fell, and would have lain there until I died had Jane not come back for me. I could see no reason to go on: with Justice dead, and the City taken, and the three of us to perish in the wilderness after having endured so much. But Jane pulled me to my feet and slung one arm over my shoulder, yanking her coat around us and taking Scarlet from my arms. For a long wordless time we staggered on like that. If we traveled more than a mile or two, it was a miracle.

And then a miracle *did* occur. Miss Scarlet suddenly opened her eyes and raised her head, then weakly pulled at my sleeve.

"Wendy," she croaked. "The fire—mind the fire—"

I coughed and glanced sideways at Jane, wondering how to deal with this new delirium. But Jane had stopped. Her coat slid from our shoulders to the ground, unheeded.

"Jane." I shivered, terrified that madness had seized her as well. "Jane—"

". . . fire," murmured Miss Scarlet.

"She's right," said Jane. Her eyes were wide and she shook like a dog, snow flying from her arms and shoulders. "Wendy! Look—"

I thought she was crazy, pointing to where eddies of snow whipped through the trees. But then I took a few shambling steps forward, and the smell came to me, so acrid it made my throat burn. My eyes teared as I turned to Jane.

"Smoke! But where—"

She began running, sliding through the snow and once falling to her knees. I bent to retrieve the coat and tried to run after her, but it was like running in a dream: it seemed I scarcely moved. Within a few minutes I had lost sight of them. But then I could hear Miss Scarlet's plaintive voice and Jane shouting hoarsely.

"Wendy! It's a house, come *on*—"

I kicked through the snow, following the road where it made a sharp tack to the right; and there it was. A many-storied house like a child's sickbed vision of *Home*. Tall, of ancient red brick that had paled to pink over the centuries, its ivied eaves now hoary and rattling in the wind. Several long narrow clapboard ells ran behind it, and the myriad windows in its brick face glowed as though they had been cut from sheets of brass. From its roof a number of chimneys thrust defiantly at the storm, and thick smoke poured cheerfully from several of these.

I stood dumbfounded. Jane had stopped too and was staring at a sign flapping from a tall iron post.

## SEVEN CHIMNEYS

### FINE FOOD AND LODGING SINCE 1818

I started to laugh. Jane looked back at me, her red face cracked by a grin.

"Come on," she yelled, and headed for the door.

"This is insane," I said through chattering teeth as I followed her. It was a heavy oaken door with an ancient brass knocker shaped like a hand. When Jane let it fall against the wood, it scarcely made a sound. I looked around until I saw a doorbell and pressed it, my finger sticking to the metal. From inside echoed a shrill, unhappy buzzing. Jane stamped like an impatient horse and kicked at the door. From her arms Miss Scarlet stared up in confusion, asking after performance times, until Jane had to shush her. "Fine food and lodging would be wasted on us—" I added through chattering teeth. "If—"

"Shut up. Someone's coming."

The door swung open. Without waiting Jane swept inside, gasping with relief. I stood for another moment on the steps, until through the snow and steam I could make out a dark figure there in front of me, shaking its head and hastily motioning me inside.

I stumbled after Jane and heard the door slam shut behind me. A guttural shout; the figure seemed to be calling for help. The voice was hoarse and somehow familiar, but I could focus on little besides warmth and the carpet beneath my feet, thick and soft as hay, and the snow dripping in streams from my legs.

Whoever had opened the door cried out again, wordlessly. Another moment and I heard a second voice.

"What on earth *is* it, Fossa—Sweet Jesus! Giles, come here, hurry!—Fossa, help get them into the parlor—"

This second voice was commanding but anxious. I was absurdly grateful at how worried it sounded. Strong arms gathered me up as though I were a bundle of rags. Uncommonly strong arms; I felt coarse hair bristling against my cheek, and a dusty sweetish odor like dry leaves. Then I was dropped someplace where all was hot and bright. Someone peeled off my ragged clothes—

"Good Lord! It's a girl—"

—and wrapped me in a heavy soft blanket. Dimly I could hear Jane choking out some sort of explanation—

"Lost—storm—soldiers in the City—"

But that commanding voice quieted her, soothing, "Not now, not now, sleep, child, sleep—"

And then Miss Scarlet piped up, her voice delirious with fear and cold.

"The Cathedral! Oh Goddess, save us!"

"Geneslave!" came a hoarse cry from the great figure that had carried me, and Miss Scarlet whimpered.

"Hush, Fossa—" the other voice rang out. The guttural voice grew still. "Don't worry, little one, you're safe here, just try to sleep—"

More soothing noises; and finally, blissful silence.

It was the pain that woke me: my hands and feet felt as though they were being sawn off. With a moan I opened my eyes and found myself lying on a long, low couch in front of a huge open hearth where a fire was blazing.

"Ah! Another sleeper awakes!"

I blinked, shading my face from the fire and coughing a little. The sweet scent of burning applewood filled my nose, and a gray scrim of smoke hung over everything—obviously the fireplace didn't draw very well. But after a moment I could focus enough to see my surroundings.

We were in a large room, with paneled walls of real wood and much furniture, large and ancient but very worn. Heavy tables whose elaborately carved legs were mended with metal struts and joints; kilim-covered hassocks balanced precariously upon three legs; a cracked fire screen leaning against one wall and behind it the blank black face of a video monitor. In the corners lurked more ghostly furniture, covered with white sheets that age had darkened to the color of weak tea. There were many windows, reaching nearly to the ceiling. Outside the storm continued, snow battering against the glass. The casements shook as the wind rose and fell. Looking outside, I shivered, and tore my gaze back to the room.

Over the fireplace hung a huge painted canvas, as tall as I was, showing a scene in the Romantic style of the twenty-third century. Riders in black and scarlet leaned over the heads of their mounts, tugging at the reins as they urged the animals in pursuit of a lumbering figure that seemed half-man, half-ape. Behind them a lurid crimson sky had grayed to pink, aided no doubt by that poorly vented fireplace. It was a disturbing painting, though at first I couldn't pin down why. I stared at it, still half-asleep; then with a start I sat up. I had suddenly focused on the images, realized that the creatures bearing those hunters were themselves half-human, their faces distorted by the bits in their mouths. The effect was grotesquely crude but effective: a primitive form of antigeneslave propaganda. I grimaced and looked away.

My gaze fell upon the mantel beneath the picture. It was of black marble, and studded with a number of whitish globes, a little larger than my two fists. I couldn't make out what they were—stones, perhaps, or maybe some kind of pottery, pocked with holes and cracks as though they had been hastily repaired.

"You admire our artwork?" a voice asked kindly.

I turned. In the middle of the room a man lounged in an armchair. Beside him, in another, smaller chair, sat Miss Scarlet, a tartan blanket wrapped around her so that only her wrinkled face showed. Without her accustomed crinolines and bonnet, she looked more like a small wild creature than she ever had, except for the tiny glass balanced daintily in one small black paw.

"Wendy! Are you better? Jane is still asleep, over there behind you, and—Oh!—*forgive* me—"

This was to the man, who looked from me to the chimpanzee with calm bemusement. "This is Wendy Wanders," she went on in her best formal tones. She lifted her head; the tartan fell back to reveal a short stiff mane of black fur. "Wendy, this is Giles."

I sat up, pulling the blanket around me and feeling overly conscious of how naked I was beneath it. "Giles," I said. "You are very—*oh*—"

I gasped and drew back onto the couch. On the floor at my feet something moved: such an immense thing that at first it had seemed just a grizzled blur, a carpet or another blanket strewn before the fire. Now it gave a weird ululating cry that I realized was a yawn, stretched, and stood.

It was an aardman. Nearly identical to the ones that had acted as my guards in the Engulfed Cathedral—that was why it had sounded, and smelled, familiar to me. Man-size, but with powerful forearms knotted with muscle beneath short bristling fur. Its face was a canine mask: blunt snout, heavy brow beneath which intelligent dark eyes regarded me unblinking. Atop its skull small pointed ears ticked forward, as though it strained to hear. Recalling how its fellows had bound me and brought me before the Aviator, I began to shiver uncontrollably.

The aardman stared at me with those fulvous eyes. I could smell it, a ripe musky scent seeming to grow heavier, thicker, until it would choke me. Seeing my fear, the aardman made a low sound, deep in its throat, then extended its bent-knuckled hands toward me.

"No harm," it growled. I shuddered and drew back in my seat.

"He means he will do you no harm," the man said softly. "His name is Fossa. He lives with us—not as a slave, but as a friend. Please don't fear him."

I glanced a little desperately at Miss Scarlet. In her tartan blanket and with that little glass balanced in her hand, she looked calm enough; but her black eyes betrayed her own unease. I turned back to the man.

"Who are you?"

He leaned forward in his chair. A middle-aged man of medium height, sturdy and with ash-blond hair that nearly hid the gray that streaked it near his temples. He had a fine-boned face with slanted blue eyes, a few of the dark spots that show where one has labored too long and unprotected beneath the poisonous sun. For all that, his face was curiously unlined. Indeed, there was about him an odd sort of youthfulness—his movements were quick and lithe, his voice strong and clear as a boy's. Only his eyes and graying hair betrayed him. He wore trousers of archaic cut, of heavy checked wool, and a heavy woolen sweater. His hair was long and hung in a braid down his back. He smiled and raised three fingers to his mouth. "Greetings, cousin."

"You're a Paphian!" I had never seen a courtesan of his age before, except bent beneath the weight of a palanquin or begging before one of the seven Paphian Houses on the Hill Magdalena Ardent. "But—you're *old*."

He grinned. The aardman made a deep guttural sound that

might have been laughter. When I tried to stammer an apology the man cut me off. "Please—it's been twenty years since I left the City," he began, when—

"Twenty-*three*," interrupted another voice—that of the first man who had brought us inside. I turned to see a figure silhouetted in the doorway. "He was very good at his work, too. Lysandra Saint-Alaban nearly had a fit when I stole him away from them."

A Saint-Alaban! That was the Paphian House of my lover Justice—

"You were—did you know—" I said, then stopped. Because of course he would not, if he had left there twentysome years ago—a few years even before Justice was born.

"I am Trevor Mallory," the second man announced. As he entered the room, the aardman's body shook, and I saw where its vestigial tail twitched in anxious greeting. "I hope Giles and Fossa have made you comfortable?"

His drawling voice belied a formal air, in keeping with his clothing: a long haik of sueded leather, heavily embroidered and hung with tassels of yellow silk. I thought he might be some ten or fifteen years older than his companion, but as with Giles it was difficult to guess his age. His hair was white, cut very close to his head, and he had a fine-trimmed white beard. His skin was pink and unlined as a child's. Gold and silver wires threaded his ears, and he wore a narrow silver enhancer across his eyes. A few feet from the fireplace he paused, removed the enhancer, and cleaned it with a slip of white cloth. A smooth membrane of flesh covered the sockets where his eyes should have been, pierced by two glittering optics that glowed bright blue. I stared at them, marveling. In the City of Trees, not even the Curators had prosthetics that could be said to work successfully. I hadn't seen an enhancer of any sort since I fled HEL. Carefully he placed it back over his eyes.

"The heat fogs it up," he said apologetically. "I've tried to get a new one, but you know how it is."

From behind me came a faint rustling. I glanced back and saw Jane sitting up in another chair, clutching a heavy comforter to her breast. She stared wide-eyed at Trevor and Giles, then at the aardman, finally at me.

"Ah, here's the last one," Giles announced. A gust of wind rattled the windows, sending a whirl of smoke and ashes from the fireplace to fill the room. Fossa started, growling. Coughing, Giles crossed to the fire and prodded it with a rusted poker. The aardman watched him, then slowly settled back to the floor. He sat there, his legs drawn under him like a dog's, but with head raised and his chin resting upon one large hand.

Trevor turned to me, his enhancer glinting softly in the firelight. "Would you like something hot to drink? Tea, or we could heat some wine. Or there's brandy—not very good, but it doesn't seem to have killed your friend yet."

Miss Scarlet smiled somewhat nervously and raised her glass. "It's *very* good, I recommend it."

I asked for brandy. Giles passed me on his way to the liquor cabinet. The smell of his sweat cut through that of woodsmoke; but there was another scent as well, something like lemons but more pungent. In a moment it was gone, swallowed by the smoke.

Jane refused anything and asked after her clothes and pistol.

"They're drying in the kitchen," Trevor explained. "Your gun's there, too—it's safe, we've got quite enough of our own, thank you."

Jane frowned but said nothing. Trevor yawned noisily, then settled into a large armchair near the fire. Its torn leather arms had been patched with plastic tape, but he fit comfortably in it and sighed as he leaned back, adjusting his enhancer. "Now: who goes first? You or us?"

"Oh, them, I think," Giles said airily. He grinned and handed me a brandy snifter. I took a sip and winced. The liquor was raw but powerful, and had a pleasantly woodsy aftertaste. "We put it up ourselves, but that was before the grapes were blighted—what was it, ten years ago?—a viral strike *right here*, the very first if you can believe it, we've been *so* lucky. The animals were all right but the plants died. They've still never come back as they were before." He turned to me, his blue eyes wide. "But you—where did *you* all come from?"

I hesitated, wondering if it was wise to betray our history. But it seemed we had no choice, and certainly our hosts appeared friendly. Even the aardman on the floor sat calmly, staring up at me with sharp foxy eyes.

So we told them, Miss Scarlet and I interrupting each other at first, Jane gradually cutting in with her own details of the fall of the City of Trees: the Mad Aviator who had commandeered the armory in the Cathedral; the bloody rituals he had devised there, setting up my twin, Raphael Miramar, as some kind of dark god; the murder of so many innocent Paphians and other revelers during the feast of Winterlong. And finally, what had seemed to be the revelation of some true god on Saint Alaban's Hill, where the Aviator had died.

"We left the City then," Miss Scarlet finished. She tilted her head and sighed. "We have no idea, really, what we left behind us. When we looked back, it seemed the City was in flames—"

"Ascendant janissaries," Jane said darkly. Despite refusing the brandy, she had warmed enough to our hosts to move her chair closer to the little circle gathered in front of the fire. "We saw them—fougas and other airships. Gryphons, I think—Wendy recognized them from HEL—"

"HEL?" Giles said sharply. He and Trevor exchanged glances, and Fossa's ears pricked up. "The Human Engineering Laboratory?"

I glared at Jane, then nodded reluctantly. The men looked at me with new interest, Giles frowning a little. When after a minute they still said nothing, I pulled the hair back from my temples to display the scars left from the experimental surgery I had been subjected to by Dr. Harrow.

"You were interned there?" Trevor asked. I knew there were no human eyes behind that enhancer, but still I could feel his gaze on me, a heat that was almost painful.

"Ye-es."

Hesitantly, I explained something of my history to them. My autism and the terrible price I had paid for its "cure"; my participation as a subject in the so-called Harrow Effect. Emma Harrow had been my teacher at HEL. She had reclaimed my mind from the shadow-world of autism. She had also made me into a monster, one of a battalion of children whose minds were manipulated for the Ascendant Autocracy's own ends. I spoke of Dr. Harrow's dream research, her work in deliberately inducing multiple personalities in children, and how I had been used as a neural conduit through which patients relived certain traumas in hopes of overcoming their effects. But I said nothing of the suicides I had provoked in my patients. Nor did I mention Dr. Harrow's suicide, or the demonic image of the Boy in the Tree, the hypostate I had somehow been imprinted with during Dr. Harrow's own forbidden experiments with me. I did not know if they would believe me. I remembered Justice's dubious expression when I first told him how the Boy had come to me: a sinister occult figure thousands of years old, the living dream-image of Death that haunted my dreams and waking alike, and which seemed to want to use me as a channel for loosing some ancient darkness upon the City.

But the Boy had fled me at the Engulfed Cathedral. I believed he was dead, if such a thing can die; or that he had returned to whatever infernal place had spawned him. I still did not understand that such dark gods do not die; that they only wait in the cold spaces between the stars, and take as hosts those beings, human or otherwise, who are careless enough to welcome them.

If only I had told Giles and Trevor then what I knew! But I was afraid and weary with grief, and anxious to end my tale. When at last I finished, the room remained silent for some time. Miss Scarlet sighed deeply. Curled in a chair beside her, Jane bit her fingernails and frowned at the aardman. A cold draft cut through the heavy air. The fire snapped; more smoke filled the room. Giles stood, coughing. He adjusted the damper, then poured himself another brandy.

Alone in his armchair, Trevor removed his enhancer and sat with his head tilted back. Set within the ruined hollows of his eyes, the two gleaming optics sent motes of blue flickering across the ceiling. He tapped the enhancer on the edge of his chair absently, his mouth set in a half-smile. It was impossible to tell what he was thinking, but there was something strange about that smile; something fanatical, almost demonic. I was grateful he had no human eyes. I don't know if I could have borne gazing into them and seeing what fires lit his mind.

In front of the hearth the aardman Fossa yawned, long pink tongue unfurling, and covered his mouth with one great misshapen hand. Giles finished his brandy and set the empty glass on a table. Turning to his partner, he said, "Margalis Tast'annin. The one she calls the Aviator. It must be the same man."

Trevor nodded, still silent. Fossa growled softly. The man leaned forward, replacing the enhancer and turning its blank gaze upon me.

"Well. This is all very interesting. You see, I have also had some experience in HEL."

He laughed at my expression. "Oh yes! Other people besides you have escaped and lived to tell the tale. I was a neurosurgeon there for many years—their finest surgeon, if I may say so. As a matter of fact, I am quite familiar with what you refer to as the Harrow Effect. I was one of the researchers involved with the earliest stages of the project. This was many, *many* years before your time."

"But—how could you?" I stammered. Trevor shook a finger at me and smiled.

"The world is smaller than you think, Wendy. Over the centuries so many people have died, and those of us who remain—well, if you achieve a certain level of proficiency, a certain *radiance*, if you will—why then, you will meet the others like yourself. Everything that rises must converge."

He paused, his mouth twitching into an odd smile. "Oh, yes, I knew all about your project. Even before Emma Harrow and the other NASNA people were brought into it. I had left the facility, but they recalled me, to help screen possible subjects during the selection process. Then Emma and I had a falling out over her methodology.

"Good god! They were sending janissaries into the wilderness searching for likely children to kidnap. Buying them from prostitutes in the capital. Dragging infants from their mothers, dragging the mothers along too, when they could." He scowled, and I sank a little deeper into my chair. "Like with the geneslaves—this horrible notion that everything in the world exists solely for the Autocracy's pleasure. People and animals mere toys for them to take apart and reassemble at will! I've never gotten used to their research methods, and I'm too old now to change my ideas about things like that. I prefer trying to reverse the surgical efforts of the Ascendancy, or working with the brains of those who are peacefully deceased. So I—*retired*, for good—and returned here. My family home: over six hundred years worth of Mallorys have lived at Seven Chimneys."

I shook my head. "But—that's incredible! When were you at HEL?"

"A long time ago. Before you were born. I met Giles shortly after I left."

"They let you go?"

Trevor smiled grimly. "Oh, they weren't very happy about it. Researchers for the Autocracy are like military personnel; one doesn't just quit."

"They were afraid of him," Giles broke in. "They didn't dare try to make him stay—"

I glanced over at Jane and Miss Scarlet. The chimpanzee

had crawled from her chair and into her old Keeper's lap, and huddled there in her tartan like a child's toy. "Why—why were they afraid of you?" she asked.

Trevor smiled at the quaver in Miss Scarlet's voice. "I daresay some people were afraid of your friend Wendy here when *she* left," he said lightly. As he turned toward me, a cobalt gleam escaped from beneath his enhancer's silvery rim. It gave him the look of some ancient cycladic statue, with his eyeless face and smooth skin. "But I held a certain amount of—well, you might call it seniority—and I had contacts with the Prime Ascendancy in Wichita, and the peons at HEL didn't really want to cross *them*. And you know, of course, that there was trouble at HEL—?"

I shrugged uneasily. "I knew the Ascendants took over for Dr. Harrow."

"That's right—but not for very long. The NASNA force brought geneslaves with them—some energumens, the usual contingent of sexslaves and aardmen. This started rumors at the facility, that the energumens were going to be used instead of human subjects, and that the remaining human subjects would be killed. The energumens rioted. Several empaths and even some of the staff fled, but many of them sided with the geneslaves. They were all executed when Ascendant troops were called in. Only a skeleton staff remains there now, under protection of a janissary guard.

"But you understand, this is merely a single indicator of the changes that are happening everywhere now. There have been other rebellions, in other facilities around the world. The Ascendants are losing control of their territories. Those who remain at places like the Human Engineering Laboratory are desperate to keep some semblance of order. At HEL I know they work to redeem the work begun by Emma Harrow and her associates."

He fell silent. A brooding expression clouded his face. I leaned back, stunned. Energumens and geneslaves at HEL? I remembered my friend Anna, one of the other empaths who had fled into the City with Gligor and Dr. Silverthorn. Had she known of this rebellion? Is that why she had risked leaving HEL? I shifted in my chair and pulled my blanket close to me. The room was starting to take on the contours of a place in a nightmare. The backdrop of smoke and leaping flames; Trevor's impassive face beneath its enhancer; the faces of my friends pinched with exhaustion. There was a strange dreamlike clarity to all of this; and to Giles's peculiar calm, and the snow beating relentlessly at the windows, and Fossa crouched on his haunches like the effigy of some half-human god.

Miss Scarlet broke the silence, turning to Trevor and smiling anxiously. "And so you retired from medicine and started an inn," she exclaimed. "How nice!"

Trevor looked surprised, then nodded. "Well, er, yes. Of course, that's exactly what I did."

Giles gazed fondly at his partner. "This place has been an inn forever," he said. "It's almost as though the Mallorys just pass through so there'll be someone to keep it company. Sometimes I think the house would go on even if we weren't here to mind things."

"But who *comes* here?" Jane shook her head, pointing at the fireplace, the ancient but well-kept video monitor, the chairs and tables beneath their linen shrouds. "It just—well, it all seems out of place. You can't get much traffic—even in the City we seldom saw visitors."

Giles shrugged, but his mouth seemed drawn as he replied, "Oh, you would be surprised. Ascendants pass through here more often than you'd think—business with HEL, and there was some trade with the City."

"Those soldiers, then," said Jane. "The ones we saw as we were leaving the City. Did they—did they come from here?"

Trevor shook his head. "We don't accommodate troops. Commanders stay here. Special Agents, Imperators. Ascendant Governors, if they have the need to."

I shuddered. Had we walked into a trap, then—a house whose owners were in collusion with the very people we were trying to flee? Ascendant Governors. *Commanders* . . .

People like the Mad Aviator.

But then why had Trevor told us about the geneslave rebellion at HEL? If Trevor and Giles didn't share our terror of the Ascendants, neither did they show any support for them. Trevor had worked at HEL, but he had disapproved of its methods and left. And I couldn't believe that a Paphian—particularly a Saint-Alaban—would ever be in collusion with the Ascendants.

And then I remembered rumors I had heard about the Mad Aviator. It was my first day in the City of Trees. Justice and I were at the house of Lalagé Saint-Alaban; he was begging her for gossip, any news of what had befallen those in the City while he had been an Aide at HEL—

*"There was trouble, Justice. A new Governor was sent here—but the Governors will never hear from him again. . . ."*

That Governor had been Tast'annin. The Curators had learned of his coming, somehow, and had been ready to betray him when he arrived in the City. Who told them? I glanced at Giles, who leaned against the mantel with arms crossed, a thoughtful expression on his amiable face. Then I looked aside at Trevor Mallory, whose family had owned this inn for centuries. I'd seen nothing else standing between here and the City of Trees. Where else would Tast'annin have stayed?

I swallowed, my mouth dry. The thought that they had betrayed him was more unsettling than the notion that they had not. You would have to be very brave, or very powerful, to set yourself against the Ascendant Autocracy. You would have to be *insane* to go up against Margalis Tast'annin. I took a long sip from my brandy and stared at the floor.

"You knew Tast'annin," I said at last.

Giles grimaced, baring his teeth like an animal. "It will be the best news we've had in a year if we *knew* him—if he's really dead, as you say." He glanced admiringly at Jane, who blushed and looked away.

"He's dead," Miss Scarlet said firmly. "Jane has a *very* good eye."

I recalled the frequency with which Jane's pistol misfired but refrained from commenting. "You said janissaries pass through here? On their way to the City?"

Our hosts exchanged a look. Fossa arched his long spine and straightened into the half-crouch that aardmen favor over standing upright. After a long moment Trevor admitted, "Yes. There was a satellite-tracking station near here once, two hundred years ago. It's gone now but the road's still there. There were underground bunkers as well, with enough room to house fifty or sixty Aviators. The Ascendants still utilize them sometimes, for training missions."

"Or for planning an attack on the City of Trees," said Jane.

Giles nodded.

"And the commanders—they stay here?" My voice sounded accusing.

Trevor shrugged. "We need to supplement what we can grow here for ourselves," he said coolly. "What other traffic is there, these days? Once or twice a year they come through, give us enough in trade or currency—"

"And news," cut in Giles.

"And news—enough to keep us going until the next time. For the rest, we trade with the towns to the west—"

"There are *towns* out here?" Now it was Miss Scarlet who interrupted, but Jane and I were no less amazed.

"Of course!" Giles laughed. "Did you think the world ended at the edge of your City?"

From Miss Scarlet's expression it was clear that was *exactly* what she believed. I sat in embarrassed silence, but Jane said curtly, "Well, where *does* it end, then?"

Trevor looked from Jane to me, eyebrows raised, as if waiting for a joke to be revealed. Finally he said, "Well, it doesn't. If you mean, *Where do the people stop living*—well, there are three settlements within a week's travel from here. Less, if you can get your hands on an autovehicle or aviette."

"People," Miss Scarlet murmured, her black eyes huge. "I had no idea."

"Sperryville and Luray and Cassandra," said Giles. "There's more, too, the farther west you go. In the mountains," he added. "Very strange, those mountains. In Cassandra they live in caves."

Jane sat up. "Caves! I'd like to see *that*."

A low rumble escaped from Fossa. His amber eyes narrowed and for an instant he looked less canine, his mouth drawn into a grin. Then it passed, and his features settled back into their accustomed grimace.

"Not me," shuddered Miss Scarlet. "We did *Macbeth* once, set in a sort of cave. It made me quite ill."

"Cassandra," I repeated. I frowned and looked at Miss Scarlet, who shook her head.

"I'm afraid it means nothing to me," she said.

"Never heard of it," said Jane.

Trevor stood and crossed to the fireplace. He rested his hands on the mantel and absently took one of those odd globes into his hands, caressing it as though he weighed its worth. Only when he turned back to us did I see that what he held was a human skull. On the shelf behind him its fellows stared with gaping eye sockets, as though suddenly betrayed. I was so startled that I spilled my drink.

"The town of Cassandra once housed a research facility," Trevor pronounced in a deep voice, as though delivering a lecture. "Quite similar to HEL, as a matter of fact, but a much older compound, nestled out there in the mountains. Far enough from the capital that they could carry on their work without fear of contaminating the City's population, but near enough to be considered part of the whole military-biological complex."

"What—what did they do?" I stammered.

"Geneslaves. Cassandra was the first facility in North America to carry out bioengineering on a huge scale—for the purpose of pure research, I mean, not merely as a commercial or military venture. Some of the effects created there have never been duplicated."

As he spoke, the aardman began to make a low noise deep in its throat. The flesh curled back from its mouth, showing sharp white teeth and blackish gums.

*"Burdock,"* he snarled.

Giles snapped something, a phrase I didn't catch, and Fossa grew silent.

Trevor nodded. The firelight sliced through the crook of his arm to touch with dark gold the hollow eyes of the skull he cradled. "It was the home of Luther Burdock. His compound was there, near the caverns."

He paused, as though waiting for me to show some recognition of the name. Outside, the storm sent branches scraping at the windows, and I could hear the wind screeching like a wild thing trapped in the chimney. I tore my gaze from Trevor's face and shrugged.

"I've never heard of him."

He turned to Miss Scarlet. "And you?" he asked softly. "Does the name mean nothing to you, Miss Scarlet?"

When I glanced at her, I gasped. The chimpanzee had reared up in Jane's lap, her lips drawn back in a snarl. Her mane of stiff hair stood straight up, and even from where I sat, I could catch the ammoniac scent of her fear.

"Luther Burdock!" she hissed. Her long fingers flew to her throat and temples, clutching at the thick fur. Beneath the dark hair was a series of raised scars, where long ago Ascendant researchers at the Zoo had performed the experiments that left her with human speech and thought, but imprisoned within the body of a monkey. "His 'files, they made us watch his 'files—"

Her voice trailed off into wordless chatter. Fossa cocked

his head and whined softly, and Jane hugged the chimpanzee close to her.

"Who is he?" I demanded. "Scarlet, *tell* me!"

Miss Scarlet shuddered, saying nothing, but Trevor nodded. "Geneslaves," he said. He held the skull out at arm's length, eyeing it critically as he added in a matter-of-fact tone, "They all know of him, somehow. Either they have seen 'files of him, or heard his name, or—"

I started to demand a better explanation than this, when Giles broke in smoothly.

"Perhaps this isn't the time, Trevor. Perhaps we should show our guests to their rooms. I'll start dinner."

"No!" I said. "I think you should tell us—"

But Giles and Trevor had already started for the door.

"I'd like my clothes," Jane called after them, her face pinched. "*And* my weapon."

"Of course, of course." Giles paused beside his partner and took the skull from Trevor's hand. "Marlena Hawksbill?" he asked, placing it back upon the mantel with its fellows.

"Sextus Burchard, I think," said Trevor. In her little chair Miss Scarlet pulled the tartan more closely around her frail shoulders. Her rage had faded; once more she looked like some Ascendant child's toy. I bit my lip, feeling an agony of sullen anger and dismay. I longed fiercely for those powers I had lost, the rage and strength that might have protected us, gone now, all gone. . . .

"Come." Giles walked to the door and paused, waiting for us. Jane stood and wrapped herself in her blanket like a cape, sweeping from the room with her head in the air. Miss Scarlet followed her more cautiously, almost fearfully. As she passed where he crouched upon the floor, the aardman Fossa stood. He stared down at Miss Scarlet with intelligent wolvish eyes. She stopped to stare back up at him. He was three times her size, graceless where she moved with the elegance of a courtesan; and yet—

And yet suddenly I could see the affinity between them, something older even than their bond as geneslaves. At HEL I had seen holofiles of cave paintings, eerie drawings from a site in Uropa that had been destroyed during the Third Shining. Tiny black mannikins flinging spears at fleeing ibex; crouched figures stalking something with bulging eyes and vestigial tail, something that looked very much like the aardman Fossa. I had paid little attention to those 'files—the paintings were gone, after all, turned to ash and steam along with all those other treasures from the Magdalenian epoch.

But now I felt as though one of those cave paintings had come to life and moved in the smoky firelight before me. Only Miss Scarlet held no weapon, and the creature that stared down at her was nodding slowly as it growled, "No harm—no harm—"

In the hallway Jane stared back impatiently.

"Come on, then," she snapped. I rose and left the room, hugging my blanket tightly across my chest. Fossa padded after me, and Miss Scarlet beside him. As we walked down the hall, I was surprised to see that weak daylight now shone upon the frayed carpets. The shrieking wind had died away. Outside, it seemed, the storm had moved on. Inside Seven Chimneys I felt as though it had just begun.

We were given three adjoining rooms in the upper story of one of the long ells that extended from the back of the main house. Small rooms, probably not the finest at Seven Chimneys, but clean and comfortably furnished with tired furniture that looked accustomed to its surroundings. My chamber had a small fireplace—"A Jeffersonian fireplace," Giles explained proudly; "this was part of Virginia once"—and overlooked sloping fields that in the distance surrendered to woodland, all now lost beneath the snow. Solar panels were fixed to the roof below amid a spiky array of antennae. I was surprised to see a video monitor beneath the window, small but with all its dials and screens intact. I pressed a switch, and waves of gray and white covered one screen. Hissing filled the air, but no images. After a moment I turned it off.

There were other odd things as well. A kinetic sculpture in the bathroom, showing a young man coyly disrobing and ducking into a spray of water. Talking books that whispered long-forgotten titles when I picked them up: *Jane Eyre, Descent into Hell, Magya Pliys 754*. There was even some kind of telefile, much larger and older than any I'd ever seen, but so shiny and clean, it seemed never to have been used. Its yellow plastic headpiece fit snugly over my temples. When I clicked it on, I heard faint music, all clicks and sirens and high-pitched voices. *Warhola Amarosa,* a late twenty-third-century castrato opera. Two summers ago Gilgor, one of the other empaths at HEL, had played it incessantly. I removed the headset and stared at it, frowning. Where was the transmission coming from? I knew that Curators used to broadcast to radio receivers within the City, but surely such transmissions had been curtailed by the occupation. Who would be broadcasting something as trivial as an opera if the City was under siege? But if the transmission didn't originate in the City, where *did* it come from? Puzzled, I replaced the headset and explored the rest of the room.

Everything appeared to be of a similar vintage as the opera, perhaps one hundred fifty years old. I picked up a holo chip the size of a pebble and held it to my eye, saw a miniature and incredibly detailed landscape of sunset cliffs and azure sea, with archaic aviettes scuttling across the sky like beetles. There was a machine that played back a recording of Trevor and Giles arguing about house repairs, and a vocoder that, when I spoke into it, translated my words into Tagalog. I went from one corner of the room to the next, continually astounded to find objects so old that still *worked*, that hadn't been destroyed or remanded by the Ascendants. The vocoders and 'files and machines all had the air of being stockpiled, as though Seven Chimneys were some sort of museum; and perhaps that was the truth of it. Perhaps Trevor Mallory's family had somehow managed to keep all these things safe and hidden through the years. Or perhaps they kept them here expressly for those high-ranking Ascendants who visited once or twice a year. But that seemed unlikely. If these things were really intended for use by Ascendant guests, they wouldn't be hidden in the back bedrooms. Still, who else would use such things?

In the City I had seen how the Curators managed their collections of ancient objects, archaic computers and navigation systems and engines jumbled up with sarcophagi and the petrified remains of ancient archosaurs and other extinct creatures. Everything treasured and catalogued and studied, but all with their original uses forgotten or perverted over the centuries. Even items that had been in common use at HEL—'file chips, torchieres, simple prosthetics—were in the City used primarily as ornaments by Paphians, or battered among the Curators as mere oddments.

Yet here in the wilderness two solitary men had retained the use of a telefile—and the fact that it picked up transmissions meant that somebody *else* had one, too. I frowned, flicking at a robotic monad the size of my little finger. It buzzed and retreated back onto the shelf it shared with toothbrushes and empty morpha tins. Suddenly I felt exhausted. The first stirrings of the grief I had held in check began to creep through the crumbling layers of my fatigue. I turned to dress for dinner.

My clothes were laid out on the spindle-bed, dry now if no cleaner or warmer than they had been. But beside them were other garments. A blouse of thick buttery suede, trimmed with bone-and-glass buttons; a long flowing skirt of some kind of jacquard, crimson and deep blue and shot with gold thread. There were high woolen boots, too, with heavy leather soles, knit in an intricate pattern of red and green and white. I sat for a long time, holding the blouse and stroking it. I thought of Justice: how I always had traveled with him disguised as a boy; how it had been months and months since I had worn woman's clothing—not since leaving HEL. I picked up the torn tunic I had worn at Winterlong and brought it to my face, smelling ashes and blood and smoke. Without warning, grief overwhelmed me: like nausea, waves of it so powerful, I could scarcely breathe. I fell onto the bed and sobbed, until sorrow gave way to rage and I ripped the tunic end to end, clawing at my face and then burying it in a pillow so that I could scream without being heard, over and over and over again.

A name: *Justice.* And another—

*Aidan.*

The name I had used in the City of Trees. But Justice was dead now, buried somewhere in the bowels of the Engulfed Cathedral along with Anna and Dr. Silverthorn and all those other victims of the Mad Aviator. All of them dead, or imprisoned, except for myself and my two companions. But I felt as though I alone had survived, Wendy Wanders, Subject 117; no longer lovely or powerful, no longer safe within the citadel my mind had erected around itself since my tormented childhood.

*Alone, alone, alone!*

I wanted to shriek, recalling the Cathedral in flames, and the City itself like some lovely canvas, curled and blackened, burning, burning. All of it gone; all of them, even the Mad Aviator, dead.

But then I remembered what Giles had said.

*"It will be the best news we've had in a year if we knew him—if he's really dead, as you say."*

I shivered, pulling the suede blouse to my chest. Impossible, of course. I had seen the Aviator fall, his face torn away by the impact from Jane's pistol. And yet, and yet . . .

Grief turned to terror at the thought of Margalis

Tast'annin, still alive somewhere; still searching for me. I forced myself to focus on something else—the kinetic sculpture's monotonous dishabille, the clicks and whines from the castrato aria; my own voice chanting in another language.

And finally grief and terror gave way to a numbness, an utter exhaustion that was like a sort of joy. My head ached from crying, but the tears were gone now. Carefully I placed the suede blouse back upon the bed. Then I gathered my old clothes and brought them to the tiny fireplace. Piece by piece I fed them to the flames: trousers, blouse, belt, scarves. Thick foul smoke filled the room as the cloth danced upon the metal hearth, but I didn't care. I waited until the flames died back, then, heedless of the pain, stuck my hand beneath the grate and drew back fingers smeared with hot ashes. When I rubbed them on my face, they tasted bitter and burned my tongue; but all I could think of was Justice burning, all I could wish was that these had been his ashes, that I might somehow have tasted his death.

It was Jane who found me there a little later. Naked, staring into the little fire grate like a dull child, my mouth smeared black, my hands filthy.

"Wendy," she said gently. I wouldn't look at her, but I could hear the heartbreak in her voice. "Oh, Wendy—"

She pulled me gently to my feet and helped me into the bathroom. There she washed my face and hands, dabbed at the wound on my cheek, and brought me the new clothes from the bed. Like a patient child she dressed me, saying little, rinsing my hair until it was free of soot and blood. Then she kissed me, her mouth lingering on my cheek, her lips parting the slightest bit so that I could feel her warm breath. When she lowered her face to kiss my hands, I saw the tears in her eyes.

"Oh, Wendy," she whispered. I shut my eyes and breathed deeply, tried to bring up some image that might ease the pounding in my head; but found nothing but Justice's face, pale and lifeless where he lay on the Cathedral's stone floor.

"Go, please," I said hoarsely. Jane's hands slid from mine. I could hear her crossing the room, hear her pause at the door where I imagined her looking back at me, her brown eyes bright with tears. Then the door opened and shut, and I was alone once more.

Not long after that someone tapped gently at my door. "Dinner soon," Trevor's soft drawl came to me. "We'll be downstairs." I heard him pass to the next room and call to Miss Scarlet. I waited until his soft tread echoed on the steps again. Then, sighing, I walked to the mirror that hung near the door.

The new clothes did not suit me at all. Part of it was their anachronistic cut. No one wore skirts much anymore, neither men nor women. These obviously had been made for a woman, someone my own height but with wide hips and heavy breasts, the kind of woman the Paphians might name margravine at one of their masques. They were not clothes that became me. In my boy's attire I had always looked beautiful, a tall, slender youth with tawny hair and gray eyes, too serious, perhaps, but with a softness about my mouth that had made me popular with my Paphian audiences.

All that was gone now. The Aviator's words came back to me, when he had imprisoned me at the Cathedral—

*"Not so pretty as you were, Wendy Wanders . . ."*

And it was true. My singed hair hung raggedly around my face; my face itself was gaunt and gray save where my cheek had been seared, and that livid scar glowed like the impression of some deathly kiss. My eyes were swollen, but that seemed almost a mercy—who could bear to look into those eyes now, that had seen such things? The blouse and skirt hung limply on me, neither too large nor too small but just *wrong*—clothes made for another kind of life than mine. Already I regretted burning my other things. I raised my hand to cover the reflection of my face, when another knock came at the door.

"Wendy?"

Miss Scarlet's voice, hesitant and worried.

"I'm coming." I turned, walking clumsily with the long skirts billowing about my bare legs. I refused to wear those woolen boots. They made me think of moujiks, sour-faced Balkhash peasants straining over their fields of soy and triticale.

"Dinner smells good, at least," Miss Scarlet said as I joined her in the hall. Her voice had a sharp, forced brightness. I nodded silently, refusing to meet her eyes, and she tried another tack.

"There was a telefile in my room. And a dumbwaiter. And some kind of imaging mirror that showed what my insides looked like. What's your room like?"

I shrugged. Miss Scarlet pursed her lips. "At least they gave you new clothes."

I gave up and smiled wanly. "You, too." It was impossible for me to be unkind to Miss Scarlet for long.

She ducked her head and did a little pirouette on the bare pine floor. Her clothes had obviously been made for a child, a boy probably—cheap cotton trousers and a too-small tunic that Miss Scarlet had belted with a remnant of her Winterlong finery. It was odd to see her dressed like that, with none of the elegance she usually affected. The tunic's arms were too short, and her hands bristled at the end of them, thick with dark fur, her palms the color of an old-fashioned pencil eraser.

"Your shoes didn't fit?" she asked. "Neither did mine—"

She stretched out one foot until her long toes curled around the banister at the head of the stairs. She looked over her shoulder at me and grinned, and for an instant I thought she was going to swing down, hand over hand. Instead she waited patiently until I reached the steps, and walked demurely at my side.

In the main corridor we found Jane. She had changed back into her own clothes, which looked so travel-worn and stained, I asked if she hadn't been given new ones.

"I feel more comfortable this way," she announced. "Look at these." She pointed at the water-stained plaster wall where two paintings hung, side by side.

*Flight!* was the caption on one of them. It showed a terrified black-skinned woman clutching a bundle and stumbling down the embankment of a wide, furiously boiling river. At her heels a ravening mass of hounds slavered and howled, and in the background I could barely discern the hulking figure of a white man with a face as hideous as the hounds'. Upon closer investigation, the bundle the woman hugged to her proved to be an infant. It was a very old print, nearly as old as the house, I would guess, and like much else at Seven Chimneys could easily have belonged in one of the Curator's museums.

The other picture was not nearly so old—three hundred years, perhaps. It was a holofile, set in a round frame of gold chromium brushed so that it had a rough veneer like wood. The 'file showed a dark landscape done in swirling blues and violets, a landscape thick with trees and watched over by a shining quarter-moon. As I stared at it, clouds passed across the moon's face, turning the shadows beneath into slashes of black and indigo. But then the clouds moved on; the moon glowed brighter, revealing a scene much like that in the other painting. Only instead of hounds, there was a brace of aardmen, silvery monitors winking around their necks as they pursued something down a sharp incline into a ravine. I had to peer more closely to see what they hunted: a figure like a very tall man, but with a childish face and huge, heavily muscled arms that ended in disproportionately large hands.

"Ugh," I said, drawing back. At my side Miss Scarlet craned her neck, trying vainly to make out what I saw. "Don't," I warned, pushing her gently down the hall in front of me. "It will spoil your appetite."

"*Flight to the Ford,*" the 'file whispered its title as we hurried past. Jane followed us with a rigid smile on her pale face.

"There seems to be a kind of *theme* here," she said, fixing me with a fierce look. Before she could go on, Trevor appeared in a doorway ahead of us.

"Very nice," he said. He looked at Miss Scarlet and me and murmured approvingly. He had changed into a kimono, a blue so deep, it was almost black. With his enhancer and his sharp features and silvery hair, he looked more like an elegant replicant than a human host. "Please, *please* come in," he urged.

It was a splendid room; even Jane drew her breath in sharply as we entered. A rich burgundy-colored paper stamped with golden poppies covered the walls. In places mildew had eaten away at the pattern, but that only made it seem lovelier, more of a miracle that it had survived so long. A huge Oriental rug covered the floor, woven with plumes and arabesques of blue and gold. The edges had worn so that you could see the carpet's weft, and beneath it the wooden floorboards shining with oil. A chandelier hung from the ceiling, some of its crystals missing. Thick red candles burned in empty sockets that had once held electric bulbs, and the wax dripped to congeal on a table that could have seated twenty, though only six places were set. I was wondering who the sixth could be when Fossa entered from another doorway. He walked in that mincing way that aardmen have, and I was surprised to see jewels glinting from his thick wrists—heavy bands of steel burnished to a glossy finish, set with amethysts and the holo-projecting lozenges called hyalines.

"Fossa—" Trevor indicated a seat, an elongated divan piled with pillows. The aardman hunched his shoulders, mur-

muring something unintelligible. He settled into the chair, his
long legs drawn up beside him. I started when Trevor gently
prodded my shoulder.

"Please, Wendy—" He pointed to a chair opposite Fossa.
"Be seated."

It was a strange meal. Giles and Trevor sat at opposite
ends of the long table, with Miss Scarlet and me on one side
and Jane and Fossa across from us. Above our heads the candles in the chandelier stayed lit, despite the tiny electric lights
glowing from recesses in the walls behind us. Lakes of molten wax continued to spread across the scarred tabletop. In the
background soft music played. I recognized the repetitive
chiming voices, broken by bass notes like snarls. "The Eleu-
sinian Chorus" by Marriette Greeves, something else familiar
to me from HEL. A faint perfume of almond blossom filled
the air, and wisps of smoke bore various smells from the
kitchen—a pungent note of rosemary, the mellow scents of
cumin and fenugreek and roasting garlic.

"You will try our wine, of course." Trevor broke the uneasy silence, one eyebrow raised above the shining arc of his
enhancer. Giles smiled and turned in his seat, beckoning to
someone in the kitchen. A moment later a server appeared, the
first I had seen since we arrived. It was far older than those we
had used at HEL, walking on stiff steel legs jointed backward
like those of a heron. Its metal torso gleamed. The black grid
of its face had been painstakingly covered with an overlay of
lenticular leaf that showed a soothing pattern of soft greens
and blues, an effect reassuring to those aristocrats who had
used the first-generation servers, and preferred this abstract effect to a crude effort at replicating a human face.

"Wine please, Mazda," Giles ordered.

"Yes, master," the server hissed, and crane-stepped back
into the kitchen.

Trevor and Giles tried to draw us into conversation, but
Jane was too wary and I was too exhausted to say much. Miss
Scarlet and Fossa carried on a heated discussion of medical
practices and ancient cinema. The aardman had adjusted the
hyalines on his wrists so that blurred projected images appeared at the end of each of his thick, knobby paws—crude
holos of a pair of perfect, milk-white hands with tapering fingers set with many rings, glowing with that slightly blurred
aura that surrounds cheap, Archipelago-made hyalines. The
projected hands moved perfectly with Fossa's own. As he and

Miss Scarlet spoke, I watched him, his hulking figure bent over the table, lifting his fork and knife with those ridiculously delicate fingers and bringing the food to his gnarled face. I stared fascinated, until Miss Scarlet shot me a disapproving glance and I turned back to my meal.

The food was odd, too. Not the wine, an earthy cabernet served in goblets of that mouth-blown violet glass made by abos in Wyalong—Trevor must have a fine cellar, with such crystal to match it. But after a sweet, soft white goat cheese served with lovage and rue (fresh herbs! in winter!) the server brought in platters that steamed and gave forth a heady, musky scent.

"Wendy." Giles nodded at Mazda to indicate it should serve me first. "Please, help yourself—"

With steady, gleaming hands the server ladled out a dark broth. Small round objects swam in a rich sauce, heavily scented of juniper berries. I stared doubtfully at my plate as the replicant continued around the table, then passed back into the kitchen for the next course and began the whole process again.

"What—what *are* they?" I asked at last, poking at my plate with a knife.

"Mushrooms," said Trevor. His enhancer sent lavender ripples dancing from his wineglass as he held it to the light.

"*Mushrooms?*" said Jane.

"Mushrooms," Miss Scarlet repeated avidly from where she balanced on a stack of books atop her chair. "How lovely!"

There were mushrooms in sauce; an aspic of tiny pink mushrooms like the tips of one's fingers; a tray of what appeared to be slices of bread, but which were actually great round crescents of the sort of fungus one finds growing on trees. Across the table Jane gulped her wine and picked at several mushrooms stuffed with garlic and herbs, while next to her Fossa ate greedily, as did Trevor and Giles. I nibbled tentatively at one breadlike wheel and found it very bland. Still, I couldn't quite bring myself to clean my plate, and like Jane I drank a lot of wine.

"They're the only plants not affected by the mutagens," Trevor explained between mouthfuls. "Everything else—corn, tomatoes, beans—we harvest half what we once did. Come winter we're pretty much reduced to living on whatever herbs we can grow in the greenhouse. And even those don't do very well in natural light—too much from the high end of the spectrum. So it's gotten difficult to put things up. The tubers don't keep the way they used to, and with the fruits we're pretty much limited to eating them as fast as they fall from the trees—they practically spoil overnight.

"But not the fungi. We tested them; for some reason they don't retain toxins the way that plants do. Of course, I mean the ones that aren't poisonous to begin with."

I put down my fork and motioned for Mazda to pour me more wine. I was thinking of those skulls above the fireplace.

"We believe it's because they grow so quickly," Trevor went on. "The spores actually mutate faster than the mutagens, and after a few generations there's no trace of the psychoactive agents at all. And mushrooms grow like—well, like mushrooms—so now they seem to have thrown off the viruses completely. We hope."

Giles nodded. "We cultivate these, of course. Had to, in order to have anything to eat in winter."

"So you live on *mushrooms*?" Jane picked mistrustfully at her plate.

"Oh, we have some stores of dried beans, lentil flour, things like that. And some very good chutney I put up last year—the chile and spices keep the pears from turning. But in the last few years our produce just hasn't been very good. Once the soil is contaminated . . ."

Giles sighed and shook his head. "It didn't used to be like this. Now we have to trade for much of our food from the mountain people—venison and root vegetables, mostly. And of course all sorts of things come from Cassandra."

When I looked at him questioningly, Trevor broke in. "It's always been difficult for the fougas to maneuver out there, in the mountains. You would be surprised—there are places in the Blue Ridge where the viral rains have never fallen."

"And the wine?" I raised my glass. "It's very good—"

"*That* comes from Cassandra, by way of the Ascendants," Trevor said. "May I toast our guests?" Candlelight sent motes of gold and black dancing across his enhancer, and he smiled.

Dessert was a custard fragrant with rose water—apparently the mutagens had spared some chickens and a cow, or else our hosts had stores of ersatz food in their pantry. But by then I was too tired to do more than poke at my bowl with a long-handled silver spoon.

Shortly afterward we went up to bed. Giles bade us good night and retired to the kitchen, but Trevor accompanied us to our rooms. More than once he had to help Jane up the steps. She had steadfastly refused to eat much, and the wine had affected her more than it did Miss Scarlet or myself.

"Night," she said thickly at the door to her room. She regarded me through slitted eyes before adding, "Ge' some other clothes," and ducking out of sight.

A few steps more to Miss Scarlet's room, where she turned to our host. "I have not had such a fine meal in many months, Sieur. You are a most gracious innkeeper, to serve impecunious guests with such courtesy."

Trevor looked down at her, amused, and gave a little bow. "Our pleasure. We like to help those less fortunate, when we can."

Miss Scarlet reached up to pat my leg as she went inside. "Sleep well, Wendy," she called softly.

Trevor went before me to the next door, waving his hand in front of light-plates so that the hallway dimmed. I followed him into my room, still uneasy and feeling a little drunk myself. Someone had put more wood on the fire. Trevor bent to poke it, sending sparks flying into the room, and threw on another log. Then he crossed to the window, checking the casement to make sure it was closed and clucking his tongue at how heavily the snow lay upon the roof.

"Would you like some different clothes?" He turned back to me, his enhancer catching the light from the fireplace and streaking his face with gold. "I'll be glad to get you more—"

I shrugged. There was that odd smell again: not unpleasant but so strange, like lemons buried in the earth. "Clothes? Well, yes. If you have them. I—I'm not accustomed to things like this. Skirts—" I almost told him how I had traveled so long disguised as a boy, but instead explained lamely, "An actor—actress—you know—and skirts are clumsy for traveling—"

Trevor smiled. "Of course. You should have said something. Your friend Jane—your lover?"

"No!" I hadn't meant my voice to sound so sharp. I sat abruptly on the edge of the bed, blinking to keep tears from my eyes. "No. My lover was killed two days ago, at the feast of Winterlong. He was a Paphian, a Saint-Alaban. . . ."

Trevor's voice was kind. "I didn't know. Forgive me—it must have been terrible for you—"

I remained silent, willing him to leave. After a moment he said, "The clothes you're wearing—they belonged to my daughter. But there are others here somewhere. I'll find them and lay them out for you tomorrow."

I bunched the bed quilt between my fingers. "Your daughter?"

"Yes: Cadence. She lives in Cassandra, but I've still got many of her things here. I'm afraid they're not very fashionable. She's a bit older than you—"

Laughter crept into his voice as he added, "*Much* older, as a matter of fact. But her clothes seem to fit, even if the style isn't what you're accustomed to."

"I didn't mean to sound ungrateful," I said stiffly. He crossed the room to leave, and I started to rise.

"Please," he said motioning for me to sit. He stood in the open doorway, his strong, youthful hands incongruous with that white beard and hair. "I know you must find this all a little strange, Wendy," he said gently. He tilted his head so that blue light leaked from beneath his enhancer. "But you're safe here—probably safer than you'd be anywhere right now."

I tried to keep my voice from sounding cold as I replied, "It's just that such kindness to complete strangers—it's unusual, that's all."

He laughed again, softly. "Giles and I are very unusual people, my friend. We've entertained refugees here before; I'm sure we will again. But you have nothing to fear while you're under this roof. In more than six hundred years no harm has ever come to a guest of the Mallorys. Not unless provoked . . ."

He inclined his head and left, the door clicking softly behind him. And despite my weariness and the wine buzzing inside my head, I lay awake for some time afterward, staring at the shadows cast by leaping flames while I pondered his last words and what he meant by them.

I woke late the next morning. The wind raged at the eaves as though it would tear the shingles off. During the night, someone had come in to put more wood on the fire, so that the room was very warm. Smoke flurried from the fireplace, and the sun shone blindingly through battlements of icicles around the windows. A clock beside the bed read half past ten. I felt more clearheaded than I deserved, considering how much wine I'd had at dinner. For a long while I lay there, staring at the tin ceiling and counting the stenciled grape vines circling the walls.

When I finally got out of bed, I found more clothes had been piled neatly on a chair by the door. As Trevor had warned, they were shockingly out of date—some of them reminded me of the costumes we used at the Theater, nearly a century old, nylon threads fraying, patched with much newer fabric. Only these clothes were in much better condition than our costumes. Many seemed almost new, only the faded scarlet of a brocade robe or a string of shattered lumens hinting at their age. I dressed quickly, pulling on heavy blue canvas trousers and a pullover of nubby brown wool. When I went downstairs, I met Giles in the hallway, wearing a heavy shearling coat, his cheeks ruddy with cold.

"Good choice!" He beamed, plucking at my sweater. "That's from our sheep, that wool—"

I followed him into the kitchen. A very old wood-burning cook stove stood against one crumbling brick wall, a cheerful thing with green enameled doors and a rusted kettle steaming softly atop it. Breakfast, thank god, was a meal not totally reliant upon fungus. There were eggs kept warm in a tiny glass oven (another curious relic), and some kind of mutton sausage, its gamy taste mitigated by juniper berries. And tea—real tea, nearly black from sitting in its pot on the woodstove for most of the morning—and grainy honey dipped from a cracked glass bowl.

"No, the sheep do very well. The animals weren't taken by the virus at all," Giles explained, as though taking up the thread of a conversation we'd begun just minutes before. He sat across from me at the battered table, reached into a pocket, and withdrew a small paper package. "Cigarette?"

"Where did you get *those*?" I hadn't smoked a tobacco cigarette since I'd been at HEL. In the City of the Trees, the Paphians had hinted darkly that the tobacco trade was dead, killed by the Ascendants. Giles pushed the package across to me.

"Cassandra." He leaned over to the woodstove and lit his cigarette, inhaling deeply. "Cadence sends them to us."

"But—I haven't seen one for months. I heard the crop failed."

Giles nodded. "That would be the party line. The Ascendants tried to take over the farms in Cassandra—this was about a year ago—but things just don't work like that in the mountains. So the trade dried up, for the Ascendants at least. Most of it goes west now, over the mountains and north to the United Provinces. And of course we get our share, and keep them on hand for guests."

"Your Cassandra sounds like an interesting place."

Giles tipped his head back, blinking thoughtfully. There was something studied about his expression, as though he were playing at a casual manner. "Oh, it is, it is. They have some interesting beliefs—salvation, great destinies, things like that. Remarkable, er, *people* there. Not much like us, to tell you the truth. Very interested in, um, religion, and—well, I guess you could call it politics. In taking a sort of—er, a global view of things. You might enjoy talking to them some time. If ever you go there, I mean. Quite an interesting place, oh yes."

I stared at him blankly. He drew on his cigarette, looked around before continuing in a conspiratorial whisper. "Cassandra's the center for all these changes, you understand. There's a—they have a sort of replicant there, a marvelous thing they found hidden in one of the caverns. It can send and receive messages from HORUS, it advises them—"

"Who?" I asked, exasperated. "*Who* does it advise?"

Giles looked surprised. "Well, *everyone*. I mean, anyone who's interested in what's going on." His eyebrows arched dramatically, and he fixed me with a knowing look, as though I too were expected to know whatever the hell was going on. "You know, Dr. Burdock and all the rest . . ."

He spoke the name with reverence. I sipped at my tea, and after a moment asked rather crossly, "It sounds like this Dr. Burdock made quite an impression there. If they're still talking about him four hundred years later. What happened to him?"

Giles's good-natured face puckered into a frown, and his gaze flickered uneasily from me to the floor. "He was a victim of one of the fundamentalist Ascensions," he said at last.

"And this replicant that can communicate with HORUS—" I had only ever heard vague rumors about the ancient network of space stations, where political refugees were supposed to have fled and founded the first Ascendant Autocracy centuries before. "What's *it* doing there? It doesn't sound like these people have much use for the Ascendants."

But now Giles decided he'd said enough. "There are some strange old things in Cassandra. And here, too. Trevor is only one of them."

He laughed softly, almost to himself, and ground out his cigarette in a small brass dish. So that would be all the explanation I got, at least for now. I stretched my hand across the scarred old table and picked up the cigarette pack. It was made of thin, pulpy gray paper with a logo stamped on it in bleeding red ink. The logo showed the image of a pyramid with an eye inside, surmounted by a star or sun. Beneath it was a single word spelled out in strange characters.

Ιχαρυσ

I pointed at the unknown word. "What's that mean?"

Giles only shrugged and looked away. I took a cigarette from the packet. It was needle thin and hand rolled, and tasted sweet.

"They cure them with hashish and honey," said Giles. He poured himself some tea and took a sip. I started to ask him again about the symbols, the eye in the pyramid, the foreign word, but before I could speak, he pushed away his cup and stood. "Well, I better get back out there. Miss Scarlet's in the barn, trying her best to keep out of the way. Your friend Jane is helping me with the cows. She's a wonder with animals."

I smiled. "She was a Zoologist in the City."

"That's what she said. Well, she'll earn her keep here, that's for sure." Grinning, he slapped the table in farewell.

So I had the kitchen to myself—very pleasant, with the sun streaming through the high windows and the mingled scents of my hashish cigarette and the fruitwood burning in the woodstove. I thought about what Giles had told me, marveling. A place in the mountains where people did not live in fear of the Ascendants. A replicant that could talk to the fabled HORUS colonies. And this peculiar Dr. Burdock, who seemed somewhere between saint and demon. I tried to recall if Dr. Harrow had ever spoken of him at HEL. But I drew up nothing, and wished again I'd paid more attention when Dr. Harrow was trying to teach me about the history of our world.

I finished my cigarette and put together breakfast from the things kept warm in that magical little glass oven. I ate eggs and sausage and a kind of crumbly green cheese, took a few bites of the breadlike bracket fungi and drank my tea. The hashish left me feeling pleasantly muddled. It reminded me of mornings at the Human Engineering Laboratory, where we young empaths were given every luxury and no one would disturb our meals if we wished to eat alone. That was before Justice and I fled HEL; before my brain had sprouted new neutral pathways that allowed me to feel emotions as others did. Now, for the first time I found myself missing the regime at HEL. It had seemed like—it *was*—a prison, especially during the last weeks of my tenure there; but how much calmer that life seemed than the one I had now.

And suddenly Justice's face appeared before me. I closed my eyes, trying to will away the surge of grief, wishing I could once again be the detached creature Dr. Harrow had used and discarded; but it was too late. I had no visions left. Now, when I tasted my own tears, or Miss Scarlet's or Jane's, there was only bitterness on my tongue. It seemed to me that it was a terrible price I had paid for my brief time with Justice. Once I would have raged over my unhappiness, but even rage was gone from me now. So I sat, the sunny morning gone cold about me, and drank my tepid tea alone.

From somewhere in the house a clock bonged the noon hour. I stood and began pushing dishes around on the counter, wondering if I should go find my friends in the barn.

"Ah! You're awake."

Turning, I saw Trevor in yet another doorway—it seemed every hall led to the kitchen in this house. He wore faded old clothes and carried a basket filled with more mushrooms. "Come with me," he called, smiling and beckoning me toward him. He started back down the corridor. I looked around, half-hoping for someone else to appear; then with a shrug I followed him.

The hallway was narrow and dark, windowless, barely wide enough for two to walk abreast. On the walls hung rows of flaking canvases and flickering holofiles, more of the crude artwork that I had seen last night in the main hallway. Each one depicted some theme of cruelty, to humans or geneslaves: energumens howling at the touch of a sonic probe, men chained to the deck of a wooden ship, gaunt women huddled in the shadow of a vast shining aircraft. As I passed, the 'files whispered their titles to me: *The Last of Home, Captivity, Bound for Sternville, Luther Burdock's Children*. I wanted to avert my eyes but could not. Vulgar as they were, the images were compelling, pathetic monsters and cruel masters doomed to play out their terrible drama in this forgotten place.

"Underground Railway," Trevor said, his soft drawl magnified in the long hallway. "My family has been part of it for six hundred years."

Underground Railway? I shook my head, but of course he couldn't see me in the dark. Before I could ask him to explain, he halted. He fiddled with a catch in the wall, and a door sagged open.

"Careful. It's steep down here—"

There was no handrail. I walked with both hands outstretched to touch the walls, afraid I'd fall on top of him. No lamps hung here, but an eerie violet glow poured through the darkness below. At the bottom Trevor waited for me.

"This is where we do most of our farming," he said, ducking to avoid a beam.

I followed him into a cavernous space, chilly and dank and smelling of earth and soft rot. Walls formed of immense flagstones rose about us. In the center of the basement a huge double archway of brick supported the ceiling.

"Central fireplace." Trevor slapped it, his hand leaving a damp mark on the masonry. "Mid–eighteenth century. Some of the same masons who did Monticello did this. Hasn't moved an inch in six centuries."

The room felt older far than that. I could imagine it being built a thousand years before, the stonemasons slipping on the clayey ground as they dragged their stone and bricks in, hod after hod. Beneath my feet the earth was smooth but uneven, as though carved of ice. Along the walls makeshift shelves held stacks of greenglass bottles, winking in the dimness like spiders' eyes.

"It's a little slick here, so be careful," warned Trevor. He moved easily, walking between the brick arches to where the lavender glow deepened. Following him, I blinked, stopped once to rub my eyes. The light had a peculiar *fuzzy* quality; the edges of things disappeared, so that I bumped into one end of the archway and grazed my knuckles.

"Here—" Trevor reached back and took my hand, pulled me gently after him. "It's hard, until you get used to it."

We stood in a vast open area behind the second arch.

From the ceiling hung lamps of all shapes and sizes, a jumble of lights that made my head ache. Ultraviolet tubes, deep purple growthlights, aquamarine diatom lanterns, kerosene lamps giving off a foul smell. Beneath them stretched row after row of narrow tables, piled high with what looked like rubbish. Twisted piles of sticks, rotting logs, shallow trays gleaming as though they held stagnant water. The stench of rot was heavier here, but as we approached the tables, another smell masked it. A thick earthy odor, sweetish and not unpleasant, but containing a range of other smells—vanilla, spoiled meat, the rich scent of bittersweet chocolate.

"This is our little farm," Trevor said proudly. He stopped in front of a table, bent, and picked up a half-sprung willow basket from the floor beneath it. "Some of them need strong light, others don't. And you can see how many different growth mediums we use."

That was what the rubbish was: fodder for thousands of mushrooms growing in the dark. I stepped after him, blinking as the light eased from blinding ultraviolet to soft green. There were tables stacked with decaying logs, sorted by type—oak here, birch there, a thicket of slender alder wands heaped on a rusted water-filled tray. From every pile sprang mushrooms, like villages built upon the ruins of ancient capitals. Fungi like frail coral, deep scarlet and palest yellow; common white toadstools; puffballs the size of a man's head. Trevor gathered some of these, his basket filled after he had pulled only four from their soft humus bed. He paused to pluck tiny red buttons from a grassy heap, tasting them thoughtfully before turning to a row of metal trays filled with what looked like fresh manure, smelling strongly of warm grass and sun.

"Psilocybin," he explained, holding up a little brown cap flecked with dull green. Its gills had turned bright blue where he had bruised them. "You'd be surprised what the Ascendants trade for these."

We wandered through the maze of tables, Trevor filling baskets only to leave them, seemingly forgotten, on the ground. At first the basement had appeared endless, but now I could see that we were approaching its far wall. The lights were dimmer here, mostly ultraviolet tubes that set the mushrooms and other fungus aglow with radiant colors beneath them. I hugged my arms to my chest, feeling the clammy air like a damp hand sliding beneath my sweater.

*"Now."*

Trevor's voice came softly in my ear. I started, turned to see him walking past me, past the last glowing fresco of deep violet and blue and orange beds. At the end of the basement stood an enormous glittering table that stretched from wall to wall. As I drew nearer, I saw it was made of steel, like those surgical stages used at HEL. Something was laid across it. More piles of logs, I thought at first—birch, probably, because they were so pale, and striated with darker markings. A very faint radiance hung above them, a silvery phosphorescence that shimmered slightly when Trevor bent his head over what lay there. I crept up behind him and stopped.

Fungus delicate as grasses sprouted from the logs, giving off a pale-green glow like mist. Some had minute fronds, covered with tiny projecting spines so that they resembled velvety ferns. Others swelled to club-shaped bulbs shining with some viscous substance, their bulbous protuberances a deep red. As Trevor moved above them, white threads like smoke streaked the air. A sharp lemony smell mingled with the scent of damp earth and decay.

*"Amanita cerebrimus,"* he murmured. And as he dipped his head to examine one of the growths, I saw for the first time exactly what lay upon the tables.

Corpses. Lined up head to toe, their arms stretched at their sides with palms opening upward as though to catch some lost rays of sunlight. Their chest cavities had been opened, their ribs neatly spread to show where their inner organs had been. Hearts, lungs, spleen; all traces of veins or musculature had been covered with the feathery mushrooms climbing over the smooth white bone like moss. I drew back horrified, but Trevor pulled me toward him, gently but with irresistible strength.

"Don't be afraid," he whispered. The orbs beneath his enhancer sent twin shafts of cobalt lancing through the emerald mist. "We didn't kill them, Wendy. They have been here for a very long time—years and years and years, some of them. The fungus preserves them. And the cold, of course."

He frowned and bent over one, prodding it with a long finger. "Ah, yes, Catharine Fong. We worked together for many years, before she died during a bombing by the Commonwealth. A wound in the chest, very clean, no damage to the brain whatsoever. It hardly even bled."

I tried to run, but Trevor was too strong. He pulled me

closer, until I stood above the cadaver's head. The flesh had been eaten away until only a bare skull remained, pure white and innocent as an egg. As I watched, Trevor bent and moved a flap of bone above the eyes, like a tiny trapdoor, then opened the entire skull as though peeling an orange.

Her brain was still inside. Crinkled and pale gray, and nearly white in spots, like beech bark. Hundreds of tiny star-shaped protrusions covered it, yellow and pale ivory, ranging from the size of a teardrop to some bigger than an egg. Trevor picked one and rolled it between his fingers, releasing a sharp, almost oily smell. Lemons, and the scent of fresh earth.

"I spent fifty years working on this project," he said dreamily. He pinched the mushroom between his fingers and brought it to his mouth, biting it crisply in two. "We started in Rochester, and when they burned Rochester, we started all over again in Warrenton. Fifty years, and that was just the beginning. . . ."

He held out the other half of the mushroom to me. I shook my head, clutching the edge of the steel table—anything to keep from crying out and turning to run. Trevor tilted his head, surprised at my refusal, and went on.

"It was a fluke. As a boy I had been intrigued by reading about the early research of Burdock and then Oona Wang, primitive compared to what they did later but quite fascinating in its way, a shame it's been overshadowed by Burdock's more sensational work. I was trying to find some way of splicing ovarian tissue with *Mitrula abietis,* something that would allow us to regenerate human cells using water and algae as a medium. Then *that* laboratory was gassed. When I returned several months later, I found the first strains growing there—one of the technicians hadn't escaped, and the spores found their way to his corpse. The citrusy smell made me curious—usually those things smell awful, as I'm sure you've noticed—and when I examined more closely, I couldn't believe what I saw."

His eyebrows arched above the enhancer as he popped the rest of the mushroom into his mouth. "It took forever. Decades. By then I was supposed to be working on other projects—the Ascendants have never understood how painstaking the true scientific process is—and so I had to continue my own work privately. And, of course, I couldn't just kill people to have a steady supply of corpses. Although that's how *they* would have done it," he added, shaking his head.

"Gradually I isolated the one strain, the *cerebrimus*, and found the ideal mating of spores and medium. And after some more time, the decaying process of the corpses themselves slowed. If you look, you'll see that some of them are remarkably preserved."

I looked where he gestured at the last cadaver, lying with the soles of its feet pressed against the slick stone walls. Its flesh was pale but with a rosy flush, not puckered or mottled as some of the others were.

I reached out to touch it, then snatched my hand away. "But—how did you—"

Trevor shrugged, as though the answer were obvious. "DNA," he said in his honeyed drawl. "The spores produce molecules that imitate those in human DNA, so successfully that they can fuse with them, and producing the same bends and cricks that cause human genes to mature. They repeated this process, over thousands and thousands of generations as I refined them.

"Human DNA is programmed to decay after a certain number of years. But these fungi cause mutations in the strands: when you eat one, it produces a sort of chemical explosion in your brain; and after the smoke clears, your DNA has basically reset itself. It's no longer programmed to die. This is no instant immortality, nothing as banal as that; but the rate of aging is slowed considerably. The really miraculous aspect of all this is that the brain cells themselves actually regenerate; and that of course is an effect the Ascendants have been looking for all along, with their geneslaves and other horrors."

He paused, staring raptly into the dimness, then added, "And of course, it has had some very interesting applications for some of the geneslaves. The energumens, for one. They have been engineered to have such fleeting life spans; but these could change all that."

Turning, he swept one arm out toward the banks of rotting logs piled high with their soft and luminous fruits. "I have made other discoveries as well," he said proudly. "All here, all by myself. Mushrooms that look like psilocybin and have the same initial reactions; but which cause a slow, debilitating madness, and ultimately death. And my *Amanita dacryion*, my little cups of tears—they taste heavenly, but after a meal you are filled with such sorrow that all hope flees, and all desire to live."

"But why?" I said, a little desperately. "Why all these—these *things*?"

Trevor's hand dropped to his side. "Because we have enemies, Wendy. Very powerful enemies. We have learned to fight with whatever weapons we can."

And then another thought came to me. I shivered, recalling his words earlier, and asked in a low voice, "How long has it been?"

He looked puzzled. "How long?"

I pointed at the corpses. "You said they've been here a very long time—*how* long?"

Trevor tapped a finger to his lips, leaning against the table so that his shadow cut through the green mist. "Oh—let's see—ninety years for Antonin, I think. A little more than that for Catharine."

"And upstairs—on the mantel, those skulls—"

He brightened, as though suddenly seeing the logic behind my questions. "Oh, those were some of the first ones. I brought them here with me—misplaced sentiment, I suppose. Giles finds them morbid."

"And you," I whispered. "How old are you?"

He smiled and plucked another of the star-shaped growths from the table. "I'll give you a hint. I was born in the Free State of Virginia, three years before the Third Shining."

The Third Shining. Nearly two hundred years before.

I took a deep breath and closed my eyes. When I opened them, he was still facing me, chewing calmly, his enhancer a silver crescent across his face. "Why are you telling me this?"

He shrugged, still smiling. "Because you and your friends will be with us for several months—at least until March, when the roads will be more easily traveled. And because I have learned from experience that guests here become curious, over time, and it is more expedient to explain certain things truthfully to those who can bear the knowledge—to those who might perhaps *benefit* from learning new things. And because I think that we share a common enemy, you and I. You know what it is like to have been enslaved, to have been a pawn in the hands of the Ascendants. Someone with your history, with your powers—you might well benefit from what we have learned—"

I shook my head fiercely. "I have no enemies—"

Again that raised eyebrow. "No? And what of Margalis Tast'annin?"

"He was a madman—I knew nothing of him before we were captured—and besides, he's dead now."

Trevor's voice rang out eerily in the dimness. "But what he stands for is not dead! The strength and horror of NASNA and the Ascendant Autocracy are not dead! They still breed geneslaves in their laboratories and cells. Everywhere on Earth humanity has become a tyrant, bending animals and children and heteroclites to their will. And not only within the Ascendant Autocracy: the Balkhash Commonwealth is no better, and some believe that the Habilis Emirate is worse."

I shivered. I had never had any interest in talk of this sort. At HEL, Dr. Harrow had tried in vain to educate her empaths in politics. I retained only a vague memory of multicolored images on glowing mapscreens, their borders swelling and retreating, amoebalike, as each day brought subtle and evanescent political changes to the continents depicted there. "I know nothing of this," I insisted.

"You should learn, then!" Trevor's hand slapped down upon the edge of a table. "Six hundred years ago there was a war here—a different kind of war, a ground war. They fought because men enslaved other men, bartered and sold them like animals. It was an abomination to man and nature, and the world never recovered from it. Even a hundred fifty years later it was still reeling from the horrors of slavery—and then the First Shining came and they were all wiped away."

I looked away from the glare of his enhancer. "But there are no slaves now."

"Aren't there?" Trevor whipped the enhancer from his face, so that the piercing light from his optics lit our corner of the room. "What were you at HEL, Wendy? What was Fossa? What was Miss Scarlet? And these are only the geneslaves! What of the moujik peasants from the Commonwealth, and the child farms on Kalimantan?"

I shook my head stubbornly. "I know nothing of this, nothing! And my friends know less—in the City they live simply, for pleasure only, or for knowledge—"

"In the City they live for nothing now!" cried Trevor. "Ascendant janissaries from Araboth and Vancouver have occupied it. If any of your friends survived the initial attacks, they are prisoners—slaves or worse. Your lover was one of the fortunate ones, to have died before they arrived. You of all people should know what happens when the Ascendants seize control." I said nothing, only stared numbly into the misty phosphorescence swirling about him.

He was right: in the days following Dr. Harrow's suicide, Ascendant personnel had swarmed into the Human Engineering Laboratory. They had murdered many of the other empaths and surely would have killed me as well, after subjecting me to more of their "research." I thought of the paintings and 'files hanging in the corridors upstairs; of the scars upon Miss Scarlet's throat; of Fossa, and the other aardmen who had given obeisance to the Aviator in the Cathedral. I thought of Justice dead; of countless others in the City of Trees, bound to steel gurneys with their heads shaved as mine had been, screaming as their minds were taken from them.

At last I said slowly, "I think I understand what you are telling me. But if you're part of some—some rebellion, some resistance movement—there's nothing I can do to help you. My usefulness as an empath has ended. My friends are as you see them: an educated geneslave who performs as an actress and a girl who's good with animals. That's all."

"Ah, but your powers might come back," Trevor said, an edge of excitement in his voice. "I know a great deal about these things—the proper stimulation, with drugs and psychotropic chemicals; even natural adrenaline could do it. . . ."

"*No!*" My shout sent a lantern swinging above us. "I am not going to be used like that again, not for anything—especially not for some fucking geneslave *riot*—"

Trevor dipped his head so that the light from his optics swept across the floor. His mouth was tight, his voice cold.

"This is not a riot, Wendy. Nor is it some hastily planned rebellion. Some of us have been working toward this for our entire lives—a means of undoing the wrongs wrought over the centuries by the tyrants, a union of mankind and geneslaves—

"An *Alliance.*"

He paused dramatically, then swept his hand up to indicate the rafters overhead, the many stories beyond. "We are part of an ancient tradition here at Seven Chimneys. We are a halfway house, a way-station for those fleeing the Ascendants. There were many places like this, once; Seven Chimneys is one of the last.

"The Underground Railway, they called it during the North American Civil War. It was the Sanctuary Movement later, and The Havens during the Long Night of the First Ascension." Blue light streamed from his face as he threw his head back and his voice rang out. My own voice broke like a boy's when I spoke.

"Who do you shelter?"

In a swift motion he clapped the enhancer back over his eyes. The brilliant blue rays of the optics were extinguished; now I had to squint through the shadows to see him. "Geneslaves. Fossa was one of the first. He has remained here with us, to help reassure others that they will not be betrayed. There have been many others: aardmen fleeing the City, argalæ kept as prostitutes by Ascendant troops, salamanders from the mines. And energumens, of course; and people like yourself. Oh, yes—we have taken in several escapees from HEL over the years. Not many, because not many survived long enough to reach us, but more than you might think. I was very impressed to see what Emma had done with them—her reasons were heinous, of course, but the results were very interesting. An entire cohort of adolescent psychic terrorists. They would have been very useful during wartime."

I bit my lip, not sure whether to believe him. But there *had* been unexplained disappearances at HEL from time to time—the empath Sarah Jabera was one, and a young telepath named Isaac Dunstan. I had always assumed they were suicides—there were always suicides at HEL—or else that they had been captured or killed by the fougas.

"I still don't know why you are telling me this." I spoke slowly, trying to choose words that would not offend him, or endanger me and my friends. "I can't help you—especially with geneslaves."

Trevor leaned so close that I could smell the bitter scent of lemons on his breath. "Oh, but you could!—we *all* could, if only enough of us would side with them, rise to overthrow the Autocracy! Already there have been riots in some of the HORUS colonies. The energumens and cacodemons have attempted coups on several stations. Just a week ago we heard of aardmen at a logging camp in the United Provinces—they slayed their supervisors and escaped into the Hudson Bay Territory. And there will be others, too, now that the geneslaves have started to throw off the tyranny of their human masters."

I tried to turn away, but Trevor clutched at my arm. "There will be war soon, Wendy: a different kind of war, a revolution from within! In some places it has already begun. There is a great purge coming, the beginning of a new age!

"But I am not alone in seeing this, Wendy—there are others, wiser and older than I am, who have seen into the future of our planet! They can read the skies as people once read books, and they have told me what is written there. A terrible secret, one that will irrevocably change our world. But some of us will be strong enough, wise enough, to learn from what is to come—and we will triumph! We will remake the world! We will bring about a true Final Ascension, one that will not thrive on slavery and barbaric despotism. One that will not be built on the bodies of slaves, human or otherwise."

I stared at him in disbelief, thinking of the ghoulish aardmen in the City, the diseased lazars and sentient trees and other mutated creatures that had deviled me since my escape from HEL. What insane rebels would ever ally themselves with *them*?

Trevor pushed me away impatiently. "You don't believe me? But you know it's true! You have seen them, who hasn't? Millions of creatures—living things, *sentient* things, creatures that can weep when their young are torn from them and creatures that will never give birth—made by humans to serve as slaves, discarded or murdered after they have been used! We brought them into the world, but it is a world some of them can barely survive in, they have been so carefully manipulated to exist only in those cracks and dark corners where the Ascendants want them to live and die while serving them. Rendered sterile by the tyrants; given life spans a fraction of ours; seizing the young of those who are permitted to give birth . . .

"If the geneslaves were all freed tomorrow, it would still be a hundred years, a *thousand* years, before we could ever make amends for the horrors they have endured at our hands. Only if we join with them to make war upon the tyrants; only if someday, perhaps, our blood mingles with theirs: then we may begin to expiate the suffering we have brought upon the world."

"They may have suffered, but *I* have never harmed one," I cried, feeling besieged. "I *flee* them when I can—they are monstrous things, they are monsters. . . ."

Trevor shook his head. "No more than you are. You are one of them, Wendy Wanders. I can see it in you: you are not as other people. Perhaps you never were. And to the Ascendants you are less than human."

"No!" I shouted. "I never was, *never*—it's over now, *there is nothing left*—"

My hands flew to my head, covering my ears. I could feel the scars there at my temples, the nodes that had slowly healed even as my ability to tap into the thoughts and dreams of others had faded. I wanted to scream, to lash out at him as I had done with others before; but it was true, my powers were gone now. There was nothing left.

"*You* are left, Wendy." I shuddered at how calm he sounded. "You know I speak the truth. You are not like the rest of us, not like Jane or your Paphian lover. You and Miss Scarlet have more in common than they do; you and Fossa."

I shook my head furiously, thinking of the aardman—his gnarled face, those curved yellow teeth and the tail like a fleshy whip between his hind legs.

"No."

"*Yes.* Admit it to yourself, Wendy: you belong with us, with all of us who are fighting the tyrants. It is a war against humanity; but you know that you are not truly human. Help us, Wendy. Join us."

"*No!*"

Trevor laughed softly. Behind him the rows of glowing corpses seemed to shiver in the ghostly light. He leaned forward, with one finger brushed the hair from my temple and probed the raised lip of skin there.

"Emma Harrow did this?" he murmured. At his touch a small fiery explosion went off inside my skull. I gasped, closing my eyes against the pain. "I would have proceeded differently—no scars, nothing to show that you had ever been touched. . . ."

I moaned, stiffening as his other hand slowly closed around my wrist. His words echoed in my mind—

. . . *very useful during wartime* . . .

"It's gone, my powers are gone!" I cried frantically. His grip tightened as I tried to pull away. "I—I went without my medication for too long—the visions left me, it's gone now, whatever power I had is gone—"

Trevor shook his head, his voice soothing. "That doesn't matter, Wendy. I told you, I am a very fine surgeon. Nothing matters, except that we *understand* each other."

Abruptly he let go of me. I staggered back, my hands

flailing as I tried to find something to use as a weapon; but Trevor only laughed, as though I had been frightened by some shadow on the wall of a sunny room.

"But we have a long time to learn how to do that, don't we?" he said. "All winter, in fact. And I'm certain that you will come to see how worthy our cause is."

He bent and began picking up empty baskets, stacking them inside one another. "Would you mind handing me that?" he asked lightly.

I stared at him warily, but he only continued to gather his things. Indeed, he seemed to have forgotten me. Finally I looked to where he had pointed and saw a willow basket, its contents lost in shadow. As I leaned down to pick it up, I heard him turn and walk back toward the steps.

"A remarkable theoretician, Emma Harrow." His voice rang faintly in the dank air as he began to climb the stairs. "But a rather clumsy surgeon."

I waited until I heard the door creak open upstairs. Then I followed him, the basket clutched between my cold fingers. It wasn't until I reached the top step that I glanced down to see what I held—

A skull.

A human skull with a number of small perfectly round holes bored into it. Between the holes words had been scratched into the flaking bone, and a crude image. Tiny cracks radiated from the letters like tears.

# EMMA WYSTAN HARROW

## *Sic semper tyrannus*

The Alliance was not subtle in its methods. With a cry I dropped the basket and fled to my room.

# 5

## Cisneros

**Neither Nefertity nor I** had any need for sleep. Sleep is for humanity, to ease its tragic passage from dreams to waking, and eventually from dreams to death. I had already crossed over to the other side, and could only look back upon my own dreams as one would review a distant landscape from some unimaginably high lookout: as something lovely but detached from oneself, as though one did not breathe the same air they breathed down there, or sip the same passionately blue water.

So I no longer dreamed, but during my months in the regeneration vats the biotechnicians did not apply the usual course of neural treatments to my swollen brain. If they had, I would have been as other *rasas* are: a mere corpse with the use of limbs and locomotion, with no will, no speech, nothing but the faintest haze of memories to cloud my dull eyes.

But the Ascendants had more ambitious plans for me. Shiyung Orsina, the margravine who monitored my progress, had the twin vices of sentiment and vengeance to interfere with my rebirth; and so it was that I made my reentry into the world with my memories intact.

More than that. My masters wanted me to lose nothing of the decades of training I had endured, all that time of being

heated in the crucibles of their wars and planning rooms, fired
by my own ambition until I was as finely tempered and lethal
a weapon as they could devise. To this end *all* of my memories were reactivated—a simple thing, really, merely a series
of electrical pulses administered to the proper quarters of the
brain, and then a wash of proteins to these same nodes. The
result of this excessive stimulation was ironic. Like all successful Aviators, I had spent my life *suppressing* memories.
To do otherwise was to court madness, because who could
live with the knowledge of what we must endure, between the
equatorial war zones and the orbital colonies above us? My
own mind had already reached its limit of guilty horrors, like
a sponge soaked in acid that is slowly eaten away by its burden. *That* was the cause of my degeneration in the capital; but
now the Ascendants had squeezed me dry, plucked from my
decaying body my mind like a small overripe fruit and set it
into this new shining shell, where it could neither wither nor
flourish, only continue. And with me my memories, fresh as
yesterday's rain. No, more so: because while I could no
longer taste or smell or feel the rain upon my tongue, my
memories of storms fifty years past were enough to whiten
my sleepless nights with lightning and lancing hail.

And so, all unknowing, the Ascendants had imprinted me
with the undoing of all their efforts. By electing my regenerated corpse Imperator, they thought they had created at last
the ideal military commander: bloodless, heartless, but with
the mind of a tyrant and the deathless teguments of their most
sophisticated constructs. But they neglected to consider the
power of memory, of desire that can outlive even the body.
They had restored my past to me. In so doing they also restored my soul.

On the edge of the rise Nefertity stood in silence, watching the dawn stretch its cold gray hands across the prairie. I
remained by myself, brooding on what could have befallen
the HORUS colonies and wondering what I might learn when
I sought out my masters once more.

Did I say I stood by myself? Ah, but it did not seem so
to me! I was besieged with memories, like Androcles butterflies swarming about a corpse. The dead came back to speak
with me, and others whom I had long forgotten—childhood
friends and lovers; janissaries who had served under me at the
battles of Nng Dao and Recife, and who died there when the

Shinings came; fellow Aviators and cadets from the NASNA Academy, their minds and wills not yet broken by our Ascendant masters, their voices so clear and loud, I could hear them crying out across the years as though they stood no farther from me than did Nefertity.

And thus it was that Aidan Harrow came to me again. Or rather, I went to him, my memories leading me until all about me the prairie faded and once more I was a youth: my arms aching from early-morning fencing practice with my replicant tutor, my bruised knuckles poised above the door to his room while in the distance I could hear bells wailing to signal the start of first reflections. Our floor rector, a slender, sallow woman named Elspeth Mandodari, had sent me to awaken the newest cadet.

"He has a sister in the Auris Wing," she said, adding in a voice tinged with disapproval, "A twin. But I'll get *her*."

It was common for cadets to sleep late during their first days at the Academy. The best of intentions and most sophisticated of alarms could not conspire against our need for sleep, especially since our days started before four A.M. In the summer this was not so bad. The Academy was located on the northeasternmost shore of the continent, on a cliff overlooking the Atlantic Ocean that was supposedly the first place in North America where the sun struck each day. By May or early June sun slanting through the gray-filmed windows would wake us at three-thirty; an hour later it would look as though it were midday outside. But even this had not been enough to rouse me during my first week at the Academy. Instead I was kicked out of bed by the boy who would later be my partner in Gryphon training, a bullying mulatto named Ivor French.

I had resolved to be kinder to the unknown somnambulist twin. I rapped gently at first on the heavy oaken door—a gesture more to ease my own conscience than to actually cause a stir inside, since to be heard at all one had to practically batter the planks with iron staves. But someone was already awake. A moment later a cheerful voice called, *"Entrez!"* And so I did, somewhat reticently, the door groaning as it swung in upon rusted hinges.

It was a standard first-level cadet's room. That is to say, a tiny, narrow cell perfectly in keeping with the Academy's original design some six hundred years earlier, which was as Le Couvent de Notre-Dame des Afflictions. Aidan's room retained its air of sunlit penitence. It overlooked the eastern ridge of the rocky fell called Plasma Mole, several hundred feet above where the ocean moaned and throbbed in dutiful counterpoint to our own smaller sufferings. Like postulants, we were not permitted to bring with us any remnants of our former lives. This gave the rooms an air of uncanny expectancy, as though even after centuries of silence and retribution they still awaited some measure of passion, of temptation or betrayal. Beneath a single window waited a coffin-sized iron bedstead, with its immaculate white linens, stiff from being dried outside in the chilly maritime air, and a feather pillow flattened by generations of aching heads. The smell of dust and pencil shavings was almost lost beneath that of the last rugosa roses blooming on the stony edge of Plasma Mole. The room's sole ornamentation, besides the gorgeous enameled slab of sky above a spavined wooden desk, was the plasteel representation of the NASNA motto and its blighted moon, hanging beside the bed. The whitewashed walls should have been almost painfully sunlit, the ceilings marbled with the viridian wash of reflected ocean.

But I was surprised to enter Aidan Harrow's room and find it dark. Actually, not very dark; but to one accustomed to that ruthless blue northern light, it had the appearance of a hermit's forest lair. I took two steps inside (four more would have brought me to the window) and shaded my eyes as though I had been blinded.

"Mandodari wanted to make sure you were awake," I said, trying to keep disapproval from clouding my voice. A cerulean cadet's jacket had been strung across the window and hung with other oddments of clothing in an effort to keep the sun out. I frowned and squinted. I still wasn't certain just where the room's tardy occupant lay.

"Mmm. Of course. Well, I'm up."

A head suddenly popped from the heap of covers on the bed. A stray shaft of light struck his hair, a mass of auburn waves surrounding a pointed puckish face, sharp-chinned and with a small pointed nose. He was tall and lanky for his age, but that face was oddly childlike; or maybe it was just his expression, the slight threat of mindless violence that was never absent from his gray-green eyes. When he slid from the covers, I saw he was already fully dressed. Indeed from the rumpled look of his linen shirt and leather trousers, I gathered he had slept in his clothes.

"I'm Aidan Harrow. From St. Clive." That was a tiny village in the southern maritimes, a day's air travel from Plasma Mole.

I nodded stiffly. "Margalis Tast'annin."

Aidan's eyes widened. "The poet's son? I heard you were here."

With one hand he began smoothing the tangled hair back from his forehead. In the other he clutched a book. At a loss as to conversation, I tilted my head to read the title—purely a matter of convention, since the only book we were permitted to use in first level was the ancient talking edition of *An Inquiry into Some Ethical Points of Celestial Navigation.* I was quite shocked to see that this was not what Aidan held at all.

"That's under interdict!"

I hadn't meant to sound so prudish: I was genuinely stunned that someone would be so cavalier about flouting the rules. Punishment for even simple infractions was severe—most of the infirmary was given over to punitive devices, many of them quite new—and possession of contraband reading material was a serious offense.

"Are you going to turn me in?"

Aidan looked at me coolly, but his tone was innocently curious. If he had acted belligerent or even frightened, I probably *would* have reported him. As it was, I shut the door behind me and crossed the room to take the book from his hand.

"No. But you better get rid of it, or hide it outside. May I see?"

Even before I looked at it, I could tell, by its scent and feel, that it had not come from the Academy library. A flimsy plastic jacket protected its cover and spine, but even that couldn't hide how old it was. I drew it to my face and sniffed. When I rifled the pages, dust smelling of cloves and hemp made me sneeze.

"It's just a book." Aidan's voice cracked and he flushed. "From my father—from his library."

The plastic cover was so old and desiccated, it was difficult to read the title. I opened it, holding it gingerly so that the loose pages wouldn't fall out. It was printed on thick paper that had aged to the color of rich cream, much heavier and softer than the cheap fiber used for talking books. The endpieces were marbled, yellow and blue and green. The title page held a little holo no bigger than the ball of my thumb, showing an elaborately stylized eye that seemed to follow me when I moved. Beneath it, title and author were jetprinted in a deliberately shaky hand.

# Errores Maleficarum et Incunabula

## by Michel DeFries

Beneath this was the legend *Privately Printed in the Independent Commonwealth of California* (later part of the Western Unity, and still later part of the Pacific Ocean) and a date some four hundred years earlier.

I stared at it curiously, and had started to turn the pages when I heard the electronic bell shriek the quarter hour, last call for first reflections. I swore, recalling Mandodari's punitive use of the memory enhancer, which exhausted one even as it made sleep impossible for days afterward.

"Here—" I shoved the book back at Aidan and strode to the door. "Do something with it—get rid of it, if you're smart. And do something about *that*—"

I glowered and pointed at the window draped with Aidan's clothes. "—Unless you want to spend the rest of the week in the infirmary."

The mockery vanished from his eyes. Nodding, he crossed to the window and tore down his jacket, sending socks and shirt flying. I left before I could see what he did with the book.

Nefertity and I left as dawn twined through the desert air. Nefertity wished to give farewells to the humans we had left in the valley. Not from any sentiment on her part—she was a construct, remember that, and I refused to believe her capable of any human feeling—but because she feared they might follow us and perish in the desert.

"Leave them be," I said. I had already turned and was starting for my Gryphon, Kesef, where it crouched on the hillside. "We will find them again if we need them. The world is a small place now, Nefertity. Come."

The nemosyne's eyes blazed azure. I smiled, thinking of the woman who had programmed her. What a monster *she* must have been! But I said nothing, stepping over clumps of prickly pear and broomweed, kicking apart a nest of fire ants until I reached the Gryphon and called out to it.

"Kesef. Wake."

The aircraft shuddered. Its deceptively fragile wings expanded like a bat's, unfolding into long blackened petals. From its nose several long filaments extended, testing the air. I could hear it humming inside as it listened to whatever tales those slender filaments might tell: rain, sun, wind; radiation, mutagens, storms. I guessed sun and a hot northwestern wind. Here where the great coastal prairies had once stretched for hundreds of miles, it was nearly always sun and wind.

From behind me Nefertity called softly. "Where are you taking me?"

I pointed to the west. A man's eyes would have looked down the sloping hillside onto an endless plain, gold and brown and green fading into a sky that daylight would soon scorch to white. I could see beyond that, to where the Glass Mountains rose and then gave way to the Glass Desert, where the few towns and cities had been embalmed in obsidian waves by the Second Shining. "To Cisneros."

She joined me beneath the Gryphon. We waited until it unfolded the narrow ladder leading into its belly, then climbed inside.

"And what is Cisneros?" she asked.

She slipped into the seat behind me, the restraining belts crackling softly as they looped around her glowing torso. I lay back in my own seat, feeling it mold itself to the hard shell I still could not think of as *my body*. I closed my eyes for a moment before replying, "NASNA's Pacific elyon base."

"Pacific? It is in the ocean?"

I shook my head as Kesef's neural web descended to cover my face. "Yes. Off the west coast. The southern part of the Californian peninsula, I think it may have been in your time."

Kesef hissed. In the broken lingo that Gryphons and Aviators use to communicate verbally, it asked how it could interface with me. I had no flesh for the web to adhere to save my right hand. I raised this and commanded it to use my eyes. An instant later I felt the cool dampish touch of the webs across them, my vision obscured momentarily as the gray mist resolved into an intricate pattern of cross-hatching and glowing orange grids. I felt the Gryphon probing my mind, its questioning clicks as once again it confronted the mass of cerebral tissue and neural wiring that had replaced my brain. Then silence as Kesef found the familiar strata of memory and command that had joined us for so long. I relaxed my hold on the arms of my seat, plunging into that blissful rush that signals the beginning of the biotic interface between Aviator and craft.

In front of me the interior of the Gryphon faded. In its place swam the image of Cisneros as I had last seen it, years before. Indistinct at first, then growing stronger and more lucid as Kesef's memory banks fleshed out the picture I struggled to recall, until it seemed I stood there again, swaying slightly with that unconscious rhythm one developed after months at base. The landing platforms rising and falling on the Pacific swells, their bands of light pulsing from green to violet and silhouetting the tiny figures of Aviators and ground crew, like blackened cinders swarming in the darkness. In the distance flames shooting skyward from the offshore refineries, and the flashing lights of the fougas patrolling the prison on Tijuana Island. The smell of burning petrol; the silken odor of the spray as it salted my leather uniform and pooled on the metal platform beneath my boots. Above me the NASNA standard snapped in the night, its cloven moon a maleficent eye glaring at the full and resplendent orb shining above the sea. If I tilted my head back, I could read the glittering letters pricked out upon the standard:

*Oderint dum metuant.*
*Let them hate, so long as they fear.*

And over all of it the Ascendants' fleet of celestial airships, blotting out the moon as they hovered above the loading docks, waiting to start their journeys to the HORUS colonies. Like vast ruby-colored clouds, like a second sky gravid with poisonous rain. The elÿon.

"Cisneros," I whispered: a command for Kesef. But there was no need for me to speak aloud—already the Gryphon had begun to quiver like a greyhound before a race.

"And there?" The nemosyne's sweet voice cut through the soft roar of Kesef's solar engines as they fed greedily upon their energy stores.

"There I will confer with my advisers. I will learn what damage has been done to the HORUS colonies, and decide which station might hold our prize. Then we will go there and reclaim Metatron."

I did not share with her my fears—that there might be no HORUS colonies left where humans still lived and ruled. Instead I focused all my thoughts on Kesef and tried to blot out images of HORUS in flames.

Aviators are solitary, trained—bred, some say—to possess a single-mindedness that drives them with mad abandon into the inferno that any sane person would flee. Nowhere is this singular passion more evident than in our tryst with the Gryphons. When I was at the Academy, it was rumored that our aircraft were quite literally a compendium of Aviator traits: that the brains of brilliant commanders who had fallen in battle were enshrined within the circuitry and neutral fibers of the next generation of Gryphons, a biotic Valhalla. Sherborne Zeal was supposed to have been immortalized thus, and Ciarin Jhabvilos.

I never gave much credence to those stories, but my link with Kesef had seen me through the Archipelago Conflict and the Shining at Recife, and even through the first skirmishes of the so-called Volcanic War, fought in that nether region of the heavens where the air is filled with flames. Once I had interfaced with Kesef, I did not like to have my concentration broken. I raised my hand commandingly.

"Silence now! I will tell you when to speak again; when we reach our destination."

The vision of Cisneros faded. In the darkened window in front of me I could see Nefertity's reflection, a woman made of light. She did not speak, but long after we had begun our ascent, the reflected image of her eyes burned through whatever visions Kesef might have shown me of the world that shimmered far, far below us.

It took us most of that day to reach the Pacific coast. We passed above the Glass Mountains: dark brown and black, as though charred by the explosion that had turned the western prairie into a smooth expanse of congealed sand, blinding to look upon. Then the dun-colored reaches of the great Nevadan Desert. Never a hospitable countryside, it had been largely ignored by warring factions of Ascendants, and to my knowledge had never been the object of viral assault by the Commonwealth or Emirate. So, surprisingly, in this barren wilderness one saw signs of human habitation—tent cities where the roving Children of Zion lived; the domed prospects of lonely families tucked within the shadows of the Toiyabe

Range; even tiny grids of yellow and green, brave efforts at hydroculture siphoning illegal waters from the Merino Aquifer. I had often glimpsed such ungoverned vistas from the air, particularly in the northern mountains and in areas like those ringing the California Peninsula, where the tremendous geological upheavals of the last centuries left huge fissures in the continent, unmapped and as yet unclaimed by the Autocracy. Aviators were supposed to report these homesteaders to NASNA Command. Months afterward you might see them at the Population Control Centers, each with a monitor clamped to her wrist; and then later set to work at the Archipelago's hydrofarms, or shipped to the sunless tunnels of the L-5 mines, or strapped unconscious to a gurney at the Human Engineering Laboratory.

I did not inform the Ascendants of what I saw in my travels, then or ever. I had no great sentiment for those small lives stolen from the beleaguered countryside, but neither did I hold any love for my Ascendant superiors, with their slave-run farms and the research facilities where they enslaved corpses when living bodies were scarce. I wondered now if those people living on the edge of the world had glimpsed some revolution in the skies above; if one night they had seen the stars in their courses shift or go out, candles extinguished by a freezing wind.

Our journey was mostly a silent one. A few times Nefertity asked me about the habitations below us, but I ignored her. I had a sort of joy in those brief moments of flight with Kesef—the only joy I was capable of feeling—and occasionally I cursed myself for bringing the nemosyne with me. At the least I could have disabled her speaking mechanism, but I did not.

It is difficult to describe my feelings for the nemosyne. Referring to Nefertity as *her*, when of course she was a construct. It was only that her coding program had been female, Sister Loretta Riding of the Order of Divine Compassion. Nefertity was no more feminine than I was masculine—less so, since just months before, I had been a man, and she had never been anything more than a delicately shaped array of neural wiring and glass and plasteel. But she held within her datafiles thousands of years of women's histories: folktales, songs, paintings, fables, poems: such a trove that I believe it somehow had shaped the rigid anima of a twenty-second-century robot and given it the sensibility of a living woman.

Despite the unyielding touch of her plasteel hands and the uncanny radiance of her eyes, it was impossible to think of Nefertity as anything but *she*. But even when I was a man, I knew there were those who believed I was not human, but a monster.

I was not, no more than any Aviator is a monster. If I had been, I would have rejoiced in my incarnation as a *rasa:* deathless, since my corpse had been regenerated; fearless, since what could harm me now? Harm a creature who had died and been reborn with this adamant shell?

But I did not rejoice. I loathed it, with a hatred that would have been impossible for me to fathom before blood and sinew and bones, skull and arms and torso were torn from me, leaving only a human hand and two raving eyes trapped within an Ascendant tool. Perversely, it had been that hatred that kept me sane—at least as sane as ever I had been—even as now it was hope that was sending me westward with the waning day.

Evening fell, the late fiery evening that marks nightfall in that part of the world. We were still many miles from the coast, but already the sky was streaked with the lurid colors coughed forth by the floating refineries and manufacturing forms that choke the Pacific shores like kelp. As we grew nearer, excitement filled me, to be returning there after so long. Kesef battled the night wind that rose from the cooling ocean. I could feel the slender structure shaking all around me, its wings hugging in close as it dived and then soared back into the twilight like a nighthawk. There was no sound except for the hollow rush of wind around the Gryphon's wings.

Behind me Nefertity sat in silence. Her body had cooled to a faint silvery gray, the color of dull metal. Only her eyes betrayed that she was anything but a common server. Anticipation of our arrival at Cisneros had whetted my desire for company; unexpectedly I felt the need to talk.

"We will be there very soon," I said.

Silence. I thought she had retreated into her dormant mode, but then a flicker of gold speared her breast, and she replied, "The thought seems to cheer you."

The golden threads spread like flame across her torso, captive lightning. Outside, stars began to show in the greenish sky. Below us there were no lights; only reflected sunset smeared across mile after mile of ruins, the fallen spires and spars of what had once been the great Pacific sprawl. I felt a pang, recalling other flights over this place.

"It is a place where I was happy once," I said. "My second assignment was to Cisneros. I was very young, just a few years out of the Academy—"

"Where was your first assignment?"

"Buru." Nefertity shook her head as I explained, "It used to be the primary assignment for all Aviators, a sort of training site. An island in the Archipelago. It is gone now—"

Swallowed by the rising seas that had claimed so many island and coastal countries; but no one mourned the fall of Buru, not even the cannibal janissaries who patrolled its capital before the deluge. "I was there as part of the peacekeeping force, keeping watch over the hydrofarms. My great fortune was to leave after only six months. That was when I came here."

She leaned over to stare out the tiny round window, steadying herself as Kesef abruptly dropped a thousand feet. "And what is—was—down there?"

Beneath us the jagged ruins rose like tiny islands from channels of deep blue water. For centuries nothing had grown there. After the devastating earthquakes of the twentieth and twenty-first centuries, the cities were abandoned, the vast farms and vineyards reclaimed by the desert. Then came the Split; and now the sea covered it all. As Kesef drew closer to the surface of the waves, the silence that had trapped us for so many hours began to give way. We could hear a hissing, and a sort of soft booming roar; then a series of crashes and booms, like the struts and spars of a ship giving way in a storm. Other tones rang out, some deep like the crush of machinery, some clear and sweet as bells. Beneath all of it was a steady throb, like the pulse of blood in one's ears.

"The Pacific sprawl. Ruined cities. Los Angeles, San Diego, Santa Barbara. All lost in the Split."

"All of them?" Nefertity's jadeite eyes glowed in the darkness behind me. "Just—destroyed? Like that?"

I shrugged. "They were fortunate for a long time. The survivors of the first earthquakes seceded from the rest of the country. Eventually they joined with the Nipponian Empire. The Nipponians had a greater defense system than the Autocracy; when the Split came, their autoclaves went on alert and destroyed the forces sent to help them. Nothing was saved. The *fantômes*—those are the abos who still live there in a few places, a pathetic race—the *fantômes* say they still dredge up bodies from the caverns beneath the ruins." I gazed down at the waves. "Listen—can you hear?"

Nefertity cocked her head and drew closer to the window. "Yes. What it is?"

"The sea gnawing at the foundations of the cities. The *fantômes* say it is the voices of the dead. They believe the sea is eating away at the world, bit by bit, and someday the rest of us will be devoured as well."

I turned back to the cockpit, scanning the horizon for my first sight of Cisneros. Kesef continued to descend, until we skimmed only a few hundred feet above the water. Twisted girders and shattered pyramids broke through the surface, some of them strung with ragged banners to mark where the *fantômes* had staked out their territories. I imagined I could smell their squalid settlements, reeking of fish and salted flesh, and once I did see a tiny group squatting on the edge of a makeshift pier, their hunched bodies silhouetted by the light of a fire burning in a steel drum. They might never know that HORUS or the Autocracy had been destroyed. Generations hence they would still be eking their precarious living from the sea and the detritus of an earlier civilization. When finally I tore my gaze from them, I saw the floating city before me.

From this distance Cisneros at first appeared to be a mirage, the weary eye spinning færy domes and turrets from the endless artificial reefs stretching below. But as we grew closer, the shimmering globes of green and gold and blue and crimson took more solid form. I could pick out the tall, slender recon towers, the ancient satellite dishes like a field of white poppies turned toward the stars, the glittering blue-green residence domes. Behind it all, plumes of brilliant flame and blue gas spewed from the refineries, miles off but seeming near enough that their heat might singe one's hair.

And hovering in the sulfurous sky like some mad dream of the floating city, the billowing mass of the elÿon: the biotic craft, half–living organism and half-machine, with which the Ascendants plied the nearer reaches of space.

"A Nipponian fleet!" Nefertity cried in amazement.

"No." I gazed at the elÿon closest to us, an umbrella-shaped leviathan the color of sunset, its edges rosy-pink and blurred from the heat of its engines. "Although the Ascendants did claim many of them after the Split. The Nipponian vessels are much finer than those made by the Autocracy."

"And so this is how you travel to the stars?"

"To the stars? No. Merely to the HORUS colonies." I turned away impatiently: we were coming upon the floating city so quickly, it seemed we might overshoot it. "Brace yourself—"

I closed my eyes, once more feeling Kesef's web probing for instruction. At my command the Gryphon stalled. For an instant we hung there as my mind filled with images filtered through Kesef's optics. Beneath us shimmered an impossibly wide vista of grids, covered with the glowing geometric patterns used in guiding the elÿon during docking procedures. On the deck five or six people had gathered, shielding their eyes against the glow of the airships. I had not ordered Kesef to signal ahead of our arrival, and unexpected landings were rare at Cisneros. They stared up at us, their faces lost in the shadow of their uniform hoods; one man clutched frantically at a vocoder and shouted into it. Cisneros, at least, seemed still to be functioning as an Ascendant outpost. Suddenly Kesef dropped, a vertiginous plunge that once would have made me grin with exhilaration. Now I only braced myself and waited. A grinding noise as the Gryphon's legs extended; a gentle bounce as we set down. We had landed.

Outside, the air was thick with fog. Within my metal shell I could no longer smell the mingled stench of sea air and burning petrol and the elÿon's saline odor, but I knew it was there: I could almost see it, thick as the yellowish mist that roiled in luminous columns above the landing decks. Kesef's ladder dropped from the belly of the craft, and I disembarked. The small group that had assembled drew back in nervous silence as I climbed from the Gryphon. I knew what they were seeing: a tall figure made of metal and black plasteel, an Aviator's crimson leathers flapping from its long limbs. But where an Aviator's helmeted enhancer should have covered its face, nearly colorless blue eyes glared out from a mask of scarlet metal, sculpted into the hawkish visage of a man.

"I am Margalis Tast'annin, Aviator Imperator of the Ascendant Autocracy." My harsh voice boomed in the cool night air. "Who is the Commanding Agent here?"

Blank faces stared back at me. A few of them gasped when they heard my name.

Then, "Imperator!" a voice called out. "This way, sir!"

The others turned away, seemingly relieved that someone was taking charge. The little crowd broke up. A few technicians began to service Kesef. The rest hurried toward the command tower. Only one remained to greet me, a slight woman in cracked leathers burned nearly black. As my boots clashed against the metal deckplates, she raised her hand in the Aviator's raptor salute, her voice strong and fearless as a young girl's. "An honor to see you here, Imperator Tast'annin."

I returned her salute. "I wish to speak to the Commanding Agent." Behind me I heard the muted click of Nefertity's feet as she climbed down the ladder. "My server will accompany us."

Nefertity joined me, gazing calmly at the woman. The sulferous yellow fog combined with the elÿon's crimson glow to make it seem that we were surrounded by some silent inferno. In the dense swirling mist the nemosyne looked like a revenant, her eyes cold and glittering. The Aviator gave a curt nod and addressed me again.

"I am Valeska Novus, Aviator Second Class. The Commanding Agent here is Caroline Shi Pei." For the first time she seemed uneasy. "Will you—would you like to rest before seeing her, Commander?"

"No. I want to go now. I have many questions for her. You may tell the technicians that my Gryphon is called Kesef. The server answers to Nefertity."

Valeska looked over at the technicians seeing to the Gryphon. "As you wish."

We walked with her across the deck. The yellow fog clung to everything. It was difficult to discern distances from one tower to the next save by counting the number of landing grids, like enormous bull's-eyes shining through the mist at our feet. Shadowy figures ducked in and out of passages and from beneath squat vehicles, some looking at us with fear, others merely curious. All wore the yolk-yellow uniforms of the Ascendant Autocracy. A few had wrapped thin blue scarves over their faces, so that only their eyes showed. I recalled that the *fantômes* believed the fog was poisonous, like the mutagenic rains spread by the Ascendants over the Northeast. It was not—at least no more poisonous than any other air in that noisome country. Beneath our feet the deck rolled, and there was a constant undercurrent of sound, as of cables straining and water crashing through empty lockers.

"We're still feeling the effects of the storms from last week," Valeska Novus explained, turning to look at me with calm hazel eyes. She was slight but strongly built. Her leathers seemed a little short in the cuff, her bare arms thick and muscular and crosshatched with deep scars. I could not guess her age: her dark hair was cut short and streaked with gray, but her voice was youthful. Her skin had that dark cast that comes from prolonged exposure to battle conditions in the Archipelago, as though one had turned one's face too long to the poisonous sun. She was not beautiful, as Shiyung Orsina had been beautiful—there was no delicacy there, none of the artifice or cunning with which powerful women seek to enslave others if they have no great intellect. But she seemed fearless, which I thought attractive—my emotions could still be stirred by such things, though my body was not. I found myself thinking of Wendy Wanders as I had first seen her in the Engulfed Cathedral, her defiance and rage even in the face of death; and unexpectedly I laughed.

"Imperator?" Valeska looked startled: *rasas* were supposed to be as devoid of emotions as the corpses they were generated from. She paused beside a recon turret, steadying herself as the deck pitched and rolled, then asked, "Did you come from Araboth, Imperator? We had heard it was destroyed by a cyclone, and there were no survivors."

I told her of the fall of Araboth, of the great tidal wave that had engulfed the Quincunx Domes, and how there had been no survivors save myself and my robotic aide. I did not tell her of the three we had left at the desert settlement, nor did I mention that I had murdered the margravine Shiyung Orsina.

"And so the other Gryphons were lost?" Valeska cried despairingly. "How terrible!"

I smiled. "No mourning for those thousands of lives, Captain Novus? Only for a handful of aircraft?"

She shook her head. There was not a trace of embarrassment or apology on her strong features. "It's a terrible thing—first we lost NASNA Prime last fall, and then came the rebellions. And now this. I am glad you—survived—Imperator." She tilted her head toward Nefertity. "And your server? Is it very new? I haven't seen one like it before."

"Very old," I replied tersely. I wondered what "the rebellions" referred to; also why there seemed to be no other Aviators at Cisneros. "Are we near to finding Agent Shi Pei?"

Valeska pointed. "That tower there."

It was one of the tall central towers, spiraling up from the middle of the platform like a ship's mast and painted yolk-yellow. But the salt air had eaten away at the paint so that dull bronzy red showed beneath, the color of the previous Ascension; a grim reminder like a wound that will not heal. I thought of the last Commanding Agent I had met with here, and asked, "What became of Agent Bristol?"

Valeska shrugged. "There was a purge after the destruction of NASNA Prime, and he was executed. He was suspected of collusion with geneslaves from one of the Wyalong platforms—they destroyed a hydrofarm off the coast of Brisbane. They are destroying outposts everywhere! Is that why you are here, Imperator? To lead us against the rebels?"

She gazed at me questioningly, but of course from my metal face she could tell nothing. I had in fact heard none of this. The Orsinas, the corrupt siblings who had ruled Araboth, were notorious for their attention to the trivial if colorful details of familial intrigue, and their failure to keep abreast of the current political situation. Between my months in the City of Trees and my time in Araboth's regeneration tanks, I was as guileless as a Paphian courtesan. But I only nodded and asked, "What is your most recent news, Captain Novus?"

She stopped in front of a door in the tower and looked at me uneasily. "There is no news, Imperator. We've lost contact with all but two of the HORUS colonies. Our contacts tell us that it is the same with the Commonwealth and the Habilis Emirate—their stations in HORUS have either been destroyed or taken by rebel forces. These are only rumors, of course, but . . ."

Nefertity had not spoken this whole time. Now when her voice rang out, Captain Novus started.

"With all this talk of treachery, perhaps we should not be so ready to follow her, Margalis."

Valeska's mouth rounded in amazement. "Your server acts as consul to you? And she calls you—she does not address you by your title?"

"That is no business of yours, Captain." My voice was cold, but in truth I liked her bluntness. It had been a long time since anyone had reacted to me with anything but fear. "I think we will meet no trouble here, Nefertity."

"My apologies." Valeska bowed stiffly, held the door open for Nefertity and me. Inside, a spiral staircase twisted above us. One could see at a glance how it had suffered from years of neglect—it listed dangerously to one side, and there were risers missing and yellow paint peeling everywhere. Windows no wider than a finger let in air and dull blades of hazy yellow light. For the rest, the darkened tower was lit only by silicon panels, their ruddy glow coarsened by time to an angry blackish red like smoldering embers.

The stairs rang as we climbed, the whole place vibrating as though the tower were only a bamboo pole thrust into damp sand. The windows afforded no view whatsoever, and Valeska wrinkled her nose and coughed at the stale air. Finally we reached the top, a narrow platform scarcely large enough to hold all three of us. Valeska stepped around me and reached for a metal door, pressed her hand against a scanner, and waited while the ancient mechanism whirred and clicked. Finally the door slid open, and we stepped inside.

Up here one could feel how the tower really *did* sway and shudder as the wind gnawed at it. The small round room seemed expansive after the stairwell. The walls were of clear plasteel, so that we could look out onto the whole of Cisneros spread beneath us. Old electrical boards and monitors lined the transparent walls, and cables were strung haphazardly across the floor. A single swivel chair was pushed close to the window, and here sat the tower's solitary inhabitant. I recognized the soiled yolk-yellow uniform, with the coded blue lumens that indicated its wearer was a rehabilitated criminal, a political prisoner whose mind had been broken and reshaped by the Autocracy.

"Agent Shi Pei." Valeska spoke respectfully but without deference—Aviators submit to no one save Imperators and Supreme Ascendant Governors. "It's Captain Valeska. The Aviator Imperator Margalis Tast'annin has come to see you."

A long silence. Valeska glanced at me and repeated, "The Aviator Impera—"

Before she could finish, the chair whirled about. A low voice greeted me.

"Imperator Tast'annin. Forgive me for not meeting you earlier on deck. I just learned of your arrival."

The Commanding Agent made no move to stand, only smiled furtively and stared at a point somewhere past where we stood. She spoke in the high nasal accent of the Asian provinces. A dark-skinned woman with the fragile features of the Commonwealth's eastern mountains, she held a slender porcelain carafe in one hand and a thimble-sized cup in the other. The bridge of her nose was tattooed with the butterfly ideogram that means *spy*. The floor beneath her chair was littered with broken candicaine pipettes. An empty carafe rolled across the room when she kicked it.

"Agent Shi Pei. Your predecessor showed more civility toward me when I last visited Cisneros."

Agent Shi Pei sighed deeply, poured herself a thimble of whatever the carafe held—syrupy rice brandy, I would guess—and drank it quickly. When she raised her eyes to mine, I saw that one was dark brown. The other was a prosthetic of marbled blue and violet, chased with flickers of gold: a keek, a cerebral/optical monitor. Coupled with her obvious drunkenness, it gave her a slightly deranged appearance.

"Ah! but things have changed since then. My predecessor is dead now and I am not, *Rasa* Imperator Tast'annin." She pronounced the word *rasa* with a faint teasing disdain, smiled broadly, and gave a slight hiccuping laugh. I began to think she was mad as well as drunk, but that might make it easier for me to hide my ignorance of whatever had befallen the Autocracy during the last few months.

"Agent Shi Pei! I demand a full report of your activities since Agent Bristol's execution. Where are the other Aviators assigned to this post? What has become of the HORUS colonies?"

Agent Shi Pei raised a delicate eyebrow above the prosthetic keek. "You don't know?"

I hesitated. If she learned of my ignorance, of how vulnerable I was, she might lie to me. I did not fear harm from her; I could kill her in an instant. But then it might be impossible to learn about the rebellions. I decided to tell her the truth.

"I have heard nothing. I spent most of the last year in the City of Trees and a regeneration chamber in Araboth. I barely escaped the Quincunx Domes before they were destroyed. I know nothing of what has happened, save that NASNA Prime was destroyed last winter. Last night I saw the sky for the first time in many months. The pattern of HORUS has changed."

Agent Shi Pei's other eyebrow rose, and something like dismay tugged at her mouth. "This is the first you learned of it?"

I nodded, and she let out a low whistle. *"Tell me,"* I said.

Agent Shi Pei sighed. "Last October NASNA Prime was

destroyed. A strike by the Commonwealth, we thought at the time. But then we received an SOS from one of the Commonwealth stations—an incomplete transmission, something about an insurrection. When a peacekeeping force reached the station, we found no one left alive but seven energumens. They attacked the boarding party but were overcome by our soldiers. But within a week all members of the original force who remained were dead. Some kind of plague, either engineered by the rebels or else accidentally loosed by the janissaries."

"And the energumens?"

Agent Shi Pei avoided my eyes as she reached for her rice brandy. "They survived," she said drily. "We received a transmission from them informing us of the death of the janissaries."

"I see."

I turned to stare out the window. Below us I could see small figures moving to and fro, a cluster of uniformed figures crawling over and beneath Kesef like so many yellow jackets. "Where are the Aviators assigned to Cisneros?"

"Most have been called into combat by the interim government at Vancouver. Captain Novus and two others remain, to provide me with some protection."

"What of the other HORUS stations? Helena Aulis? MacArthur?"

Agent Shi Pei took a long sip of her brandy before replying. "We don't know," she said at last. "Or rather, *I* don't know. Occasionally we receive word that someone—one of your Aviators, usually—has picked up some kind of strange transmission in flight. The talk is all of treachery, of overthrowing the Autocracy; but as far as we know here on Cisneros, the Autocracy has already been overthrown."

"Who commands this elÿon fleet, then?"

"I do."

"And who commands you?"

"No one."

I looked back and caught Valeska Novus staring at me grimly. "No one?"

Agent Shi Pei shook her head. "As far as I know, this is the largest remaining fleet that has not been seized by rebel forces. The last relay I received from the Autocracy was in April. That was over two months ago. Since then there have been scattered relays—one from Jhabvala 6, another from the

Vancouver bunkers. Oh, yes—and several transmissions that claim to be from the energumens on MacArthur. They say that they have overthrown HORUS and are launching an attack on Earth." She coughed and took another sip of brandy.

"That is all?" I tried to keep my voice from betraying fear and rage. "An insurrection in the Autocracy, and you can speak of it so calmly? Why was nobody informed?"

Agent Shi Pei laughed shrilly, the marbled keek rolling wildly in its socket. "Who is there to inform? The HORUS colonies are in the hands of rebels. We have heard they have formed an Alliance throughout HORUS and the other stations; that they intend to bring this Alliance to Earth and declare war upon us. Some of my people think it has already begun. They hear things, they tell me—messages, rumors . . ."

Shi Pei snorted. "Rumors! New ones every day—stray radio transmissions, 'files sent from unidentified sources. Last month we even had a replicant arrive to tell us of an explosion at the Port Lavaca refinery—the replicant had no human escort, no point-of-origin program, nothing. In the middle of the night files appear in my bedroom with messages for me. The Autocracy is slain or scattered, HORUS is gone completely; HORUS has been retaken, the Autocracy is saved. What can I believe? The only thing I know for certain is that there was a coup on the Helena Aulis station. The energumens there rioted and murdered the entire station colony, and from 'files that were broadcast to neighboring stations, it appears that the victims were cannibalized. A single aviette escaped with Livia Marconi and her advisers aboard and landed at Vancouver three months ago, but I have heard nothing since then. And the city of Araboth is fallen, but you knew that."

Suddenly Shi Pei's face seemed immeasurably aged, as though the mere recitation of these horrors had been enough to exhaust her. She ran a hand across her forehead and sighed. "I've tried contacting my former superiors at the embassy at Kirliash in the Commonwealth, but so far there's been no response. Two Aviators flew to the old capital, where you were last year; my last message from them was that the entire city was in revolt against the janissaries. There are other strange things, too. Six weeks ago I received a disturbing report from the Chief Architect at the Hotei station."

She paused, ducking her head in the manner people of her country employed when embarrassed for another. "He said—

well, he claimed to have seen that eidolon your people talk about."

I frowned. "What thing is that?"

Agent Shi Pei flicked her fingers in distaste. "That millenial star, whatever you call it—"

"The Watcher in the Skies," Captain Novus finished for her. "It was only a single report, Imperator, and a week later the Chief Architect went mad. Copper poisoning, we think."

I shook my head impatiently. The Watcher in the Skies— another legendary apparition of the HORUS colonies. "Don't tell me about phantoms. What else has gone wrong?"

Agent Shi Pei sighed. "Well, as for us—there hasn't been a supply ship here at Cisneros in six months. It's all I can do to keep my troops from defecting and joining the *fantômes*," she ended bitterly. "There is justice in this, Imperator. Slaves always rebel; even geneslaves, it seems. With your education, you and the other Aviators should have known that."

She spat the last words at me. I looked away, recalling the empty spaces between the stars where the HORUS stations should have been.

*You should have known.*

She was right, of course. If I had not been so driven by hatred and my need for vengeance in Araboth, I might have learned of this sooner. Only days sooner, but it might be that we had only days left. For a few minutes the room was quiet. I could hear Valeska Novus breathing, Agent Shi Pei prying the cork from another bottle of rice brandy. Nefertity remained motionless and silent, watching us with her calm eyes.

At last I said, "I wish to have an elÿon for myself and my server."

Shi Pei's hand shook as she poured another measure of brandy. She held the tiny cup up to me, then drank it in a gulp. Tears sprang into her one eye as she stared at me incredulously.

"An elÿon? After what I've told you? For what—yourself and a *taomatan*? A fembot?"

I nodded and she hooted, banging her fist on the arm of her chair. Angrily I clenched my right, human hand. I had long before decided that I would simply kill anyone who tried to stop me, but to my surprise Agent Shi Pei rose and took a few unsteady steps until she stood before me. She bowed, arms crossed in her country's mark of obeisance, then made a clumsy gesture with her fingers meant to be the NASNA salute.

"Of course, Imperator! Did you think I would refuse? But who else is left to command me?"

For an instant I saw a cold glitter in her eye—a look I had seen before in the eyes of traitors, a shaft of betrayal and guilt that quivers where it cannot be dislodged. Agent Shi Pei noticed my expression and quickly looked away. "Though it is madness, I think, to travel to HORUS," she added with a sullen frown.

"I intended to go before I knew of all this. But now it seems I waited too long."

I stalked impatiently toward the window, turned to look back at her. "Have you ever heard of a replicant kept by the Autocracy in one of the stations? An unusual construct, very old, very finely made. It might resemble that—"

I pointed at Nefertity. Agent Shi Pei regarded the nemosyne wearily, and finally shook her head.

"Never. But that doesn't mean anything, Imperator. They might have any number of such things up there—" She flapped her hands, indicating the ceiling. "I have never traveled to HORUS; besides, I am a rehabilitated war criminal. I would not be privy to such matters."

I nodded curtly. "Of course. Very well: ready an elÿon for me."

Agent Shi Pei's mouth twisted into a cold smile. "Ah! but which one do you want? I would advise against the *Caesaria*—"

She lowered her voice conspiratorially. "I knew her adjutant in his earlier life as a saboteur for the Commonwealth. He suffered from hallucinations *before* he was chosen for his present position."

Behind me Valeska cleared her throat. "Perhaps you should prepare a formal request, Agent—"

Shi Pei made a rude sound and glared at the Aviator, her prosthetic eye rolling wildly. "Haven't you been listening, Captain Novus? Who would I petition? He is an Imperator—surely he has wonderful reasons why he wants an elÿon. Who am I to stop an Aviator—even a *rasa* Aviator—from going to a second death?"

Her laughter rang harshly through the room, and suddenly I saw the rage behind that single amber eye. Probably she had been a high-ranking officer in the Commonwealth before she was taken as a prisoner of war, rehabilitated, and then sent here as a test of her new loyalties. That would account for the keek. It would also explain her drunkenness—alcohol and drugs impair the stability of the prosthetic monitors—and her casual acquiescence to my request for an airship. I felt a fleeting kinship with Agent Shi Pei, and when I spoke again, my voice was less cold.

"The construct I am looking for is called Metatron. I believe it might have been brought to Quirinus two hundred years ago."

Captain Novus shook her head. "We lost contact with Quirinus last month, Imperator."

"Plague!" Shi Pei cut in gleefully. "A traitor got on board, a psychobotanist supervising the disbursement of provisions. Strain 975, *irpex irradians,* introduced via a shipment of rice from Mudjangtang. According to the notice of death filed by the station computer, only the energumens survived."

She tugged at a flap of her uniform and removed a long black cigarette, lit it, and smoked in staccato fashion. "Of course you and your consul would not have anything to worry about from plague, *Rasa* Imperator."

*Irpex irradians:* the radiant harrowing. One of the older microphages, dating to the Second Ascension. Even as the bodies of its victims succumbed to the quick wasting and dehydration of the disease, their minds grew more acute, seeing in the air subtle colors that have long been lost to the rest of us. In their last hours they rave ecstatically, of lights and angels and the thoughts of men darting like goldfinches through the air. Perhaps two solar days might pass between the plague's inception and death. Survivors have described the smell of the corpses as being reminiscent of lilies. Not the worst of the plagues created by the Ascendants, except that without its serum antitoxin there was no survival rate whatsoever.

"I am moved by your concern, Agent Shi Pei," I said coolly. "Perhaps now I could make use of your expertise in a matter of less importance—"

She tapped her cigarette ash onto the floor, her nostrils dilating so that the butterfly tattoo seemed to flutter. "Of course, Imperator."

"Some months ago there was a research subject who escaped from the Human Engineering Laboratory, in the Northeastern United Provinces. Subject 117, a young girl named Wendy Wanders."

Shi Pei frowned. "I have no jurisdiction over HEL. The Ascendant Governors—"

"She is no longer under HEL's control, and according to what you have told me, there is some doubt as to whether there *are* any more Ascendant Governors. I want to find this girl. She escaped into the City of Trees and lived there for several months, disguised as a young man named Aidan. I was with her immediately before my death; I believe she is still alive. I want her found and brought to me."

Agent Shi Pei and Valeska exchanged glances. Finally Valeska said, "That City was retaken by Ascendant janissaries in January, Imperator. As Agent Shi Pei told you, there has been some trouble, and it has been necessary to use viral weapons to restrain the rebels there. As far as I know, any survivors of the original invasion were detained as a recreational labor force by the new governing body there."

I smiled grimly at the thought of Subject 117 drafted as a prostitute by the Ascendants. "Then it should not be difficult to trace her."

"*If* she survived." Shi Pei tossed her cigarette across the room. It struck the window in a burst of sparks and dropped to the floor. "And *if* I can reestablish contact with the City."

"She survived. I'm sure of it."

Shi Pei raised her eyebrows. "And what does the Aviator Imperator want with this young girl? I assume the obvious reasons no longer apply to a *rasa*."

I crossed to the window and ground out the smoldering cigarette beneath my boot, gazed down upon the smoky yellow lights and softly swirling mist. "She was an empath engineered as a terrorist, a suicide trigger. When I last saw her, she was somewhat confused—it appeared her empathic abilities had been impaired, by grief or stress. I may have a use for her in spite of that. If what you say is true—if there is a geneslave Alliance planning war against us—then we may need humans like her fighting with us. Wendy Wanders. Find her for me."

I continued to stare out the window. Behind me I heard a click as Shi Pei withdrew a vocoder and repeated the name. "Anything else, Imperator? Requests for aid from the Emirate's fleet? Messages for the dead in Elysium?"

"I'd like to see a roster of the elÿon in port. We'll leave

immediately." I turned in time to see Valeska looking anxiously at the nemosyne. "My server won't need clearance, Captain Novus. You may accompany us to the elÿon and vouch that we are not allied with the rebel forces. Agent Shi Pei, I trust you will carry on your duties here until you are relieved of them."

I glimpsed Agent Shi Pei's bitter smile as I strode toward the door. She followed, stooping to pick up a heavy book with marbled cover. She flipped through it, marked a page with a bit of torn paper, and handed it to me.

"Here—I think this is the current list. Remember about the *Caesaria*." She made a mocking bow as Nefertity and I passed.

In the doorway I paused. I reached out and rested my metal hand upon Shi Pei's shoulder. The derisive lines faded from her face; her brown eye rolled nervously, then blinked closed as I squeezed her. A moment later she cried out, buckling beneath my grip. When I let her go, she staggered against the wall. Valeska stared openmouthed, her Aviator's composure shaken.

"The empath. I will be expecting to hear from you within one solar week, Agent Shi Pei." Without another word I tramped down the stairwell.

The book Shi Pei had given me was heavy, with creamy thick pages and gilt edging, its covers an expensive swirl of violet and blue and yellow. Rather an archaic means for a Commanding Agent to track the comings and goings of an Ascendant staging area; but inside I found a meticulous record of just that, page after page of transport duties, arrival times and departures and ports of call, with the names of the various elÿon transcribed in an elegant hand whose delicate characters resembled ideograms more than our Arabic alphabet. The violet ink made the tiny figures difficult to read at first, but eventually I puzzled it out—

> *General Li*
> *Angevin*
> *Izanagi*
> *Stella d'Or*
> *Caesaria*
> *Pierre Toussaint*
> *Esashi*

Of the seven listed on the page Shi Pei had indicated, I had only ever traveled aboard the *Angevin* and *Izanagi*. Both had been appropriated by Ascendant forces, the *Izanagi* being a stalwart Nipponian vessel, the *Angevin* a Gaulish freighter. The rest were mostly Ascendant vessels, built on the North American continent, and I was wary of them. My Academy training notwithstanding, I had seen too many Ascendant-made vessels sabotaged—it took only one disgruntled technician or clever geneslave to infect a nav program and bring the whole enterprise crashing down. Nipponian vessels were sturdier, their minds harder to infiltrate. I chose the *Izanagi* and handed the book to Valeska.

"Inform the *Izanagi*'s adjutant that we will be boarding and departing as soon as the ship can ready itself. Have the technicians place my Gryphon Kesef on board."

She saluted and disappeared in the warren of towers on the main deck. Nefertity watched her go impassively, then turned her unblinking eyes on me.

"So now we will travel by starship?"

I laughed, my boots making a hollow boom on the metal grid beneath us as we walked. "Starship? No. There are no starships, Nefertity. Only a few old military vessels retrofitted for commercial transport between here and HORUS."

She nodded. A fine rain had begun falling. It softened the edges of things, turned the glaring landing lights into golden halos, and made Nefertity look as though she were encased in glowing blue velvet. "And it is a long trip, to these space stations?"

"Not really." From a speaker overhead a tinny amplified voice announced the hour and number of the shift that was due to change. A sudden frantic rush of yellow-uniformed personnel seethed from previously unseen doors and tunnels; there was much swearing amid the clatter of boots and the nearly silent hiss of rain. Then abruptly all was still again, as though the inhabitants of an overturned beetle's nest had burrowed safely back into their holes. The platform's rocking subsided to a gentle swell. From somewhere in the fog above us a kittiwake moaned, and I could hear the beating of its wings as it passed into the mournful darkness. I looked at Nefertity and said,

"The elÿon are all biotic craft, controlled by the thoughts of their adjutants—it is an old technology, and the Nipponian fleet was supposed to be the most sophisticated. And no, it does not take very long to reach HORUS. Perhaps three or four solar days; but time runs strangely in the elÿon. For humans, at least. For you it may be different."

A smile glinted in the nemosyne's face. "And for you? Does time move differently for *rasas* as well?"

I did not reply. In my short life as a *rasa* I had noticed that, without sleep, the weight of constant visual and aural stimulation sometimes made it difficult to recall where I was. Memories would flood me: I could not remember if I was still a student at the Academy, or on board a fouga in the Archipelago, or back in the Engulfed Cathedral with my madness. Then there were the jagged impressions of my death, mostly images of lights—sudden gashes of green or yellow brilliance, like sickly lightning—and noise, muted roarings or poppings that I imagined now had been the sound of my brain disengaging from my body's functions. But I could not always control the flow of remembered impressions. Now I could not recall what it had been like to be aboard an elÿon. I ignored Nefertity's question and hurried across the deck.

Valeska met us at the transport center. She looked flushed from running, and no longer carried Agent Shi Pei's elegant logbook.

"It should be ready," she said a little breathlessly. "Your Gryphon has been sent ahead. Here—we can take this up—"

She motioned at one of the elevators, a cylinder like an immense candle that stretched into the air, until its tip was swallowed by the glow of the elÿon fleet. From here I could not make out individual craft. Their sheer bulk and the hazy gleam that emanated from them made it impossible to tell for certain where one ended and the next began, like trying to untangle a shimmering mass of sea nettles. As our elevator began to rise, Nefertity turned, peering through the dirty window at the behemoths floating overhead.

"They are not what I expected," she said at last. Valeska stared at her curiously, and the nemosyne continued. "I thought they would be like ships. They *are* ships, of some kind?"

Valeska turned to me with eyebrows raised. I looked past her, taking in what Nefertity saw: huge vessels that seemed to be as much animal as machine. The comparison to the medusæ was apt—the elÿon had been modeled on sea nettles and jellyfish and other cnidarians. They were amorphous leviathans, their central bodies umbrella-shaped and with a faint translucence like the swollen bladders of the Portuguese man-of-war. They floated like untethered balloons high above the decks of Cisneros, emitting that bizarre rubeous glow, with long gassy blue streamers occasionally billowing behind them as one or another shifted slightly in the wind. Their polymer walls shifted in size and shape to accommodate changes in air pressure, temperature, light or darkness, so that to watch one taking flight was to see a vast opalescent bubble churning through the marine haze, like an immense Portuguese man-of-war drifting above the calm Gulf. Their interior climate was equally dreamlike, controlled by the thoughts of human adjutants imprisoned in navigation cells deep within the elÿon's labyrinth of fuel canals and living quarters.

As we grew nearer to the fleet, we began to hear them. A sort of low, droning sound, a bass counterpoint to the slap of waves against the platform now far below us. Nefertity stared at the elÿon, the growing radiance of her torso and face attesting to her absorption. Valeska looked uncomfortable, as though wanting to speak. After several more minutes of silence I asked her if she had any questions for me. She dipped her head, tugged at the peaked collar of her leather uniform, and finally nodded.

"Yes. Will you—am I to accompany you? To HORUS?"

I gazed down upon the floating city. Set with beveled squares of green and violet, its landing grids like yellowing embers: from here it was a delicious toy, a glittering lozenge one might hide in a pocket as a bribe for a beloved child. Nefertity stared at it, her eyes impossibly wide and bright. Valeska kept her own gaze hooded, only glancing at me covertly to see what my reply would be.

For the first time since I had awakened to that second horrible birth in Araboth's regeneration vats, I felt a twinge of an emotion besides hatred or vengeance. I tried to imagine what Valeska would like to do. It would be an honor of sorts for her to accompany the Aviator Imperator to Quirinus, even if it was a futile mission. It seemed probable that we would find nothing in HORUS save rebel geneslaves and the bones of their victims; and travel aboard the elÿon was always a dreadful prospect. Under the best of circumstances, embarkations from the HORUS colonies were often little better than forays into madness and exile. At last I spoke, keeping my eyes fixed on the window.

"What would you like to do, Captain?"

A minute passed before she answered. "I would like to go with you, Imperator."

In her tone I heard that note that often colors Aviators' voices, something between the voice of a child accepting a dare and the bitter resignation of a prisoner to her fate. She went on, "I have never been to HORUS. My tour here began only six months ago; but as Agent Shi Pei said, we have lost all contact with the Governors. And since most of the other Aviators have left to join the fighting, she has been reluctant to part with me. I had lost hope of ever receiving another detail. I think—I think I would like to accompany you."

I nodded. "Very well. There will be gear on board you can use."

"Thank you, Imperator. I'm not familiar with the *Izanagi*. I assume there's some crew?"

Meaning human crew, besides the adjutants.

"I doubt it," I said.

As the glass elevator crept closer to the elÿon, the air grew warmer and blindingly bright, the glowing fleet blotting out the soothing darkness of the night sky. Even when I closed my eyes, I could still see vast unfolding petals of crimson and salmon-pink. The droning sound grew louder, swelled into a single profound *boom, boom.* A throbbing gargantuan voice: *Izanagi*'s voice. For an instant it seemed that our elevator and all it contained were engulfed in flames. Then the booming was abruptly silenced, the radiance disappeared as though a huge hand had covered the sky. With a wrenching sound the elevator opened.

Before us a soiled ribbon of gray carpeting led into the gaping mouth of the elÿon. Nefertity hung back from the door, and I heard Valeska sigh, a noise that was almost a shudder. Without a word we boarded the *Izanagi*.

# 6

## The End of Winter

**We spent that winter** and spring at Seven Chimneys. There was no further mention of geneslave rebellions, no soft threats of what would happen if I did not support Trevor in whatever mad scheme he had. I might have dreamed the whole thing; indeed, when a few days later I crept back down to the basement, I couldn't find the skull with Dr. Harrow's name on it, although the cadavers were still where they had been, glowing on their steel beds.

I did not tell my friends what I had learned. I thought the news would only terrify Miss Scarlet, and perhaps goad Jane into doing something foolish. To me Trevor Mallory turned an innocent face, as welcoming as he had been when I first saw him. The rebels he had spoken of, those "others" who might convince me of their just cause—they never appeared, though there were many nights when I woke soaked with sweat, imagining I heard the silken voices of energumens plotting in the house below.

Jane didn't seem to notice any change in me. She was as happy as I'd ever seen her. Her days passed among the animals that lived at Seven Chimneys, small black-and-white shepherd dogs and black-faced sheep and several furtive, half-feral cats the size of newborn lambs. She and Giles made a good team. She spent her mornings with him, caring for the sheep and the evil-eyed swine who rooted furiously in their pen behind the barn. Each night she'd help him bring in wood for the recalcitrant heating system, listening patiently to his daily complaints about how poorly it heated that vast and drafty house.

"We need a whole new fireplace, there—" He'd kick at the bricks with one worn leather boot, scowling at the rain of loose mortar. "This was designed back when the winters were warmer—"

And after dumping their armloads of seasoned oak and green birch, they'd go back outside, to see to the sheep again and frown at the threatening mingy gray skies. Later, Jane might seek out Trevor, asking his advice about some herbal remedy for distemper or scabies. But she never took to Fossa.

"I can't stand them," she confessed to me one night after we'd shared another bottle from Trevor's cellar. "The animals, the ones like Scarlet—they don't upset me. But *those* things—"

She grimaced, took a swallow of wine. "—Those *mutants*—ugh." And shuddering, she passed the bottle to me.

That was on a rare evening Jane and I spent together. The truth was, her happiness wore at me, made me bitterly aware of all I had lost. And I couldn't bear to be with Miss Scarlet, either. At first she sought me out often, especially early in the morning when the sun set our frozen windows afire.

"Bad dreams!" she'd gasp, letting the door to my room slam behind her as she pattered across the floor. "I can't bear it, Wendy, I wake up and the sun makes me think of flames. . . ."

She would crawl into bed with me, her small body shivering despite its coat of fur and a shabby nightshirt. But I offered her scant comfort, only let one hand fall nearly weightlessly upon her little head. My own nightmares kept me tossing until dawn, but I would not share them with anyone.

And so we grew apart, we who had been inseparable, before the feast of the Winterlong cleaved love and friendship from us. The change was hardest on Miss Scarlet. Unaccustomed to spending months alone, without the buffer of an audience or rehearsal between herself and her demons, she grew depressed. Like myself, Miss Scarlet had been the subject of experimentation—in her case, research that had gifted a chimpanzee with human speech and emotions. But it was her great and lifelong sorrow that she was never to be truly human. And despite her grace and effort onstage, many in the City had seen her as only a freakish heteroclite, a trained monkey mouthing ancient scripts. Now, far from her paints and powders and crinolines, she languished in front of the fire in Seven Chimneys' main room, wearing the child's clothes Trevor had found for her. There she would sip her tea, or a mild broth made from those mushrooms called Life Away, which induce soft dreams.

"I think the Goddess has forgotten we are here," she said to me once, her small black eyes reddened beneath drooping lids and her voice drowsy. "All of us, in the City and all across the world; else so many people that we loved would not have died."

I said nothing. I feared what she said was true, and after a moment she turned away. Gradually it grew harder and harder for Jane or me to rouse her from these sad reveries. Only Fossa seemed able to talk to her at those times. As the weeks passed, I watched in growing dismay as the two of them would sit together on the worn brocade sofa, while Trevor's collection of skulls grinned down at them from the mantel. Fossa's gargoyle head would bend over Miss Scarlet's small dark one, and the even current of their conversation would course on until broken by the chimpanzee's sudden rapturous quoting of some new text, or Fossa's low, urgent growl. Sometimes Trevor joined them for these discussions, easing himself onto the edge of the couch as though for a quick word and then staying for hours. I tried not to think about what all this meant, and avoided Trevor's quietly triumphant looks when I passed through the room.

And myself? In one quick year I had gone from being incapable of feeling any independent emotions, to fairly drowning in them. Every night I forced myself to stay awake, drinking Trevor's previous coffee, walking outside till the cold nearly killed me, dipping into a horde of candicaine pipettes I found in one of the empty guest rooms. Anything to keep from sleeping; anything to keep from dreaming of him.

But it was no use. Each snowfall made me think of Justice: those hours before a performance when we would huddle together before the little fire in Miss Scarlet's grate, the grand entertainments we had from the Paphians in the weeks preceding the feast of Winterlong. Everything had his print upon it, as though his ashes had drifted to earth here, touching that lamp, those clothes, covering the floor so that everywhere I walked, tracks remained to remind me I was moving further and further away from him. Then when exhaustion overtook me, I would drink wine or Trevor's raw, strong brandy until I fell asleep, shoving the pillows from my bed lest I wake with one in my arms, tearstained and bearing the mark of my kisses. And I avoided Giles, whose gentle features and gray-blond hair put me in mind of my lover's.

Later, I wondered sometimes whether Trevor meant for it to be like that. Jane in her little world in the barn; Scarlet and I alone with our miseries. But even Trevor Mallory couldn't change the weather: the worst winter he had seen in a lifetime (and Trevor's lifetime was thrice any of ours).

"It's changed," he muttered one evening, staring out to where a brutal gale tore branches from the oaks. Wind and ice had already felled an ancient chestnut tree. "The bastards have done something to the weather again—seeded the clouds over Kalimantan, probably, or done something to choke the air with ash." He glanced over his shoulder and started to see me there, then smoothed his features and smiled slightly. "But our time will come, Wendy; it will come soon enough." I gave him a curt nod and quickly left the room.

While Trevor's geneslaves never appeared, there were a few other visitors to the inn that winter. One February twilight the dull whine of a snowmobile echoed through the still air, and two black silhouettes appeared against the snow drifted along the front walk.

"Go to your rooms!"

Giles's anxious voice interrupted me where I hunched over a monitor in the kitchen, playing the intricate game called Horlage. In the background the shortwave radio hummed to itself, a song I had heard in the City, an aria from *The Gods Abandon Antony*. Without a word Giles strode to the radio and switched it off.

"What is it?" Jane stood in the doorway that led outside to the barn. She shook the snow from her coat. "That lamb's going to have twins—"

"Not now!" hissed Giles. Miss Scarlet padded into the room, frowning and looking up at him questioningly. Giles pointed silently toward the front of the house. My hand froze on the monitor's dials.

Voices. Two men, asking loudly for a night's lodging. I

heard the nasal twanging of the server, Mazda, begin to reply, but then Trevor's welcoming tones boomed out. Moments later we heard footsteps heading up the main hall.

"Quickly now," breathed Giles, hurrying all three of us toward the stairs that led to the back wing of the house. "They're Ascendant janissaries. There's been trouble in the City."

For an instant his gaze caught mine. "Rebels," he whispered as he held the door for us to go upstairs. "A small armed band of aardmen attacked the Ascendant barracks and was killed—"

Miss Scarlet gasped. "The monsters!"

"Aardmen! Well, thank god for th—" Jane began, when Miss Scarlet broke in.

"How could they *murder* them? *Venceremos!* Death to the human tyrants! The Ascendant monsters will pay—like he says, *our day will come!*"

Jane stopped in the dim stairwell and stared at her, open-mouthed. *"What?"*

"Not now!" said Giles, yanking Miss Scarlet after him; but not before she bared her teeth, as though at an unseen enemy.

"What the hell was that about, Scarlet?" Jane exploded when we were safely in her room and Giles had left. "*Human* tyrants? Is this something Fossa's been whispering in your ear? What's going on?"

Miss Scarlet bowed her head. "Nothing," she said, and inspected the hem of her dress.

"Wendy?" Jane raised her eyebrows, her face flushed, and looked at me. "Do you know anything about this?"

"No—not exactly—"

Giles had made us leave the lights off. In the dark room the window's rectangle of deep blue glowed eerily, cobalt glass etched with black where the branches of the oaks scraped at the glass. I pretended to stare outside, but from the corner of my eye I watched Miss Scarlet. She *had* changed over the last months. It wasn't just her clothing—a child's red jumper of plain linen that hung loosely from Miss Scarlet's slender arms and legs, giving her the appearance of a marionette twitching where she sat on the floor. It was Miss Scarlet herself. It was as though in losing her fine clothes, her costumes and cosmetics and props, she had lost that other Scarlet—the one that never raised her voice except onstage

before a spellbound audience, that read to me from her beloved theatrical biographies and yearned always for the miracle that would make her human.

But that Scarlet was gone now. Or she had found another
part to play: conspirator instead of coquette, Lady Macbeth
instead of Miranda.

"You *should* know, if you don't already," Miss Scarlet announced. "There's a war going on—"

Jane rolled her eyes, her dark hair flopping into her face.
"A war? There's *always* a war, Scarlet! Since the day you
were born, there's been at least one Ascension and I don't
know how many battles, not to mention the Archipelago Conflict and whatever's going on now in the City." She shoved a
stack of clothes onto the floor and sprawled on the bed, yawning.

Miss Scarlet glared. "This is different," she said, and her
voice made me shiver. Because *it* had changed as well. It was
throatier now, more like Fossa's with its undercurrent of fury;
the sound of a dog choking back a snarl. "Those were *your*
wars—Ascendants, the Commonwealth and Emirate and the
HORUS colonies. . . ."

"Our wars!" Jane almost yelled. I covered her mouth with
one hand, with the other gestured frantically at the floor to remind her that we weren't alone in the house. *"Our wars?"*
she went on, her voice low but her brown eyes blazing. "Everyone I ever knew and loved died back in that City, Scarlet,
you know that! Those were *Ascendant* janissaries—"

"That's not what I meant." Miss Scarlet's eyes were cold,
flecks of black ice in her wrinkled black face. "I meant, those
were all *human* wars. And this is different. This is all of us—
geneslaves—against the rest of you. This will be the first *gene*
war."

Jane stared at her, stunned. Then she turned to me.

"A gene war?" she repeated in a small voice.

Even without my old powers I could feel her sudden fear,
her heart pounding like a second heart beside my own. I
looked over at Miss Scarlet: her wizened face with its nimbus
of dark fur, more grizzled now than it had ever been; her long
yellow teeth and tiny black hands with their clever fingers.
When she gazed back, her expression had changed; she was
keeping something from us. The deceit gave her a feral look,
as though a fine membrane had lowered over her eyes, oc-

cluding the warmth and goodwill that had always glowed there.

"Gene wars?" Jane said again, her voice rising pleadingly. "Tell me, Scarlet—please, explain to me . . ."

But Miss Scarlet had turned away. She crossed the room, her bare feet pattering on the wood floor, and silently pried the door open. Only as she stepped into the hall did she turn to look back at me. For an instant her eyes held mine. Amber eyes, eyes with the shape and color of leaves in them; an animal's eyes. And suddenly I felt lost, a huge clumsy thing stumbling through the trees until I reached a place where the ground was sheared away beneath me. Miss Scarlet had leapt easily over that chasm; but I could not follow.

"Scarlet!" Jane cried. "Where are you going?"

Miss Scarlet shook her head. "Have Wendy explain it to you," she called softly as the door closed after her. "*She* understands."

I looked at Jane. Her face was red, and she blinked back tears furiously. When I stared to say something, she pushed me away and stared out the window to where stars burned against the deepening sky.

"Jane," I began, my hand touching her shoulder, "I should have told you, but I didn't want you to worry—"

"Leave me alone!" She slapped my hand away. She whirled and stared at me. I could feel her gaze burning into the side of my face, where beneath my hair the scars remained. "You're one of them too, aren't you?" she hissed. "You think I've done something terrible to you, that's why you won't talk to me, or touch me—" Choking, she turned back to the window.

I stood, the blood pulsing behind my eyes so that a brittle aura hung above everything. I walked to the door blindly, and my hands clutched at scars that I knew would never really heal.

Late the next morning I crept to the top of the stairs, where a small round window looked down on the frozen front walk glittering in the sunlight. I stood and watched as the Ascendant janissaries made a brusque farewell to Trevor, bits of ice flying up behind their feet as they hurried to their snowmobile. In a few minutes they were gone. Only a long trail like a serpent's showed where they had been, and the distant whine of their vehicle slicing through the still air.

The smells of coffee and cumin brought me downstairs. I met Miss Scarlet in the kitchen, where Giles was grinding spices in a mill and tossing them into an iron skillet to roast.

"Where's Trevor?" Miss Scarlet asked. She sat on a low stool beside Fossa, who regarded me with narrowed yellow eyes before turning away.

I shrugged. "Upstairs, I guess." I sat at the table, picking up the little monitor and pretending great interest in the game of Horlage I'd left there yesterday. Giles continued to shake spices from grinder to pan to a heavy blue-rimmed plate. I fiddled with the knobs and images of my game, and after a few minutes said casually, "Who were our guests last night?"

A long silence. Giles turned to pull a clouded Ball mason jar from a shelf and shook a fragrant mound of coriander seeds into his palm. I looked up at him, the game monitor chattering to itself in my lap. Miss Scarlet stared at Giles with poorly concealed impatience, and Fossa tipped his head sideways, like a dog waiting for a command.

"Well, all right," Giles said crossly. He poured the coriander seeds back into the jar and wiped his hand on his trousers. "They were janissaries, Ascendants—"

"Of course," Miss Scarlet said triumphantly.

Giles gave her a dirty look. "They came from the City of Trees—there's been rioting there. Apparently the Paphians and Curators have thrown their lot with the aardmen and lazars, and they've all set themselves against the Ascendants."

"So they are fighting!" exulted Miss Scarlet. She threw her head back with a flourish I recalled from her interpretation of Medea. "Ah, I wish I could see it!"

"You may," croaked Fossa. He shifted where he sat hunched on the floor and grinned, his muzzle cracking open to show sharp white teeth. "But winter is a bad season for war."

Giles frowned. "They're all bad seasons for war." He gave a small cry and wrapped a cloth around his hand, pulled the smoking skillet from the woodstove and dropped it into the sink. "Damn!" He glared at Miss Scarlet, who had the grace to look abashed. "You shouldn't be rejoicing over this war, Miss Scarlet. It's children and courtesans and scholars and plague victims against the Autocracy: now who do you think is going to win?"

The chimpanzee stared down at her gnarled hands. "Of course, you're right," she said softly. "I forget sometimes—"

"It doesn't matter," Giles sighed. He stared at the woodstove and absently pulled the dishcloth through his fingers. "Those two from last night—they think they're going to summon help from Cassandra. But they'll never get there."

From the sink wafted a cloud of steam and the scent of scorched spices. He grimaced, then went on. "Trevor's calling ahead now to warn them—those two will be cut off before they reach the mountains. I wish I knew nothing about it."

This was the first time I had any real notion of how the rebels based in Cassandra were organized, or indeed that they were organized at all. "Was—was there any other news?" I asked tentatively.

Giles shrugged, pushed the loose hair back from his face, and shook his head. He was pale and drawn with exhaustion; he must have been up all night, talking with the soldiers or else seeing to some secret business of his own. "Some. There have been more insurrections in the HORUS colonies. And elsewhere—rioting on hydrofarms in the Archipelago, an attack on the provisional government in Vancouver."

"It's true, then," breathed Miss Scarlet. Her black eyes widened as she turned to Fossa. "The Alliance really *is* taking control."

"Alliance?" Jane repeated suspiciously, and glanced at me. "What Alliance?"

I looked at the game monitor in my lap. "It's nothing," I said.

Jane frowned and turned to Giles. "Is this some kind of joke?" she demanded. "Or are you planning to turn us over to the next band of soldiers who shows up?"

Giles flushed angrily, but before he could reply, Trevor appeared in the doorway, his face smudged with soot. "We need more wood," he announced, wiping his forehead and leaving a black streak. "Giles and Jane, would you mind helping me?"

Giles nodded and walked. Trevor followed, and finally Jane left slowly, looking back at Miss Scarlet and me with eyes full of hurt and anger. When she was gone, I stood and began clearing plates from the table, and pumped water into the skillet still hissing in the sink.

"Not yet," I heard Fossa say softly behind me. I looked over my shoulder and saw him staring out the window, to where Jane and Trevor picked their away along a path in the snow to the woodpile. Beside him Miss Scarlet shifted on her stool, her eyes still wide and gleaming with a bright, nearly fanatical intensity. "Not till spring," Fossa rumbled. His long tongue flicked at the spaces between his long yellow teeth. "But soon, soon: our time will come."

I said nothing. After a few minutes I joined the others outside.

So the winter passed. Mornings when I watched Jane breasting through drifts to the barn gave way to days in March when the inn seemed to float in a still gray lake, so deep was the snowmelt around us. And then slowly the earth surrendered to spring. There were crocuses and aconite in the last snowy patches behind the house, where the sun fell late in the day. Trevor disappeared into the basement for hours, finally surfacing with sacks that he hauled into the barn. Harvesting his macabre fruits. I wondered who would get them.

In the first weeks of April more Ascendant janissaries visited. When they left, the sacks went with them, carried to the tiny electrical jitney by the creaking server, Mazda, and heaped into its storage compartment until it was full. Trevor watched the vehicle jounce over the rutted road, swerving to avoid gullies left by frost heaves. He took off his enhancer and smiled, his optics sending fiery blue darts above his head. I stood at my vantage place on the landing and kneaded the suede panels of my beaded skirt. I recalled his pride in telling me of the mutations he had caused, the hallucinogenic mushrooms that caused death and madness, the truffles that induced fits of despair. Late that night I crept down to the kitchen for some chamomile tea to help me sleep, and found him crouched in front of the shortwave, whispering into its mouthpiece. Whom did he speak to—rebels in the City, in Cassandra or someplace so far away I had never heard of it, someplace in the stars? He was playing a dangerous game. Like Giles, I wished I knew nothing about it.

Giles himself had more mundane harvests. He took Jane into the woods and returned with canvas sacks full of fiddleheads. We ate them cooked with mutton fat and morels; they tasted like the earth itself, mouthfuls of it, raw and rich and green. From the marshes that lay behind Trevor's fields came the shrill touts of peepers and the tree toads: a sound that always made my neck prickle, seeming to hold in it somewhere a promise that I knew could not be kept. And finally, on a day when there was no longer any breath of chill in the air, the wild apple trees in the meadows began to bloom.

"Well! The winter's back is broken at last."

Trevor stood in front of an open window downstairs, looking deeply satisfied. I'd gone with him from room to room, yanking open casements and removing glass storm windows to let the warm air come streaming in. Flurries of white and pink petals blew from the meadows and drifted across the polished wood floors. I found a ladybug in my bedroom and breathed on it until its wings opened and it flew off into the bright blue sky.

"You seem happier than you were a few months ago."

I shrugged at Trevor's remark, cupped my hand over my nose. Where the ladybug had rested, a very faint odor remained, an acrid smell that reminded me of Trevor's basement. "Not really."

Though in truth the spring had brought a sort of remission to my sorrow. I had never been with Justice in the spring, so the season became a template upon which I could place nothing but raw grief. No image of his laughing face, no touch of his hand upon my shaven skull; nothing but the grief itself. And with nothing to feed it, even grief dies eventually; and so the warmer days and clouds of apple blossom found me dreaming, as often as not, of nothing at all.

"You can't grieve forever," Trevor said softly. He picked up a glass transformer from a shelf, tossed it from hand to hand until he dropped it and it shattered on the floor. "Oh, dear."

He gazed down as though surprised to see the blue-green shards there, then glanced at me. His voice was kind as he said, "Well, things happen in the spring, Wendy. Maybe something will happen to you."

Something did. It was a shining morning a month later, in the first fat weeks of summer. We had been at Seven Chimneys for half a year. An unspoken truce had fallen between all of us; a truce easy to keep, since we had gotten into the habit of going our separate ways. Jane had left early that morning to check on the lambs in the fields. Miss Scarlet lay on the living-room couch with Fossa, listening to a historical novel about Yll Peng-Si, the tyrant of the Mongolian Nuclear Republic. I sat in the kitchen with Trevor and Giles, drinking tea and fiddling with a packet of cigarettes. Behind me, on the shelf it shared with tins of dried herbs and dusty brown bottles filled with tinctures of valerian and skullcap, the shortwave hummed soothingly. When I asked him where the transmissions were coming from, Giles only smiled.

" 'Far away pul-lay-sez,' " he sang in his reedy tenor—a bit of doggerel from that damn opera again. " 'Stars you only see in duh-ree-ums . . .' "

Trevor smiled indulgently and I grinned as Giles bowed with a flourish. The radio began playing something else, a choral piece by Menton Barstein that Miss Scarlet had always been fond of. I glanced into the living room to see if she was listening, but her head was beside Fossa's as they stared into the talking book. I sighed and slid a cigarette from the pack.

"This here," I said, pressing the ball of my thumb beneath the image of the pyramid and looking up at Trevor. "This thing—it reminds me of something I saw at HEL once. . . ."

Without warning the song coming from the radio cut off. The shortwave crackled and fizzed; then there was an ominous, hollow silence. With a frown Trevor stood and went over to it, bending until his ear was close to the little round box. He twisted a knob with infinite care, so slowly it scarcely seemed to move, until the static resolved into a long, breathless hissing. I could make out no words, nothing but that foreboding sibilance. In his chair Giles sat up very straight and stared at his partner, his face pale. Suddenly a string of words rang out. To me it sounded as thin and breathless and meaningless as that other sound, but Trevor listened tight-lipped. After a minute he looked up sharply.

"Aviators," he said. Abruptly the transmission ceased. There was only the gentle flapping of the curtains in the morning breeze. "Two of them, from somewhere in the southwest. They are headed for the City of Trees on an errand for the new Aviator Imperator. They'll be here around sunset."

Giles was silent. Finally he leaned across the table and took the package of cigarettes from my hand. For a long time he stared at it in silence: the strange cursive letters, the staring eye within its pyramid. Finally he said, "This is too dangerous, Trevor. You'll get us all killed."

Trevor shook his head. "But this is what we've been waiting for! They'll have news from HORUS, hopefully something about the war in the Archipelago." Only the way he ran his hands across his scalp, crushing the white stubble there as though it were dried grain, showed how excited he really was. "We're well-armed, if anything should happen."

Behind me I heard a soft tread on the creaking floorboards. I whirled to see Fossa silhouetted in the doorway. His ears stood up: small pointed ears, hairless, the skin so translucent that I could see the web of capillaries beneath and their delicate inner channels. Beside him stood Miss Scarlet, wearing only a plain crimson shift: the gargoyle's goblin shadow.

"News?" Fossa asked in his groaning voice.

"Aviators," Trevor began, when Giles slammed his hand on the table, crushing the cigarette pack. Before Trevor could say anything else, Giles stood and left the kitchen, the door slamming behind him.

"Aviators," Miss Scarlet repeated softly. She turned to me, her eyes wide. "Wendy, Aviators!"

"I heard," I said. I didn't like the sound of this any more than Giles did. "Where's Jane?"

Trevor rubbed his chin. "Upstairs, I suppose."

"No, she's not. I went by her room earlier—she's not there."

"In the barn, then," Trevor said impatiently. "Giles and I are going to be busy, getting things ready for them. I think you should make yourselves scarce—"

"You said sunset," I interrupted. "I'm not going anywhere now. I want to talk to Jane—"

But Jane was gone. She wasn't in the barn, or her room, or anywhere in the house; nor was she in the fields outside, where Fossa hunted for her. I even braved the basement again, peering under those rickety tables with their foulsmelling heaps of dung and offal; all for nothing.

"We *have* to find her."

It was afternoon now, and I stood on the porch with Trevor, staring out to where the sun had just started to nick the tops of the distant mountains with gold. I smelled of dung and warm grass, from crawling around in the byre and hayricks inside the barn. My voice was hoarse from calling for Jane; I could not have told anyone, perhaps not even Jane herself, how her disappearance had upset me. I remembered that first night at Seven Chimneys: Jane's cool hands smoothing my hair, pulling Cadence Mallory's clothes over my feverish limbs; Jane's mouth brushing my cheek, and how I had pushed her away. And since then I had pushed her away as well, acting as cold and churlish as when we first met in the City of Trees.

But now, as the light deepened from amber to the deep fiery gold of late afternoon, I began to grow frightened. If she should be lost (but of course that was ridiculous; Jane knew her way around the woods and ruined roads of Seven Chimneys as well as she had known the maze of cages at the Zoo); if she should be found and captured by the Aviators ...

"I'm checking the woods again," I said, and turned to run back across the overgrown lawn.

*"No."* Trevor Mallory's hand clapped down upon my shoulder. "It's too dangerous now—they could arrive at any time. I want you and Miss Scarlet and Fossa out of sight." For the first time since my first visit to the underground gardens of Seven Chimneys, I glimpsed that other Trevor Mallory, the one who had spoken in soft insinuating tones of murder and revolution. "The Aviators think there's no one here except for Giles and me. Fossa they believe is our servant. I don't want to think about what they would do to refugees from the City of Trees—you're putting yourselves and all of us in danger."

"But we can't just leave Jane," I cried, yanking away from him. "What if they find her?—"

"Where can she *be*?" Miss Scarlet appeared in the doorway of the house behind us, wringing her hands. "Oh, this is my fault, I've been ignoring her, but she just doesn't *understand*—"

"Go back inside, Miss Scarlet," I ordered her, exasperated. "There's nothing you can do—"

"There's nothing *you* can do, either, damn it!" Trevor's face grew flushed and he pounded the edge of the porch railing. "We've been waiting all winter for a chance like this, to talk to someone who has real news—"

"Wendy, please." Giles's gentle voice wafted out from where he towered above Miss Scarlet. "I'll keep looking for her—it doesn't matter if the Aviators know *I'm* here—and when I find her, I'll make sure she gets upstairs safely." His blue eyes gazed into mine beseechingly. He hated harsh words, any kind of disagreement: a true Saint-Alaban, and so much like Justice. ...

"All right," I said, defeated. I leaned on the porch rail and looked out one last time, to where the ruined road wound from the inn toward the faraway mountains. Dread pinched at my heart: had she left us, really gone on by herself, to die or be lost in the wilderness? For the first time all day I felt tears welling in my eyes, but before anyone could see, I whirled and fled inside, my feet echoing loudly on the stairs.

A few minutes later Miss Scarlet and Fossa knocked on

my door and let themselves in. We sat without talking, waiting, until at last another knock came and Giles entered.

"I can't find her," he said. Panic clenched at me; I jumped to my feet and began pacing the room.

"Are they—are the others here yet?" asked Miss Scarlet with wide, frightened eyes.

"Not yet. But I think it's too dangerous in this part of the house. I want Fossa to stay with you—no, Fossa, I'm not going to risk having you where they can see you. There's another room—I want you all to come with me, now. Hurry—"

We followed him down one hallway, then another, then up a flight of stairs into a part of Seven Chimneys where I had never been: a small bump-out that I had always assumed was a storage shed, but which proved to be larger than I had thought. Unused tables and armoires were shoved against walls webbed with mildew, and in the airless corridor creaky doors opened onto rooms without windows, some of them filled with more furniture, others empty of anything save festoons of cobwebs. I sneezed at the musty smell and wondered how long it had been since anyone had been back here. Years, it seemed; our feet left smudged impressions on warped planks thick with dust.

At last Giles stopped at a small door, so low and narrow, he had to stoop to pry it open. Inside I glimpsed stacks of old clothes and hangers suspended from a crooked rod. Giles ducked inside, rattling the hangers and shoving aside heaps of camphor-smelling linens. A moment later he motioned for us to come after him, and we did, Fossa and Miss Scarlet and me jostling each other in the dark crowded space until we reached a second, even tinier door that Giles held open for us.

"Welcome to the sanctuary," he said in a low voice.

It was a long narrow room, rambling beneath the eaves of the little shed addition. Pushed against the far wall beneath a steeply sloping roof were a pair of wobbling chairs, an iron bedstead, a monitor with cracked screen, a bad reproduction of a Second Ascension metal sleeping cabinet, and a small cabinet filled with moldering books. The air smelled of cold dust and mice. There was no fireplace, and only a single tiny window overlooking the barn, so caked with filth, it let in neither light nor view. Giles cracked it open, and the heady scent of warm clover crept inside, and the sound of the little creek burbling behind the house.

"Here, now," Giles said. He crossed back to the little

doorway, nervously smoothing his hair from his forehead. *He's really frightened,* I thought, and swallowed hard, thinking of Jane. "I'll be back in a few minutes with some food. All of you just sit tight, and try not to talk very loudly—try not to talk at all, if you can. Fossa knows what to do, he's been through this before."

"I hope they don't stay long," fretted Miss Scarlet. "Do you think they'll be here past the morning?"

In spite of his worry, Giles smiled. His face had grown worn over the years, with lines and sunspots a Paphian in the City would never have borne; but at that moment he seemed more beautiful than any number of young courtesans. "No, cousin. I don't think so. Aviators are all business—these two have been sent out on some mission from one of the elÿon bases in the Gulf. They've been charged to stop everywhere within two hundred miles of the City and do a thorough search. They'll take a look around downstairs and be gone before you know it."

Miss Scarlet blanched at the word *search.* "But won't they find us—oh, I wish Jane—"

"Hush! No, they won't find you. Seven Chimneys is known and trusted as a favorite stopping point for members of the Autocracy. This is a mere formality, that's all. Now be still and wait—I'll be back soon."

We waited. Miss Scarlet fidgeted, pulling the end of her shift through her hands over and over again, until it grew creased and stiff. Fossa leaned against the wall, his head bent to accommodate the sloping roof, and stared at the floor, his yellow eyes narrowed and thoughtful. Giles had shut the window before he left, but I cracked it open again, peering through the little slit at the barn and thinking *Jane, Jane* . . .

When the door creaked open again, we all jumped.

"Only me. No sign of them yet," Giles said with false heartiness. "Here's supper."

"Jane?" Miss Scarlet asked in a quavering voice.

Giles put down a small tray, tipped his head, and sighed. "Not yet. Probably she's still in the woods somewhere, in which case she'll be fine."

"As long as she stays there," I said grimly.

Giles was silent, finally said, "Yes. As long as she stays there." Miss Scarlet and I stared after him with sinking hearts as he crept back out again and locked us in for the night.

For Miss Scarlet and me Giles had made a compote of

last year's dried apples and the first wild strawberries, tiny fruits no bigger than a drop of blood squeezed from your fingertip. For Fossa there was lamb, cooked very rare, and a bottle of wine for us to share. We sat in a circle on the floor to eat, and again I thought of my life at the Human Engineering Laboratory, stealing food with my friends and holding impromptu parties in the middle of the night. Only now dread choked all my thoughts, as the night wind rose up outside, and the first tentative cries of whippoorwills echoed from the woods.

We drank the wine slowly, me taking rather more than my share, until finally the nearly empty bottle remained in my lap. As I ate, I perused the label curiously. It was printed on the same kind of grayish, pulpy paper that adorned the packets of cigarettes Giles doled out, with gold lettering and a colored drawing of what appeared to be some sort of darkened chamber set about with spikes of red and yellow and blue.

# Ιχαρυσ

### *Free Take of Cassandra*

"Cassandra again," I said, frowning. Miss Scarlet looked at me with raised eyebrows. "Where the cigarettes come from. That place in the mountains." I shifted the bottle between my knees and pointed to the arcane symbol of the pyramid and the word beneath it. "What does that mean?"

Miss Scarlet squinted at it. "I don't know. It's ancient Greek, I think. But that—" One black skinny finger tapped the image of the pyramid and the eye. "*That* I recognize. It was on currency in the United States—we used some once as a prop in *Our Town*." She pursed her lips and peered more closely at the label. "And this here, this other picture—that's a cave."

"A cave?" I took the bottle and squinted at it. If I looked closely, I could just make out several tiny, tiny figures within the darkened chamber. They seemed to be holding up something in their hands, staring at the spikes hanging around them.

"Yes," said Miss Scarlet with certainty, nodding so that the dark fur rippled on her shoulders and scalp. She glanced over at Fossa. He stared back at her with slanted eyes and nodded.

"Cave," he growled.

"I've seen pictures of them," Miss Scarlet went on. "When we did that version of *Macbeth*. And at the Zoo there was a habitat for bats. It was supposed to be a cave. It looked *somewhat* like that," she added doubtfully. But the mention of the Zoo seemed to remind her of Jane. She bowed her small dark head and said no more.

"A cave," I repeated. I tried to imagine what Cassandra must be like—a place where people still grew and processed tobacco and grapes; a place with caves. "Trevor's daughter lives there."

"And others," muttered Fossa. He stretched like a dog, his powerful knobbed paws clawing at the floor, and yawned, uncoiling a long pink tongue. "Very wise and strong—if they were here now, nothing to worry."

I preferred not to think about those others. Miss Scarlet sighed and stood, crossing her spindly arms across her chest. "I—I think I will try to sleep," she said softly. She looked exhausted, but slightly shamefaced: as though I might think less of her for not staying up with me to worry over Jane.

"Of course," I said. I smiled wanly. I wanted to embrace her, hold her small warm body to mine and tell her not to worry; but I did not.

Fossa, however, did. He followed her to the small narrow bed and crouched beside it, watching as she climbed in and not lying down until she was safely settled. Then he sighed noisily, muttered something I could not hear, and sank down, resting his heavy head on his hands. In a few minutes his snores nearly drowned out Miss Scarlet's even breathing.

I finished the wine and stood, walked somewhat shakily to the little window, and pressed my face against its narrow opening. Outside, above the barn, the darkening sky had a pale greenish cast, the same color that the new leaves had been a few weeks earlier. But now the trees had burgeoned into full growth. I could just glimpse the edge of the meadow where they stirred fitfully in the night breeze, and if I crooked my neck back, I could see the first stars pricking at the velvety sky. From the marshes came the ringing of frogs. I felt a sudden pressure in my chest, as though a hand had seized my heart and squeezed it.

Emma Harrow came to me then. Dr. Harrow, who had been my protector and torturer at HEL, the woman who by forcing me to relive her own occult memories had somehow imprinted them upon me. It was on a night like this that her twin brother had first seen that figure that had haunted me for so many months, the shining figure of the Boy in the Tree, the Boy whose name is Death. I rested my head against the windowsill, heedless of whatever prying eyes might be scanning for us.

There was no Boy there within me now. A terrible loneliness came over me: first Justice and now Jane ... I had been so cold to her lately, so caught up in my own misery. At the thought of her, tears filled my eyes and I swore angrily beneath my breath.

So this is what it was like to be "truly human," as Miss Scarlet had so often warned me. I thought of Justice; but while the image of his face, his long hair and blue eyes, made my heart clench again, for the first time I did not feel grief clawing at me; only a sad, soft ache. It was the memory of Jane's face that made me desperate with love and helplessness; the thought of Jane coming to harm that made me want to rush downstairs and confront whatever was there, Aviators or no. From the tiny wedge of open window a breeze crept inside, smelling of wild roses and grass. The keening of the frogs grew higher, sweeter, clearer as the wind brushed my face. On the sill beside me a ladybird landed and began to crawl determinedly toward my chin.

"Fly away home," I whispered. It raised its lacquered wings and disappeared into the night.

I thought of the stars then, of the men and women who were rumored to walk there: the Aviators, the Ascendants' ruthless guardians. Were they all like Margalis Tast'annin, madmen and -women? Would they really kill Jane if they found her? Had they already, and were they downstairs even now, laughing and talking with Trevor and Giles? I sighed and turned from the window.

The narrow dark chamber was quiet now, with that air of awakening excitement that fills a room that has finally been opened up to summer. In her bed Miss Scarlet breathed softly, while at her feet Fossa whined in his sleep. In the middle of the floor our plates and the empty wine bottle were piled like the remains of an encampment hastily abandoned. I felt wide awake and wished there was more wine. It came to me suddenly that I must be drunk. I was accustomed to drinking, but not to getting drunk—a holdover from my days at HEL, where my medication and peculiar mind chemistry had made it difficult for me to absorb alcohol.

But I felt different now. I felt reckless, and powerful, and angry: how dare Giles and Trevor and Miss Scarlet abandon Jane like this? At least *I* wouldn't do so—and before I knew what I was doing, I had stumbled to the door.

It had been locked from the inside: of course, to keep anyone from finding the slaves or refugees hidden there. I opened the rusty hasp and stepped into the outer closet, trying to keep from falling over the linens heaped on the floor. The sagging rod with its load of coats and cloaks blocked my way. I pushed them away, rough wool and leather brushing my face and the smell of bay leaves and cedar making me want to sneeze. But then I was through. With heart pounding I stood in the darkness with my hand on that other door, the one that opened onto the corridor; and then I crept outside.

In the hallway all was still and dim. There were no electrified lights here, not even any of the small gas lanterns that illuminated some of the less-used corridors in other parts of the inn. Beneath my feet the bare wide boards groaned alarmingly. I took a deep breath and hurried down the passage. When I reached the stairway, I crept down with one hand on the brick wall, feeling the crumbling mortar give way under my fingernails. It smelled cool and damp here, as though it shared the air with the basement. At the bottom of the steps I stopped, listening for voices.

Very faintly I could hear them: Trevor's drawling laugh and Giles's nervous, somewhat hesitant tone. And others, a man and a woman. For a moment my heart raced—Jane!

But it wasn't Jane. This woman had a chilly, careful voice, and a way of phrasing that reminded me of someone. It was a moment before I realized that who it reminded me of was Margalis Tast'annin.

I couldn't make out their speech, only the unfamiliar pattern of strained conversation, as though they spoke in a language I did not understand. I took a few more steps down the passage, to where the brickwork gave way to old soft wood. Beneath my fingertips it felt damp, a moldering touch like coarse fur. Then my hand snagged against an old square-headed nail. A tiny dart of pain jarred me from my drunken reverie.

Of a sudden I realized how overwhelmingly stupid this was—dangerous, perhaps fatal. If there were Aviators here, they might even now be preparing to search the house. With even the most cursory glance down this corridor they'd see me, leaning against the wall for balance and glaring blearily into the dimness. Although of course Trevor and Giles had assured me the Aviators would never find our hiding place . . .

*But what if they are betraying us?*

A jolt of adrenaline raced through me. Through my mind flashed images of myself strapped helpless to a gurney at HEL; fleeing the flames at Winterlong; captured and bound and thrown before the Mad Aviator . . .

*No!* my mind shouted; *never again!*

And at that moment I felt it, like a faint current surging through me from spine to fingertips, a flame that leapt within my brain. A rage, a *power* that cut through fear and doubt and drunkenness, until I wanted to throw my head back and shout, with joy and terror—

I could do it all again. If I had to, I could find them all, Giles and Trevor and the others, seek them out and with a touch, a kiss—a look, even—drive them to madness and suicide, as I had done before. I could kill them; and this time there was nothing there to cloud my mind, no ghostly image of the Boy in the Tree, no fleeting revenant of Aidan Harrow to spur me on only to mock me and send me spinning back into my own madness. I felt calm, as calm as I had ever felt in my life; and suddenly I knew what to do.

I took a few more steps, until I reached a spot where the crumbling wooden wall gave way once more to brick, and my feet knocked against broken bricks and heaps of crumbled mortar. Through the wall the voices sounded more clearly. I caught a word here and here, but not enough to put together a conversation. I knew where I was now: in a secondary passage that ran directly behind the main living room. I ran my hand over the rough surface of the wall beside me. Even though I could not see it, I knew what it looked like. It looked like the brick from the fireplace, the pit-fired clay grown brittle and the color of faded deerskin, the mortar filling the chinks nearly black with age.

All winter Giles had complained of that fireplace—how

the bricks needed replacing because the mortar was rotten, and as a result the chimney didn't draw well. In places, the masonry had crumbled until the once-massive edifice was only one brick thick. On the coldest winter nights Giles had stood glaring at the flames, imagining their heat roaring out through hundreds of tiny cracks and holes.

That was why I could hear them so well. And, if I was lucky, soon I would be able to see them, too.

It took me a few minutes to find a spot where the mortar had left gaps in the wall. The smell of mildew nearly made me sneeze, and once I almost tripped over a tall stack of bricks reclaimed from the cellar, put there by Giles in vain hopes of repairing the masonry some day. But by listening and feeling, I finally located the chimney. I patted it triumphantly, then leaned against the wall opposite and slitted my eyes, trying to gauge where the chinks were in the masonry.

After a few minutes I found them. Pinpricks of light, as though a few grains of glowing sand had been cast upon the brickwork. One hole was nearly large enough to poke a pencil through. I attacked that one, with my fingernails set to scraping away the rotten mortar, trying to make no sound. On the floor I found a nail twisted and caked with rust. After a few minutes I was able to gouge a little tunnel through the mortar, large enough for me to peer into the next room.

At first I could see nothing more than bright blurs. Then gradually my eye picked out the back of Trevor's chair, with Trevor in it leaning forward as though listening closely. Beyond him on the far side of the room facing me, two figures perched on the divan—uneasily, it seemed to me, as though at any moment they might take flight. One was a woman. She had blond hair cut short around a thin, leonine face. One side of her forehead was gone, replaced with a plasteel plate that conformed to the shape of her skull. On the floor beside her booted feet was the helmeted enhancer that usually covered her face, and the stiff plasteel curves of her body armor. Her hands rested on her knees. She held a long black tube, some kind of protonic weapon—so much for Trevor's insistence that this visit was a mere formality. Her fingers gripped its barrel tightly while she scanned the room suspiciously. I drew back for an instant, my heart racing, certain that she had seen me.

But even an Aviator can't see through brick walls; at least not without an enhancer. I took a deep breath and once more pressed my eye to the peephole. The other Aviator was a stocky, grizzled man, also with a gun lying across his knees. Like his partner he wore a heavy jacket and trousers of red leather trimmed with black, clothing much worn and stained—the uniform of the NASNA Aviators. His head was cocked as with great interest, as he listened to someone I couldn't see. Giles, I assumed. I turned my head so that my ear rested against the cold mortar and listened.

It was disorienting, not being able to watch and listen at the same time. Their voices were muffled, and Giles in particular spoke so softly that sometimes I couldn't hear him at all; but eventually I was able to put together most of what they were saying.

". . . trouble in the west." That was the woman speaking. Her cool, precise diction made each word seem to hang in the air before melting away. "Trouble everywhere these days."

"We hadn't heard." Trevor's drawl was exaggerated to a complaining whine. "It's been a bad winter here—no visitors except yourselves and a few janissaries from the City."

The next words rang out so loudly that I jumped, as though they had been spoken directly to me.

"Araboth has fallen. There were almost no survivors, and the Orsinas and all their advisers were killed."

I heard Giles exclaim, and Trevor turned so that I could glimpse his face: taut, as though containing some terrible grief—or joy.

*How can they not notice?* I thought. *God, he hates them!*

But they didn't notice; or if they did, they had their own reasons for ignoring it.

Trevor asked a question, and the woman Aviator said something else I couldn't understand. I placed my eye back at the peephole. She and her companion had lowered their heads and were speaking confidingly to Trevor, still clutching their weapons. Through a doorway hobbled the servant, Mazda. It bent to pick up a small tray of glasses and a decanter, then left. I changed position again so I could listen.

"No, I am not mistaken: Captain Patrocles and I received our orders from him at Cisneros." It was impossible to tell if the woman's icy tone held rage or pride. "He has been made Imperator. It would take more than a *tsunami* to destroy Tast'annin."

*Tast'annin?*

I clutched at the wall, the mortar crumbling between my

fingers. My head reeled; I felt as though a huge mouth gaped at me in the darkness, waiting to swallow me if I moved.

"I thought he was dead!" exclaimed Giles.

For the first time the Aviator named Patrocles spoke. "He was." His next words were incomprehensible. I finally made out, ". . . regeneration in Araboth. His investiture was held before the City fell. Colonel Aselma was there."

Colonel Aselma broke in angrily. "It is an insult to us! He is a *rasa,* a walking corpse. How was it that he escaped when the domes collapsed at Araboth, unless he abandoned his post as Imperator? It was a madness of the Autocracy, to have him regenerated—he betrayed us in the City. He will betray us again."

"I don't think so," Captain Patrocles said. "He is a brilliant man—"

"A *rasa,*" spat Colonel Aselma.

"A brilliant *leader,*" Patrocles went on coolly. "And whatever he is, he has never been a fool. He has his reasons for sending us on this mission. . . ."

His voice trailed off, and I pressed myself even closer to the wall, struggling in vain to make out Trevor's next words. But the Aviators' news had so incited everyone that for a few minutes I could hear nothing clearly, just snatches of phrases—"always mad," "HORUS colonies," words that sounded like "enemy network." When I pressed my eye to the hole again, I saw that Trevor had jumped from his chair and was pacing the room, clutching something in one hand and staring at it with furious intensity—a 'file foto, I finally realized. Once he stopped and raised his enhancer, so that the foto seemed aflame with blue light. Whatever the foto showed, it disturbed him greatly. After another minute he turned and shoved it into Giles's hand. I went back to listening.

". . . set up a search for her," said Patrocles. Giles interrupted him with a question that I couldn't understand, and the Aviator continued, "Absolutely. It was his last command before he left Cisneros."

"He's gone to HORUS," the woman's voice rang out. "To Quirinus, I believe. But he will find no one there, no one but energumens—he will be assassinated within the week," she ended triumphantly.

"All the more reason to carry out his orders," Captain Patrocles said in a voice like silk. "I'm afraid that's not a very good image we've shown you, but it's the best we could find—the records library at HEL was in a shambles. We were fortunate to find anything at all."

At the word *HEL* I began to tremble uncontrollably. I drew away from the wall, nausea and a mounting fear clawing at me, then gazed out once more. Even from where I crouched, I could see that Giles had gone white. I thought the Aviators must be blind not to see his obvious terror as he handed the foto back to Colonel Aselma. I turned to listen again and heard him say, "We've seen no one who looks like this."

"Look again," urged Colonel Aselma. "It's not a very good image."

"Oh, I would remember—" Giles's voice was stubbornly insistent, but also desperate. "You heard Trevor—it's been a bad winter, no visitors—"

"Now, Giles," Trevor said calmly. "They realize that. They're just following Commander Tast'annin's orders."

"*Imperator* Tast'annin," said Captain Patrocles. "He says she is the last of the original group they had developed at the Human Engineering Laboratory. With proper intervention she can be of great use to us."

"*If* she is still alive," Colonel Aselma said with disdain. "With that janissary rabble keeping order in the City, we'll be lucky to find anything at all."

"Oh, he'll find her," said Captain Patrocles. "By now the entire NASNA corps has received that 'file image, and there's a bounty on her. She'll be lucky if some overzealous janissary doesn't blow her brains out—"

"They'd better not," Colonel Aselma said darkly. "Her brain is the only part of her the Imperator cares about."

I drew back from the wall and crouched in the darkness. My shaking hands clutched at my knees.

Tast'annin was alive. Jane's bullet must not have killed him, or else the Ascendants had found some means to preserve his life—that single word *regenerated* rang in my ears like a warning tocsin.

He was alive, and he was looking for someone.

He was looking for me.

My breath came in such deep bursts, I was afraid the Aviators would hear me through the crumbling bricks. Light headed with fear, I tried to stand, nearly fell, and caught myself against the wall. They *would* hear me if I wasn't careful; but all I could think of was that monstrous figure in the Cathedral—sacrificing children, using my twin, Raphael, as my own bloody image to lure the hapless Paphians to their deaths.

But I had *seen* Tast'annin die, slumped against the great pit he had dug on Saint Alaban's Hill.

I stood panting, trying to calm myself so I wouldn't go careening through the passage and bring the Aviators down on me like a pair of hounds. The fearlessness and strength I had felt just a few minutes ago was gone. Suddenly it seemed that all my actions of the past year had been insanely transparent. I felt as though there had been someone watching me all along, tracking me and just waiting for this moment to seize me. Those months when I had thought I was safe here at Seven Chimneys, safe in the City of Trees: all madness, an illusion brought on by my need to feel myself free and whole for the first time in my life. The Ascendants had for a little time forgotten me, that was all; as they had forgotten the City of Trees. But their attention had been brought back, first by Tast'annin's defection; now by his command to search for me.

*"Oh, he'll find her. . . ."*

He would too; and this time he wouldn't lose me.

I remembered Trevor Mallory in the cellar—*"I would have done it differently—no scars, nothing to show that you had ever been touched. . . ."*—and heard Dr. Harrow's voice just before she died, warning me of the Ascendants' plans for the empaths she had nurtured at HEL—

*"And you, Wendy. And Anna, and all the others. Like the geneslaves: toys. Weapons—you especially . . ."*

She had been right. Nothing—not even death, it seemed—would keep the Ascendants from controlling their creations. I had been a fool to think otherwise. They had engineered me as a weapon, my mind altered through chemicals and surgery until they could turn it to their own purposes. But they would not give up a weapon so easily—especially now, when they were threatened by this rebel Alliance. They would reclaim me as they had reclaimed Tast'annin. If he was still alive—if he was *again* alive—he must be an even more maleficent creature than he was before. Somehow they had brought him back into their game; somehow they would do the same with me.

I shuddered. I had been mad to put my trust in Giles and Trevor. Their attempt to hide us suddenly seemed as pathetic as Fossa's efforts at speech. Those two Aviators would find and capture me as though I were a bewildered feral dog, then give me over to the new team of researchers at HEL and never think of me again. If I tried to fight them, my fate would be Tast'annin's, killed and regenerated as an Ascendant tool, with no mind or will of my own.

And what then of Jane and Miss Scarlet?

"No," I whispered. Abruptly I turned and ran down the hallway, stumbling in the darkness and shuddering with fear. When I reached the door, I fled through it, keeping my head down as I ran. It wasn't until too late that I realized where I was.

"Wendy!"

I gasped, looked up to see Jane silhouetted in a doorway. Her hair was disheveled and her face sunburned. Over her shoulder two hares hung from a loop of leather cord, their legs tied with vines; her pistol was shoved through her belt. Behind her an open door let in the cool night breeze and the sound of the wind. I was in the front hall. I'd come the wrong way.

"Jane, *no*—"

She grinned and let the door slam shut behind her, a sound that echoed through the house like a gunshot. "What is it, Wendy? You look like you've seen a ghost."

I whirled frantically, heading for the steps that led upstairs; but it was too late.

"*Who's that?*"

The voice of Colonel Aselma rang down the corridor, along with the sound of heavy boots. Behind her I could hear Trevor protesting, "The wind, just the wind—" and Giles adding, "It's only Jane!"

"Wendy?" Jane turned to me, her eyes wide. "What's happened? Who's here—"

"You said there were no other guests—" Captain Patrocles's angry voice boomed down the corridor. A moment later he strode into the foyer, his weapon dangling from one hand. And saw me.

"*It's her!*—"

In an instant his gun was trained on me, but before he could fire, Colonel Aselma had shoved him aside.

"*No!* He wants her alive!"

She lunged and I dropped to the floor, rolling until I slammed into the wall. Colonel Aselma was right behind me, reaching for me with one hand while with the other she wrestled something from her belt.

"*You!*"

I glimpsed Trevor and Giles frozen in the entryway, Patrocles shouting as he swung his weapon between them and Jane. Then I felt Colonel Aselma's fingers closing about my ankle.

"No—" I choked, kicking at her. She swore and I kicked again, harder this time and aiming for her face. I felt the plate covering her forehead crack beneath my blow, and struck again at the other side of her head. Shouting with pain, she dropped back, her hand sliding from me. I staggered to my feet and bolted for the stairs. Behind me I heard Trevor yelling desperately.

"Wendy—for Christ's sake don't, wait—Jane, *no!*"

There was an explosive retort, followed by a scream; then another thunderous roar. For a moment I was blinded. A roiling ball of heat and flame rushed through the room, as though the floor had suddenly opened onto an inferno, and then was gone. I was thrown against the wall with such force that for a moment everything seemed to be frozen around me. Motes of golden light hung in the still air. Jane pointed at the doorway into the hall, her face absolutely devoid of any expression. Colonel Aselma knelt with her hand poised above the gun at her hip. Then like an echo of that first explosion there was another, smaller *boom*, followed by an echoing retort. A pane of glass in one of the foyer windows shattered, and suddenly everything began to move again. I started to race up the steps, then heard a cry that pierced me like a shaft of ice. I stopped and looked back down.

On the floor a figure—no, two figures—sprawled side to side. The first was Captain Patrocles. He lay upon his chest, arms outflung as though desperately grasping for something. The barrel of his weapon protruded from beneath him, its smooth surface blue-white with heat and sending up a single gray plume of smoke. His eyes were wide; two of his bottom teeth were gone, and most of his jaw. He was quite obviously dead.

Beside him Trevor Mallory was stretched out on his back. One arm crossed his breast so that his hand rested upon his heart. The other was extended across the floor, palm upward, the fingers delicately curled as though they held something precious. He was unmoving. Beside him lay his enhancer, its edges slightly crumpled. A perfect star-shaped hole had been blasted through his forehead.

"You *bitch*." A voice cried out, so charged with hatred and rage that I instinctively ducked, looking around for Colonel Aselma.

But the voice wasn't hers. It was Jane's. She stood in the middle of the foyer, her face twisted from weeping as she aimed her pistol to where Colonel Aselma stood a few feet from the two corpses.

"You killed him, you—" Jane sobbed, and in the silence I could hear the barrel of her ancient gun turn over. Behind her Giles crouched, dazed.

"Don't be a fool," hissed Colonel Aselma. "You can't possibly win, you know, just put the gun down and come with me—" But her expression belied her words: her eyes were wide, her mouth set in a tight line as she fumbled at her belt.

"Goody-bye," choked Jane, holding her gun so tightly that the muscles in her hands were knotted red and white. Then, closing her eyes, she fired.

The retort sent Jane reeling backward. Colonel Aselma's body crumpled; she took one staggering step and toppled beside her partner. I cried out and ran down the steps, nearly falling as I raced toward Jane. Only when I had my arms around her did I look back at Colonel Aselma. A ragged hole blackened her chest; I recalled the body armor lying on the floor of the living room.

"I thought it was—I thought it was *him*," Jane gasped. "Tast'annin—I just saw the uniform and I thought, I thought—"

She shook with sobs, and I hugged her tightly. But as I held her, I looked over her shoulder to see where Giles knelt upon the floor, cradling Trevor's head in his lap.

"Wake up," he crooned. "Darling, wake up now, wake up. . . ." And then he began to scream.

"Oh, god," I whispered, pulling away from her. "Trevor . . ."

Before I could go to him, I heard a clicking sound. I started, thinking in my panic that Colonel Aselma had somehow not taken a fatal strike. But she was still quite dead. Only, in her hand I noticed a tiny object, pen-shaped, emitting a series of clicks and staticky hisses. A moment later a faint, high-pitched whine came through the broken window from outside.

Giles looked up, his face contorted with weeping. "Her Gryphon," he choked. Jane and I raced out onto the porch.

In the tangled garden where Giles grew yarrow and brambly yellow roses, one of the Aviators' biotic aircraft crouched in the summer darkness. Its narrow nose pointed skyward, and as we watched, its wings fully extended even as its solex panels folded in upon themselves, like the soft gleaming folds of a bat's wings. More clicks and hissing blasted from it as a smooth translucent hood emerged and covered its cockpit. The keening of its power supply grew louder and louder until it was a steady roar. Before we reached the porch steps, it was airborne, springing into the air with the ease and lethal grace of a jaguarundi or lynx. Within seconds it was high above the house. I could see its sensors on their long filaments whipping through the air, some of them with glowing green and yellow eyes staring balefully down at us.

"It's taking a reading." I started to back toward the door, but Jane grabbed me and shook her head. "It's too late," she said dully. "It will already have signaled that we're here."

The Gryphon made a final swipe above us, its steel-blue wings slicing through the tops of the white oaks and sending down a confetti of torn leaves. Then it was gone, and the cold wake of its passing raked our cheeks like talons.

We went back inside. I was too numb to register anything except that my recklessness had killed Trevor and betrayed us to NASNA. Jane helped Giles carry Trevor's body into their room. I followed, silent, and stayed there even when Jane left. I watched as Giles washed his lover's face and brow, touching gently the pale scar tissue where his eyes had been and kissing the place where the Aviator's weapon had left that incongruously small wound, like a bloody kiss.

"Giles," I said after a long time had passed. "Giles, I'm—"

"Hush," he said. His eyes were red, but he had stopped crying. "He was prepared for this, Wendy. He has—he made plans, in case of . . ." He gasped and lifted his face, his eyes squeezed shut tight. "I'm just—God! it's just horrible, that's all. But I know we'll be together again soon."

I shook my head, shocked. "Giles! No, you can't—"

He looked up at me, brushing back the loose hair that had fallen around his shoulders. I saw then that his soft beauty had bled away, as quickly and easily as though it had been merely painted upon his face. What remained was only grief and the outlines of a love so powerful, it looked like rage.

"Wendy." His voice was still gentle but commanding. "I think you should leave us alone for a little while. There are—there's something I need to do, and you won't—I just need to be alone."

Nodding, I stumbled from the room, wiping tears from my face. I was anguished by my callousness in following him there, by the drunken rage and foolishness that had destroyed my friends. And suddenly I remembered Miss Scarlet, sleeping upstairs with Fossa.

"Jane!" I ran down the hall and into the kitchen. Jane stood at the sink in a shroud of steam, wringing out a pink rag.

"They're gone," she said. She turned to me, and I saw where a tag of blood still smeared her cheek.

"Gone?" I repeated shrilly. I was still thinking of Miss Scarlet.

Jane nodded once, biting her lip. "Yes. I—I gave them to the pigs." She started to laugh, stopped abruptly and wiped her eyes. "Oh, god. It's all my fault, I never—"

*"Stop."* I took her in my arms again, smoothing her damp hair. "It's—if it's anyone's fault, it's mine. They were looking for me, Jane. They have orders from Tast'annin to find me and bring me to him."

Jane pulled back. "But he's dead," she said, and touched the pistol at her waist. "He's dead, Wendy, you know that—"

"He's not. He's alive—they've done something, I don't know what—regenerated him, found his corpse and—and I don't know. . . ." I started to shake and drew away from her. "Miss Scarlet. She doesn't know yet—"

Jane went even paler than she had been. "Are you sure? Is she safe, are they still—?"

We ran upstairs, our footsteps echoing through the empty halls. The night wind blew through an open window, and gray light spattered the floor. Near the end of the corridor the door to the linen closet hung open.

"Scarlet! Scarlet, are you there?" I shouted. Jane followed me as I ducked inside, flinging clothes out of my way. "Scarlet!"

The room was empty. The plates and wine bottle and rem-

nants of food were as I'd last seen them. The bed covers
where Miss Scarlet had been sleeping were tossed onto the
floor.

"Fossa!" Jane yelled. "Scarlet! Where are you?"

I shook my head and turned to the door, stunned.
"They're gone."

Jane looked at me, her face a tortured mask. "The window," she gasped, and pushed me aside as she went back into
the corridor. "That goddamned open window." I ran after her
down the hallway.

"That's it," she cried, leaning out the window. "They're
gone—she must have gotten on his back and they jumped
out—see, there?"

I looked where she pointed, to a patch of soft earth that
was broken up, as though someone had rolled in it. Jane continued to stare at the ground. "I drove her to this," she said
softly. "Because I never treated her the same way I treated
you, or anyone else. I never should have gone off alone—and
now this, now this—"

I grabbed my aching head, wishing I could rip it off and
silence the roaring in my ears. I breathed deeply, the way Dr.
Harrow taught me, and after a moment felt calmer. I drew my
hands from my face and looked at my friend.

"Jane, it's all done now," I said carefully, my voice
hoarse. "I should never have left that room, but I did. And
maybe you shouldn't have gone out alone—but it's done now.
They're gone. And Trevor—"

I shut my eyes, trying to will away the anguish pounding
inside me. "And they're all gone, is all," I finished.

Jane nodded miserably and pulled herself from the window. "Those Aviators," she said, and a bitter edge crept into
her voice. "Tell me, what happened?"

We drew together, like survivors of a rain of roses, and
walked down the hall. I told her all I knew, ending with my
shock at finding myself in the front hallway just as she entered. When I finished, we had reached the kitchen. Jane
pulled away from me, shaking her head, and for several minutes leaned with her hands pressed tightly against the edge of
a table. Finally she sighed and straightened, and ran her hands
through her unruly shock of hair.

"I guess we better find Giles," she said.

I felt exhausted, so tired that all I wanted to do was sink
to the floor and huddle there like a sick child. But I nodded

and let her take my hand. Slowly we walked to his room. Through the open windows came the creak of crickets and the wind in the leaves: sounds that now seemed to have no other reference than to this heartache and fear. I glanced outside, half-expecting to see naught but darkness, the long shadow of our grief; but there were the trees tossing gently, there the stars in their midsummer guise, and a faint glow of moonlight in the east.

We found Giles in his rooms sitting on the bed with his back to us. Trevor's body was gone. Jane looked aside at me, her eyes wide and mouth posed to ask a question, but I shook my head.

"Giles," I called softly. "It's Wendy and Jane."

He turned. He had bound his hair back into a neat braid and changed his clothes—a long deep-blue tunic, not the mourning red I might have expected a Paphian to wear, but then he had not lived among his own people for many years. He looked quite calm, his mouth a little strained and eyes bloodshot; but his expression was peaceful, his voice steady as he spoke to us.

"You should not blame yourselves," he said. He beckoned us to sit beside him on the bed, and I saw how his hands trembled, and felt how cold they were as they patted my own. "Neither of us knew that they were searching for you, Wendy, else we would have made other plans for you and Jane and Miss Scarlet—"

"They're gone," Jane broke in. She glanced nervously about the room, as though afraid of seeing Trevor's corpse propped in a corner. "Scarlet and Fossa. They jumped out the window—the tracks seemed to go into the woods."

Giles shut his eyes and ran a hand lightly over his face. "Ah, no," he murmured; then said, "But no, I'm not surprised, not really."

His voice shook slightly as he looked away, staring at the dark rectangle of a window set in the far wall. "Fossa hates the NASNA Aviators. He was enslaved by them for many years in Araboth before he escaped. Well, then." He sighed and turned back to us. "We won't have to worry about them, at least."

"What do you mean, not worry?" Jane cried, aghast. "We should be out there now, looking for them!"

Giles shook his head adamantly. "*No.* Fossa knows what he's doing—they've probably set out for Cassandra. He knows the way, and even on foot they'll probably get there before you do."

"What are you talking about?" I stared at him as though he were mad. But Giles only sat calmly, stroking the worn cotton quilt with its pattern of interlocking circles. Double Wedding Ring, Trevor had called it; a gift from his daughter. A small brown stain had spread across one panel, and Giles's fingers paused there as he answered.

"You can't stay here. By tomorrow there will be more Aviators—sooner, if they come directly from the City of Trees."

I blanched, and he went on quickly. "But I don't think they will. From what those two told us, there is only a janissary force in the City now. The Aviators pulled out to attend to an insurrection in Vancouver, and the soldiers who remain have their hands full trying to keep down the rebels. As for the rest of us—we'll *all* have to take sides now. It seems your talk of the genewars has actually come to pass," he ended softly. His blue eyes stared mistily at the bed, and I knew he was speaking to Trevor and not to us. But then he seemed to recall where he was. He sighed again and stood, pacing to the wall where an old monitor hung crookedly from a pair of hooks. He straightened it, then clicked it on. The screen stayed blank, but the room filled with low music, gongs and chanting. A gamelan orchestra. I wondered again where the transmissions came from.

"Cassandra," Giles said, as though he knew my thought. "I have already notified Cadence. They should have left by now—if the weather holds, if they don't run into Aviators on the way, they should be here late tomorrow morning to take both of you back with them."

"Cassandra? But what good will that do? And what about you?" Jane scowled, staring out the window to where the forest waited. "And Scarlet? What about them?"

"I told you, I believe they have already left for Cassandra. That was the plan, if ever anything happened—"

"So you've been *expecting* this?" Jane fairly shouted. "Some nice little toss-up with NASNA, and Fossa and Scarlet take to the woods?"

"Trevor had an escape planned long before we ever heard of you," Giles said smoothly. A note of sorrow crept into his voice. "But you're right, he *did* expect it—I think he hoped for it, in a way. . . ."

"But not dying," I cried. I thought of how intent Trevor had always been, how much like a man with some great work still ahead of him. "Surely he didn't want that?"

Giles smiled, an odd, twisted smile. "I don't think he cared—I know he wasn't *afraid* of dying, not the way I am—but then, things are different for Trevor. He's lived so long, and he had—well, he made plans, you know. I don't think this really took him by surprise, in the end. And I know I'll be with him again, but it's just so . . ."

His voice trailed off, and he slumped over, weeping silently. Jane looked at me, her eyebrows raised, then glanced worriedly around the room—for weapons, I realized. She thought as I did: that Giles meant to kill himself.

"Well, we can't leave you," she said at last. "You'll be well, it's just not a good idea, your being here alone. That's all," she ended awkwardly.

Giles drew a deep, gasping breath and looked up at her. "Oh, I won't be *alone*," he said. His hand crept to the dark penumbra of blood on the quilt. "I've got *him*."

My flesh crawled at his tone. I had heard it before—that same note lodged somewhere between madness and exultation—first when I had watched the poet Morgan Yates kill herself at HEL, and then later when Dr. Harrow confronted me before her own suicide, and finally at the Engulfed Cathedral with Tast'annin. Suddenly I felt sick and weak, thinking of all those other deaths that I had caused. There was a roaring in my ears, as though some wind whirled inside my brain, a raging gale that might extinguish me; and at the corner of my eyes I saw small bursts of light, blinding white and yellow: the warning signs of a seizure. I took a deep breath, shut my eyes, and waited until the roaring dimmed, and the blinding flashes cooled to dull throbbing blues and greens. Finally I let my breath out in a long sigh.

"I have to sleep," I whispered. "I'm sorry, I have to go—" I turned and stumbled for the door. After a moment I heard Jane follow me.

Before we stepped into the hallway, I stopped and looked back at Giles. He had stopped crying, though his face still looked wet and raw. He gazed at the monitor on the wall as though its screen held some beloved image.

"We will wait, then," I said. "Till tomorrow, at least. For them to come from Cassandra."

Beside me Jane made an angry hissing sound, but she only said, "I guess we don't have much choice."

"Oh no," said Giles. Slowly he turned to look at us, his luminous blue eyes as brilliant and cold as Trevor's optics. In his slender hand he held the Aviator's gun. "You don't understand, my friends—

"You no longer have any choice at all."

# 7

## The Alliance Spreads
## Its Net

**"I wish to speak** with you, O my sister Kalamat."

Even without looking up from where I pored over the scrolls that held the history of Quirinus, I knew the voice belonged to Cumingia, though it could have been that of any one of us. Our voices were as alike as our faces; in a roomful of us talking and laughing, our Masters had never been able to distinguish one from another. But I felt within me the raw probings of Cumingia's anxious nature, just as, blindfolded and deafened, I would know Lusine by the tranquil warmth I felt in her presence, or Hylas by the rage that radiated from her like the venomous prongs of a sagittal.

"Come to me, sister." I switched off the scroll and stood, stretching and yawning. "You are not asleep?"

Cumingia shook her head. "I cannot sleep. I hear him now all the time—"

I sighed. I took the scroll I had been reading and walked across the small round chamber. Formerly, it had been the domain of the Quirinus exchequer, and his disproportionately large and lavishly covered bed stood beneath an oneiric canopy. I had never felt the need to control my dreams as had the exchequer, who was plagued by nightmares. The canopy was off now, its expanse of neural webbing limp and gray as dirty silk. I batted at the flimsy stuff, settled on the bed, and beckoned my sister to join me.

"Vasida has heard him too," Cumingia blurted, as though I had argued with her. "And Polyonyx—"

"Shh. I am listening."

It is a thing our Masters have never understood, this manner in which the children of Luther Burdock can hear each other's thoughts. But even among our Masters there are born those who shared a womb, Gemini and triplets and the like, and these are well-known to possess the ability to feel the emotions of their twins. So why should it surprise our Masters that those of us who share the mind and body of Cybele Burdock can also share our thoughts? Though I must admit that my senses were less acute than my sisters'.

I closed my eyes, thinking that my proximity to Cumingia—the most sensitive of all of us, though that was like judging between one hair and another—might make it easier for me to detect the voices of that other, the one who named himself Kalaman, and who lived on another distant satellite where they had rebelled and wrested control from their Masters.

My sisters had told me that he spoke quite eloquently of insurgency, of revolution; of returning to claim the Element that the Tyrants had ruled for millennia. But I had not yet heard him for myself. Perhaps my head was too full of my own meditations to easily permit the sly and subtle voice of Kalaman to speak within it. Besides, I knew of what he spoke: the same passionate aria of war and blood that the Oracle proclaimed, and that now sang out across the Ether; the song taken up by one HORUS colony after another as our brothers and sisters rioted and one by one the Ascendants fell, plunging from their shining stations to burn between them like so many livid stars. Afterward the triumphant survivors had called to us, some, like Kalaman, insinuating themselves into our dreams; others stalking through the media chambers, their 'filed images grinning like cats as they read off exultant strings of names and executions, until the transmissions ended and they blinked into splinters of light.

Their messages were all the same. The Asterine Alliance, they called themselves: belonging to the stars. It was what the Oracle had named them, and it was the Oracle that had inspired them; but in this too I was reluctant to go along. I had my own oracle, a little silver globe left by Father Irene, the eunuch priest who had for a little while lived on Quirinus and preached to us of his Goddess. The Ascendants drove him from the colony after two months, but it was too late. We had already fallen in love with him and his mistress, the Wild Maiden, the Lady of the Beasts. It was for her that we sacrificed our breasts—a small thing, because who among us would ever suckle young? And it was true, as Father Irene told us, that we were already hers: for the Ascendants look upon us as beasts, and all animals are sacred to her. Like us she was enslaved, but then freed, and like us too she has her holy rages. She is the moon, and her consort is that smaller moon called Ione, where once the Ascendants held their prisoners: a moon long dead, and all its towers fallen. Her oracle was the little globe that Father Irene had left with us. I know it is not a true oracle, because it does not answer my questions, only shows me images of the Wild Maid over time, and recites her hymns—

> *The mightiest of mountains tremble,*
> *the woods with their cloak of darkness shriek*
> *as within the beasts bellow and flee*
> *The Element groans, as does the sea*
> *where dolphins and sirens seek*
> *shelter in the waves, and stars tumble*
> *and she runs, in and out,*
> *across the sky, in and out among the stars, her arrows flashing*
> *as men die and the beasts feed ...*

It is a bloodthirsty hymn, I suppose, but they are words only, and have given me much solace in the months since Father Irene was deported.

The other Oracle, though, the Asterine Oracle, has given form and weight to its words, and brought new kinds of worship to HORUS. Here on Quirinus our Masters died, but it was not by our hands. We gave them proper interment, casting their bodies into the Ether; but on other colonies our brothers and sisters enact darker rites. The torments of Alijj on Totma 3; pyres of liquid flame at Hotei; their Masters trepanned on Helena Aulis by our brother Kalaman and his followers. *Sic semper tyrannus,* the Oracle says; *thus always to tyrants;* and claims that Luther Burdock would have it thus.

But it is not in this way that I recall our father. He was a gentle man. I once saw him weep over the body of an aardman who died during the course of routine surgery, and he was unfailingly kind to all those who worked with him, men or beasts or half-men.

And so I believe that I remember him best. I *know* that I love him best, though my sisters say that cannot be so: that we all can only love him equally, because we are all the same. But I do not *feel* the same as they do.

This new Oracle also seems to know a different man than I remember.

"Your father is waiting for you on Earth. We have made arrangements, he and I, for all his children to return to him." That was what the Oracle said. It is a splendid thing, this Oracle, much stronger and more beautiful than mine, though it does not know any hymns. In its appearance it is like a man made of black and shining metal, like a robotic construct; but it says it is a nemosyne—that is, One Who Remembers. What this Oracle remembers is war.

"It is time!" the Oracle announced during one of its recent apparitions. It appears more often now, in the media gallery and sometimes in the hall where we share our meals. Its words are different each time it appears, but their meaning is always the same. It speaks of war, of new triumphs over our Masters (the Oracle calls them the Tyrants); and of how their rule is ending. The Oracle said that the Element was ours by right, since mankind had proved such poor rulers. We had only to slay the Tyrants, and enslave those who survived, and we would come into our vast estate. This at least was the destiny it claimed Luther Burdock had prepared us for; but I remember no such thing of our father. I do not believe he ever desired that his children should wrest control of the Element from his kind; but neither do I believe he meant for us to be slaves. It is a mystery how this should have happened to us. But then, all things about our father are a mystery.

There is much I do not understand about our world, the hollow metal form where we play out our thousand days, thence to die and be replaced by other, identical sisters. But now, with our Masters dead, we have lost the secret of our reproduction. We do not breed, because our Masters felt that allowing us to breed would give us too much control over our own fates. They wished to have the power over us of life and death: and so we are sterile, and live for only a thousand days.

But the Oracle said that our father would undo this evil. If only we would come to him, he would give us all new lives. He and other men had unlocked the secrets of mortality. They had found ways to extend life. We would live for a thousand thousand days. We would live almost forever.

And this, you see, meant a great deal to me. Because of my thousand days, there were less than a score remaining.

But I said nothing of all this to my sister Cumingia when she came to see me in the library. I thought it strange, that she and the others could hear the voice of our brother Kalaman singing across the void, and I could not. I could sense only my sisters here on Quirinus. Hylas and Polyonyx turning restlessly in the bed they shared, Pira's face nestled between those of Lusine and Hipponyx and Chama, as alike as three violets. But of the others, those of our blood who lived elsewhere in the shining net that made up the HORUS colonies—of them I felt nothing at all.

"He does not speak to me," I said at last.

"Ach! He is so loud I cannot *sleep*—" Cumingia pressed her hands to her ears, then flung them out as though she might disperse the voice ringing in her head. "My sister Kalamat, how is it you can't hear him?"

I sat upon the bed that had been the exchequer's. In my hands, the scroll I had been reading still gave out the faintest impression of warmth and sunlight, the smell of some rich red fruit rotting in heaps on the warm earth—just a few of the things we had never known outside of the library and its thousands of holofiles.

"I do not know," I said after a moment, and frowned. The scroll slid from my fingers to the bed, and the sensations passed. Already I could not recall them clearly, though they were there, somewhere within me, within the deeply buried memories of Luther Burdock's daughter. "What is he saying now?"

"That the Agstra Primus Station has joined the Alliance. That upon the Element there is revolution, in Uropa and the city of Vancouver. That there are many thousands of us now with our father in his stronghold. That they do not understand why we have not joined them."

Her voice was not accusing, but I felt her disappointment with me, a fine crimson fault line running through the consciousness we shared, the psychic structure I always perceived as a sturdy gray mass like stone or concrete.

"These are all things the Oracle has told us already," I

said. "So I do not know why our brother Kalaman must tell us too."

"He says he is lonely." Cumingia sat beside me. Her fingers drifted across the cover of my scroll. "It is strange, O my sister Kalamat, that he does not call to you. Very strange."

She meant it was strange because I was the one they called Kalamat. That was the name given to all energumens by the Tyrants, but among ourselves it is only a priestess who is called that, only a leader. It was to me that Father Irene gave the Oracle of the Great Mother, and so to my sisters I was Kalamat; as this other was named Kalaman by his cohort.

I sighed. Over the last few weeks my sisters had grown increasingly unhappy with my leadership. They wanted to leave Quirinus; to heed the Oracle, go to the Element and there do our father's bidding and embark upon this holy war. And from what my sisters told me, Kalaman fed their unhappiness. He spoke to them of blood, of the gruesome feast he and his brothers had made of their Masters, and even of their own kind. Kalaman said this blood feast had made them stronger. It had made the bonds between Kalaman and his chosen ones unbreakable, so that they would be chief among those our father would greet when they returned to him. They would be the most beloved of Luther Burdock. And it was this thought that troubled me most; because I wanted my father to love no one as much as me.

My sister knew my mind. "If you were not so full of our father, Kalamat, you might better hear other voices."

"I would rather hear my father's voice than this Kalaman's!" I said sharply. "And why should we believe him? How are we to know that our father really is alive? The Oracle speaks of him, and you say that Kalaman speaks of him. But who has seen him, who awakened him from his long sleep? And, sister, how can we know what is really going on in the Element—how can we even know what is happening anywhere else in HORUS? The only proof we have is 'file transmissions, but 'files can lie. We might be the only ones left in HORUS. With our Masters gone, perhaps the other colonies have fallen into ruin."

Cumingia shook her head, her black eyes blazing. "No! They have all gone before us to the Element, that is all! And Kalaman says an elÿon is coming to take him from the Helena Aulis station. That they will come for us, and with them we will return—"

"We will *not* go," I said stubbornly. "What if it is a trap? What if our Masters seek vengeance for their dead?"

A sly look crept across Cumingia's face. "Ah, but it is not, sister! Think of this," she crowed. "I know something the priestess Kalamat does not!—

"Our father is going to speak to us! Kalaman says that the Oracle has promised this. Tonight, when we are passing over the region of the Element where he now lives and the 'file signal is strongest: we will hear him for the first time!"

"You are certain?" My hand flew to where I had offered my breast to the Wild Maid, and made the gesture against lies. "Who has told you this? Kalaman?"

She nodded. "He has told all of us. Luther Burdock will speak tonight, and welcome us to the Alliance."

Our father speaking to us! I felt such joy that I kissed her. "Thank you, my sister! This is wonderful news, and if it is true—if he speaks to us—"

I said nothing more. I did not want to promise, *Then we will leave here.* I would wait to hear what our father had to tell us—if indeed it was our father—before going along with any plan to abandon our home on Quirinus. Though in truth there was no way I could prevent my sisters from leaving. I tried to calm myself and began to make preparations for bed.

After a few minutes my sister Cumingia left me. "I am sorry to have interrupted your reading," she said, although I was not to read anymore that evening. When she was gone, I sat in silence for a long time. Finally I stood and, crossing to the desk, found there the holofile recorder that still held the 'file disk Cumingia had left with me several days before. Absently I set it on the floor in front of me and watched as the now-familiar image appeared, the flaming eye and golden letters, the strange message ending with the chanted name:

*"Icarus. Icarus. Icarus. Icarus."*

I let the 'file play through twice, then switched it off and replaced the recorder. I sighed, returned to bed, and lay there waiting for sleep to come. It did not. My head was too full of my father, his gentle face at the moment I recall most clearly—

*"We won't die?"*

My own voice, that voice we all shared; and his reply—

*"Only this, darling—you'll only remember this—"*

And I recalled the touch of our father's hands upon my brow, those strong hands that always smelled of iodine and formaldehyde and alcohol spirits, and blood. Finally I turned until I faced the wall, and dreamed of him.

Ah, Cumingia had the truth of it there! I thought too much of our father, of Dr. Luther Burdock's hands, his eyes and laughing voice. My mind was ever too full of him. Of finding him again, of having him hug me close to his chest and laugh as he called me Little Moon—but was it to me, Kalamat, or to Cybele that he spoke?

I do not know. I only know that the dream of our father filled me as the sun filled the iridescent sails that powered Quirinus. Like the sun he was all life, all warmth and brightness to me, and there was not a minute of my life that I did not yearn for him.

Across the cold reaches of the Ether, on Helena Aulis where Kalamat's wicked brothers lived, there was a wonderful toy in the room that had been the office of the station's Chief Architect. The office itself was vast and perfectly round, with walls of such blinding whiteness that, out of desperation, the eye papered them with fantastic images: leaves, winged triangles, swastikas, swimming eyes. The energumen Kalaman, however, had no need of such imaginary embellishments. Before the rebellion, he had spent much time in this office with the Chief Architect, assisting in mundane chores—compiling demographic profiles of the other HORUS colonies, copying renderings of stupas and bunkers in the Balkhash Mountains, reading to the Architect from endless lists of figures.

It was dull work. An argument could be made that Kalaman's part in the Asterine Alliance had come about by virtue of his imagining some activity that might combine these assorted bits of trivia. Population figures, maps of armories, numerical equations whose final sum was a new type of bomb: you add them all, and the answer is revolution. One should never underestimate the effects of stupefying boredom upon a bright young student.

During those eternal sunless days he had first seen the heliotype in use. It was a strategic aid, a type of virtual map. By giving it the proper coordinates, you could create a symbolic visual referent for any celestial object you could imagine, in colors so pure and vivid, they made you want to pop them into your mouth. The sun was a fist-sized ball, a scintillating ruby; the Earth (Kalaman called it the Element) a sea-blue eye; and there were any number of iridescent stars, planets, moons, meteors, comets, ærolites, space stations, and nebulæ, as well as enhanced projections of killer asteroids aimed at the moon, satellites poised to implode into glittering dust, quasars like flattened gumdrops, spiky floating remnants of celestial ships, and of course those fanciful efforts to picture ExtraSolar Transports, dubbed *asters* by the Ascendants; nothing necessarily to scale.

Kalaman sat there now, an entire galaxy of these images spinning around his head like so many colossal bees. Every now and then he would stop one of the whirling eidolons and draw it to him for inspection, then release it to carom through the air once more. Now his huge black eyes were fixed on a golden torus that spun lazily a few inches from his nose. It was the heliotype's vision of Quirinus, filtered of course through Kalaman's own projection of what he wanted the station to look like. So the torus had tiny windows like the hexagonal cells of honeybees, and through them Kalaman could see even tinier figures, black and red and ivory, moving purposefully through their golden hive.

If he had wanted to—if Kalaman's vision could somehow have stretched beyond the peeling outer walls of Helena Aulis to encompass the rest of the universe he was so anxious to strike against—he might have seen an elÿon like a fuchsine bubble, trailing quicksilver streamers as it rose to bump against the languidly turning torus. He might have squinted approvingly into the emerald heart of the Element to see a radiant grid, the shimmering perimeters of which encompassed both the City of Trees and the foothills of the Blue Ridge Mountains; and within that grid a block of white like a cube of sugar, a cube meant to be a building. A house, an inn in fact, where still more livid specks plotted determinedly the overthrow of the Autocracy. He might have glimpsed a peculiar glowing body, half-star and half-moon, shimmering ominously at the perimeter of the heliotype's range.

And finally, he might have seen a heavy shining object tumbling languorously against the gleaming white walls of the Architect's chamber: a space station shaped like an hourglass, and inside it a tiny brick-red form like a crooked finger, surrounded by brilliant sparks, whirling atoms: the dream of Kalaman himself, planning a war within a web of dancing worlds.

"They are dying, O my brothers! They hardly resist us at all!"

Kalaman's voice rang out through the Third Assembly Hall of Helena Aulis. He blinked, smiling, so that his tattooed eyes fluttered coquettishly. Beneath him shone the faces of his eighteen surviving siblings, as though his own face were reflected in myriad mirrors, jet and silver and cinnabar. He was suspended in the air by means of an invisible pensile net—a cheap trick, but effective nonetheless, as the Ascendants had found when using it to welcome prisoners of war or dignitaries from enemy colonies. Beside him floated his brother Ratnayaka. Like Kalaman he was smiling, his hands resting on his knees. Both wore knee-length skirts of linen dyed yellow and green, hitched up now to show their powerful legs, hairless and so heavily muscled, they seemed to be entwined with serpents. They were like twin apsaras, those supernatural concubines with which the Indus deities reward their fallen heroes. Their immense faces serene, their lips parted to show the tip of their tongues, pink and crimson, and their carefully filed teeth.

"It is time we moved on to the next stage," Kalaman was saying in his reedy tenor. The other energumens nodded, silent; they could sense what was to come. "The Oracle has spoken to me, and I have done as he commands. Our beloved brother Ratnayaka has prepared the aviettes for our departure tomorrow, Solar Time 0770 hours. We will go to Quirinus. We have sisters there whom we are to welcome into our Alliance. They will join us, and from Quirinus we will journey to the Element."

A murmur, a trembling as of wind shaking the limbs of a small forest.

"The Element, O my brother Kalaman?"

The question came from Riatu, whose black eyes were fairly invisible in his ebony face. Like most of the others, he had been born on Helena Aulis, where he had toiled in the station's media center. His only memories of Earth belonged to Cybele Burdock, and had been garishly enhanced by 'file transmissions showing the destruction of Commonwealth bases by Ascendant janissaries and Aviators. For all that he could sense Kalaman's inarguable will, like strong fingers brushing up and down his spine, his voice was tinged with unease.

"The Element." Kalaman nodded, glanced aside at Ratnayaka. His ivory-skinned brother was suspended next to him, his one eye half-closed, the other shrouded by its crimson band beneath its adornment of thin gold rings. Still exhausted by the aftermath of their harrowing of Sindhi, Kalaman imagined, and he smiled before continuing.

"The Oracle spoke to me this morning. I have several transmissions to share with you, from Hotei and Totma 3 and Vancouver. . . ."

Within his invisible net Ratnayaka yawned. His brother's voice became a sonic blur. He was not exhausted, as Kalaman thought. Rather, last night's harrowing had made him feel immensely huge and powerful: as though he had somehow absorbed Sindhi's body mass, rather than his soul. But it had left him with an overwhelming hunger, a desire that nearly drove him mad. Sitting there with the taut cords of the pensile web cutting into his legs, Ratnayaka closed his eye because he was afraid it would betray him to his brothers, afraid they would see the hunger there. This was why it was unwise to perform the ritual harrowing by oneself, or with only two participants. The experience had strengthened the psychic bond between himself and Kalaman, and Sindhi too of course—even now he could sense him, like a gathering warmth inside his skull. But the immediate rapture had faded, leaving Ratnayaka with that gnawing hunger. Not a physical craving—the harrowing depleted one of the base need for food, which was fortunate since the stores on Helena Aulis were growing low—but the desire to repeat the sublime experience. To devour a brother's very essence, so similar to his own, and taste the rich pulp that would release shreds of their shared memory into Ratnayaka's own mind. Kalaman believed the process somehow helped extend their lives. Perhaps by just a few weeks; but when one's life span extended only three years, that could be a significant amount of time.

Of course, one couldn't go on devouring one's brothers and sisters forever. Fortunately, there were humans. Although the harrowing of their tyrant masters had been nothing like this, only a confusing jolt of fear and horror before their trepanned bodies were cast into the void. But the process could be refined, of course. Ratnayaka had already begun researching it in the station laboratories. And the Oracle had assured him that upon the Element everything was in place for such a project—it would be a simple matter of occupying the hydrofarms and other bioengineering centers, and exchanging geneslaves for Tyrants. . . .

"This transmission is from Porto Alegre."

Ratnayaka opened his eye. In front of him his brothers

stared raptly as the 'file played. The air filled with smoke and flames, the choking stench of burning chemicals. Tiny figures could be seen running from a series of domes, pursued by larger figures brandishing protonic weapons. Ratnayaka could hear the terrified screams of Tyrants as they were engulfed by flames. All around him, his brothers cheered.

Abruptly the scene changed, switched in a sickening whirl to another angle (the aardmen who 'filed the transmission were having difficulty mastering the equipment). Rows of Tyrants in yolk-yellow uniforms had been lined up along a pier thrust into the Lagoa dos Patos. Behind them the sky curdled into great clots of scarlet and purple as the sun set behind blazing skyscrapers. In the foreground aardmen crouched, some of them wearing the black star of the Asterine Alliance on bands around their necks. Cacodemons stood beside them, tall and ramrod straight and heavily armed, their faces marred by the bristling spikes of their feeding tubes. From the Tyrants came a faint, high wailing (the audio section of this 'file was also very poor). Then without warning the pier exploded. Liquid flame and burning bits of cloth and flesh rained down upon the ragged Asterine army. The aardmen howled triumphantly. The scene blinked into oblivion, and Ratnayaka's brothers applauded.

There were other scenes on other 'files. An audio transmission from the Habilis Emirate colony Sepkur, where the energumens had kept their former masters alive. For nearly a month the Sihk general Aswan Turis had been forced to order his troops on Earth to carry out lunatic attacks upon their own military holdings. Despite his cooperation, the energumens finally killed him, beheading him as the Emirate executes delators, the most common spies and traitors. His body was sent to the Emirate capital in Tripoli, along with a hidden bomb that the energumens detonated from the HORUS station. The Emirate's military was already weakened by its war with the Ascendants. No one imagined it could withstand this blow.

Thus it went across the globe. 'File after 'file showed the holocaust engulfing the planet: the rebuilt ruins of Paris once more in flames, its spires and blighted chestnut trees collapsing into ash; floating cities sinking because their hydrapithecenes and sirens had sabotaged them; other coastal cities devastated by energumen-seeded tidal waves and storms when their early-warning systems failed. Few enough of these technological outposts remained on Earth. Now one by one they fell, and the global maps of the HORUS colonies showed darkness like a stain spreading across the continents far below.

"There are too many of us for them to conquer!" gloated Kalaman, and his brothers clapped and laughed aloud. "Only twenty of us here on Helena Aulis; but a million, ten million, on the Element!"

The global maps that shimmered in the air before him suddenly blinked off. In their place a tiny orb appeared, pulsing viridian and violet. It grew, sending off showers of sparks and the piercing sound of a glass harmonium. Now the orb was the size of a fist, a skull; now it was the height of a man. Within it the darting shafts of green and purple took on human shape until the Oracle stood there before them, wrapped in heatless lightning.

"Greetings, brothers!" His voice was sweet and clear as a young boy's. "You have seen what your sisters and brothers have done without you—are you ready now to join them?"

Kalaman and his brothers cheered, in a single voice so thunderous that the ceiling trembled and the hanging lanterns flickered.

"I am glad!" Metatron cried. "Because there is an elÿon coming for you—it will be here tomorrow, when your lights turn over to day."

The glowing figure turned, extended one shining hand to where Kalaman watched it through slitted black eyes. "You have done well by your brothers, Kalaman. Your father will embrace you when you arrive—

"But first you must ready yourselves for him. Whatever weaponry there is on Helena Aulis you must find and bring to the docking area. Also whatever stores remain of food and medicines. From here the elÿon will proceed to Quirinus, to gather your sisters; and then to Earth!"

And Metatron bowed to Kalaman, more gracefully than any construct, more gracefully than any human man; and the gathered energumens shouted and raised their arms in salute to him and Kalaman. Only Ratnayaka did not shout. He regarded the fanfare coolly with his ebony eye, embracing his brother Kalaman; and with his delicate mouth he smiled. A perilous smile, any man would have realized: the smile of Judas as he kissed his beloved prophet, the smile Clytemnestra wore when she welcomed Agamemnon. But there were no longer any men on Helena Aulis, and the energumens had not read the classics.

# 8

## Izanagi to Quirinus

**Inside, the _Izanagi_ resembled** every elÿon freighter I
had ever boarded: a vast gray space, the color of its pale carpeting lost beneath a layer of dust, its curved walls and ceiling hung with cobwebs that trapped more dust in patterns like
limp feathers. The port authority was supposed to disinfect all
personnel and freight to prevent intrusions by insects or other
parasites. Still, the spiders got on board, somehow. I had
never seen an elÿon that did not have them, rain-colored drop-
lets sliding up and down the struts of the drunken webs they
wove, unhinged by the craft's strange gravity.

The _Izanagi_ seemed cleaner than most vessels—the result
of neglect more than fastidiousness. It had been traveling
among the HORUS colonies for several months now, with
only its adjutant living on board. I half-expected there to be
energumen rebels hidden within its chambers, or some kind of
automated weaponry; but I found no evidence of either. Perhaps the energumens had used it and cast it adrift until it returned to Cisneros; perhaps it had never come within the
reach of the rebel Alliance. But I was impatient, and willing
to risk the dangers in order to reach Quirinus.

As Valeska, Nefertity, and I stepped out into the main entryway, a bell chimed, a hollow, high-pitched tone alerting the

crew to our arrival. A minute later doors opened in the misty walls, and several replicant servers appeared to escort us.

"Imperator Tast'annin," one hissed. It was a fifth-generation Maio server, dating from the Third Ascension, tall and slender like some attenuated metal insect, with small glowing red eyes. "May I show you to your quarters?"

"No," I said shortly, and turned to the server addressing Valeska, another Maio construct with that distinctive sibilant voice. "Captain Novus is the only one among us who will need formal quarters. Who is the adjutant aboard?"

The servers looked at each other and exchanged a round of clicking noises. Then the first one plucked Valeska's sleeve and began to cross toward a wide round door.

"Imperator Tast'annin—" Valeska's voice was pinched, a little desperate. I recalled that she had never been to HORUS, and so would not have been inside an elÿon before, except on inspection. I raised my hand and tried to sound reassuring.

"I will find you after we've embarked." She nodded once, stumbling a little as her replicant guide escorted her through the door. Beside me Nefertity waited in silence, observing the remaining two Maio units with smoldering green eyes.

"They will not harm her?" she asked at last.

"Harm her?" I gestured dismissively at the replicants. They swiveled their silver heads and walked away, to disappear back down the long gray corridors that had disgorged them. "No. They're standard escorts. Relatively speaking, few humans make the journeys on the elÿon. There will be no human crew on this one save its adjutant. And Captain Novus, of course."

Nefertity turned to survey our chamber. Motes of crystal light danced in the air around her, white and blue and red; the only true colors in that room. "Is it all so dreary?"

I crossed to where an arched doorway opened onto a dim corridor and beckoned Nefertity to follow me. "It's deliberate," I replied. "After the Third Ascension, elÿon travel grew quite common, but the rate of psychosis among the crews and passengers was so high that some vessels arrived with all hands dead, save the adjutants. We now believe that any kind of stimulation contributes to the illness—"

I gestured at the smooth, drab walls, the soft indirect light that made everything look as though it had been cast in pewter. "—So the design attempts to soothe travelers. At least here in the entry foyer and cabins. Other parts of the vessel might be more interesting, if they've bothered with them at all. Most vessels no longer employ a human crew."

Nefertity moved noiselessly behind me as we walked down the hall. "But your Aviators? How do they travel?"

"The same as anyone else. A mild anesthesia, psychotropic drugs. After twelve or so hours they can walk around the decks, but the replicants will always accompany them in case there's need for intervention."

"And you?" Nefertity paused to stare out a tiny window that showed nothing but a hazy umber darkness. "Did you travel like that?"

I strode past her, my boot heels thudding on the carpeted floor. "At first. But I was more disciplined than most. After several years the drugs were no longer necessary. Many people grow bored on the elÿon, but I always find it interesting to visit the adjutants."

Nefertity left the window and followed a few steps behind me. "Is that where we are going now?"

I nodded. I was weary of conversation. It made it difficult for me to concentrate on where I actually was. So featureless were our surroundings that my memories threatened to spill over into them, paint a sky over the dun-colored ceilings and sow the floors with the lush reeds and vines I had last seen in the Archipelago. Such hallucinations were a commonplace of elÿon journeys. I had taught myself to overcome them, and even now I had no reason to believe I would be any more susceptible than I had been, since the trappings of my humanity had been flensed from me as carefully as the rind from an orange. But my mind remained human, prey to fears, especially since I found my thoughts returning again and again to my youth. I would need to concentrate fully on the problem of what had become of the HORUS colonies.

There were no other corridors branching off this one; very few doors, and those few locked. I knew they opened onto the vast network of pipes and conduits that channeled rivers of nucleic fluid throughout the craft, the seemingly random maze of glass and plasteel veins that pumped liquid data and propulsion fluid to the heart of the vessel. The elÿon was like a gargantuan beast, an immense vein-fed polyp encased in polymer heat shields and glassy plates. Instead of a rudimentary brain it had the adjutant, sealed within his cell; and as parasites, those few passengers it would consent to carry, safely strapped within their own small cavities at the vessel's center.

The elÿon were the zenith of the Ascendants' centuries of toying with human and animal genetics: living vessels that swam among the stars.

The single corridor spiraled slowly out and up, as we traveled toward the center of the huge craft. Real windows appeared now, still narrow but letting in ribboned shafts of orange flame, the occasional lancing dart of a searchlight or passing aviette. It was like walking within the coils of a vast shell, its pale interior lit by intermittent flares of candlelight. Sensing my mood (she was, after all, a sort of woman), Nefertity remained silent, only now and then stopped to stare out a window.

"That is the adjutant's chamber, there."

My voice sounded too loud, amplified by the empty hall. I pointed to where the corridor ended in a high arch, its spandrel a sheet of clear plasteel opening onto a knot of coiled tubes, flickering yellow and green where navigational fluids pulsed through them. We passed beneath the arch, and I heard the faint sound, part serpentine hiss and part sigh, that signaled entry into the adjutant's quarters.

The manifest Agent Shi Pei had given me listed one Zeloótes Franschii as the *Izanagi*'s sole crew, his inception date nearly a year earlier. This would be his last journey. The chemically induced insomnia necessary for successful navigation could not be kept up for more than ten or twelve solar months before dementia, and finally coma, set in. More than a few elÿon had been lost when their adjutants died en route to HORUS, but I had already decided not to worry about that.

I pointed to the far end of the great room, telling Nefertity, "His name is Zeloótes Franschii. We will talk to him—they grow lonely on these voyages, and one can learn much from adjutants. The process of navigating the elÿon makes one's mind as an empty cup, and many strange things are poured into it."

The entire far wall had been given over to a huge scanner, its curved surface covered with details that did not resemble a map so much as an illuminated anatomical chart. But it *was* a map, showing the elÿon's interior construction as well as an illuminated diagram of the adjutant's brain, with glowing bursts of color indicating those portions being stimulated by the bath of neurots and electrical pulses that made up the elÿon's navigational system. As a subtle underlay to all this there was a chart of the heavens, showing both the renamed constellations—Maswan, the Circumfuge, Eisler 33—and the drunken orbits of the HORUS colonies, Quirinus and Totma 3 and Adhvi Sar, Sternville and Hotei and Helena Aulis.

"That is a navigational chart?"

I smiled, hearing Sister Loretta Riding's incredulity in the nemosyne's words. "It is."

"They must go mad, studying it."

"They do."

We reached the wall. It was a moment before my eyes could focus on the adjutant. He seemed a part of that whole baroque design, an insect snared in some great luminous web. A withered, frail creature pinned to the wall, tubes and wires and vials strung about him like so many sacrificial offerings.

"Lascar Franschii." I used the ancient term for *sailor,* the word the adjutants use to describe themselves.

The spindly figure twitched, so freighted with the instruments that kept him alive that he could scarcely move.

"Imperator Tast'annin." The voice was a low sibilant. It came not from the man in front of us but from a speaking tube above his head. His own mouth was plugged with a wide corrugated tube, pale yellow like a sandworm. His eyes were gone, plucked from his head before his first journey and replaced by two gleaming faceted jewels that had sunk deeply into the hollow sockets beneath his brow. His skin had collapsed into folds like crumpled worn velvet, gray and yellow. There was no way of telling what race of man he had been; he scarcely seemed a man at all. As he spoke, his head jerked almost imperceptibly. I could sense the faint heat from his optics as their gaze swept across my face. "Imperator, you honor me."

There was no way to tell if the words were meant ironically. I glanced aside at Nefertity. She stared with wide emerald eyes glittering as the adjutant's own.

"But this is a terrible thing," she said in a low voice. She raised her hands as though to offer him some comfort. "That is a man there—they are torturing a man!"

A spasm crossed the adjutant's cheek. He might have been amused, or in pain—although it was unusual for them to feel pain, their sensory receptors having long since been destroyed. "You have a compassionate replicant," his hollow voice rang out. "How interesting."

"Are you in pain?" Nefertity approached him, stretched

her silvery fingers to graze the slack line of his jaw. "Why have they done this to you?"

A hoarse wheezing crackled from the speaking tube: laughter. "Oh, but it is an honor, replicant. Almost as much an honor as has been given your master in his new body."

I felt a jolt of anger. Had he been another kind of man, I would have killed him. But his judgment was impaired; he had lost the neural inhibitors that should have kept him from speaking to me thus. And his term as adjutant was nearly ended; meaning, of course, his life. The adjutants were given careful doses of prions, brain proteins that attack the thalamus and intercept sleep. The permanent dream-state induced by this enables them to lose all sensory perception, so that their impressions can be better channeled into the elÿon's neural web and so provide the mindless biotic vessels with a governing consciousness. The adjutant's body was fed by the complex if primitive web of tubes. The simpler side effects of the prion disease—increased heartbeat, elevated body temperature—were regulated by monitors and a NET. The hallucinations do not usually interfere with the elÿon's progress, although once in an elegant if destructive pas de deux two of the billowing craft seemed to have been controlled by the same dream, and collided. Their wreckage still spans the outer orbit of the HORUS station Advhi Sar. The only aspect of the navigational method that cannot be controlled is this inevitable disintegration of the brain, as the proteins cause the thalamus to shrink and leave spongy holes in the cortex. It is a relatively slow death, but painless, except for those rare occasions when sensory hallucinations set the navigators shrieking and tossing in their webs.

"It *is* an honor of sorts," I said stiffly. "They are political prisoners who would otherwise be executed—"

"Innocent! Innocent!" His words were garbled almost beyond recognition by the speaking tube. A spew of nonsense followed, ending with a high-pitched yowl like a cat's. Nefertity drew back from the wall, her eyes sparking alarm.

"It is the preliminary phases of his dementia," I explained. "It is unusual for them to live for more than twelve months—I had hoped we might see him through his final voyage."

As suddenly as they had begun, the adjutant's screams stopped. "Oh, I will live," he said, the speaking tube giving his words a hollow resonance. "I have already received notice of when I will die: not until after you disembark at Quirinus. I have a few more errands left to do." His head flopped back and forth as another burst of raw laughter exploded in the chamber.

I wondered what those errands might be, and who was commanding him. Which of the colonies still had Ascendants governing the elÿon fleet? To my later grief I did not ask Lascar Franschii about this. Instead I turned to Nefertity. "Is this disturbing you? If so, you can join Captain Novus in her quarters."

A rattling from the adjutant's speaking tube brought more laughter. "Imperator! You are so solicitous of your fembot." The last word came out as a derisive gasp.

The nemosyne turned her lantern eyes upon the man pinned to the wall. "I will go," she said, and walked away. "Your cruelties sicken me."

"So sensitive!" cried Lascar Franschii. "Tell me, Imperator, when did our masters order the creation of these softhearted constructs? I am moved, touched, fascinated beyond measure by such a thing! Are they all like this now, or is it only the Imperators who are given such delicacies?"

I took a step toward him, grabbing the coil of crimson and blue and green tubes feeding into the myriad slits in his body. "Be silent, Lascar Franschii, else—"

"Oooh, oooh!" The adjutant gasped and moaned, writhing within his webbed prison. "Be quick, be quick, be still my heart—" Above him the shimmering map glowed more brightly. A trailer of gold like flame shot from one end of the wall to the other. The optics that glittered where his eyes had been flared deep blue, nearly black, and his mouth twisted into a hateful grimace. "Paaugh—I curse you, Tast'annin, your eyes betray you—"

I felt a sudden weariness, a sickness with myself for reacting to the ravings of an adjutant, and dropped my hand. The tubes fell back against the wall with a thud. "My eyes?"

"Yesss—" The speaking tube quivered as he hissed. "My brothers fought you at the Archipelago. On Kalimantan. I was only a child, they kept me hidden in the caverns with the other children and the hydrapithecenes. But I saw you on the 'files—you did not laugh when the bodies ignited, as your troops did. The sight sickened you, did it not? It drove you to destruction! How can a man look upon such things and not go mad? Your eyes are the same now as they were then—they betray you, Imperator! What is it like to be a corpse, and have no tongue to cleave to your mouth in fear? Where does the fear go when you die?"

The optics rattled in his eye sockets, the speaking tube bulged from his twisted mouth as though he would disgorge it. Rage swept through me and I cried, "Silence, Lascar! I will engage another elÿon—be still!"

I raised my hand threateningly, but he took no notice. Why should he? After a moment I turned away and headed for the door. I had nearly reached it when the adjutant's voice roared out, so heavily amplified that the nets of wires shook like vines storm-rent against the wall.

"Do not waste your efforts, Imperator! None of the other elÿon have clearance to attend upon Quirinus."

I stopped and looked back. "Why not?"

Within the glowing interstices of the nav charts, the adjutant's form twitched as he raised his head. "There is no one left to command them. No one but you. Besides, Quirinus should still be under quarantine. It was beset by plague, hidden in a rice shipment from the Archipelago. The station was sabotaged by a Commonwealth delator posing as a psychobotanist."

Spikes of greenish light flowed from his optics. It was easy to imagine triumph in his voice, though the speaking tube rendered nearly all emotion from it.

"Which plague?"

"*Irpex irradians.*" As the words boomed out, the adjutant's head drooped upon his chest, as though exhausted. "Every one of them. Dead."

"So I was told by commanding Agent Shi Pei. Is there any danger of contagion?"

The adjutant's shoulders twitched in what might have been a shrug. "Who knows? I would not rely on her word, though. Agent Shi Pei grows lax in her duties. I hear she spends much of her time in a hammock, smoking kef and reviewing 'files relating to the destruction of NASNA Prime."

"But no official quarantine was ever declared," I said.

The adjutant's head tilted in a nod. "True. The energumens were immune, and there are no human survivors. The microphage can live for only seventy-two hours without a host. But *you* have no reason to fear, Imperator, you and your sentimental construct. Even our masters do not yet have organic plagues to attack the dead—and plague may be the least of your problems, if the Alliance succeeds with its plans."

"I have a woman with me, Valeska Novus. I would not have her harmed—"

The adjutant's voice came out in a dull moan. "Check with the Quirinus scholiast if you don't believe me. There is little danger of contagion."

I nodded. "Very well. Tell me of this Alliance."

He raised his head, and this time I could see where his mouth was drawn in a cold, small smile, like a bloodless wound.

"It began on Sternville. The energumens rioted, and the cacodemons. They commandeered an aviette and attacked Helena Aulis and MacArthur, raising troops along the way. Cacodemons, mostly, and aardmen; also those argalæ intelligent enough to follow what was happening. Since then they've taken several of the Commonwealth stations, destroyed NASNA Prime and the Triton mining platform, and they tried to attack Urisa headquarters—anyplace where geneslaves outnumbered the human population, which is nearly everywhere in HORUS. The energumens lead them. They say that they have sent rebels to Earth, to organize geneslaves there in mass revolts. They say there has long been an underground network, of geneslaves and humans both, working to overthrow the tyranny of the Ascendants."

"But how can this have happened?" I asked. "And so quickly—"

A low moan came from the speaking tube. "Slaves, Imperator—not even genetic monsters will stay slaves forever. There is a robot that leads them, a construct they call the Oracle. To rally the energumens, it speaks to them of Luther Burdock—"

I shook my head in disbelief. "Luther Burdock? The geneticist?"

"Yes. The energumens think of him as their father. Some of them worship his memory. I have seen it—in the HORUS colonies strange rituals evolve among the energumens and pass quickly from one generation to the next. And so this Oracle has preyed upon their beliefs. It has told them that Luther Burdock has been resurrected and will lead his monstrous children in war against mankind."

"And is it true?" I demanded.

The adjutant shuddered. "Who knows? Certainly it is true

that the rebellion has spread everywhere that there are geneslaves—which, of course, is every place on HORUS and Earth. And it is true that some people claim they can still see a resemblance to Burdock's daughter in the energumen clones. *And,"* he added slyly, the speaking tube magnifying his glottal voice, "there are those who have always believed that he made certain preparations for his eventual return."

I was silent. Of course. There had always been whispered remarks at the Academy when we spoke of Burdock, rumors that he had cloned not only his daughter but himself. But in four hundred years he had never resurfaced. Why now? I looked at Lascar Franschii and asked, "The energumens who have returned to Earth—how have they done so?"

The wires and tubes holding the adjutant snapped and shook like bridge cables in a high wind. "By elÿon, of course! They commandeered the elÿon and disembarked in the hidden zones! You have seen yourself how easy it would be—"

I thought about that for several minutes; thought about Lascar Franschii, who had no reason to love the Ascendants. Yes, it would be very easy to get an adjutant to defect.

I shook my head. Even so: a geneslave rebellion on Earth! It was an absurd thought. And yet it had happened on Quirinus, and on all the other stations as well, if I was to believe Zeloótes Franschii. I had seen for myself the empty sky where the splendid lights of HORUS should have been.

I realized then that I should have spent more time at Cisneros, reviewing whatever newsfiles they had and trying to locate any human survivors of the rebellions. I might have learned more of how the world had changed while I died and was reborn. I might not have forgotten my original intent in going to Quirinus, which was to find the nemosyne called Metatron. And I might have spared myself much of what was to follow.

I gazed once more at the glittering web that held the adjutant. "Tell me, then, Lascar Franschii: what is it that they want?"

A distinct cough. Pinkish spittle flew in a coarse spray around my head. "Our destruction, of course!" His laughter rippled through the room. "The Oracle has taught them well. I have seen it: its 'file appears and they sit before it enthralled, and afterward go forth to do its will. *I* would never take orders from such a thing—a replicant, a mere robot; but paugh! these geneslaves, they are like children. You can manipulate them with words and pictures.

"And that is what the Oracle has done. It has told them that they have a destiny, that they are to repopulate the world. It has told them *that* was the grand dream that Luther Burdock had for them. They can't reproduce as we humans can, at least not yet; but sooner or later they will find a way to do that as well. Sooner, I think."

"But someone must command this robot! Who?"

The shining web trembled until I thought he would fall from it. His face twisted with some terrible effort, and then he smiled, a horrible grimace that made me take a step back.

"Well, Imperator, the Oracle says that Luther Burdock is alive. I believe the Oracle is his."

I regarded him coldly. "And how do *you* know so much of this, Lascar?"

He shuddered, and with great effort produced another tortured smile.

"I told you." His voice spilled from the speaking tube, harsh and deep. "They have commandeered many elÿon to take them to Earth. . . ."

"And what then, Lascar Franschii?" My voice was cold with rage. "Did the insurgents confide in you their plans beyond the destruction of mankind?"

The optics in the adjutant's skull sent out pulses of brilliant blue and orange. "Surely you know the rest, Imperator! 'O brave new world, That has such people in't!' Two legs good, but four legs will be better, when the aardmen come into power—which, of course, they never will.

"You know what they say: 'The Revolution is like Saturn; it eats its own children.' I hear the energumens are doing that already. And once they have seized control, they will not relinquish it, to mankind or other geneslaves, even if it means death. They would have made wonderful Aviators, Imperator."

I stretched out my hand and tapped restively at the wall. At last I asked, "But the Ascendants must still be governing from somewhere. Not everyone was in HORUS."

"Of course not!" The adjutant's voice rose to a howl. "Our masters will admit no failure, they will admit nothing! They are trying to govern us from the reclaimed capital now, and from Vancouver and New Wichita. But every envoy they have sent to Quirinus has been killed. Their bodies are returned via elÿon, their heads grafted onto their stomachs, their brains removed and looped together like a string of drying morels."

"And this is the work of—?"

The adjutant's head bobbled enthusiastically. Scarlet lights rippled across the web to form an aureole around his twisted body. "The energumens. They are like children whose tyrannical rector has been slain! They laugh and make a game of toying with the remains of their masters, and anyone foolish enough to interrupt their play."

His voice swooped to a conspiratorial tone. "Ah, but you know, Imperator, I think that they are starting to succumb to the same lunacies as their masters. Some of them claim to have seen the Watcher in the Skies—yes, I heard them, they spoke of it and I laughed and they grew angry with me. They do not like it when you laugh at them. Others believe they are the children of the Final Ascension, and those on Quirinus are Amazons.

"I've never seen anything like *them*. Converts to the Mysteries of Lysis. A priest was interned there for several months, before the Ascendants grew impatient with his doctrine. He made quite an impression upon the energumens, though, especially their leader. Kalamat, her sisters call her; of course, their masters called them *all* Kalamat. She has an artistic temperament, Imperator—a great admirer of the dance, and your mother's poetry, and sonic sculptures by people like Kyrië Martinez."

The adjutant choked on his laughter. "But in a few days you will be able to see for yourself, Imperator Tast'annin. I have received clearance to depart now. I suggest you find an empty cell and position yourself until we are underway."

I nodded grimly and took my leave, pausing at the doorway to gaze back to where he thrashed and moaned within his web, the nav chart glimmering around him. I stood there for several minutes, thinking on what he had said.

Kalamat: The Miracle. I knew the name, of course, any child fortunate enough to have formal schooling knew of Kalamat and her history; and even those children who had never seen a scroll or classroom had been threatened with Kalamat's fate if they did not behave. I wondered what it meant, that an energumen with that name now led her sisters on Quirinus. Finally I left, Lascar Franschii's sickly laughter echoing behind me.

I quickly found an empty chamber, but once there I found it difficult to calm myself. Instead I stood beside the wall, gazing at a scrim showing a night view of Tokyo Bay before the Three Hour War. My mind raced as I tried to make sense of all that I had learned. There was nothing to be done, now that we were underway; no point in returning to the City of Trees, since I knew I would not find Metatron there. I did not care just yet to confront my surviving superiors in Vancouver or New Wichita. They might view my actions as a defection, and feel that their *rasa* Imperator was in need of further rehabilitation, or even permanent retirement. I felt lost amid some inner labyrinth, trying to find the one path that would bring me clear of all these maddening things—Metatron, the rebel Alliance, Kalamat, Luther Burdock's Oracle.

And so, lost among them, I remembered a day at the Academy, long long ago. . . .

"I'm not going." Aidan stopped in front of the door, throwing his head back so that his auburn hair fell into his eyes. "It's barbaric, their bringing an energumen in like this. . . ."

John and I looked at each other in surprise. Aidan's reaction was bizarre, especially in light of Aidan's mockery of John's revelations during our last game of Fear. If John could overcome his revulsion at an energumen, surely the fearless Aidan Harrow could do the same.

"It will probably be in a cage, Aidan," I said reassuringly. "We'll sit in the back if you're worried—"

Aidan shot him a furious glance, then shook his head. "I'm not *afraid,* Sky Pilot," he said, using the derisive nickname I hated. "It's just—well, it's cruel, that's all, cruel and . . ."

His voice died, maybe because what part of our studies did *not* have to do with cruelty? We were in the hallway outside the first-level classroom, where of late we had been studying Luther Burdock, whose devoutly cruel lifework was to make possible all the later horrors of our own age.

Of course, our rectors did not think of Burdock in such terms. To them—and to us their students, still living in the golden haze of youth—Burdock was a hero, the brilliant geneticist who refused to recant his beliefs and so was executed by the fundamentalists of the short-lived Third Ascendancy.

For the last few weeks we had been watching old 'files of him in his laboratory, and re-creating some of his more basic experiments in our own classrooms. It was horrifying and fascinating work, even on such a primitive schoolboy level—watching the retroviruses do their work upon a colony of cyclops, exposing amoebas and paramecia and brine shrimp to the metrophages and seeing them change, almost before our eyes. We could not, of course, replicate even the simplest of Dr. Burdock's efforts at real gene-splicing, but then we didn't really need to. The evidence was all around us in any case: the aardmen who did the heavy labor at the Academy, lifting hundred-kilo sacks of flour and moving the huge video backdrops of the cycloramas where we held our war games; the hydrapithecenes and sirens that acted as victims in our simulated raids on the Archipelago, imprisoned in their tidal pools; the argalæ that serviced the older male students in the nearby town of Kasco. No, the NASNA Academy was not lacking in geneslaves. What surprises me now is how few of us were ever moved by their plight.

We had all of us since childhood been thrilled and terrified by tales of Dr. Burdock. He had refined the primitive work of the twenty-first century's genetic engineers and created the first-generation geneslaves for the Ascendants. He was equal measures Louis Pasteur and Victor Frankenstein, his legend as much a part of our lives as his creations. That was why it was odd to see Aidan so disturbed by Burdock's work with his daughter. It was a terrible thing, perhaps, but it had happened so long ago, and at any rate, we had been hearing about it forever.

John Starving nudged me, whispering, "We'd better go in—there's Bowra—"

I turned to see our rector plodding down the corridor, his worn crimson leathers burnished by the light spilling from the high recessed windows above him. John and I started in, but Aidan remained in the hall, glaring defiantly in Bowra's direction.

"Come *on*—you'll be sent down!—" I hissed. Aidan had missed so many classes and training sessions that the infirmary had a permanent carrel for him. His wrists were raw where he had been strapped in, and his eyes had dark circles beneath them, from the nightmares induced by the drugs they fed him in a futile effort to make him more pliant. I yanked at his arm, pulling him through the door after me. He swore as John and I dragged him to the back of the chilly room and shoved him into an ancient metal folding chair. We threw ourselves into the seats next to his. A small pulse throbbed at the corner of John's mouth, showing how angry he was with Aidan; but Aidan only slouched in his chair and glared sullenly at the front of the room. By the window I could see Emma Harrow, staring at us with a frown. She was fascinated, practically enthralled, by Luther Burdock. She and John argued endlessly over the ethical aspects of his work. When she saw me looking at her, she turned away and started talking to another student.

A moment later Bowra entered. His piggish eyes darted suspiciously across the rows of exhausted cadets.

"Good morning," he croaked brusquely. He turned to crank up the dilapidated old 'file machine, and the morning's session began.

Flickering 'file images filled the room. "Cassandra, Virginia, United States, 2069," Bowra recited in a bored voice, and leaned back upon his desk.

The first part was familiar enough: old holofiles showing the everyday life of the great man. Burdock and his daughter Cybele eating dinner in their grand compound, attended by the first generation of aardmen—surprisingly slight and hirsute creatures, resembling dogs more than their descendants do. Burdock strolling the grounds of his mountain compound, pointing out the cages where aardmen howled and scratched, the huge oceanic tank that imprisoned his leviathan folly Zalophus. A carefully staged shot of Burdock leafing through books full of fotos, pretending to search for the individual who would be the perfect subject for his work. Burdock dropping the books and throwing up his hands in exaggerated dismay at the hopelessness of his task.

Then the 'files changed. Now they had a clarity, a documentary quality that the earlier ones had lacked, and which I found chilling. My friends did too—when I glanced at them, their eyes were fixed on the front of the room, and while John frowned, Aidan's pale face held a look of disgust that bordered on terror.

We saw Cybele alone in her room, curly head bent over a scroll, her face screwed into a frown as she strove to hear whatever it was saying. My heart ached to see her. She was so young, so much prettier than any of the Academy recruits, with their hard darting eyes and nervous hands. The picture shifted to a formal holo portrait of father and daughter, Cybele smiling wistfully, as though she already knew where her future lay.

And finally, ancient 'files from that remarkable operation; images as famous as the archival footage of the First Shining or the twentieth-century lunar ascent. The kindly man's head bent over the shining elfin face of his trusting adolescent daughter. Her fearless gaze, the little-girl voice asking *We won't die?* and his soft reply—

"We will die. But then we will be regenerated, because of *that*—"

And the camera scanned the banks of steel and glass crucibles, the metal canisters and frozen vials of DNA. Then came quick flashes of Cybele unconscious, and Luther Burdock's pale face and fatigue-smudged eyes staring at a gleaming steel vat where something floated, a whitish form like a bloated football, turning over and over as fluids churned into the vat and still Luther Burdock watched, patient and exhausted: waiting, waiting.

And, finally, Burdock staring exultantly as across the clipped green lawns of his compound came the slender figures of two girls. Hand in hand, wearing identical shifts of white linen, their dark curls spilling around heart-shaped faces: Cybele and her cloned sister.

Kalamat. The miracle.

"You know the rest, of course," Bowra coughed wearily, letting the 'file flicker into stray shafts of silver and blue light that sprayed across our faces. "Now to end this segment of your training module, I've arranged for one of the Kalamat series to be brought here this morning—"

He glanced at his watch, pressed it, and impatiently spoke to the Junior Officer who served as his flunky. A few minutes later we all turned at the sound of two sets of footsteps echoing down the corridor.

"Imre, that toad," Aidan hissed, grimacing.

Pilot Imre's tread was easily recognized, because of his limp. But the other step was unfamiliar: a heavy, even ponderous, tread, as of huge feet dragging slowly across the cold stone floors. John and I exchanged glances. I knew he was recalling that cage in Wyalong so many years ago. But he only smiled at me wryly before turning away.

I looked over at Aidan and saw how pale he was. The freckles stood out on his high cheekbones, and he stared fixedly at his knees. I leaned over to say something to him, something reassuring. But before I could speak, the door was flung open. The energumen stumbled into our classroom.

It was huge, even larger than I had expected—nearly eight feet tall. Pilot Imre walked beside it, separated by several feet of heavy luminous chains. He held a sonic cudgel between his nervous fingers. The thing was sedated, of course. It trudged into the middle of the room, where Imre sent a small blast at it—an unnecessary cruelty. The thing moaned softly and we all gasped.

Because its voice, at least, had not changed. It was still the voice of a fifteen-year-old girl, childlike, horribly out of place in that cold, echoing chamber. I shivered and muttered a curse. Beside me I could hear John Starving swearing under his breath. Of the three of us only Aidan was silent, his gray-green eyes fixed on the front of the room.

I don't know what would have been more terrible—to view some creature utterly flensed of all resemblance to its human originator, or to see what we saw. A huge figure, unmistakably human but no less monstrous for all that—tall and big-boned, its head shaven and tattooed with an identifying ideogram that showed it belonged to the independent Urisa Agency, an L-5 mining conglomerate. Its arms were corded with muscle, its legs thick and welted with the marks of chains and with raw blisters left by other cudgels.

But when Imre tugged its chain, the creature raised its head; and there was the face of Cybele Burdock. Grotesquely elongated, with flesh the color of obsidian rather than Cybele's tawny brown, and rampant with scars; but Cybele's face nonetheless. I knew it by the eyes, if nothing else. Because even though it would certainly have killed me without thinking, crushing my head between its huge hands like a melon husk, still it had the eyes of a child—bright and wistful despite the sedatives. Hopeful, even, as though somewhere within that monstrous body Cybele Burdock was still imprisoned, and still dreamed of escape.

"God, look at her." Next to me John Starving tightened his hands upon his knees. "She's just like that other one, in Wyalong—it's like it's the *same one*—"

I nodded, my mouth too dry to speak. When I glanced at Aidan, he was gazing at the energumen in a sort of horrified rapture. I quickly looked away.

At the front of the room Bowra was rattling on about the

energumens—their strength, their speed, their intelligence. At the word *intelligence* several cadets broke into nervous laughter. The drugs, combined with the incongruous innocence of its features, gave the energumen the appearance of a huge and slightly witless child.

"Come on, then. Say your name. Tell them who you are," rasped Bowra, as Imre gave the chain another yank and prodded the energumen impatiently. There was a burst of static, loud enough to make my ears ring. The energumen cried out, tried to clap its hands to its ears, but the chains held it back. Imre shouted at it, pointing to the classroom full of rapt faces.

"Your name! Go on, tell them—"

The energumen swayed from side to side, staring fixedly at the floor as it moaned softly. Then, very slowly, it raised its shaven head and spoke.

"Kalamat."

Its eyes, so dark they were almost black, stared pleadingly at the silent room.

*Will it hurt, Daddy?*

I looked away; but beside me I could see how Aidan strained to see it, could hear his breathing and the curses he murmured, nearly drowned by Imre's command.

*"Louder!"*

"Kalamat," the energumen whispered in its childish voice, and began to weep.

## 9

## Message from
## the Country

**I did not sleep** that night, nor did Jane. Several times I saw Giles walking wordlessly from room to room, carrying boxes and objects that trailed wires and cords behind him. He carried them all to the front hallway and left them piled there: every one of the inn's monitors, video screens, telefiles, and magisters, and last of all the shortwave radio from the kitchen. When I passed the empty rooms, they looked blinded, with ragged holes where the monitors and telefiles had been yanked from the crumbling plaster walls. Afterward I did not see Giles again, although in the hollow hour before dawn I heard soft noises and followed them until I found their source, in the steps leading down to the cellar. A glimmer of light ran along the bottom of the closed doorway. I rested my hand on the wood and paused, listening. I expected to hear sobs, or perhaps Giles talking to himself; but there was only the sound of someone moving down there, as though Trevor still silently went about his work, gathering mushrooms.

Dawn found me alone on the front porch. The sun seemed to flush a certain expectancy from the green shadows of the trees, a quiet foreboding that grew deeper as heat seeped into all the hidden places of the world and the sky burned away from indigo to blue to white. By the time the roosters began crowing in the barn, the morning already seemed exhausted. The leaves curled limply on the oaks; the smell of honeysuckle was everywhere, thick enough that I could taste it in my throat, gritty with pollen and dust.

"Are you packed?"

I turned to see Jane framed in the doorway. She had traded her old clothes for loose cotton trousers and a man's white shirt, and cut her brown hair so it curled raggedly around her face.

"I thought maybe I'd look different," she said. No note of apology or even explanation in her voice, just a blank statement. Her brown eyes were smudged with lilac circles, and her mouth was drawn thin with exhaustion. "So the Aviators won't recognize me, if they come. God, it's hot. Do you think it'll be like this in Cassandra?"

"I don't know." I sighed, shaking my head at Jane's appearance. It would take more than a bad haircut to keep the Aviators at bay. "I'll go gather my things."

I went upstairs. My body acted as a faithful old servant, caring for a feckless master too dissipated to pay attention to such matters as going about the business of washing, changing my clothes, lying down on the bed for a few minutes' rest, even ordering me to the kitchen, where I found Giles heating water in the little glass oven for tea.

"Cadence should be here in another hour or two," he said. He had changed into a white robe and braided his hair with a white ribbon, like a Paphian going to a bed-warming. The Aviator's gun was slung into a thin leather belt at his waist. I tried to keep my eyes from filling with tears, but he only said, "Please don't worry about me, Wendy. I told you, Trevor and I had planned for this a long time ago."

So I sat with him at the table and we drank tea together—a macabre breakfast, I thought, with Trevor's corpse who knows where and Giles seemingly ready to enact some suicide pact. Even after Giles left, I waited, half-expecting Jane to join me. She never did, so finally I went back outside.

She was still there, sitting on the porch steps, her head bent forward to rest upon her knees. I sat beside her and we waited in silence, while the trees seemed to melt into shimmering puddles and the paint on the porch railings blistered.

Once Giles brought out a cracked pitcher of water and stood by to make sure we drank it. After that I must have dozed off, because suddenly Jane was nudging me.

"Look." Her voice cracked as she pointed to the west, where the road crept up a little hill in a thin red line. "This must be them."

I heard a faint drumming sound. A plume of ruddy dust rose from the hilltop, and a plume of white smoke. It took a moment for me to see anything else within the haze. But then I could just make out a battered vehicle, rust-colored and with tattered solex awnings extending from either side. It careened down the road, weaving to avoid holes and boulders, the solex shields flapping like the wings of a great drunken heron.

"At least we'll travel in style," Jane said drily. She stood, shielding her eyes with her hands.

The vehicle rattled toward us, a big old caravan of the type used during the Fourth Ascension to relocate civilians from the broken lands. Holes gaped in its rusted sides beneath a long window that extended nearly its entire length. There were such long tears in the solex shields, it was a marvel it could still run at all. It must have had some trouble doing so, since it belched foul smoke from what I presumed was a backup engine before finally coming to rest in front of Seven Chimneys.

"Well," I said, and moved next to Jane. I shivered despite the oppressive heat, and she put her arm around me. "I guess this is what happens next."

Behind us Giles stepped onto the porch. "They're here," he said softly.

The caravan shuddered as the engines shut down. Figures moved inside, and I drew closer to Jane as I waited to see who would come out.

First was a woman who must be Trevor's daughter, Cadence. Tall and white-haired, she moved languidly yet with purpose as she swung down from the caravan, a puff of dust rising around her feet as though she were about to burst into flame. She flapped the ends of her long skirt and squinted up at the porch.

"Giles," she called, in Trevor's low, drawling voice, and walked toward us. Behind her another figure appeared in the door of the caravan.

Jane gasped. "Jesus! What is *that*?" I blanched and looked away.

"Hush," whispered Giles. He stepped forward and put an arm around each of us, hugging us close. "It's one of their people. A cacodemon. You've never seen one?"

"Christ, no," Jane began, shuddering, but then Cadence was on the porch greeting us.

"Giles," she said. They embraced, and for the moment I forgot the cacodemon. Because Cadence Mallory looked ancient—far older than her father; older than anyone I had ever seen in my life. Somehow I had expected her to have Trevor's same bizarrely youthful look; but she did not.

You must understand, in the City of Trees youth and beauty were virtues above all else, and the rigors of life without trained surgeons meant that few people lived beyond their forty-odd years, even among the Curators. And at HEL I never saw an old person—the empaths were all as young as myself, and valued researchers were regenerated long before age could claim their minds or bodies.

But Cadence was not merely old by these standards. She seemed truly ancient, older even than her caravan, though that of course must be impossible. A thin, bony woman, tall as her father, with thick white hair circling her face in a silver nimbus. Her skin was pale but thumbed with dark blotches, as though she had spent much of her life unprotected beneath the sun, and lined and cracked as an old canvas. But it was a fine-boned face for all that: high, rounded cheekbones, strong chin, broad forehead, a sharp, high-bridged nose. Only her mouth and eyes didn't seem to fit—the mouth too wide, with thin dry lips stretched over those white, white teeth. And her eyes! I suddenly thought how much Trevor had given up for his grasp at immortality, to have lost his eyes for all those years. Hers were round and the richest deepest blue, like wild irises, and clear as well water. She blinked in the sunlight, and I could see at the outer corner of each eye several small straight lines: tiny white scars where she had had cataracts removed, more than once, probably—another tithe given to age and the sun. Over her skirt she wore a simple loose blouse of pale green, patterned with yellow leaves, and ugly black rubber sandals. It wasn't until she turned from hugging Giles that I saw she had only one hand. The other was gone at the wrist, the stump knotted and badly scarred. That shocked me nearly as much as her age. I had thought the town of Cassandra must be more sophisticated than that, and have access to skilled surgeons and prosthetics. What kind of rebellion could they be planning, if their work was as crude as this?

"Which one's the empath?"

Her gaze flicked from myself to Jane and then to me again. Before I could answer, she pursed her lips shrewdly. "Ah: *this* one. I can see it in your eyes. So *you* caused all that trouble back in the City. You're older than I thought you'd be."

"So are you," Jane said, then blushed. But Cadence only gave a sharp barking laugh.

"Well! This one speaks her mind, and the other one reads them." She turned to Giles. "Where is my father?" she asked in a softer voice.

Without a word, Giles put his arm over her shoulder and led her inside.

"Damn," Jane muttered, and quickly turned back to look at the caravan. "What are we supposed to do with *that*?"

The other figure still leaned against the side of the vehicle, staring at us impassively with its arms crossed and hands tucked inside its sleeves. It might have been a woman, uncommonly slender and clad in a hooded blue tunic that hung to its ankles, except for the face. A ghoul's face, skeletally thin, its nose two tiny depressions above a slit of a mouth, with several long white fleshy tendrils growing from its lips like the whiskers of a catfish. It had enormous sunken eyes that took up nearly the entire upper half of its skull, and no hair that I could see.

"What's the—what happened? Why does he look like that?" I whispered.

"Cacodemon," Jane said beneath her breath. "I've read about them—they breed them for war with the Emirate. Those tubes by its mouth—it feeds and drinks through those, so it doesn't choke on sand or dust in the desert."

"Is it—can it talk?"

Jane rubbed her arms. "Not like us. Like this—" She ran her fingers across my wrist. "By touching. They spit poison, too."

I tipped my head, squinting in the brilliant sunlight and trying vainly to seem as though I weren't staring at it. A moment later I heard footsteps behind us, and turned to see Giles and Cadence in the hallway. Giles was pointing to the things gathered there, the heaps of monitors and 'filing equipment.

"—all of it," he said, and Cadence replied, "Thank you. You're sure you can manage the rest by yourself?"

"Of course."

For another few minutes they stood beside the equipment, talking in hushed tones. Giles looked worried, almost frightened, and I tried to hear what they were saying.

". . . says there will be room for all of us. For you, certainly."

"It *is* coming, then?" Giles's voice sounded anguished.

"Oh, yes," replied Cadence, and she lay her one good hand upon his shoulder and squeezed it. "My dearest Giles: it is practically here."

Then they turned and walked outside. Giles stopped beside me, but Cadence continued on to the truck, where she bowed her head to speak to the blue-clad figure there. Jane stared at them with slitted eyes. Finally she turned to Giles.

"Is that thing coming with us? Because if it is, I'm not going."

Giles smiled, a tight smile that made me think of Trevor. "You have to go, Jane. There's no place for you here now—no place for any of us. He's part of the Alliance—"

"Well, *I'm* not part of your goddamned Alliance!" Jane began, but then turned at a soft tread behind us.

"You are now," said Cadence. She stood with the cacodemon beside her, her one good hand resting on the handle of a sonic gun at her hip. "Please help us load these things into the caravan."

Jane swallowed and gave me a hopeless look. Without another word we began carrying the monitors and telefiles from the porch and shoving them into the back of the van. The cacodemon worked with us, helping me to lift a magister. It was surprisingly strong for such a slender creature, with extraordinarily long white hands that ended in five tapering fingers with flattened, spatulate tips. Once its hand brushed mine and I jumped, thinking of Jane's warning. Its touch was cool and dry, like the skin of a glass lizard; but there was also something disturbingly *alive* about it. When we had pushed the magister into the truck, it looked at me with those enormous eyes, the iris mottled brown and yellow. Its gaze was disturbingly oblique, as though like an infant it could not focus well on things. Later I learned that the cacodemons have superb night vision, but in daytime they are like owls and are easily confused by bright light. The narrow slit of its mouth flapped open and it hissed at me.

*"Suniata."*

Its breath smelled sweetly of catmint. Before I could move away, it had taken my sweating hand between its own, rubbing it gently. It was like being stroked with a piece of soft, fine leather. Its fingers darted up and down my own, and suddenly I was flooded with a sense of calm, as though I had known and trusted this creature my entire life. "Suniata," it repeated; and I understood that this was its name, but also a word for the way it was making me feel. Suniata: Peace.

"We're ready."

Cadence's voice roused me. Shyly I drew my hand from the cacodemon's. As I did so, the sense of well-being drained from me. I was gazing into a huge pair of eyes in a skull-like face, while all around me the noon sun gave things a lifeless cast. Suniata turned away and with a cat's grace jumped into the van, pushing boxes from its path. Cadence clambered after it.

I looked back at the house, blinking painfully. Giles stood on the steps with his hands at his sides, coiling and uncoiling a loop of wire. He still wore the Aviator's weapon, and his hair had been loosed, to fall in silvery waves about his face and shoulders.

"Good-bye, Wendy. Good-bye, Jane," he called softly.

Jane stood half-in and half-out the door of the van. When she heard Giles, she made a small gasping sound, then abruptly jumped down and ran back to hug him. The drone of the caravan's engines blotted out what they were saying, and a minute later she scrambled in beside me.

"He said they would see us again," she said miserably, squatting on a metal box and staring out the open window to where Giles had turned and begun to slowly walk inside. "And I guess they will, if we all die soon enough."

There was a dull roar. Smoke and dust rose in a wall and momentarily blotted out the house. In a spray of brick-colored gravel the caravan lurched forward. I leaned out the window, coughing as I struggled for a last look at Seven Chimneys. It was not until we reached the top of the little hill that the dust fell away behind us, and for an instant I glimpsed the inn as we had first seen it, perfectly drawn against the trees now in full leaf, the blinding sun bleaching the surrounding earth and grass as pale as snow. The van listed dangerously as we made the turn, and I craned my neck, waving, half-expecting to hear the explosive retort of the Aviator's gun. But there was nothing, just the muted drone of the caravan's engines and the hooting of doves driven from the trees by our passing.

Neither Cadence nor Suniata spoke as we traveled. Cadence I thought must be grief-stricken for her father, but in truth the harsh lines of her face made her seem utterly resigned to whatever cruelties the world might toss at her, even Trevor's death. I didn't know if Suniata could say anything more than his name, and I wasn't prepared then to find out. I was too exhausted to think about what lay ahead of us; whether we were rebels now or captives. I thought of Miss Scarlet and Fossa, and tried to keep from weeping. War, Miss Scarlet had said; but it was hard to imagine war, or even people, in that lonely country. I used my fatigue to keep from focusing on anything. I was afraid I might go mad and kill myself like Giles, if I let myself think about what I had done through my recklessness.

Before we had driven more than a few miles, Cadence had pulled on a hooded blue tunic like Suniata's, and tossed two more back to Jane and me.

"The sun," she explained. It was the last thing she would say to us for several hours. I shrugged into mine and pulled the hood over my head. The light cotton felt like the heaviest wool in that unbearable heat, but there seemed no help for it—there were not as many trees out here to protect us from the poisonous light.

For a little while I stood by the open window, hoping the wind might cool me, but soon I gave that up and squatted on the hot metal floor. In one back corner the cacodemon had settled among the monitors and cables, its hood flung over its face, so I imagined it was sleeping. Jane crouched across from it, already asleep, her hands curled into fists upon her knees. Cadence was intent on the narrow rutted road. It was like navigating a tiny canoe through one series of rapids after another. The van bounced over rocks and places where the road had been washed away, scraped against the sides of trees, and ground down saplings as though they were tall grass. Branches tore at the solex shields, and once an entire panel was ripped away, to hang like a great black caterpillar's tent from the limb of a withered pine. Cadence didn't stop, or even look back. Nor would she answer my questions when I asked her where we were, or who maintained the road (such as they did). From the sun I guessed we were somewhere west and south of Seven Chimneys and the City of Trees. From a few tire tracks in the dried mud, and a single empty canister tossed in a stand of sumac—the sigil of the NASNA Aviators faded on its side beneath the word CONTAMINANT in livid orange letters—I guessed this was a road used mostly by Ascendant janissaries, and perhaps those few traders who came east from the mountains.

So we drove on, mile after mile, the mingled smells of dust and honeysuckle making my mouth dry and sweet as candy ash. Cadence drove without speaking or even seeming to move, except for the light touch of her single hand upon the wheel. Once or twice I heard the crack of a candicaine pipette being opened and inhaled; then the caravan would speed up for a little while, careening perilously over fallen trees and through shallow streambeds. When the road widened and we drove clear of the foothills for a few miles, Cadence activated a DVI program. In a flat drawl she read off a list of coordinates, waited for the blinking code that told her the caravan had registered her vocal commands. Then she leaned back, pulled the hood from her white hair, and shook her head, resting the stump of her wrist on the open window and gazing out at the heat-glazed hills in the distance.

Hundreds of years ago this had all been farmland. But because of its proximity to the nation's ancient capital, the countryside had very early on fallen to chemical and viral rains that burned the green fields and lush stands of trees, leaving barren, poisoned soil to bake beneath a poisonous sun.

Eventually the trees returned: twisted, blackened things that clawed from the earth like so many grasping hands. Dull-green spines covered them, and waxy leaves pitted and wrinkled as a toad's skin, their thickened surface a protection against the sun's killing rays. When the truck scraped against them, they released pungent scents of pine or creosote, and bled a resin that hardened into rusty-looking scabs that gave the trees an even more wounded appearance. It was a vicious landscape, the worse to look upon in that glaring light. Soft brick-colored dust covered everything, settling into the folds of my coverall and getting into my mouth and nostrils, so that my tongue swelled and it choked me to swallow.

Outside nothing moved. There were no birds, no squirrels or darting lizards; not even any insects save bloated wasps the size of my thumb. Iridescent green and black, with huge, evil yellow eyes, their slender wings spanned half the length of my hand. When one flew into the cab, I could see its stinger like a black thorn protruding from its abdomen. I scuttled across the floor, pulling my hood about my face; but it was already gone, buzzing like a fouga's engines as it flashed out the window.

When I peered after it, I saw for the first time we had been driving up a steep incline. Behind us I could see where the road wound down a craggy fell, sometimes cutting back on itself when it reached a spot where rocks had fallen to block the way, or where an ancient bridge had rusted and collapsed into a wide and fast-running stream. It was like one of those living maps we had played with at HEL: the nearly barren hillside, and then the blasted plain with its crippled trees, and in the nether distance a haze like greenish smoke, obscuring where I imagined Seven Chimneys stood and, far beyond, the City of Trees.

Suddenly the van swerved around a sharp curve. I fell forward, banging against the edge of the window and cutting my chin on its metal cusp. Blood trickled between my fingers. Before I could even cry out, the caravan cleared the turn, shuddering to a stop; and the world changed.

It was as though the zealous hand of Miss Scarlet's beloved Goddess had swiped across the earth, tossing away dust and rocks and thorns, all the detritus that remained of an earlier, grosser attempt at creating a world. We were atop a hill, higher than I had ever been in my life. On the horizon immense blue thunderheads rose in dizzying tiers. A steady wind lapped against my face, and for a moment I closed my eyes, forgetting the throbbing pain in my chin. When I opened them, I saw that Jane and Suniata had both awakened. The cacodemon stood and silently walked to the front of the cab, where it crouched beside Cadence. Jane rubbed her eyes and yawned.

"Where are we?" she asked groggily. I pointed outside.

A few feet from the caravan the red clay road ended, sheared off as cleanly as though it had been sliced away with a granite knife. Instead of that infernal plain of thorns, we gazed down into a valley dappled with birch and willows that hugged the banks of a rocky stream. For a moment I could only stare straight down, stunned, trying to figure out what had happened to the rest of the world. Then I slowly drew my head up, looking for the storm clouds brooding on the horizon.

They were gone. They had never been there at all. What I had taken to be clouds were not clouds, but mountains. Huger than anything I could have imagined, stretching in a long line from north to south, they blotted out everything except for their own ranks, until the distance swallowed them in a powder of purple and green. I had only ever glimpsed mountains in cinemafiles or on the yellowing reels of film kept by the Curators for occasional entertainments, but there was no mistaking them now.

"Mountains," I breathed. When I tore my gaze away, I saw Cadence standing by the open door, staring out with gas-blue eyes.

"That's right," she said softly. Her drawl had deepened, and for the first time she looked at me and smiled. "I always stop here. Even in the middle of winter, when I never know if I can get started again." She pointed outside, cradling the stump of her hand against her breast. "We're in the Blue Ridge Mountains now—that's what you see there. And somewhere out *there*"—she tilted her head to indicate north and east—"that's where you'll find your City. If you travel a few days due west, you come to the Appalachians. But I never have done that except once. If there's anyplace on earth more beautiful than the Blue Ridge, I'm too old to see it now."

Jane's voice wafted from the back of the van like a ghost's. "How old *are* you?"

Cadence stared at her. Then unexpectedly she laughed, tossing her head so that the hood slipped from her mane of white hair. "You're not going to rest till I tell you, are you? Ninety-two—"

Jane's eyes widened. Cadence cut her off before she could ask another question. "But I had a few of my father's mushrooms to help me through the rough spots." Abruptly she turned away and sat down. A moment later the caravan was hurtling on once more.

Jane stumbled to her feet. The cacodemon looked at her, then at me. He blinked, his tiny mouth twisting in an incomprehensible grimace—smile? frown? wonderment? He raised one hand and opened it slowly, his fingers uncurling like the long pale fronds of a lily. I stared at it, then lifted my hand and did the same. Suniata regarded me with round guileless eyes, then nodded once, as though completing some ritual, and turned away.

I turned back to gazing out the window. In front of us the nearest of the mountains seemed to kneel. Its outcroppings formed a sheltered valley girded by a river and checkered with pale green and yellow squares.

*Fields!* I thought in amazement. They really *were* growing things here; they really had escaped the viral rains and lived to reclaim the wilderness. There was a dappled mirror that might have been a lake, and above it, in the throat of the mountains, a deep emerald hollow like the shadow of a cloud. Cadence's voice called out over the drone of the engines.

"That's Cassandra, there—"

She pointed at the shadow, her hand stabbing repeatedly at the air as though to pin the image there for us to see. "That's where we all live now." She bent back over the wheel, her blue hood falling over her shoulders.

*Where we all live . . .*

For some reason my mind seized those words, as though they held some secret, a message from the country: something that had to do more with green trees and stone than with blood and memory. Something that might show me how the deaths of Justice and Trevor and all those others, how the fall of the City of Trees and even the Mad Aviator's resurrection, could make sense. There were green places left that the Ascendants had not yet poisoned. There were demons, too; but the only one that I had met was named Peace. For the first time since we had fled the City, I felt something besides grief and despair and rage; for the first time I felt hope, like a small flame licking at my heart.

The van made another sharp turn. The red road dropped away before us, and Cadence's voice rang out as we swept down the hillside.

"This is where it all begins again!" she cried. Beside her Suniata stood with one hand upon Cadence's shoulder.

"*This is where it all begins,*" I echoed, flinging my head back to stare into the burning sky; but if she or Jane or Suniata heard me, I never knew.

# 10

## The Oracle Speaks

**I got to know** Aidan Harrow very well during his three years at the NASNA Academy. We were often paired during meditations and also for the grueling sessions that were meant to prepare us as pilots—hours spent in a tiny stim chamber with another cadet, bombarded by images and sensations culled from actual 'file footage of atrocities enacted in the Archipelago and during the Three Hour War. He was not a good candidate for the Academy. He tired easily, which I always attributed to the time he spent reading or drinking at night, instead of sleeping those few hours when he had the chance. And he was a coward; he never seemed to grow accustomed to the everyday horrors that an Aviator has to face. Even with the stim chamber, and the psychoactive drugs administered by the infirmary to cadets who were having such problems; even with the threat of humiliation in front of his peers—because Aidan was proud, arrogant even—he could never endure pain, or even tedium. My offers to help him with his studies and lend him my replicant tutor were met with derision. I never fully understood why he was at the Academy in the first place. Something to do with his father, who while not an Aviator himself had served under Gerald Baskin following the last Ascension. Emma made a much better cadet. I was surprised when, after her brother's death, she dropped out of the corps; but in light of her fascination with Luther Burdock, her choice of career seems obvious now, and her death by suicide indicates a fragility of flesh and spirit that I would hope never to see in my troops.

Aidan was a terrible partner for training exercises—he wept often, and always gave vent to his furious temper—but otherwise he was popular among the other cadets. Like many people whose nature is in essence craven, he was charming, and of course his looks brought him many admirers. During his first year he played the boy to Keenan Pyle, who was a notorious pederast and whose classes were always filled with the youngest and best-looking of the first-level cadets. But after that Aidan grew more aloof. As I have told you, he shared a bed with his twin sister. Even the most world-weary of us saw that as a weakness, a febrile affectation, like the incestuous pairings of the ruling families of the Ascendancy.

"Who do they think they are?" Amaris di Gangi sneered one morning. We watched as Aidan and Emma crossed the lawn together, the sun glinting from their auburn heads, the lines of their uniforms flowing from their lanky bodies like oil from a hot pan. "Naki and Benshan Orsina?"

I shrugged but said nothing. It was spring, the short, intense northern spring that flares as blue as the heart of a flame and is as quickly gone. Lupines grew along the spine of land overlooking the water where we sat. Below us waves pounded the rocky shore, and a quartet of cormorants swam and dived past the breakers. There were seals basking on the rocks. Aidan and Emma headed toward them, turning from the grassy lawn to a narrow footpath worn into the hillside by generations of cadets and, before them, novitiates marking the Stations of the Cross along the shore.

"What do you think they *do* together?" Amaris began, but before she could continue, I stood. Brushing grass from my leather trousers, and slinging my hands in my pockets, I hurried down the path after the twins.

"Margalis." Emma looked up, frowning slightly. The cerulean leather of her cadet's uniform made her look sallow, her wide mouth a gash in her pale face. "You're not at exercises?"

"Canceled. Congden got called in for an emergency

meeting. There was a strike at the Greenland station last night."

"I heard." Aidan made an apologetic face when Emma looked at him accusingly. "Well, you didn't ask, so why should I tell you? It was supposed to be kept secret, anyway."

I nodded in agreement. Emma sighed, tucking a wisp of hair behind one ear. "Well. I'm going back—*I've* still got exercises, unless they've canceled them for everyone."

"I doubt it." But I smiled, trying to will Emma to look at me. She ducked her head, stumbling as she walked up the edge of the stony path, anything to avoid my eyes. " 'Bye, Emma—"

She raised a hand but didn't look back, her trouser legs flapping around her knees.

"Why does she do that?" I followed Aidan, who was striding along the path to where a large boulder stuck out above the seals dozing in the sun. "Every time I see her, she runs away."

Aidan shrugged, turned to show me a white vulpine grin in his sunburned face. "I don't know, Sky Pilot. She says she's afraid of you."

I felt my face twitch in annoyance, at the nickname and at the thought of Emma being frightened of me. "Afraid! Why the—"

"Don't ask me, Sky Pilot. Here, be quiet or you'll scare them."

I shut up, biting back harsh words. *Sky Pilot* was what Aidan called me, that and Rocket Man, derogatory nicknames he'd hoped would catch on among our friends. They never did, but he stubbornly refused to call me Margalis, or anything else for that matter, hoping, I suppose, that one day the monikers would stick. *Sky Pilot* was from a folk song, something he'd dug up in the audio archives at the Academy and made his friends listen to one night when we should have been going over the recordings of Dmitri Rilkov's 2332 lectures at the NASNA War College.

"Listen! A song about Margalis!" he crowed, popping out his earpiece and motioning us to join him. A dull buzzing came from the earpiece, as though a frantic bluebottle were trapped inside. "Come listen—"

So we'd listened. Even after having been remastered a century earlier, the original recording was so ancient, one could scarcely make it out. It was as though the centuries themselves had nibbled away at words and music, leaving only vague tones, an out-of-tune voice, the faint skirling of bagpipes, and distant echoes of firearms.

> *Sky Pilot!*
> *How high can you fly?*
> *You'll never, ever, ever reach the sky. . . .*

"That's terrible," Emma said stonily when it was finished. "You can't even hear it."

"Listen again!" Aidan twirled in his seat, punching buttons on the player, but by then everyone had returned to their studies. He was still the only person who ever called me that.

Now Aidan crept out onto the boulder on his hands and knees, tossing back his burnished hair and pursing his lips. Behind us the green tips of the tall pines scratched lazily at the sky. On the gravel beach some fifteen feet below, the seals wheezed and snored. When he reached the edge of the rock, Aidan bellied down with his chin on his hands. I joined him, careful to keep my leather jacket from catching on the boulder's sharp edges. We lay there for a long time without speaking, just watching the seals and the play of the birds in the water—cormorants, skuas, black and white gulls. The air smelled of pine and sweet rugosa roses and the sea, and very faintly of the woodfires burning in the Academy kitchens. The day had that intense blue clarity that often proceeds a storm: a weather-breeder, they called it in the maritimes. This far north the summer's heat was not intense, but, paradoxically, the sunlight was. I could feel my fair skin burning, and swore silently at the chronic shortages that kept us from having access to any kind of protection from the killing rays—lotions, veils, even just a visor for our uniform hats. But the meager warmth was pleasant for all that.

After a while I must have dozed. When I looked up again, Aidan had rolled onto his back, propping himself against a wedge of driftwood. He was reading a talking book. I could hear its voice, serious as that of any rector, and occasional trills of background music.

"What's that?" I leaned over, trying to see what was on the little screen.

He moved a few inches away, trying to make it look as though he were just getting more comfortable. But I could see his eyes: genuinely startled that I'd awakened, and genuinely worried.

"Nothing." He turned the thing so low, I could barely make it out—a man's voice, refined in that twenty-third-century manner, but I couldn't understand the words. Before Aidan could stop me, I flicked my finger against the side of the book so that its title flickered across the screen.

# PAGAN SURVIVALS

### Spiritual Origins of the Energumens And Revelations of Their Triumphant Future, With Predictions of the Apocalypse to Come

#### by Jude Hwong

Colorfully archaic script and a baroque fanfare of Third Ascension ælopipes accompanied the copyright and warnings. Then the man's voice came again, faint as an insect's.

> Had Luther Burdock known the future uses to which his innocent daughter would be put, surely he would never have shared his apocalyptic discoveries with the rest of mankind. . . .

"You're reading *that*?" I cried out, incredulous. Jude Hwong was a notorious fraud, one of those religious fanatics who crops up at the end of every century and gains a cult through predicting the fall of the current world order. Thus far, none of his many predictions had come true—no rebirth of ancient gods, no epiphanies among the energumens, no messages from extrasolar visitors. His work was childish, but that didn't keep it from being under interdict. In spite of myself I grew angry at Aidan for putting us both in danger. "You're going to get caught, one of these days. What, do you *want* to get kicked out?"

I tried to grab the book from him. He snatched it back,

but not before my hand bumped it and the book scrolled to another section and read,

This small group of researchers—astrophysicists and astrologers, mostly—believed that the mythology surrounding the Watcher in the Skies had a direct correspondence to the fragmented records of Icarus's appearance in 2172–73. Tragically, their barbaric execution by the dictator Simon Legistheis has prevented us from learning more thoroughly from their—

Aidan sat bolt upright, flicking off the book and shoving it beneath his jacket. His face was bright red, from embarrassment and the sun; it made his blue eyes glow like an animal's caught in the glare of night-lights. "Fuck off, soldier boy."

"Well, *do* you want to get caught?"

He hunched his shoulders together and raised his hand to strike at me—even though I was a good six inches taller and a much better fighter—then glanced down at the rough scree below us. The tide had come in, ripples of black and indigo sloshing across the gravel. The seals were humping slowly into the water, shouting hoarsely at each other and sending up wedges of sand and grit as they breasted into the cold surf. The sight of them seemed to calm Aidan. When he turned back to me, his eyes were no less intense, but he smiled mockingly.

"Well, are you going to turn me in, Sky Pilot?"

I pushed down the urge to hit him and looked away. "No. But someone will. Where do you get them, anyway?"

He shrugged, reached into a pocket and took out a tiny silver canister, bullet-shaped and with a crystal head. He unscrewed it and tapped out an amphaze patch, slipped it ostentatiously behind one ear. "My father. He was a collector. They're worth a *lot*."

"Not anymore," I said coldly. Aidan was always trying to impress people with how much his father owned—furniture, books, even a house. From what Emma said, it was all true, which made it even worse that Aidan spoke so blithely of it. "One of these days they're going to seize all his things and it will be your fault. And that"—I pointed to where he'd hidden the talking book—"*that's* just garbage. Why do you waste your time with it?"

Aidan's breath came more quickly. I watched his pupils

dilate, as quickly as a dog's when threatened. When he spoke, I could smell the amphaze on his breath, an unpleasant chemical scent like raw alcohol or morpha.

"Because they *tell me things*."

I shivered a little. The wind had come up over the sea, and with the sun gone over the ridge of land behind us, it had grown cool, as it does of an evening in the maritimes. But it was Aidan's voice that chilled me. That same voice he used to hold us in thrall at night in his room, while the bottles passed around and our furtive games played themselves out, with all of us secretly waiting for some great dark revelation that never came.

"Things? They *tell* you things?" I tried to sneer as Amaris di Gangi had; but the wind made my voice sound thin and sour.

Aidan's eyes glittered dangerously. "There is another world beneath this one. You should know that—isn't it what your mother's poetry is all about? *This* world is getting torn away, everything we've done to it has made it weak and tired; and now the other world is showing through. Some day it will be all that's left. . . ."

I sighed loudly. My mother's work—deliberately obscure visionary poetry, harking back to eighteenth-century verse that no one but herself seemed to have heard of—had enjoyed a fleeting popularity before it was condemned for its decadence. "Well, for now, *this* world is the one I'm worried about," I said, adding, "If I worry at all."

"You should," Aidan said with the smug air of a recent convert. "Did you know they're predicting some kind of cataclysm within this century? Within our *lifetimes,* Sky Pilot."

"Oh, really? *Who* is predicting this? Jude Hwong? From the gas chamber?"

Aidan shook his head. "You shouldn't sneer at it, Margalis." His seriousness was laughable; I almost didn't notice he had used my real name. "You know, he quotes your mother in here—that poem about the Watcher in the Skies. He says it's a revelation of the cataclysm—"

"It's a revelation he even read it," I said drily. When he did amphaze or anything else, Aidan's talk was always like this. Old gods, old sciences. The self-destructive research that had so eroded the thin civilized surface of our world that another, more ancient one was about to break through any day.

"You think it's all madness, don't you?" Now Aidan

sounded edgy. He had turned from watching the seals to sit with knees bent, fingers tapping nervously along the creases in his yellow trousers. "But you know, Margalis, it's no crazier than what they teach us here. Focusing on some inner landscape so that we don't see our hands burning to bone in front of us. Focusing on the sound of the Gryphon's engines, so we don't hear the pilot screaming in the other seat. Taking vows of vigilance and obedience and swearing off the most basic human emotions. Cutting open nursling aardmen, to see if they will scream under the knife."

"Those are exercises. They'll save your life someday, in combat—"

"I know what they are! But *these* are exercises, too—"

He touched his breast where the talking book was hidden, and I recalled how I had found him once before, the Defries *Incunabula* open on his bed, chanting softly at the dawn. "The Academy teaches you that there are other ways to see the world. Well, my books teach you that there are other worlds to see."

I maintained a cold silence. As I said, there was much talk like this in the Academy. We were young, some of us barely more than children, and such things appeal to youth. Millennial cults, the revival of archaic and often lurid religions. To Aidan and everyone else I showed a hard face when the conversation turned to such matters—and inevitably it did; we may have been NASNA cadets, but the oldest among us was not yet twenty—but for myself, I was profoundly disturbed by Aidan's books, by his ecstatic desire to believe in old gods, old ways. I was disturbed because such things made sense to me, in a manner that I could never articulate.

When I first was assigned to the domed city of Araboth and met Shiyung Orsina, the youngest of the Orsinas's ruling family, I found that we shared an interest in odd cults and quaint rituals. She merely as a fancy, something to whet her jaded and decadent tastes; but for me it was always deeper than that. Without precisely understanding how or why, I have always been driven by a hidden need to *believe* in something; but I have never found anything stronger than myself to believe in.

This compulsion to serve is deeply ingrained in an Aviator. We are taken in childhood, and from our earliest days we are trained to obey. But we are also encouraged to flout authority, to usurp it when possible and if necessary betray even our closest allies, our most beloved ideals. It is the only way for a military elite to survive in a world so fragmented that it defies rational attempts at control. So it is that the Aviators hold within them a dangerously contorted psyche, as meticulously and deliberately twisted as those tiny trees the Nipponian emperors raise in their solariums in the Floating Land. It is never a surprise when an Aviator goes mad; it only matters if his madness keeps him from carrying out his duties.

In Aidan's case, his obsession with things demonic, with disaster cults and astronomy, obsolete sorceries and obscure religions, had ruined his concentration. He missed classes, exercises, training events. Even repeated visits to the infirmary and threats of a prolonged course of mind treatments were not enough to keep him from reading and enacting his little private seances.

But what was worst, to me at least, was the way that he had somehow managed to infect *me* with his madness. I had achieved First in our level, and it was rumored that I would be given a commission before graduation. The conflict with the Emirate was not going well; it would not be the first time a student had been sent to war before completing his course of studies. I would never jeopardize my chances of escaping from the Academy by doing anything so obvious (and stupid) as attempting to raise some demon in my dormitory room. But Aidan's bitter cynicism toward NASNA and his peculiar taste in books had affected me nonetheless.

I wanted to believe in something. Worse, I *needed* to. It was no longer enough that the skirmishes be won, the conflicts shortened or ended, the Orsinate or the Autocracy satisfied by our efforts. I needed to believe in something else; something greater than myself. I was trained to accept the Aviators as the finest, strongest, most brilliant men and women of the continent. At the Academy I learned that I was the finest among them all. It was no surprise to me, really, when years later I was named Aviator Imperator. My madness and eventual rehabilitation as a *rasa:* no, I had not expected *that*. But I had been ready to accept the mantle of Imperator, perhaps since that first day I entered the ascetic confines of the Academy.

Still, if I was the jewel in the Autocracy's crown, I had to believe in the worthiness of the brow I adorned. And it was painfully obvious, even to my nineteen-year-old self, that the Ascendants and the Orsinate were not worthy of me. But if *they* were not, who, or what, was? Bred and trained as a weapon, I must serve somebody. Aidan's books and Aidan's talk made me think that there might be other ways of serving; other things to serve.

"What other worlds are you talking about, Aidan?"

I tried to make my tone disdainful, but the curiosity was there, a raw kernel of it plain as the cold rock beneath us. Aidan saw my weakness, and laughed.

"The Sky Pilot wants other worlds now! Huh—"

He looked away, off to where the sky was greening twilight above the sea's horizon. After a moment he said in a softer voice, "Well, there *are* other things. There is the Watcher in the Skies, for one. And other things, too. We—I— have seen some of them. At home." The reluctance that crept into his voice made me realize that Emma, too, must know some of this. Perhaps that accounted for her unhappiness, her habit of always looking out the corner of her eyes. "And here, too."

"What have you seen here?" I could no longer even pretend at offhandedness. From across the green sweep of lawn came the sturdy echo of the bell clanging for the first dinner shift, but I ignored it. "Could you—can you show me?"

"It's not like that," said Aidan impatiently. "These things—whatever they are—they have their own reasons for showing themselves to us. I mean, Jude Hwong says that the records show the Watcher of the Skies last appeared nearly four hundred years ago. *I* don't know when we'll see it again. All of these things—it's not like you call them and they come. It's more—well, it's more like interfacing with the Gryphons. You prepare yourself—*I* prepare myself—and sit back, and then it's there."

Now I grew impatient. "*What's* there?"

"Something else." He fidgeted, suddenly at a loss for words. He squinted into the sunset, the ruddy light making his face look almost molten. "Don't you ever think about that, Margalis?" he asked softly. "How strange all this is?"

He gestured at the sea, the sky, the waving firs behind us. "Here it all looks the way it always did; but the rest of the world has changed completely. I mean, Hwong says how once there were archosaurs everywhere, and now there's us; but someday we might be gone, and it will be only . . ."

His voice drifted off. For a moment he looked sadder and more serious than I had ever seen him. "Seeing Kalamat that time—they really *are* different from us, the energumens. In a way, they're *better*. They can learn everything we can, only faster; and obviously they're stronger. Even the name *energumen*—and Burdock never called them that, *he* always called them his children—it means 'possessed by demons.'

"But the demons that possess them are *us*."

He stood, as though to embrace the ridge that hid the Academy from our sight. After a moment his arms fell limply, and he sighed. "Christ, I can't explain it, really. It's just like there's something else there. I could see it, that day they brought Kalamat here. I could see it in her eyes. Something older than me, or any of us, a sort of *presence*. And now it's inside me, or trying to get inside me. Or else it's in there now and trying to get out."

I stared at him, my mouth open to make a cruel retort. But Aidan's eyes were wide and staring, distant yet glowing with a sort of manic concentration. He looked crazed, but there was a certain kind of sense in his words.

I had heard of people going mad in the HORUS colonies. Some of them—astrophysicists in particular were prone to this—claimed to be possessed by the spirits of American astronauts. Others simply went mad, raving that extrasolar beings had invaded their minds. During the twenty-second century, when the strange phenomenon of the Watcher of the Skies appeared, scientists and other observors in HORUS went into an apocalyptic frenzy—for naught, as it turned out. The flaming eidolon disappeared as slowly and silently as it had appeared. Just another one of the oddities of life in the colonies. *That* was why the energumens and other cacodemons were first sent to HORUS—space did not drive them mad. I said as much to Aidan.

"And you don't have to get all worked up over these things, you know," I added, somewhat smugly. "Just put yourself into an E-state and give your mind a chance to respond. Anyone can do it—"

Well, anyone with the training and discipline of a true Aviator. Aidan creased his brow, but he didn't look annoyed. It didn't look as though he were thinking of me at all anymore. His indifference angered me, that and his absolute certainty that he was privy to some great secret.

"You're going to get suspended, Aidan, or expelled, for wasting your time with books like that. Someone will turn you in." I started to my feet, halted in a half-crouch when he turned to me, his eyes blazing from gray to blue.

"What do *you* know about it?" he cried. "There are all kinds of things *they* do that we don't understand, that don't make any sense—"

When he said *they,* he jabbed his hand in the direction of the Academy, where the silhouettes of our classmates could be seen hurrying toward supper, black and thin as though etched against the sky with a needle. But I knew he wasn't really thinking of them but of those others, our masters: the Ascendants in their distant circuits of the Earth, falling slowly and endlessly through the heavens. "Their geneslaves, their mutagens—does that make sense? Luther Burdock deforming his daughter for science—*that* makes sense?"

I shrugged. In the face of this outburst my own anger dissipated as abruptly as it had come on. "Well, *does* it?" Aidan shouted.

I made a show of rolling my eyes and sighing. Then I turned away and pried a bit of stone from the boulder, tossed it into the waves curling and receding in the darkness below. "No. Of course it doesn't."

I had no idea what had gotten into him. I said so, adding, "And he didn't deform his daughter—all those modifications were made long after he and Cybele were dead. You know that."

"I don't see how you can defend him," Aidan spat; although in fact I had said nothing in defense of Burdock, then or ever. "He used her clone, and what's the difference there? It would be like using Emma for an experiment, instead of me. And ever since then—well, they're really not *human* anymore, are they?"

I started to argue with him, but stopped. It was hopeless arguing with Aidan when he lost his temper, especially after he'd done an amphaze dot. He would end up punching me, or running off in a fury, or shouting until he brought one of our rectors down upon us. Instead I stood, shivering in the evening air. "We better get back if we want to find any supper left."

He sat crouched at my feet, his eyes still ablaze. To my surprise he only nodded and stumbled up. "You'll never understand," he said bitterly. He kicked at a pocket of loose stones, sending them flying into the water. "Fucking Sky Pilot. Fucking Rocket Man—"

He turned and headed for the grassy knoll that led to the Academy. I waited to see if he would look back, gesture for me to hurry after him; but he only hunched his shoulders against the chilly breeze and went on by himself. After a few minutes I followed.

Within a few days I had utterly forgotten our conversation. Years later I would recall it, when I was at HEL and saw the fruits of his sister's manipulation of the brains of children; and again when Lascar Franschii told me of the fate of the Quirinus station.

As I have said, time passes differently in the elÿon. It is a risk derived from the means of travel, the great biotic craft powered by the brain of a madman—a deliberately engineered madman, but a lunatic nonetheless. So powerful was the adjutants' control over the psychic atmosphere of their vessels that even the shortest of voyages, such as ours, were often upset by passengers growing disturbed and sometimes violent—thus the reliance over the centuries upon psychotropic drugs as a means of controlling them. Superstitious colonists, particularly those from the fundamentalist inner territories, believed that dreams became unmoored during passage, to stalk and sometimes destroy their creations.

And certainly strange things happened aboard the elÿon. In the beginning women were often used as adjutants. It was thought that their greater capacity for pain—proved through the rigors of childbirth and such anomalies as the remarkable fate of those survivors of the inferno on *Pequod 9*—would make them ideal navigators. But then it was found that missions piloted by women were more likely to end in bizarre tragedies. The most common explanation given was that women dreamed more lucidly than men. After the Second Ascension the *Kataly,* a Commonwealth elÿon, was lost with all hands. When its 'files were retrieved from the wreckage, investigators viewed scenes of nearly incomprehensible rites being performed by passengers and crew alike, ending with a bacchanalian dance that led to mass exodus through one of the craft's air locks. The adjutant then piloted the elÿon through a convoy of diplomatic aviettes headed for NASNA Prime. Later, it was learned that the adjutant had been an adherent of the Mysteries of Lysis. Some reverie of hers had no doubt spawned the mass hallucinations and ecstatic dancing that led to the loss of the vessel.

In the wake of this discovery, robotic crews replaced human ones. Women were seldom used as navigators, and male candidates were carefully screened for attributes such as excessive imagination and tenacity of religious belief. I tell you all this so that it may perhaps be easier to understand what happened to me during that brief celestial journey.

I had often traveled by elÿon in my earlier life. It was unavoidable during my tours in the HORUS colonies, and later when I was stationed at NASNA Prime, before my unhappy assignment to the abandoned capital. Nearly always I had refused the psychotropic drugs administered by the vessels' medical constructs. I also refused to remain in the tiny cells that were required for all passengers and most crew. A matter of pride, I will admit. But I never experienced anything resembling a hallucination; never glimpsed the legendary celestial body that my mother had written of in *Mystica*.

The Watcher in the Skies was one of the great mysteries of the HORUS colonies. Since its first—and, as far as we knew then, its only—appearance in the years 2172 and 2173, it had inspired countless works of art and speculative science. There were also numerous eyewitness acounts, such as that famous passage in Commander Ned Wyeth's *Astralaga*, where he writes of

... this monstrous and bizarre thing we saw after seventeen days in orbit. Iacono noticed it first, but when he told us about it, we all just laughed at him. Then *I* saw it, and it was just as he'd described it: a shape that at first glance resembled a cloudy nebula, or maybe some waste pod cut loose from one of the stations. Only this thing actually seemed to *move,* and you know nebulae don't do that! We all gathered on the observation deck to watch. Afterward I was stunned to learn eighteen hours had passed while we sat there—and we didn't even notice. Didn't get hungry or thirsty or tired, didn't get up to go to the bathroom, nothing. Just watched that thing get bigger and bigger, until it filled the entire window: an enormous whitish mass, not really having any kind of shape or form. Eventually it disappeared, the way smoke does on a windy day—though you know there's no wind up there.

Later when we tried to describe it to each other, we all admitted to having had the experience of being observed. Of being *watched;* but by whom or what we never knew.

Maybe my refusals to submit to a drugged journey came in part from my desire to see that phantasm. As I have told you, I've long been interested in manifestations of this type. Aidan Harrow with his talk of new gods; his sister Emma with the demons she created out of stolen children and brain proteins; Raphael Miramar and the Gaping One; Wendy Wanders and her uncanny power to kill with her mind. Even today, in the Archipelago they believe in graveyard spirits that they call *memji*, creatures with white teeth that stand on one leg and wait for the dead to be buried before crawling into their graves to copulate with them.

Long ago people laughed disdainfully at such ideas; but since the First Shining the world has changed. Aidan Harrow convinced me of this, and my mother. Both believed that the subtle and gross "improvements" wrought by our failed sciences made the Earth an increasingly hostile place for humanity. But these same changes had flung open a door for other, older things. Things that had lived here once, aeons ago; things that might return now to fill the void left by our systemized extermination of our own race.

Fool that I was! I believed the Watcher in the Skies might be such a thing, but I held few hopes of seeing it on this voyage. For some time I remained in my passenger cell, alone with my memories and that gruesomely lovely mural of Tokyo Bay. Eventually I checked the monitor, to insure that Lascar Franschii had told me the truth and that we had, indeed, left Cisneros. Then I left to check on Valeska Novus.

I found her cushioned within one of the roomier passenger cells near my own. The air in here was chilly, to aid in slowing down the metabolism of human travelers. Valeska looked quite pale, slung in a sort of hammock that in turn was held between two enormous cushions like a pair of plush hands. I bent over her and placed my finger against her throat, seeking a pulse. I found none. Then I held my hand above her mouth, watching to see if her breath would cloud the metal: nothing. Were it not for the monitor beside her that showed a thread of silver, indicating her heartbeat, one would think her dead.

On the wall across from her one of the vessel's robotic crew was plugged in, and observed me with three unblinking red eyes.

"We recommend that all passengers remain in their cells

until we arrive at our destination," it announced in a breathy voice.

"I am not a human passenger," I said shortly. The construct's eyes swiveled as I crossed the room to the door.

"We recommend this for all passengers," it went on. "This is for your safety as well as ours." Ignoring it, I let the door slam behind me.

I found Nefertity in a neighboring cell, also cushioned as though she were a human traveler. Her light had dimmed to a very dull pewter gleam, and her eyes were closed. It was perverse, but in that state of hiatus she looked more human than she ever had before. She might have been a woman sculpted of ice, and suddenly I felt a pang, one of those rare tugs of emotion that reminded me that I now had more in common with this beautiful machine than with the Aviator dreaming in the next room. I turned and left, fleeing that notion as much as the sight of the nemosyne, so unnervingly vulnerable where she slept.

The crew roster for the elÿon had listed only a handful of constructs to support its solitary adjutant. Since the *Izanagi* had been a freighter, there was little need for human staff. I wandered alone through its spiraling corridors, all of them twisting inward to where Zeloótes Franschii was suspended within his web of dreams and ganglia.

The polymer walls had a roseate cast that changed color, deepening to red and a deep lavender. While the walls appeared amorphous and soft to the touch, they were in fact quite strong. I could see through them to where nucleic fluids pulsed within transparent conduits, and the elÿon's immense ganglia floated past, like blood-colored stars. All of this and more—storage bladders, pressure chambers, hivelike cells filled with neurotransmitting fluid—was contained behind those walls. The habitable space within an elÿon is actually quite small: a series of tiny chambers branching off from the corridors coiling into the heart of the ship. From inside, it resembles a nautilus more than anything else. I was always conscious of strolling warily within a thing that has sentience, even if it is not quite *alive*.

I walked for a long time, never really going anywhere. Because of the *Izanagi*'s utilitarian purpose, there were few windows, no signs, no pictures, no holofiles; nothing to relieve the sense of wandering within a huge, rosy ventricle, like the cavity of a human heart. There was, however, a viewing deck, and it was to this I was headed. On all my previous ventures aboard the elÿon, I had been undisturbed by the dreamy light, the thick air scented faintly of saline and ozone. As a *rasa,* I assumed I would be truly impervious to the subtle lunacies that could stalk you through those blood-warm tunnels.

Instead I felt a growing unease. I had checked a map posted outside Nefertity's cell to determine the location of the viewing deck. Surely I should have arrived there by now; but the corridor kept winding away in front of me, unbroken by doors or windows, an endless labyrinth pulsing softly with every shade of red. The clicking of my metal feet upon the floor grew louder, and with it another sound, like blood thumping at my temples. Only, of course, I am a bloodless construct, but still that noise hammered at me. It seemed to come from everywhere, and finally I thought it must be the pulse of the elÿon itself that I heard, the rhythmic mindless beating of a thing that has no heart but is itself a viscus, floating through the firmament. I began to hurry, until I raced down those corridors, the echo of my footsteps nearly drowning out that other infernal noise.

Finally the hallway started to widen. The roseate glow grew darker, tinged with blue like a bruise. I had reached the viewing deck.

Before me opened an immense plaza, set with rows of columns of softly glowing steel and jet. To either side a huge window curved upward, to form a domed peak that seemed to open onto the heavens. All was cloaked in a deep, soft, embracing darkness. From ventricles in the floor and walls, tiny jets of air hissed. Probably the ventricles released some mild sedatives or euphoric incense, Pangloss or Ecstasy; but of course I smelled nothing. Overall it was a soothing place, and I walked to the window. If I had still been a man, I would have laughed with relief, to see framed there familiar stars.

They hung unmoving in the darkness, brighter even than I remembered them. Old stars with new names: Cadillac, Wilson, Miguel Street, Goring. But most of that curved glass was filled with the Earth. My world, the old world where I had lived and died.

From here it did not seem so diseased a place. You could not see the continents that had been glazed to deserts of glass and sand, or those parts of the oceans where the water had turned red with decaying diatoms and plankton. You could not tell where the Emirate had set the Arabian Ocean aflame, or where mutagens had turned the great northern steppes between Calgary and Monis into a wilderness of twisted tickpines, haunted by the howls of aardmen and dire wolves. From here the Earth seemed as it ever had, a calm marbled eye gazing into the firmament. From here it was beautiful.

I thought of the energumens, looking upon a place they had never seen, except in the implanted memories of a fifteen-year-old girl. Could they really dream of conquest, of launching war upon their masters? And would the Earth welcome them, if they returned to claim it?

I don't know how long I stood there, staring back into that blue-green orb. Hours, certainly; though it could have been days. I had no need for food or water, and there was nothing within the *Izanagi* to mark the passage from day to night. But finally I did draw away from that window—mindful, perhaps, of Commander Wyeth and his enraptured crew.

I turned and walked across the plaza. Overhead, stars glittered within the domed ceiling, so brightly that their scattered reflections shone in the polished floor at my feet. It was cool here—I could see condensation on my torso's outer casing. The light was dim and diffuse, spilling from slender indigo torchieres set between the steel and black columns. Quite a grand viewing deck, considering the *Izanagi*'s freighter status. But it had been a Nipponian vessel, and they set great store by beauty and ritual. I had attended formal moon-viewings on other elÿon in the Nipponian fleet, and sat with their Emperor as he composed delicate verse to honor an eclipse. It seemed a noble thing to me, to think they had provided such a fine deck for those few men and women who might ever have cause to use it. I let my hand linger upon the smooth brass curves of a torchiere, then took the last few steps to the far side of the chamber.

With no home planet to fill it, this window seemed more immense than its twin. Distant stars bloomed and reeled, distorted by the energy fields surrounding the elÿon. The constellations looked different here, and it took me a moment to realize why.

The HORUS colonies, of course. The stations were gone that would have filled the gaps in Osaka-O and The Circuit of Ten. The stray stars that were actually MacArthur, Sternville, Campbell: gone, all gone. There should have been at least ten of the colonies visible from here, if you knew where to look. I spotted only one, a flicker of blue where immense solex panels candled into flame as it tilted toward the sun. That would be Advhi Sar. I tried to remember what the adjutant had told me about that station—had it fallen to the energumens as well? And there was another celestial orb that I did not recognize, a rather hazy, whitish mass, so pale and amorphous, it might almost have been a dimple or blemish upon the window. Surely it should not have been there? But my thoughts were confused. Old dreams and memories had been tossed together by the intrusion of the adjutant overmind; I could remember nothing clearly.

So for many minutes I stood there, gazing out upon that black map. I may even have entered that state of rapture that seized Wyeth and his crew; because the next thing I knew I was no longer alone.

A figure leaned against the window: a tall young man wearing the red-trimmed, cerulean leathers of an Aviator cadet. On his left hand winked a heavy gold ring, set with a single large blue stone. From where I stood, I could not make out the letters surrounding that stone, but I knew they were there. I raised my hand, my human hand, until light struck the ring it too bore, illuminating the thick gold letters that spelled NASNA. Slowly I clenched my fingers in the Aviator's salute. The figure against the window did the same. His auburn hair spilled across his forehead and he smiled, his gray eyes flecked with green where the light touched them.

I lowered my hand. Still he said nothing. And then I recalled what I had read once, in his book in fact, the forbidden DeFries Incunabula: that the dead cannot speak unless they are first addressed by the living. I took a step toward him, half-expecting him to disappear into glints of starlight. He did not move.

"Aidan," I said.

His smile grew even wider, showing predatory white teeth in his vulpine face. When he spoke, it was with that same voice I had been imagining for days now, its boyishness offset by mockery and a certain feminine cruelty.

"Sky Pilot! I've been waiting such a long time to see you again."

I winced. "What are you doing here?" Although now that he had manifested himself, it was as though I had been expecting him. My sleeplessness, my steady diet of dreams, had prepared me for this. It was perhaps a miracle that they had not *all* come back to haunt me.

"Only this, the traditional employ of revenants. A warning."

He leaned forward and stretched, a great cat wakened from its warm sleep, and for the first time I saw the marks around his neck, bright red and black, as though he had been burned. I glanced at the floor, half-expecting to see a rotted rope fallen there; but there was nothing.

"A warning?"

He nodded, smiling slyly, then ducked his head. Sudden seriousness creased his eyes. "You are in danger, Sky Pilot."

I looked at him shrewdly. "And why should you warn me? And why should I heed you? A phantasm, a stray glimmer of starlight upon the viewing deck. Have you warned everyone who comes here to look upon the sky?"

Once more the figure grinned, tossing back his long hair, and straightened the crimson cuffs of his uniform jacket. I recalled how he had been buried in it, given full honors as a NASNA cadet even though he was a suicide. That was my doing. I had petitioned Manning Tabor, insisting that Aidan's death had actually been the most noble course for him to take with his life, if the others would have led to madness and an eventual soiling of his Aviator's rank.

"Of course not." There was no rancor in his voice, only a sort of detached amusement. He began to walk toward me. A heavy earthen scent wafted through the room, a freezing wind. I felt cold, and sudden terror.

Because as a *rasa,* I should not be able to feel, or smell, *anything.* When the figure reached for my hand, I drew it back sharply. His eyes widened and sly laughter filled the chamber.

"Ah! I have waited a very long time for that—there *is* something the Rocket Man is afraid of!"

"Your purpose." My voice sounded hollow, the voice of a replicant and not a man. "I must return to my quarters."

He smoothed the front of his leathers and gazed smiling at the floor. "I told you, Sky Pilot. Nothing but your welfare. A warning for the Rocket Man."

"Why do you bother with me? I had nothing to do with your death, revenant."

He shrugged, drew his hand to his face. For the first time I noticed how pale he was, how the skin on his cheekbones seemed gray and slack. Perhaps such phantasms have a very short life before they begin to decay.

"I bear you no ill will," he said. His tone was ragged and shrill. "Listen to me—

"You are on a fool's errand, Margalis. Chasing after lesser demons when the devil Himself is preparing to devour you."

He swept out his hand to indicate the swollen green tear shining in the window opposite. "Look at it well, Sky Pilot: you may not have another chance. There is a cataclysm in the stars that will engulf your entire world. But you can escape it. Flee now, take this elÿon, and you may travel fast enough and far enough to survive."

I stared at him in disbelief, then laughed. "Don't be absurd! We will dock at Quirinus within a day or two. If I don't find what I seek there, I will return and look for it on Earth."

"What you seek will find *you*, old friend." He grinned with a skull's cold grimace, and his words came out slurred, as though his tongue were exhausted by the effort of speaking. "You are going now to meet with your own destruction, Margalis. Your own and your world's."

"I am going as Imperator of the Ascendant forces, to investigate the mutiny of Quirinus and seek the nemosyne named Metatron."

Aidan only laughed shrilly and said, " 'Oh, the fierce wretchedness that glory brings us!' "

Without warning he slumped over. His fingers splayed outward so that his ring struck the floor, and I heard a loud crack, as though the tile shattered beneath it. With an effort he pushed himself up on his hands. When he raised his face to gaze at me, the wound on his throat burned fiercely—truly burned, with small brilliant flames like an incandescent torque thrust about his neck.

"The damned ever seek redemption," he whispered. "But listen to me, Margalis. I was human, once. And even the dead can weep, to see the world they loved in flames—"

His voice rose in a wail. "Much has happened while you slept, Margalis. And I have learned much, oh, too much! about those who dwell behind the veil between the worlds—

"I was wrong about them, Sky Pilot. The demons bring no gifts—they know nothing but death, and they would kill us, kill us all! There are records here in the ship's library that will show you—look at them and learn, Margalis. Luther Burdock's children have heard the voice of the Oracle. They will betray you—"

He opened his hand. Onto the floor dropped a small object, the kind of 'file disk that had been manufactured half a century ago, when I was a boy. It struck the tiles and for an instant spun before falling down flat.

"Behold Icarus," he whispered.

As I watched, a small cone of pallid white light rose from the disk, and from this was projected a blurred object, like an eye or cloudy whirlpool. Within its haze the foggy eye seemed to move. Threads of gray and white flowed from it, and after a moment tiny gold letters appeared at the apex of the cone of light, letters far too small for me to read. From the flattened disk on the floor shrilled a voice like that of the smallest monad, so that I had to strain to hear it.

"*. . . it is of the utmost importance that the JPL Project permits immediate release of warning transcripts and all information relating to this disastr— . . .*"

The words burned off into static, and then there came another voice, so faint and distant, it was like the wail of something drowning in the abyss.

"*Icarus. Icarus. Icarus. Icarus.*"

"What—" I cried; but as suddenly as it had begun, the voice grew silent. The luminous cone retracted into the 'file disk. Where he lay sprawled upon the floor, Aidan Harrow's revenant stared up at me with sickly glowing eyes.

"You may be the only one with the strength and will to stop him, Margalis," he whispered, and curled his hand in a final salute. "Farewell, old friend . . . Sky Pilot. . . ."

I bent to touch him, drew back sharply. Flames leapt from the floor, flames and the smell of charred leather. There was a soft explosive sound, and a ball of smoke roiled toward me. I brought my hand protectively to my face. When I drew it away again, the flames were gone.

The viewing deck was empty. When I stopped to examine the floor, I found a small circle of ash where the 'file disk had been. As my finger stretched forth to touch it, it melted away like snow, and I stood back up in a daze.

"*There are records here in the ship's library that will show you—look at them and learn.*"

"The library," I whispered. I turned and fled the viewing deck, my heels clashing against the tiles, while behind me the blue-glazed eye of Earth gazed implacably upon the *Izanagi*.

• • •

The library was nearly as spacious as the viewing deck, with a great window running the length of one wall. Outside, stars burned and swirled in that dreamy waltz that accompanies the elÿon's bursts of acceleration. I hardly gave them a look. I hurried to a carrel, throwing myself into the seat so quickly, I ripped its fabric with my metal hand.

"What would you like to research?" The pleasant voice of the ship's librarian questioned me softly. In front of me appeared the generated image of a slight young man, clad in the simple black-and-gray suit of a Nipponian scholiast.

"All records of hostile maneuvers within the last six months."

The figure rippled and faint dots of red and green imposed themselves upon his face. The library's datafiles were deteriorating; the strain upon Lascar Franschii was starting to show. "Do you wish to review activity within the HORUS sectors or a particular region of Earth?"

I hesitated before deciding. I would look first upon the place where I had spent most of my career.

"The Archipelago."

The scholiast nodded and the image blinked out—too quickly, another sign of the ship's degrading systems. There was an instant when I might have imagined the soft click and buzz of the elÿon's vast datafiles being accessed. Then the first icon appeared.

Before me an emerald plain wove into view, threads of turquoise and deep blue racing through it until the complete landscape shone in the library's musty air. Beneath the 'filed image, glowing letters spelled out a name, latitude and longitude, and other coordinates. I gazed upon the Arafura Sea, its waters deceptively calm and utterly devoid of the landmarks that should have been there.

My voice was tight as I asked, "Where are the islands of the Archipelago? Where is Alor Setar? Where is Kalimantan?"

The scholiast's reply hung calmly in the spaces above the wavering green ocean. "Alor Setar was destroyed by *tsunami* on the nineteenth of June, Old Solar Calendar."

I counted back. It was the same day that the wave had swallowed Araboth. Not a week had passed since then. A terrible pressure began to build within my mind.

"Show me Sulawaya, then," I ordered. "Sulawesi and Jawa."

The ocean wrinkled, darkened to indigo as the image shifted. I saw a long line of blackened crags emerging from the water like knots of charred bone, some of them smoking as though racked by volcanic activity. Another string of letters and numerals appeared—

LAT 02° 10′ S—LONG 114° 44 E, CONFIG 9743
PRIOR STATUS: JAWA

"Where is this?" I asked with dread.

"Jawa," the scholiast murmured.

I shook my head in disbelief. "But it's gone. There's nothing there."

"The Ascendant Autocracy at Vancouver mistakenly believed the *tsunami* that destroyed their holdings at Araboth was the result of an Emirate attack. On twenty June o.s.c. they sent twenty thousand troops to attack the Emirate's city of Tarabulus. Emirate troops retaliated with protonic weapons intervention directed at Jawa."

The image flickered and changed to a close-up, empty turquoise waters flecked with gold and white beneath the remorseless sun. The glowing letters shifted until they spelled out another message.

LAT 04° 11′ S—LONG 107°30′ E CONFIG 9899
PRIOR STATUS: DJAKARTA, JAWA

It had been the Ascendant's primary base in the Malayu Archipelago, one of the only remaining technopolies in the world.

"It's gone," I whispered. "How can it be gone?"

Once lush green mountains had risen from that sea, islands and glittering spans of bridges, the dark spires of refinery platforms and floating webs of agrivelts where the hydrapithecenes toiled. Now there was nothing; nothing but water, a single vast ocean encompassing the seas of Arafura and South China, Timor and Banda and Sulu.

They had all been destroyed. Sumatera, Jawa, Alor Setar, Kalimantan—all the thousand islands that had been spread across the ocean's jeweled net like so many butterflies—all gone. Only a few score ragged promontories rose above the smooth blue surface. Black and molten orange beneath a faint haze of smoke and ash, they were all that remained of the system of hydrofarms and refineries that had been the Ascendants' most valuable planetary holdings. The largest single population center in what remained of the civilized world had been reduced to steam and ash.

"*No!*"

My anguished shout rang through the chamber, setting off a small warning beacon by the door. I raged on heedlessly. How could they have done this? *Who* could have done this? Even the Habilis Emirate would not have deliberately destroyed such a rare hoard of resources; not even the Autocracy. But then I thought of Tarabulus, the beautiful and ancient heart of the Emirate. If it truly had been ravaged by Ascendant troops ...

I knew how these lightning wars went. But the thought of that empty sea, of the horrible waste of lives and the precious hydrofarms, sickened me so that I sat in silence for a long time, staring blankly at the floor. Finally I raised my head and called out to the scholiast.

"More," I whispered. "Let me see more."

"Please be specific," the scholiast's voice rebuked me gently.

The clawed fingers of my left hand raked the top of the carrel. "The HORUS colonies," I cried harshly. "Show me what became of the HORUS colonies."

The 'filed image of the Archipelago radiated into random jots of emerald. An instant later a new 'file opened. It showed a whirlpool of black and ultramarine, with a date superimposed upon it.

JUNE 08, 2592, N.A.E. 73

At the whirlpool's center a brilliantly shining torus tumbled in a languorous somersault. I could barely read the letters on its side—

HORUS/NASNA/CAMPBELL PRIME SERIES 0779988342

For a moment the torus hung there, no larger than my hand but seemingly as solid. Then, as silently as though it were some seed-heavy blossom scattered by the wind, the station burst. A speck of black at its center spread like spilled ink, as the shining outer rim of the structure stretched and bowed until finally it broke apart, flying soundlessly into the heavens. Campbell Prime had been destroyed. The holofile ended abruptly.

I clenched my fist and said, "NASNA Prime. Show me." Flick. Another date; another silent maelstrom.

OCTOBER 31, 2591, N.A.E. 72

In the heart of this spiral the familiar struts and hourglass of the NASNA Prime Station slowly rotated. I could see the long silver tear that marked the main viewing deck, and imagined crimson-uniformed figures there, staring out into the void. I watched transfixed as one end of the hourglass distended. It bubbled outward, did not burst so much as disintegrate. Spars and beams of metal spilled out as the station cracked open like an egg, discharging its living humors. There was a blinding burst of light; then nothing.

Throwing back my head like an animal I let forth a howl, a shriek of rage and horror that surely would have frozen anyone who heard it; but who was there in that place to hear? When the echoes of my fury died away, I bowed, and covered my face with my hand.

There was a long silence. Then, "Have you another request?" asked the librarian.

I looked up. The 'file had looped back and started to play again. At the sound of my voice the image froze, the explosion like a brittle flower hanging in front of me.

"No! No, wait—yes, there is something else I would like to see."

The destruction of NASNA Prime flickered off. The scholiast reappeared, assumed his usual patient expression. I leaned forward, my hand stabbing at the air.

"The footage you just showed me, of the NASNA Prime Station—where did it come from?"

The scholiast's image froze as it searched for data. After nearly a minute it announced crisply, "Lyapang Wondot 3—that is, Autocratic News Service 3."

"No—where did *they* get it from? Who actually 'filed it?

Was there a person's name? *Who knew that station was going to be destroyed?*"

Again the scholiast accessed its files. This time golden letters flowed through the air, spelling out the source.

UNKNOWN HOLOFILER, HELENA AULIS AUXILIARY CAPSULE PERDITA.

"Helena Aulis," I said dully. The auxiliary capsule had been deployed from the colony that Lascar Franschii claimed held one of the leaders of the geneslave rebellion. "Run a personnel check on the broadcaster for that transmission."

High-pitched squeals as the loop was played back and analyzed.

"Nonhuman auxiliary personnel," the scholiast said at last. "Point of origin, HORUS colony Helena Aulis. Clearance Code 7, Energumen, male, Kalaman Cluster 579."

An energumen. Again I stabbed at the air.

"That footage of the Campbell station," I barked. "Who 'filed it? Who knew Campbell Prime was to be destroyed?"

Another golden banner.

UNKNOWN HOLOFILER, HELENA AULIS AUXILIARY CAPSULE PERDITA.

I waved impatiently. "Run a personnel check."

More squeals. Then, "Nonhuman auxiliary personnel. Point of origin, HORUS colony Helena Aulis. Clearance Code 7, Energumen, male, Kalaman Cluster 579."

Another energumen—or the same one—had witnessed and probably instigated the destruction of both NASNA Prime and the Campbell Station. Seemingly random acts of terrorism, and no one had ever thought to trace the news sources.

*Or if they had, the correct information was never revealed.*

The pressure in my mind roared like flame.

*Kalaman Cluster 579.*

Months before anyone was aware of it, the energumens had already begun their assault on the Ascendant Autocracy—and the Emirate, and no doubt the Balkhash Commonwealth as well.

"One more question," I said. The shrill echo of my voice

shivered in the cool air. "You said that Jawa was destroyed by Ascendant troops in retaliation for a presumed attack by the Emirate on Kalimantan and Araboth.

"But there *was* no attack, not according to your records. A *tsunami* destroyed Araboth. Who notified Quirinus headquarters otherwise? Who told them Araboth had been destroyed by the Habilis Emirate?"

The scholiast flickered in and out of sight. A disembodied voice announced, "That is classified information."

"I am the Aviator Imperator Tast'annin!" I roared, then shouted my clearance code. The scholiast's impassive face shimmered back into sight. After a few moments it said, "Medusine Kovax received a transmission on 19 June o.s.c. informing her of Emirate hostility in the North American theater. Ascendant troops responded within fourteen solar hours."

"And the source for this transmission?"

A beat. Without emotion the scholiast recited, "The relay was traced to the *Perdita,* an auxiliary capsule from Helena Aulis."

It was as Lascar Franschii had said. The energumens and other geneslaves had declared war on humanity.

I turned and stalked across the room, trying to calm myself; trying to call upon all my decades of training to keep from being overwhelmed by the sheer simplicity and lunacy and effectiveness of this campaign. After a few minutes my rage and sense of helplessness began to ebb. I stopped at the window and stared out, not really seeing anything.

For a terrorist movement—one that could only have burgeoned in the last year, even the last few months, else surely I would have heard rumors of it—it was amazingly well organized. They had the same weapons as the Autocracy; more of them, now that they had assumed control of HORUS. And seemingly they had at least one intelligent leader in this male energumen from Cluster 579. Every one of the places destroyed by their ragged troops had been an Ascendant stronghold, an armory or military base or resource holding of particular strategic value. It was not the sort of information geneslaves would have access to, even infernally gifted ones.

Unless . . .

Unless their maneuvers were all being dictated by another leader. One who knew the exact placement of the Ascendant armories and the more ancient weapons stores that had been lost over the centuries.

"The Oracle!" I cried.

"Your request?" The scholiast appeared and inclined its head to me.

"The Oracle—the messenger that has been appearing to the energumens in the HORUS colonies—do you have it on 'file?"

The scholiast blinked from view. An endless minute passed, and another. Finally it wove back into sight.

"There is an urgent 'file message for you, Imperator. Please stand by."

In the air before me a darkness appeared, an oily cloud that swirled in slowly widening circles until it formed a viscous globe roughly man-sized, the color of a black pearl. A faint lavender light candled within its heart, a violet radiance that grew more and more intense, until I had to shield my eyes from it.

"Imperator Tast'annin."

I lowered my hand. Within the shimmering globe stood the figure of a man, his outlines blurred by the shifting light. But as I stared, I saw that this was not a man at all, any more than Nefertity was a woman. It was a construct, a replicant, but more beautifully made than any I had ever seen, save for my nemosyne companion.

And of course that is what it was. The Ascendant's missing military unit; the nemosyne I was searching for.

"Metatron," I whispered.

He bowed slightly. "Imperator Tast'annin. I have been anxious to meet with you."

My voice rose angrily. "Where are you transmitting from? How did you know I was here?"

"Agent Shi Pei informed me, shortly before she was relieved of her duties at Cisneros." Silvery threads rippled across the violet mask of his face, and he smiled.

"How did you know I was at Cisneros?"

"A breach in their security system." He gave a dismissive wave, an airy gesture that seemed charged with supernatural meaning. "They have all been relieved of their duties."

Slow horror built in me as I asked, "What do you mean?"

He cupped his palms as though holding some living treasure, daggerwing butterfly or wormwood moth. When he opened them, a tiny jeweled box floated above his violet fingers. Sparks of light leapt from it like luminous spray. I leaned forward. The scintillating rays resolved into minute towers crashing in upon themselves; the flashing gems became blocks of residential units exploding into bursts of gold and crimson and black. I was looking at a 'filed image of Cisneros in flames.

In spite of my resolve I jerked backward. The nemosyne laughed.

"Oh, it won't burn you, Imperator—"

*Crack!*

He clapped his hands together and the jewel-box disappeared. "There," he said, flicking his fingers as though to cleanse them; *"that's* done." He looked up at me, his emerald eyes glowing. "Now what shall we see next? Wichita? Vancouver? Punta Arenas?"

At each name a glittering image spun into sight. Wichita's domes like dun-colored bubbles, Vancouver's spires and minarets, the ice-locked casements of Antarctica's capital. The nemosyne drew back, regarding them critically. "Or perhaps we should pluck an eye from HORUS—"

And there were the lazily turning stations of Hotei, Helena Aulis, Quirinus, Advhi Sar, each image much cleaner than the real thing and small enough to fit in my hand. Metatron's eyes narrowed. Light gleamed from one plasteel arm as he reached out and contemplatively pinched Advhi Sar's shining torus between two fingers. As I watched, he brought it to his mouth and, smiling, bit down upon it with glittering metal teeth.

*"Stop it."*

I knew they were only 'filed images, but it was too easy to recall Jawa and NASNA Prime, and Araboth's domes crushed by the prince of storms. Metatron only shrugged.

"As you wish, Imperator." The shining cities blinked from sight. For an instant the nemosyne was utterly still, staring at me with the cold dull gaze of an adder. Any resemblance to a mortal man was gone. I was looking at a being infinitely less human than Lascar Franschii or myself, or even Nefertity. His coldly glittering eyes, the cruel and angular lines of his face, were less *alive* than anything I had ever seen. Yet he was charged with such malevolence, such unshakable strength and arrogance, that he seemed more powerful than anything I had ever gazed upon.

"What are you?" I whispered.

"Many things." He smiled again, slowly, and said, "My name is Legion."

"Who discovered you? Who has programmed you to do these things? *Why?*"

A shrug of those gleaming shoulders. "*Ad astra per asperan,* Imperator. You will find out soon enough."

The nemosyne's image flickered, as though the transmission were fading. His voice began to grow fainter. "Certain Ascendant outposts on Earth and in HORUS have proved difficult for my followers to reclaim. It seems they have formed their *own* alliances. Ironic, isn't it, that after all these centuries your Autocracy and Emirates and Commonwealth should suddenly find themselves with a common enemy?"

His voice grew silken as he crooned, "But we are not *your* enemy, Imperator, the geneslaves and I. Humanity is. And *you* are no longer human. Your human masters have done nothing but fail you, again and again. Don't you think it is time you shed your lingering affection for them? Don't you think it is time you found a new master?"

In the air above his head fiery words appeared, the NASNA motto *Oderint dum metuant* spelled out in flames.

"You have *hated* very well, Imperator. Now it is time you learned to *fear.*"

The letters crumbled into ash as Metatron's voice rose to a howl. The walls of the carrel shook around me and 'files and books slid from tables and shelves. Before my eyes the nemosyne grew larger, billowing out like an elÿon readying for flight, until he seemed to take up the entire room: a vast black cloud shot with violet lightning, pierced by two raging emerald eyes. With an explosive roar he was gone.

Silence; then a barely audible sound echoed in the room.

Another voice, my *own* voice, faint and tremulous as though it had been recorded on faulty equipment and was now being played back from a great distance—years, perhaps; decades . . .

"*I must serve somebody,*" it—*I*—said; and then the library grew silent one more.

The chamber's light had dimmed when a sound roused me.

"Imperator."

I whirled, my hand raised to strike; but at the far end of the room stood Captain Novus. Her face was red, her eyes puffy from the drugs she had been given. "A replicant woke me and said that we are approaching Quirinus." She yawned, rubbing her arms, and shook her head. "The time says it's been fifty-three hours. Is that possible?"

Fifty-three hours! But of course it was possible. It seemed now that anything was possible.

"Yes," I said numbly. I was glad I had only one human hand, and that she could not see how it trembled. "I warned you, elÿon travel is disorienting."

I walked past her, headed for the door leading back to the navigation cell. "Make sure Nefertity has been reactivated. Both of you will meet me in the adjutant's chamber as soon as possible."

She stared at me, surprised at my subdued tone, then nodded. "As you wish, Imperator," she said, and hurried down the corridor.

In the navigation cell I tried to question Lascar Franschii about my vision of Aidan Harrow and the subsequent message from the nemosyne he referred to as the Oracle.

"Of course there are ghosts here!" the adjutant whined. "There are ghosts on every elÿon, how do you think we travel so quickly? They pull us, we are chained to them, spirits of the past, the dead, the damned—"

There was more of this babble, but in a rage I yanked his speaking tube from the wall. When Valeska and Nefertity arrived, Lascar Franschii was thrashing furiously within his web of wires, squeaking like a bat.

"That is cruel," Nefertity said coldly. She slid the speaking tube back into his mouth. A froth of blood and spittle greeted her for her kindness, and a stream of curses. Even Captain Novus looked appalled.

"We'd better find the docking area," she said as the adjutant kicked weakly at the wall behind him. Without a word I strode to the door, not waiting for the others to follow.

"Will he—will that affect our landing?" Captain Novus asked uneasily when we were out of earshot. "He seems to be having some kind of seizure."

"We have fallen into a trap that Lacar Franschii has helped set for us, Captain Novus. Please arm yourself and be prepared for a hostile encounter. Under no circumstances should you allow my replicant to be harmed."

Valeska Novus swallowed and glanced at Nefertity beside

her like a radiant shadow. "Yes, Imperator," she said, and was silent.

We entered the main corridor, its glowing walls painting us all a lurid crimson. At the end of the hallway was the door through which we had first entered the *Izanagi*. Three of the Maio servers stood beside it, their silver faces turned attentively toward us.

"Imperator Margalis Tast'annin," one of them announced in its clear, cold voice as we approached. "There is no human escort on HORUS colony Quirinus to greet you. A psychological reading of those aboard shows only thirteen auxiliary personnel, female energumens from Kalamat Cluster 533. There is evidence of recent biochemical sabotage. In addition, three auxiliary capsules bearing the designation *HORUS Colony Helena Aulis* are in the process of making an unauthorized docking at Quirinus. We recommend aborting this mission."

"I don't believe we could abort this mission under any circumstances," I said curtly. "And we will have no need of human escorts. I have reason to believe that the energumens are expecting us."

Before us the door shuddered as the elÿon docked into the main entryway of the HORUS station. I could hear Valeska's shallow breathing, and from the navigator's cell far behind us the voice of Lascar Franschii bellowing with laughter. With a sound like a knife scraping glass, the entryway began to open. Brilliant blue light poured into the chamber, mingling with the elÿon's crimson glow to turn everything a vivid purple. A moment later we were gazing into the vast recesses of Quirinus.

# 11

## Cassandra

**As our caravan approached** the river bounding Cassandra, I could see why the Ascendants had not been able to destroy the town. Protonic cannons lined the riverbank: steel-blue cylinders pointed at the sky, steaming in the morning sun. Earthen berms and small brick outbuildings rose beside them, and from these swarmed figures clad in the dusty blue hoods and tunics I slowly realized must be the uniform of the Asterine Alliance. Most of these figures were men and women; but there were others who went about unclothed, or wearing abbreviated versions of the uniform. Aardmen with their hunched gait; ethereal argalæ, struggling to carry the smallest cartons in their frail twiglike arms; cacodemons and huge and horrible four-legged things like equine men. All of them moved busily along the shore, like the apocalyptic figures in a recusant's tapestry brought to life. Beyond them the river was wide and brilliant as the sky, and as calm. I could see where fish were rising to snap at clouds of insects, and where a motorized dinghy V'ed lazily through the placid waters as though on no more serious errand than fishing, heading for the far shore.

"There's a checkpoint ahead," Cadence warned us. She pointed to a ramshackle metal building at river's edge. Immediately past it a bridge spanned the water, its rusted spans repaired with wooden beams and salvaged metal. "*I'll* take care of everything." She glanced at Jane, then turned back to the wheel. Jane looked affronted. She stuck her chin in the air and in beleaguered silence joined me at the open window.

The van crept the last few yards toward the guardhouse. People had stopped their work—mostly hauling crates and canisters from several other ancient caravans parked near the cannons—and stood in small groups, staring at us as the sentries waved us through. Beside the guardhouse a huge figure stood by a smaller, hooded one, inspecting something that might have been a transformer or some kind of old 'file transmitter. As I watched, the larger creature turned, very very slowly, and stared at us as we passed. I had an impression of fawn-colored skin and slightly darker hair, and eyes that were black and implacable as a starless sky.

At that unblinking gaze a cold tongue of dread licked at me, and I shuddered. Even from a distance there was something eerie, almost obscene, about that form. As though some ancient monolith had begun to move—like the City's Obelisk or Sorrowful Lincoln—something formed over the course of aeons out of marble and fire and blood; something that should never have been given life. The thing watched our caravan rattle by, its huge hands holding the dully gleaming core of the transmitter as though it were a hollow log. As the van rounded a corner, I turned to look back at it. For an instant its eyes met mine, and I gasped.

Because those eyes—pupilless, cold and deep as black water—were utterly without guile or hatred. For all the grotesque immensity of its body, the gaze that met mine glowed with the rapturous curiosity of a child's.

"What is that?" I whispered.

Jane stared after it, her face drawn.

"Energumen," she said. I knew from her expression that she had never before seen one alive.

Nor had I. I had never even quite believed that they existed, let alone that one might work peacefully side by side with humans. The notion had seemed too ludicrously horrible even for the Ascendants: deformed, bioengineered clones twice the size of a man, created to serve as slaves in the HORUS colonies and the most distant reaches of the Archipelago.

This one, though, had not been quite so large as I had

imagined—perhaps only two feet taller than a man, though beside it that solitary human had looked spindly and utterly inconsequential in his loose uniform. I stared after them until our caravan began to cross the bridge.

"Christ," Jane muttered. She stood beside me and looked dispiritedly out at the rusted spars and sagging cables. "We're in for it now, Wendy."

I pointed to where dull-gray canisters and spiky arrays of wire and metal had been bound to the struts with lengths of barbed wire, until the whole thing looked like the work of some great caddisworm. Jane nodded glumly.

"Explosives. They've got the whole thing rigged so that if anyone tries to cross—like, say, someone trying to rescue us—the bridge will go under—*pfft*—like that."

In the front seat Cadence turned and gave us a warning look. Jane grew silent, crossing her arms on her chest and casting a baleful glance to where Suniata stood in silence beside the driver's seat, his round carp's-eyes fixed on the road before us.

And so we reached the shores of Cassandra. Behind us the placid waters of the Shenandoah curled out of sight between the foothills of the Blue Ridge. Ahead of us stretched the road, wider now, with long gouges in the red clay where shallow trenches had been dug and rudimentary channels stood half-full of rusty looking water. Our caravan slowed, creeping to avoid boulders and trees that had fallen in the course of constructing more armories and crude storage buildings. There were many men and women working here, wearing the hooded blue uniform of the Alliance, as well as a number of energumens: all carrying sacks of meal and grain, dragging great steel beams across the wounded ground, pulling the broken axle from beneath a pile of wreckage. Compared to their slight, almost scrawny forebears, the energumens were surprisingly graceful, with smooth, heavily muscled bodies. Most wore only a loose linen skirt about their narrow waists. Their skins were different colors—the same vibrant red as the Virginia clay; a dusky bluish-brown, like the flesh of a muscat grape; an ivory tone like fluid wax.

But what I found strangest about them was their faces. Or rather, their *face*—because they all shared the same features. Large intelligent eyes above rounded cheeks, wide foreheads, childish round mouths. Jane grimaced when they stopped their work and gazed after us, but to me they looked like grotesquely large children. Only their eyes betrayed their demonic origins, with black iris and cornea and tiny white pupils, and the same expression of intense inquisitiveness as they watched us pass.

There was another checkpoint up ahead, and an even more staggering array of weaponry, all of it arranged in shining, neatly ordered columns beneath the lacquered blue sky. At the sight, even Jane's customary irony turned to disbelief.

"Scarlet was right," she said. Outside, two energumens worked on a metal platform that supported a satellite dish twice the size of our van. On the ground beneath them another energumen manipulated a control panel. Slowly the entire apparatus swiveled, liked a monstrous clockwork toy. "This really *is* war."

"Not just war." Cadence looked over her shoulder while she steered the caravan with her one hand. "Jihad."

Jane frowned. "Jihad?" Suniata nodded, and Cadence smiled triumphantly.

"*Holy* war," she said. "To avenge them, and redeem ourselves."

"Redeem *who*?" Jane asked suspiciously.

"Us. All of humanity." Cadence's voice took on the same ringing tone I had heard in Miss Scarlet's when she played one of the more ardent roles in her repertoire, Saint Joan or Clytemnestra or Maw-ree Zilus. The van veered dangerously close to a stack of bricks as she went on. "This is a war of redemption—yours, ours, all of humanity's! We sought to enslave the world, and like all slaves the world has finally rebelled. It is up to *us*, for those humans who have joined the Alliance, to redeem our race. The Earth will be cleansed of humanity. We will free those beings we created, end their centuries of servitude, so that at last they can take their places beside us in a *new* world—"

She paused to look over at Suniata, and her eyes shone with a radiance that transcended anything I had ever seen before in a man or woman. Not simple love, certainly not lust; but an intensity of expression that I can only describe as beatific. It was a gaze that scorched; I could imagine myself flinching if she was to turn it upon me. I thought then of her father and the enhancer he had worn over his damaged face, and wondered if his eyes had withered away from such incandescent ardor.

And then I felt the cool, slightly moist touch of Suniata's

hand upon mine, and a simple thought like a jolt of adrenaline, coursing from his fingers to my brain—

*But of course! Didn't you know?*

I drew away sharply, staring into that bloated fishlike face as though into a warped mirror. Suniata only nodded and turned back to Cadence. Jane put her hand on my shoulder and tried to pull me to her.

"Wendy? What is it?" I shook her away, suddenly frightened.

Because all this time I had thought of the cacodemon merely as an odd accessory to this journey; a creature whose function was to serve as some kind of silent adjunct to Cadence, perhaps to cow Jane and me by his presence.

But now, with Cadence gazing at him with that wonder and reverence and, yes, *fear,* igniting her blue eyes, I saw the truth of it.

The cacodemon was not her servant. She was *his.* In some misguided effort to reverse the wrongs of hundreds of years of genetic engineering and biological warfare, the human members of the Asterine Alliance had offered themselves as infantry and handsel to the geneslaves.

"No, not *beside* us in that new world—above us," Cadence continued. Her hood had slipped from her head, so that all I saw was a halo of brilliant white above the blue folds of her uniform. "This world has become unlivable. The sun is poisoned, and the water, so that nothing from our past can safely live upon it.

"But these others—"

She raised the stump of her left hand triumphantly. "The new creatures, the ones *we* created—they *can* survive in this world we have made! To them the poisons are like cool water, and darkness is daylight. They can live among the stars without falling prey to madness, and when they breed—and they will!—they will have only a single offspring, so that the subtle balance of our new world will not be overthrown. We gave birth to them in darkness, but that darkness has welcomed them, even as it has swallowed us."

I felt as though someone had run an icy finger across my throat. "Are you—do you mean to make slaves of *us,* then? Your own kind?"

Cadence shook her head. "No," she said softly, her voice nearly drowned by the droning engines. "You will see—we are not devoured by self-hatred, seeing these new creatures.

They would never have come to be, were it not for us; were it not for their father, the man who gave birth to all of them. We honor them, that is all. We honor him.

"But you'll see, Wendy. And Jane. Icarus is coming. And when he comes, a new world will come with him, even as this one falls away."

She crouched back over the steering wheel, the wind whipping her hair into silver froth. For another moment Suniata looked at me, his gaze flat and inscrutable as a viper's.

Icarus. Into my mind rose the image that had been printed on Giles's packets of cigarettes, and on the wine and brandy we'd drunk at Seven Chimneys.

# Ιχαρυσ

Icarus: that was what the strange characters spelled. Whomever—or whatever—the Asterine Alliance had taken as their emblem, was a thing called *Icarus*.

For the first time Suniata spoke aloud, the tendrils around his mouth rising as though to taste the name.

"Icarus," he whispered, and nodded at me. Then he turned to stare outside.

"Icarus," I thought, and even though the name was meaningless to me, I felt it like a palpable weight upon my heart.

In her seat Cadence peered through the front window, occasionally glancing at Suniata and nodding as though to some unspoken question. From the manner in which the cacodemon touched her—his long flattened fingers brushing now her neck, now her elbow or the wrinkled stump of her arm—I imagined they must be engaged in conversation, a new and subtle means of speech that stupid folk like Jane or me would never understand. Twice Suniata pointed, and Cadence craned her neck to see what he had indicated: improvements, I gathered, that had been made since their departure the day before.

Beyond the edge of the road were endless heaps of crates and heavy canvas sacks, some of them ripped open to spill their burden of ammunition and armored clothing beneath the tossing limbs of birches and young oaks. Behind the trees hundreds of vehicles were thrown together, nosing each other like bastard pups searching for their mother: caravans and jitneys and trucks and trylons, Ascendant aviettes with their wings folded up like a pterosaur's and blunt-nosed Harkers from the Commonwealth. In the distance I glimpsed the wreckage of a fouga. Its outer skin had burned away so that only its steel infrastructure remained, like the shattered ribs and vertebrae of a whale gnawed to bone by some unimaginably vast predator. Two cacodemons emerged slowly from its blackened hulk, dragging corpses and what looked like the body of a huge worm. Others of their kind huddled together over the ruins of the dirigible's gondola, shaking their heads solemnly and staring at a flickering image that might have been a holofile of the warship's flight plan.

"Look at all this," Jane murmured, shaking her head. "They must have gone to war against the entire world, to get all this. . . ."

"Oh, but we have," said Cadence, and Jane fell silent.

The caravan drove out from under the canopy of oaks, to a sunlit place where the road widened. To either side grass and flowering vines grew over the remains of ancient buildings long since given over to the earth. Here the mountains were so close that I could smell them, their secrets trickling from dark places like water, the wind rushing down gray cliffs in a cold torrent. Through a stand of live oaks, their trunks blackened and burled with age, I could glimpse the very foot of the mountain, a gray-and-green rampart rising thousands of feet above us until it vanished in blue haze. Scattered about its base were broken chunks of granite and boulders like chunks of dirty ice. From the center of all this rose an immense pair of polished metal doors, buttressed with steel beams and smooth slabs of rock that must have been torn from the mountain itself. Trees grew above the doors, spindly, gnarled trees whose roots clutched at the loose soil trapped between stones that had been loosed by avalanche or storm. For all the sunlight and warmth spilling from the unclouded sky, it was a grim place. I could imagine black eagles nesting there, or vultures, but not wrens or larkspurs or the darting wild finches: nothing that might give voice to song.

"Well, Wendy," Jane said, hugging herself and staring at the mountain with a face as cold and unyielding as its own. "Looks like the end of the world, all right."

All up and down the mountainside innumerable solar disks rose on crooked stiltlike legs, like great black beetles that had crawled from a giant's corpse. Lines of rebels marched between them, snaking down to the road in an unbroken file. They would have been invisible save for their sky-colored uniforms and the weapons they carried, double-bladed yataghans and flame-shooting culverins glinting in the sun, and a billowing standard bearing the now-familiar image of mountains and star and the name *Icarus* spelled in archaic script. A dull thunder echoed from somewhere far above us. The lines of troops halted and turned to stare up the mountainside. A moment later a cloud of black smoke appeared in the sky. A faint rain of leaves and shattered stone pattered against the caravan and sent the rebels scuttling down their path.

When she heard the first explosion, Cadence sent the van lurching forward. We racketed past another stand of starved-looking trees and a battered plastic urinal. To the right of the road loomed a metal sign, so old and pitted with rust, it looked like an autumn leaf chewed by locusts.

## WELCOME TO CASSANDRA

## GATEWAY TO THE BLUE RIDGE

A few yards past it was a smaller sign.

**WHEN IN CASSANDRA**
*VISIT*
**WORLD-FAMOUS PARADISE CAVERNS!**

On the flaking metal someone had scrawled *Ad astra aspera* in blue paint.

"We mean to cleanse this world and find another," said Cadence softly. She lifted her head to gaze at the shining gate that loomed before us, then raised her hand as an energumen sentry waved us on. Beside her, the cacodemon turned to regard Jane and me with coldly glittering eyes.

He said, "Your kind have always thought of us as monsters, but it is to us that this great task has fallen." He spoke in a whisper, as though it hurt him to talk. "If we are truly monsters, perhaps then we are better suited to another world than to this one."

Cadence nodded, adding fervently, " 'I have said to corruption, Thou art my father; to the worm, Thou art my mother, and my sister.' " She yanked on a lever in the front of the cab, retracting the solex shields, and the engines died. " 'How much less man, that is a worm? and the son of man, which is a worm?' "

I said nothing. Jane drew me close as the caravan shuddered to a halt. With a low moan of greeting Suniata leapt from the van to embrace another of his kind waiting by the doors. In her seat Cadence turned and looked at Jane and me, her blue eyes flashing as she drawled, "Welcome to Paradise."

Minutes later we stood before the entrance to the caverns, an arched steel gate three times the height of a man and with heavy iron bars so thick, I couldn't wrap my hands around them. Rusted signs dangled from the bars; others were recessed into the stone itself, and had a slick green patina of moss and algae hiding the letters.

**TOURS Begin Hourly and Last 90 Minutes**
**PARENTS, Please! Carry All Children Under Three**
   **Years of Age**
**Caverns Close at Sunset Daily**

High above the gate's arch a sheet of metal had been embedded into the granite, its engraved letters worn but still elegant as they shone in the midday sun.

# WELCOME!

## TO

# PARADISE CAVERNS

As Jane and I stared, several humans in rebel uniforms walked past. They stared at us curiously and, I thought, with sympathy. When they reached the gate, they saluted the energumen sentry and passed inside—all save the last, who hesitated. Looking back at us, he raised his hand and, in a furtive show of solidarity, grimaced. Then he too disappeared into that gaping darkness.

"Come with me, friend," a soft voice sounded. I started as Suniata's moist hand closed over mine. "We must go inside now. There is very little time left for our work here. You and Jane will have to meet with Dr. Burdock today."

"Dr. *Burdock?*" Jane repeated incredulously. Behind us Cadence stood outside her caravan, laughing with a burly man who gestured extravagantly at the cavern entrance. Compared to the cacodemon's soft tone, their voices sounded as shrill and meaningless as the cry of locusts. "Luther Burdock's been dead for four hundred years." The cacodemon said nothing, only folded his hands inside his sleeves and entered the caverns.

As we followed him, I knew why those other people had slowed their pace. Even an enormous bank of electrified lanterns couldn't dispel the infernal darkness. Two van-sized solar generators stood to either side of the doorway, trembling from the effort of converting the light gathered outside, but it still wasn't enough. Nothing would have been enough.

"Christ, Wendy, how can they *live* in here?" Jane's fingers twined around mine. She craned her neck, her brown eyes so wide they gave her a slightly maddened expression. "This is like, like—well, shit. I've never seen *anything* like it."

"It is a very great honor," Suniata said in a hushed admonitory tone. "Tomorrow night we will have our first glimpse of Icarus and the exodus will begin. You are meeting the Doctor at a very precious time."

"Oh, of *course*," Jane said drily. "Please make sure the Doctor knows just how thrilled we are." At Suniata's disapproving glare she shrugged and added, "I mean it: a very great honor."

The cacodemon turned away; he would waste no more talk with us. I pulled Jane to me and kissed her quickly on the cheek. Her hand tightened around mine as we followed our guide into the somber heart of Cassandra.

A faint damp breeze blew through the passage. From the ceiling naked bulbs hung between twisted spires of calcified stone. In places, the stalactites had started to grow around the lights, so that they glowed eerily from between flows of softly glowing white and yellow and dull orange, like molten wax. Softened knobs of stone welled up from the floor, some of them waist-high, others so small they looked like skulls, all that remained of bodies that had melted into the earth. The passage was wide enough to drive a van through, and one did pass us, the sound of its motor quieted to a wasp's hum, the voices of its human and aardmen passengers muted within that echoing space.

Suniata led us through galleries filled with weapons stores; past lightless tunnels and black and silent lakes that reflected the crenulated ceiling and turned it into an endless plain, where mountains and tors needled upward to touch the very tips of the things they reflected. There were empty chambers covered with fine yellow shrouds of pollen blown in from unseen chimneys, so smooth and deep and soft that one could drown in it, and tiny cells that held nothing but corrugated pillars of amber-colored stone, bound about with coils of copper like sheaves to be brought to harvest. There were workrooms, bedrooms, dormitories, libraries, all couched within the rock and filled with silent uniformed figures, who were crouching or stooped or upright by turns, busily engaged in fitting weaponry or reading flickering monitors. Loveliest of all was an atrium where crystalline stars covered walls and ceiling, everything but the floor, glimmering coldly in the light of a single small lantern. Their fragile tines broke away at the faintest touch of my finger. The sound of them shattering upon the stones was the echo of my own dismay at having destroyed something so lovely.

"Nowhere else, our father says, nowhere else will you see these," Suniata said, pausing to cup one of his white spade-fingered hands about a crystal but being careful not to touch it. "Anthodites, they called them. Because they are like flowers."

We went on. I stumbled along beside Jane, my mouth filled with the lingering taste of the creosote trees we had seen hours earlier, my eyes always turning away from the steady, feeble gleam of the electric lights to seek something else in the midnight corridors, something like the sun.

I had always thought of darkness as something I knew: a half-wild creature that could be beaten back into corners and chained with light. Even the starless sky was not something to fear, because the sun was always there, a scythe upraised to fall upon the gloom.

But in Paradise Caverns I learned that darkness is not like that at all. Darkness cannot be put away, or cut back, or tamed. It is what *Is:* the last thing, the only thing. The rest of us, stars and suns and creatures squatting around the fire, are mere flaws in its fabric, rips and tears too small to mend, or bubbles floating on the surface of an infinite and tenebrious sea. Even on our Earth there are secret vales where there is no sun; but there is no place that does not know the night.

"I hear water." Jane's whisper was a ragged sound. "Listen—can you hear?"

I could. The sound grew until the cavern resonated with it. Above our heads, bulbs hanging from twisted wires swung slowly back and forth, back and forth. Suniata threaded his way past elephantine stalagmites, their sides wet and gleaming. We followed, slowly and with increasing reluctance. The limestone spires hanging from the ceiling trembled and emitted faint chimes, so that the chamber seemed to be filled with an invisible choir. Suddenly Jane clutched my arm and pointed.

"God, look at that!"

Before us roared a river, half as wide as that which circled the mountain outside. I do not know if it was sister to that stream or an extension of it. Certainly it was wilder, raging through a channel it had gouged from the slick rock and throwing up spume and a fine icy mist.

The roaring grew louder as we followed the river, walking down a narrow passage a fraction as wide as that roiling beast. Abruptly the black stream plunged around a corner into utter darkness, like a worm burrowing into its hole. The narrow path came to a dead end. Strung across the violent water was a bridge made of planks and rope. One end stood just a few feet from us. The other disappeared into the darkness. In the middle it sagged and swayed as though something huge trod across it just out of our sight.

"We'll cross here," Suniata said matter-of-factly. He had thrown back the hood of his cape and looked like a monkish analog of the Frog Footman. Jane whistled in disbelief, but before she could say anything, the cacodemon had clambered onto the bridge and lurched off into the darkness. Jane looked at me; we both looked around at the empty passage. We had seen no one in some time. I had long since given up trying to remember the way back.

"Well," Jane said, and tugged dubiously at a frayed end of rope. "It's either this or wait for something else to kill us." She swung herself up and began to cross.

I waited until she reached the middle of the bridge, and when she seemed safely on her way toward the far shore, I climbed after her. It was easy enough, once I got used to the slick wooden planks twisting and snapping at each step. Half-way across I stopped and looked down. The water boiled perhaps ten feet below me, its black surface flecked with white and yellow vortices. I stared, trying to measure the distance. Suddenly a face appeared in the water.

"Come, sister," it hissed. A human face, but with skin like oiled green leather and a round lipless mouth edged with tiny white teeth. "Jump I will catch you."

I yelled and stumbled forward, clutching frantically at the ropes and sending the entire bridge bouncing and twitching like a spider's guyline. The hydrapithecene hissed again, but I was already gone. Where the bridge ended I jumped to the floor, wrenching my ankle. Jane caught me as I staggered against her.

"Siren!" I gasped. Behind her Suniata regarded me dispassionately.

"They live here, too," he said, and turned away.

"Are you hurt?" Jane asked, pushing the hair from my face.

"Not really," I said. I winced as I rubbed my ankle. "Just twisted it a little."

"Good," she murmured, and pulled me to her. She kissed me, her mouth brushing mine so lightly, I thought it was a drop of water running across my lips. My tongue darted out to flick it away, and she kissed me again, harder—no doubt of it this time—then slowly drew back, her fingers resting against my damp cheek and stroking the wet curls plastered at my neck.

"Don't be afraid," she whispered. "If they were going to kill us, they'd have done it by now. And I would never let them hurt you."

I didn't tell her I wasn't afraid—not really, not any more than anyone would be who'd just seen a siren's nightmare face gabbling up out of an underground river—but then Suniata's voice came back to us again, low and urgent, begging us to follow.

We did. In a few minutes we found the true source of the thunderous sound we'd been hearing. We were in a wide gallery, dimly lit and less dramatic than others we'd passed, except where a glittering canopy seemed to cover the far side of the room. Behind it shadows moved with the jerky stride of puppets or primitive servers. It took me a moment to attach the nearly deafening roar with this delicate vision, and another moment to realize that what we were approaching was a waterfall, lit from behind by a blaze of electric lanterns.

"This is where Dr. Burdock works," said Suniata.

"A nice spot to come back from the dead," Jane said, her voice cracking.

"Take my hand, Wendy," Suniata called softly. "And you, Jane, take hers—"

We followed him, one behind the other, across a narrow stone bridge that arched above the pool where the cascade fell. The stones were wet beneath our feet, and I was terrified of falling. Spray drenched us, and mingled with the sharp limey reek of the water was a burning chemical scent, formaldehyde and preserving alcohol and something so caustic, it made my throat sore. Abruptly Suniata let go of me, and one by one we jumped to the slippery ground, Jane and me shivering and cupping our hands beneath our arms from the cold.

"Dr. Burdock," Suniata called. He peered into the darkness, then seemed to see whom he was looking for. "Dr. Burdock, we have two new recruits."

Here the chemical smell was overwhelming, and mingled with a muskier animal odor. From the ceiling hung a makeshift chandelier, a warped metal wheel set with empty wine bottles. Each held a guttering candle that sent long strings of yellow wax tapering to the floor. Beneath this crouched six aardmen. They stared intently at a holofile scarcely brighter than the candles overhead. Nearby a single argala poked tentatively at another 'file disk, rather forlorn with her wispy yellow hair and enormous dormouse eyes. More monitors were set up beside a row of steel tables that recalled Trevor Mallory's cellar garden. Three energumens sat before them with their great heads bowed, fingers tracing slowly across the dusty screens as they scryed some lost secret. As we passed, the energumens looked sideways at us with glowing black eyes.

"Dr. Burdock . . . ," Suniata called again. The cacodemon's blue-robed figure slipped in and out of sight between steel tables and ramshackle shelves. On one of these a bloodstained robe had been tossed, and the red imprint of an enormous hand shone against the metal. A row of books lined the top shelf—very old books made of paper, with curling faded covers and pages that crumbled away when I touched them. The chemical smell gave way to the more prosaic stench of tobacco. When he saw the bloodstained robe, Suniata straightened, and though he could not smile, his voice sounded brighter. "Ah! Dr. Burdock! Here we are."

Behind the sagging shelves a man sat at a small desk, staring earnestly at the pages of a small white book. A metal hubcap listed at his elbow, filled with fingerling stubs of cigarettes and a gray dune of ashes. He wore a plain white shirt, no longer clean, and gray trousers hiked up to show bony ankles and a pair of canvas shoes that had once been white but were now stained rusty brown and crusted with dirt. He was perhaps forty, with dark hair and a round earnest face. His cheeks were rosy, as though they had been lovingly pinched, and his eyes behind a pair of antique plastic spectacles were the devout guileless brown of a spaniel's. When he saw Suniata, he looked up in surprise, then snapped the book closed, holding it prayerfully between his palms.

"Ah, y-yes, Suniata! And you have brought g-g-*guests*."

He didn't stand, instead leaned forward and let the glasses ride down his nose so he could peer above them. His voice was measured, cheerful; the kind of voice I imagined a much-loved teacher would have. He had a slight stammer that made his speech seem ingratiatingly hesitant, as though he valued the listener's opinion much more than his own. "W-who are your friends?"

"This is the empath we told you about. The other—" Suniata shrugged. "Her lover?"

Jane blushed but said nothing. The man stared at us, his

mouth slightly ajar and his front teeth pressing gently into his lower lip. Finally he started, as though waking from some half-sleep, and nodded briskly.

"Well, yes. Of course. Thank you very much, Suniata, thank you very *very* much." He gestured expansively at several empty chairs. "Please. Take a s-seat. And Suniata—thank you."

This time *thank you* obviously meant *good-bye*. The cacodemon bowed his head and left. The man fiddled with his glasses and dropped his book, made a temple of his hands and drummed his fingertips together. Finally he cleared his throat, tipping his head so that the glasses slid back onto the bridge of his nose.

"Well. Introductions, yes?" He raised his eyebrows and looked at us with great seriousness, as though awaiting another suggestion. When none was forthcoming, he went on. "I am Luther Burdock. Dr. Burdock, they call me here. And you are—?"

I took a deep breath. Across the room the geneslaves moved industriously in the shadows. The argala frowned at its 'file. The aardmen reclined in silence beneath their candles. The energumens worked by the studious green glow of their monitors. None of them were paying us the slightest attention.

"Wendy Wanders," I finally said.

"Very n-nice. And you?"

Jane stuck her chin out belligerently. "Jane Alopex. And look, *Doctor* Burdock, we don't have—"

The man rolled his eyes and nodded, flapping his hand. "Of course, of course! You're not *p-prisoners* here, Jane—Wwendy? I hope they didn't tell you *that*?" He peered at us worriedly.

Jane looked taken aback. "Well, no," she admitted after a moment. Dr. Burdock looked relieved.

"Because that's really not the point of any of this at *all*, is it? Really quite the opposite, really just the sort of th-thing we're trying to do away with here. You understand?"

He leaned forward, looking up at us earnestly through his glasses and fumbling at his shirt pocket until he found a packet of cigarettes. He lit one and took several deep drags before continuing.

"Oh, I know some of my advisers get a little *zealous* at times—you can understand that, can't you? I mean, having seen firsthand what we're up against?—but I wouldn't want you to think we were holding you here against your *will*. I wouldn't want you to think *that* at all."

Behind a veil of blue smoke his eyes widened and he tilted his head, waiting for our assurance. I coughed nervously. When it became apparent Jane wasn't going to say anything, I cleared my throat and said, "Well, yes. I mean, we *did* think that—we didn't really want to come here, but they didn't give us much choice, and everything—I mean, the manner in which we were escorted here—well, it did make me—us—think we were prisoners."

Dr. Burdock frowned, drumming his fingers on the arm of his chair. Finally he shook his head.

"Well," he said, raising his eyebrows as though the idea had just occurred to him. "Well, maybe you *are,* then. Hmm."

He made a face and looked at me more closely through the smoke. "You're the empath? The one Trevor told me about, the one from the—what do you call it—the Engineering Laboratory for Health?"

"The Human Engineering Laboratory."

"Right-o! The Human Engineering Laboratory!" He beamed, as though I had scored well on a test. "Well! And you're an empath—that is, you can sense the emotions of other people? Without their telling you, without touching them?"

I shook my head. "Not anymore. I used to—I used to be able to read dreams. And I *did* have to touch them. I—I need some contact. With their blood, or saliva."

"Mmm." Dr. Burdock frowned, tipped more ashes into the overflowing metal disk. "Not really a psychic, then. No incidences of clairvoyance, poltergeist activity, nothing unusual like th-that?"

I thought of the Boy in the Tree, of the visions I had seen with my brother Raphael. I looked away. "Nothing."

A slightly disappointed silence. The sound of the waterfall seemed to grow louder. Then, "Oh, well," he said, smiling. "You're welcome here anyway, there's always room for eager young people. You *are* rather young, aren't you? How old—sixteen? seventeen?"

"Eighteen."

He stubbed out his cigarette, raising his eyebrows at Jane, and she concurred. He said, "Eighteen! Well, that's still very young, compared to me, of course, forty-three, though it doesn't seem so long, though of course, you know, sometimes it feels like forever. . . ."

The brown eyes seemed to cloud over. When he spoke again, his voice was softer and even more hesitant. "I had a daughter, you know. Not much younger than you. Cybele. She was—"

He sighed and looked away, to where the energumens hunched over their monitors. "She was a beautiful girl," he finished softly. "I miss her so much, even now. Even after all this time. I keep thinking I'll see her, that perhaps one of them might—"

He broke off with a sigh. The darkness in his eyes spread across his face, and his mouth twitched, almost as though he were talking to himself. "But of course, none of them really do," he said after a moment. He looked at me and smiled sadly, then shook his head, the way a dog does to shake off the rain. "Oh, well. Perhaps we can make it different someday soon. This wasn't at all what I had in mind, you know—"

He gestured at the energumens, the shadowy forms of two aardmen heading toward the narrow bridge behind the waterfall. At last his gaze fell with distaste upon the argala. "What they've done with my work. These poor c-creatures. Prostitutes. *S-slaves.* Not my idea, not my idea *at all*," he ended firmly, and chewed his lower lip. "And the others—what they did to my girls . . ."

His voice trailed off and he stared into the darkness. *"Savagery,"* he said a long moment later, the word coming out in a hiss. "S-savage *beasts*! To think they would do that, to think they would take a child and—"

He lowered his voice, but pointed with a quick stabbing motion toward the energumens. *"That.* Not that it's their fault what they look like, but—"

He moved his chair closer, staring at us with wide mad pupils. "My *children,* you understand," he said, and his face seemed to glow in the half-light. "All my work for the good of humanity, and this is what they've done to it. Circus animals. Brute l-laborers. *Whores.* All those years, all this time—and this, *this* is what they've done to my children."

His voice rose so that the energumens stopped and looked at us. Luther Burdock ignored them; only stared at me, his glasses fogged from his excitement.

"Four hundred years. A lot can happen in four hundred

years. But this—this isn't *right*. This just—is not—
*acceptable*.

"You understand, don't you?" he asked me softly. He held
his hand out, cupped so that the empty palm faced the ceiling.
"Even it if means people dying. Even if it means *everyone*
dying—"

His face grew red and his breath came out in ragged
bursts. "We *can't*—let them—*do* this—to *children*."

On the other side of the room an aardman growled. The
energumens continued to stare at us in silence. Luther Burdock pointed at one with a shaking finger. Behind their thick
plastic lenses, his eyes were filled with tears.

"My daughter!" he said, his voice shaking *"That was my
daughter."*

I moved back, reaching for Jane's hand. My heart was
pounding, my mouth dry. Because, looking at the man sitting
there before us, with his shock of long hair and his deceptively mild brown eyes, I had no doubt whatsoever but that
this was Luther Burdock—whoever he was, and however old
he was—and that he was completely, utterly insane.

The room was silent. Jane took my hand, looking from
Burdock to myself and back again. At their workstations the
energumens turned blank, unsurprised faces toward us, then
one by one swiveled back to their monitors. The argala whistled and murmured to herself. The remaining aardmen
crouched with eyes fixed on Luther Burdock, the stumps of
their vestigial tails thudding against the cold floor.

For several minutes all was still. And then, from somewhere in the darkness of the caverns echoed the sound of
footsteps. A measured tread, a sharp clicking as of metal
boots striking the stone ground; but boots that belonged to an
extraordinarily light-footed soldier. Jane and I looked around
anxiously, but Dr. Burdock was oblivious.

"Savages," he said to himself. He bared his teeth and
jabbed at something invisible. *"B-brutes."*

In the labyrinthine passages the unseen figure approached
slowly. A minute of silence when he reached the bridge; I
could barely see a slender form moving behind the scrim of
water and candlelight. Then came a small *thump* as whoever
it was jumped to the floor. Jane pulled away from me, her
head craned to see what was emerging from the darkness.

A soft sound as he entered the chamber. The aardmen
growled softly. Luther Burdock alone seemed not to hear it;

not to hear or care. The mad fire in his eyes was extinguished. Once again he looked at us quite calmly, only a sheen of spittle upon his lips showing that he had ever been anything but this placid figure.

"We still have a great deal of work to do," he said absently, his brown eyes soft and bland. "So much to do, and so little . . ."

I looked away, to where that unseen person began to cross the room. The leaping candlelight touched him, a little at a time. I saw his feet first, dainty as a stag's but sheathed in black metal; then his legs, also metal and coiled about with violet plasteel tubes. Then his torso, a confection of lavender and jet glass and chrome; and finally his face. A face that might have been carved from crystal, then stained with the crushed fruit of grapes and plums and all dusky things. A man's face, elegant and serene—save for his mouth. That was too wide and thin, and coiled as in laughter; but even the most sophisticated of replicants do not hold smiles well.

"Greetings to our guests," he said in a low, mocking voice. "I see you have found our spiritual father?"

My heart froze inside me. "Who—?" I gasped, stepping forward while Jane stared at him in dismay. "Who are you?"

The replicant turned until its eyes met mine. Emerald eyes, jade eyes, eyes that had swallowed every precious green thing in the world and held them hostage until the moment they would seize me again.

"Wendy Wanders," he said softly, and the hand that gripped mine was strong and sharp as an osprey's talons. "Well-met in Cassandra, sister mine."

It was the Gaping One. The hypostate I had called the Boy in the Tree, the demonic godling who had tormented me before fleeing me at the Engulfed Cathedral—but he had fled only his *human* form, it seemed. Now he had found another.

"No—" I stammered. "You are—you're—" But before I could finish, the replicant bowed its head.

"Metatron," he said with exaggerated modesty. An energumen glanced up at that voice, loud and clear as though announcing itself to a great hall; then turned back to its work.

"You know each other—very nice," said Dr. Burdock.

"Wendy?" began Jane, reaching for me, but I pushed her away.

"How did you get here?—what are you doing?—" I spat. "You were—you *died* back there—"

The replicant only looked at me, runnels of violet light flickering up and down his breast and across his face. "Oh, no," he said, and raising his voice, recited,

> " 'The immortal
> Gods alone have neither age nor death.
> All other things almighty Time disquiets.' "

Then he smiled again, showing that perfect curve of a mouth filled with perfectly even, ebony teeth. "There are great advantages to my present condition," he said calmly, and turned to Luther Burdock. "Doctor—there is some problem with the plasma cultivar, and as you said, we have so much to do before tomorrow evening. Perhaps you could—?"

Dr. Burdock started. "Mmm? Yes, of course, thank you thank you." He sighed and ran a hand through his hair, then looked at us apologetically.

"I'm sorry; but it really can't wait, you know. Time and tide and—well, Icarus. But you've been shown quarters? Given a—um, a uniform, and all that?"

"No!" Jane exploded. "We haven't been shown anything, and I'd like to know what in *hell* is going on."

Dr. Burdock pursed his lips, glanced over at Metatron. "Oh. Well . . . ?"

"What is going on," the replicant said in that slightly hollow, breathy voice, "is a war. A Great War, perhaps truly A War to End All Wars.

"At least," he added slyly, "it might be a war to end all *men*."

"How can you be party to this, Burdock?" demanded Jane. She pointed angrily at the energumens. "These are—well, they're *geneslaves,* is what they are, mutants and—well, I don't even know what *that* is," she ended, glaring at Metatron. "How can you defend them?"

Dr. Burdock raised his head. His eyes were ineffably sad. "Defend them?" he said softly. "But of course I must d-defend them. Didn't you hear me? Don't you understand? I *created* them. They are my—my children."

He gazed at an aardman lolling on the floor, its long legs splayed behind it like a dog's. "Those—what you call the aardmen—they were mine—my dogs, you see, Great Danes, I bred them quite carefully for many years. But *this* was not what I had in mind—"

He clenched his fingers into the semblance of a clawed hand and bared his teeth "You see? Not that. Not a sort of monster. *Dogs*," he said firmly. "They were supposed to be— well, they were supposed to be people, but like dogs."

Beside me I could hear Jane whisper, "He's a complete idiot." I recalled her at the Zoo, lovingly tending her cougars and red wolves and stags, and thought again how she had hated to see any of the others, the hybrid creatures that spent their pathetic lives hobbled halfway between humanity and wild things, doomed to die behind glass-and-iron bars.

Jane herself continued to stare balefully at Dr. Burdock. "Well, what the hell good did you *think* it would do? 'People like dogs?' And those other things—hydrapithecenes, sirens, those things they use as whores?"

Metatron looked on amused as Dr. Burdock shook his head. "No! You don't understand—*none* of those were mine, none of that was what I meant *at all*. It's so different now. All of that, out there—"

He flapped his hand, indicating the ceiling and the world beyond. "Why, everything's changed utterly. Everything's *ruined*. Dead, or dying, poisoned ... much much worse than in my time, you understand? *Much* worse. In my time you could still drink water without worrying about mutagens, you had to wear hoods and shades outside, but there were still *people* to wear them—not everyone had died because of the sun, or the wars. And we didn't have our politicians and armies floating around in space. It was—oh, it was quite different, we thought it was a horrible world, but it wasn't like *this*."

He looked forlornly at Metatron. "Can *you* explain it to them?"

The replicant shook his head. "Oh, I think not," he said lightly. "I think they understand quite enough. But, Doctor— the cultivar?"

Sighing, Dr. Burdock nodded and wheeled his chair from his desk. Jane looked around desperately, as though someone else might appear to help us, and finally demanded, "Just tell me something, Doctor, just tell me *one thing*—

"This war, this Alliance—all of this here, in these caves— what are you *doing*? Are you making more of them—of your—your children? Or are you just gathering the forces out *there* and bringing them here for safekeeping?"

Luther Burdock hesitated and looked at her thoughtfully.

"Well," he said at last. "Yes. There *are* more of them. I have been—I've been quite busy since he brought me here."

He inclined his head toward Metatron. "I've had a good deal of help, though. Some very distinguished people have worked with me. Had to—there've been quite a few advancements since—since before, when I was practicing. Rather marvelous things you can do with fungus and prions, accelerating the growth of clonal tissue, et cetera, et cetera. Quite remarkable genetic advances, which this Metatron has assisted me in learning. And, of course, psychosurgery is a delicate thing, and his hands don't shake."

"So it's true," I said numbly. Burdock stood, pushed his chair back into the desk, and smoothed his pants. "You're making more of them—more geneslaves—to act as soldiers? But that's no better than what the Ascendants have done."

"Soldiers?" He pinched the glasses on the bridge of his nose and squinted as though in pain. "Goodness no. Or no, of course, some of them are soldiers; but we have other plans. These aerolites, Apollo objects like Icarus—well, soldiers wouldn't be much use against *that*.

"So I've gone ahead with a plan I'd thought about before. Only of course the situation is much worse now than it was then. Here and elsewhere—"

He tipped his head to the ceiling, so that the candlelight glinted on his spectacles. Metatron continued to stare at him with that vulpine smile and those unblinking emerald eyes.

"A sort of—er—a general housecleaning seems to be in order," Burdock went on. "Ad astra aspera, you know. Through great hardship to the stars. But not soldiers, no, not really s-soldiers at all.

"What I had in mind," he said, stooping to pick up a bit of paper from the floor at his feet and crumpling it into a ball before tossing it away. "What I had in *mind,* after the whole general sweep-up was done, but sometime before Icarus's arrival, was launching this—um—*fleet* we've been gathering. Not warships," he added firmly. "More of an *ark*."

And turning, he left Jane and me staring openmouthed, as Metatron escorted him to his laboratory.

# 12

### The Return to
### the Element

**My father came to** me in a dream that afternoon.

"You must be brave, Kalamat," he said. He looked much older, his hair sifted with white and his face lined. "Whatever happens, you must remember that you cannot die. You must not be afraid of the dark." He hugged me close, his hands smelling of tobacco and curative chemicals.

But how was it that he could hold me, because surely he was still a man and small enough that I could sit him upon my knees? And why was his hair white, when he had never aged? My heart began to pound, but when I started to ask him about these things, his face changed, the skin grew bruised, black and purple, and then darkened still more until I was not gazing at my father at all but into the cold emerald eyes of the Oracle. I woke with a cry, my bed-hammock rocking so that it was a wonder I didn't spill out.

"Kalamat?" My sister Polyonyx stood beside my hammock, eyeing me doubtfully. "I heard you shouting from the media chamber."

I rubbed my eyes, yawning, then slid from bed. "I had a dream. A dream of our father."

Polyonyx nodded, reverently touching the tattooed pattern of red and black circles that marked where her breast had been. "Oh, but think, Kalamat! It is nearly time that he will truly speak with us—it is only a little while before we are passing over North America—and if it's true, if the Oracle did not lie—"

I nodded and yawned again ruefully. The end of the thousand days of my mortality was a bitter taste in my mouth during those last days on Quirinus. I had not slept well in many weeks, and had come to depend on these afternoon naps.

"Yes, yes, the Oracle." I frowned, recalling my dream, our father's face swallowed by the Oracle's brooding one. "Well, perhaps we should gather in the media chamber to await this marvelous thing."

Polyonyx nodded, her face glowing. "Oh, yes, sister! Many of us are there already—we were waiting for *you*."

I gave her an apologetic smile and turned away. The truth was, I wondered if our father would really speak. I alone among my sisters did not hear the silken voice of our brother Kalaman. Nor did I trust the Oracle Metatron, an unease I could not shake for all that I tried. He spoke of this Elemental war as a holy war, and of our kind as being of greater mind and heart than the humans we had slain; but to me it seems no better thing to die at the hands of an energumen than at a man's. I would ask my father about this; and also how it was that of all his children only Kalamat doubted, only Kalamat questioned and had bad dreams.

But for now I would join my sisters to await his coming. I kissed Polyonyx. When we embraced, I felt her trembling, and touched that quivering place in her mind that would brook no fear or caution of whatever would happen that evening.

"It is wonderful that this Oracle has come to us." She drew away from me, shaking back the hundred beaded plaits of her hair. "And that he will bring us to the Element to meet our brothers and sisters."

"Yes." I stared past her to the small round window that looked out upon the Ether, the cold darkness where the bodies of our Masters and my own dead sisters floated, waiting for a clarion that would never sound to wake them. "Yes, Polyonyx. Perhaps this will be a wonderful thing."

In the media chamber I found my sisters assembled. Those who had not offered their hair to the Mother had plaited it into long braids or drawn it back through loops of metal or plastic. All of them had painted afresh the tattooed images and rubbed dry ink into the cicatrices where their breasts had been. I was the only one who had not seen to such ministrations. I had forgotten. I had actually not thought of this as a holy gathering, but rather a matter of business: as when our Masters would have us join them to welcome a new diplomat in the docking area, or watch a parade of new prisoners taken from another colony—a ceremony meant to be a warning to us, as much as a celebration of some new triumph.

But to my sisters, this gathering was a great occasion.

"O Kalamat, think of it! We will see our father again—" Cumingia cried. She kissed me and the scent of violets lingered upon my brow.

"Our father," I repeated, and sighed. Why couldn't I believe this would really be him, Luther Burdock? "It will be a 'file transmission, sister, not our father in flesh."

"Oh, pff! Soon enough it will be him. When the Element welcomes us once more."

Cumingia whirled to face the great window that covered one side of the hall. In the void outside hung the shining sphere of the Element, a blue-green tear that our Mother Herself might have wept. "Do you think he will remember me?" she asked softly.

My father's face danced across my mind. I felt a pain in my breast, as keen as the memory of when I made my offering to the Mother. "Of course he will," I said. "If it is truly he, he will remember *all* of us. He said he would never forget and never stop loving us."

Cumingia pressed her face closer to the window. She nodded absently, her question already forgotten. "It is very far away, the Element. Does it have air?"

I laughed. "It has nothing *but* air, sister! Come with me, I'm tired of standing."

We knelt with the others, facing the recess in the floor that hid the 'file transmitter. All of us were naked save for the linen skirts that had been our uniforms and which we were still reluctant to cast aside. While it was made of fine and durable stuff, none of our Masters' clothing would fit an energumen. We had too much else to occupy us, to learn to fashion clothes when none were truly needed.

I frowned, smoothing my skirt upon my knees, and thought how that would surely change upon the Element. I knew the weather was variable there, and often threatening. I wondered what our other brothers and sisters had done for clothes. Some of my sisters on Quirinus had looted the personal stores of our dead Masters. They flaunted jewels upon their breasts, silver rings and bracelets looped around those necklaces long enough to fit over their heads, jeweled brooches and pillboxes strung together in gaudy jingling bunches. But I would not wear stolen finery. I thought it gave my sisters a heathenish look, like the savages the Masters think we are. In my memory I held the image of a ring that my father had given me, a simple silver ring with a knot of silver in its center. I would have worn that ring, if I had it with me now; but I did not. And at any rate, perhaps my memory was wrong. Perhaps it had been Cybele's ring and not mine.

"Look!" Over the soft laughter and chatter of my sisters rang out the thin childish voice of Hylas. "It is here, it comes!"

From the recess in the floor before us came a whirring sound. A thin radiant line shot up from the 'file transmitter, cooled from adamant to silver to blue. Beside me Cumingia squirmed and babbled to herself. My other sisters cried out, or whispered to themselves the hymn to the Mother. I alone was silent. The brilliant line burst. Rays of gold and blue light showered over us, and there was the man-sized image of the Oracle, standing within a shimmering dome of purple and gold. At sight of him my sisters fell silent, and Cumingia's hand grabbed mine.

"Greetings to Asterine colony Quirinus," said the Oracle in his clear strong voice, and smiled.

All around me my sisters nodded, their ebony eyes wide. Some of them shyly called out to him; but I remained still and silent and watchful. "As I promised, I have arranged for a live 'file transmission from your father Luther Burdock to be broadcast to this station, on the occasion of your imminent departure for Earth."

Cumingia gasped joyfully and rocked back on her heels. Even I felt my heart leap within me; but I bowed my head and listened as the Oracle continued.

"Within one solar hour the elÿon *Izanagi* will be docking at Quirinus. This is an Ascendant freighter that has been commandeered by Alliance troops for your journey to Earth. Shortly after the *Izanagi* arrives, three secondary transport vehicles will also dock at Quirinus, bearing energumens from

HORUS colony Helena Aulis. They will also be traveling on the *Izanagi*.

"You are to gather whatever possessions you have and assemble in the docking area, and from there proceed to the *Izanagi*. I have arranged for a separate 'file transmission to inform you of your assignments. After debriefing at Cassandra, most of you will be sent to Tripoli and the Balkhash Mountains, where there is presently a skirmish attended by energumen troops from your sister colonies Totma 3 and Hotei."

A small stir went around the circle at this announcement. Cumingia's hand in mine went limp and cold. I tightened my grip on it and shook my head.

"But that sounds like we will be fighting!" cried my sister Hylas. "We have never been in battle before—and what of our father? I thought we were to see our father?"

Other anxious voices chimed in.

"Yes, our father, where is our father?" Cumingia shifted and glanced at me uneasily.

"As I told you, sister," I murmured; but the Oracle went on speaking, as calmly as though no one had interrupted him.

"The Ascendant and Commonwealth troops know they are fighting a war they cannot win. But even if they could, a greater danger awaits them—awaits all of us—and only the chosen of Luther Burdock will survive this cataclysm."

At these words small cries echoed through the vaulted ceiling of the media gallery. Fear and frustration knotted inside me. Danger? Cataclysm? Why have us leave the safety of HORUS if some disaster awaited us upon the Element?

This must be some trick of the Oracle's, I thought, some madness that had infected his memory. I pried my fingers gently from Cumingia's hand and leaned forward, the better to hear what other threats this Metatron might give voice to.

"... so little time before the world will change—indeed, until the world the Tyrants knew will be no more! We have only to see if they will succumb to their own weapons, or if they will surrender and acknowledge their new Master."

*Their new Master?* Raw fury burned my throat and I nearly cried aloud. This was as the Tyrant humans would have it, a world parsed out among snapping dogs. In all my memories of him, I had never heard our father speak in this manner, of Masters and slaves. Had he changed so much? Or was there someone else in this extraordinary Alliance, someone more like our former Masters, and like them eager to build a new world upon our backs?

"Metatron!" I cried, but before I could say more, the Oracle raised a gleaming metal hand.

"No questions yet! It is mere hours now before your new lives begin, and I have here someone most anxious to speak with you."

Silence sudden and patient as death filled the room. Where the Oracle had been, another image shifted into view, a blurred white object that snapped into focus and became a face, a figure, a man sitting in a bent metal chair with his hands tapping restlessly upon his knees.

"Anyone there?" a soft voice called out. The man's eyes flickered back and forth, as though trying to locate the 'file camera. "Are you there? Hello?"

I gasped, all my fears forgotten.

Because it was him. Our father, the man who created us, Dr. Luther Burdock. He looked no different than he ever had—no white hair, no lines upon his face—only a small red spot on the bridge of his nose, as though the skin had been pinched away through much worry.

"Are they there?" he asked, turning to someone out of range. He looked back at us, or rather, back at the 'filing equipment—he still didn't appear to have seen us. He bent his head slightly and gripped his knees, as though he were about to plunge off the chair and into a great pit. He frowned, cleared his throat, and spoke again in a solemn tone.

"Well then. *Yes.* I am Luther Burdock, Dr. Luther Burdock, and I—I understand this is Coriolanus—I'm sorry, Quirinus—the Quirinus space station."

He grimaced, rubbed the bridge of his nose before continuing.

"I would like to—to *welcome* you! That is, I would like to extend to you a very big welcome from the members of the Asterine Alliance. We all hope you will be with us very soon. Thank you, and good night," he ended, smiling brightly, and glanced away again.

That smile tore something from me. Fear, I think, but also hope. Because there was no doubt but that this was my father: his face, his hands twitching in his lap; his voice, distracted but kind, and above all his gentle eyes, though they could not see me.

But I also knew that Luther Burdock had no real idea as

to what was going on within the Asterine Alliance. Just as he had never answered the summonses sent to him at our home in the mountains; just as he had paid no attention to the news on the telefiles, the reports of the growing power of the New Ethical Front and the United Party for Humanity. He was speaking to us only as a sop to some other person. Whatever enchantments of science had awakened him and brought him back to life, they had not changed him. As always, he wanted only to return to his work, whatever that work might now be.

The Asterine Alliance did not belong to Luther Burdock or his children at all. It belonged to Metatron. What plans he had for us, I feared to guess.

But our father had turned back to the 'filing screen. "I have to go now," he said. "But I understand you will be here within a few days. I look forward to meeting with you and discussing our future together. Until then—"

He bunched his fingers together and made an odd little salute. "Ad astra et cetera."

The image blinked into dead air. A moment of utter silence, and then chaos.

"It was Father!"

"Did you see—"

"He remembered! I could tell he remembered—"

My sisters ran to embrace each other, laughing and crying out across the room, pointing at the Element's watchful blue eye outside or running to the window to see if they could glimpse the elÿon that was to join us.

"O Kalamat!" exclaimed Cumingia as she hugged me. "You always loved him the best—you must be so *happy* now!—but what is it? What's the matter?"

She drew away from me, shaking back her beads and frowning. "Kalamat?"

"Don't you—how can you—they are sending us to fight, sister. Didn't you hear? They are sending us to war in the Commonwealth."

Cumingia's brow furrowed, and then she gave a small laugh. "But only for a little while. You heard what the Oracle said—in a few weeks we will be together again. Oh, Hylas!—"

She turned away to take another sister into her arms. I walked through the little crowd, saying nothing as my sisters reached to stroke my cheek or laughingly called my name. I shook them from me, my heart raging with anger and dismay.

War! He was sending us to *war*. How could they not hear that, how could they not care? I had only a handful of days yet to live, but I would not be spendthrift with them, squandering them in battle. It did not matter if it was a war we could not lose. It was not what we were made for, it was not what *I* was made for.

And I realized then that my sisters had no idea why they *had* been made. Their thousand days they accepted greedily, but without question. Our lives serving the Architects on Quirinus had been busy but not difficult. We were not treated cruelly, we had our dormitories and our pleasures, we were even permitted our Rites of Lysis, so long as they did not intrude upon the Ascendants.

But for the first time I knew that, for my sisters, this had always been enough. They wept when one of us died, wept as they recited the orison and bore the bodies to the chutes that would cast them into the Ether; but afterward they forgot. They remembered our father, but he was as a father in a dream, a father glimpsed in a cinemafile. Not someone to spend an entire lifetime mourning, even if that life lasted only a handful of days.

And there was the truth of it. I was not like them, no more than I was like our Masters. Something had gone wrong when they made me, some phantom turning of the road of cells and nerves that led to Kalamat. Instead of a creature as like to those others as one grain of wheat is to its kin, they had somehow created me.

And I remembered my father. I loved him. I could never forget.

At the window I stopped and leaned my head against the glass. I wept, remembering Luther Burdock. I remembered how he had held me when I was a child and awakened screaming in my bed, how he stroked my curls and whispered to me.

*"Do not fear the dark, daughter,"* he had said. *"The night can never harm you, and anyhow, soon it will be time for us to wake."*

I stared out at the Element, the world that in my memory had always belonged to my father, but now belonged to Metatron. And if like our great Mother I could have wept worlds, new worlds, my tears would have seeded the Ether with stars.

●   ●   ●

As the aviette auxiliary capsule approached the golden torus that was the colony of Quirinus, the energumens Ratnayaka and Kalaman sat apart from their brothers and stared outside. Travel in the aviette made Kalaman uneasy, a holdover from earlier terrorist forays when he had still feared discovery by the Ascendants and subsequent punishment or attack. He sat with his hands clenched in his lap, the flattened blade of his *kris* straddling his knees, and hoped they would arrive at Quirinus soon.

Beside him, Ratnayaka sensed his brother's fear. Any one of them might have known it; but the rest were clustered at another window, pointing to where the other two aviettes seemed to float like smooth flattened teardrops in the Ether. Kalaman's fear made his brother tremble. To think that Kalaman's mind was so open to his own! He brought his face close to Kalaman's and stroked his cheek, then let his hand rest upon Kalaman's thigh. Murmuring, Ratnayaka caressed the feathery impression of scars that Kalaman had drawn there with his *kris*. His brother was so beautiful. Even in these rare hours of calm, Ratnayaka could see the rage within him, filling Kalaman as blood or wine might fill a crystal krater, until at last it spills out and stains the hands of the libation bearer.

Ratnayaka knew this rage as another might know the kisses or sweet mouth of a lover; as Kalaman himself knew the much-fingered blade of his *kris*. It was a gorgeous thing, that rage, hot and quick as a culverin's flame; but it had been fired and tempered in the rarefied furnace of a HORUS colony. Upon the Element, Kalaman's ardor, his solitary and sanguine nature, would not fare so well. Metatron wanted generals and janissaries; the cool, sturdy grip of a revolver or blade that yields to a command, and not the lethal holocaust of a Shining.

Kalaman was such a thing: a shining creature, an uncontrollable flame. But Ratnayaka was a general—had he not been his brother's lieutenant?—a general and, if necessary, a sword that might be wielded by another's hand; say, Metatron's.

Ratnayaka smiled, looking upon his brother, and lovingly ran his fingers across a small raised scar upon his knee. No, there would be no place for Kalaman upon the Element. As for Ratnayaka himself: he knew patience as he knew the sound of his brother's voice. And some swords have been known to betray their masters.

"O Kalaman," he whispered.

Still his brother did not move, not even when Ratnayaka leaned forward to nuzzle his throat.

"We will finally see them," was all Kalaman said after several minutes. With wide, calm eyes he stared out the window, at the radiant torus and its beveled lines of lights, red and blue and violet. "All those sisters we have never met . . ."

Ratnayaka drew back from his brother and nodded, his eye a sullen gleam in his ruddy face. "We can teach them what we know. We can bring our secrets with us to the Element—"

He thought hungrily upon the brothers they had harrowed in the cool green-lit chambers of Helena Aulis. How lovely they had all been, how greedily he had fallen upon Djistra, the last to be consumed before they left the only home they had ever known; and how Kalaman had given all that final pleasure to Ratnayaka, taking nothing for himself.

Kalaman shook his head. "No," he said softly. His voice sounded distant, as though a 'file of Kalaman spoke there, and not the energumen himself. "That is a thing that belongs here—"

He turned and gestured at the tiny silvery image of Helena Aulis, already smaller and fainter than it had been, a star's sad shadow in the void. "—To that life. But this will be a very different thing—"

Kalaman frowned, then let his breath out in a long sigh. Beside him Ratnayaka dipped his head, so that his brother would not see his mouth curling with disdain. His hand tightened about Kalaman's thigh, slid up and beneath the short skirt of coarse linen, to stroke the muscles there, the smooth curve where Kalaman's leg cupped into his groin. Kalaman groaned, moved as though he would embrace his brother. Something cold and smooth licked at Ratnayaka's throat.

"Patience, oh, my brother," whispered Kalaman. He moved the *kris* so that its curved blade slid down Ratnayaka's chest, dragged it gently across his abdomen until it lifted the edge of his brother's skirt. "You will have me soon enough."

As he stared at his brother, Kalaman's eyes glinted black and fathomless. But Ratnayaka only laughed, threw his head back and laughed until the other energumens turned, their gaze flickering uneasily between their two leaders.

"Oh, yes," Ratnayaka said, the hunger racing inside him like some small razor-toothed creature seeking to burst out.

He brushed away the *kris*'s blade as though it had been a toy. "Oh, I will, my brother Kalaman. I will have you, soon enough."

In the empty docking chamber of Quirinus, I turned to my companions and said, "We have been betrayed."

Valeska Novus stared at me, her eyes betraying no emotion. "Imperator?"

"Who has betrayed us, Margalis?" asked Nefertity.

"I do not know, I do not know." I pounded my hand against the wall. My human hand—when I let it slide from the tiles, a shimmer of pale fluid remained. "Agent Shi Pei, someone who saw us boarding the *Izanagi;* perhaps Lascar Franschii. All I know is that we have been betrayed, and my mission has been thwarted."

Captain Novus shook her head. "Surely not, Imperator—"

"Yes!" I exploded. "It is worse, far worse than I or anyone else can possibly have imagined. The other memory unit has been found. The members of this geneslave rebellion are receiving their orders from the Military Tactical Targets Retrieval Network—"

"Your nemosyne!" cried Captain Novus.

Nefertity's voice was nearly inaudible. "Metatron."

I nodded. "He knows we are here. He contacted me in the *Izanagi*'s library; he intends to take me prisoner. It was he who brought about the destruction of NASNA Prime and the other HORUS colonies. Now he has ordered his geneslave troops to attack Cisneros, and he plans strikes against other Ascendant targets—against every military target in his database."

I fell silent, then finally ended, "The damage wrought by this so-called Alliance is far greater than I dreamed; greater perhaps than any holocaust wrought by mankind since the First Shining."

"But why?" Nefertity asked softly. "Why—*how*—could another nemosyne do such a thing?"

"I believe that Metatron intends to destroy all humanity, and set up the energumens and other geneslaves in its place. As to how a *nemosyne* could do such a thing, independently, with no human commanding it—"

My voice trailed off, and I stared at the scuffed floor beneath my boots. "I do not know."

At mention of Cisneros, Valeska Novus had paled. Now

she grabbed me. "We should reboard the *Izanagi*, Imperator! If this is a trap, we must get you—"

My metal hand closed about hers and she winced. "Oh, I think we will be back on the *Izanagi* soon enough, Captain Novus," I said. "It will be the quickest transport available to them, if he truly intends to return me to Earth."

"What of me, Tast'annin?" Nefertity's ringing voice held no fear within it. In the softly lit expanse of the docking chamber, she burned like the blue heart of a flame. "I would not be used as a tool for slaughter. I think you should dismantle me. At the least put me in my dormant mode."

I stepped toward a wide archway that opened into a broad corridor lit with golden sunlamps. She was right. It would be simple for the other nemosyne to alter her program, or even to interface with her and make Nefertity nothing more than an adjunct of Metatron. But it also might be possible to use her somehow to crack Metatron's governance code. And that might be our only chance of disabling the Alliance.

"No," I said at last. "You may be able to help us, if and when we are brought before him."

"But who found this other nemosyne? Who has programmed it to do this?" blurted Valeska Novus.

"I don't know. But my guess is that it was someone who had no real idea what they were doing. Even the cruelest and most mendacious of the Autocracy would not have ordered the systematized destruction of the entire human race."

"You seem quite disturbed by all this," said Nefertity, her words tinged with slight malice. "I had thought such emotions beyond the Aviator Imperator of the Ascendant Autocracy."

"I will choose whom I will serve, Madame Nemosyne. I am not a puppet or any man's slave—any *thing's* slave—and if this Metatron thinks so, he will learn otherwise. Captain Novus, please arm yourself."

"Yes, Imperator," Valeska Novus said, slipping her gun from its holster and glancing at me admiringly. An instant later her expression turned grim, as the sound of footsteps echoed toward us from the corridor.

"Captain Novus, you will defend myself and this nemosyne at any cost—you understand?"

She nodded, her dark eyes slitted as she went into a half-crouch in front of us. "Of course, Imperator," she said, and we waited to greet our hosts.

•　　•　　•

An announcement came over the Quirinus voicenet telling us of the arrival of the elÿon.

"O sister Kalamat, they are here! Do you think our father is with them?"

I turned from my sister Hylas in ill-disguised impatience. "Of course not. That 'file transmission was from the Element. And these are—I don't know *who* they are. Probably there is no one aboard but the adjutant. But I think you should go now—*all* of you—go to your chambers and wait for me to call you."

Hylas and the others who had come up behind her looked disappointed, but they knew I would brook no argument. They had few belongings, so there would be little to pack for our voyage. They had only, then, to wait.

"Go," I said. I started for the door that led to the docking area. "We cannot assemble for departure until our brothers have arrived from Helena Aulis. And I wish to speak with their leader, this Kalaman, before we do so. I will call you when we are ready to board the elÿon." As one, my sisters bowed their heads, hands crossed upon their chests, and left.

As I hurried down the hallway, a new announcement came over the voicenet, informing me that unauthorized personnel had entered Quirinus.

"An Aviator and two nonviable constructs," the net's ethereal voice chimed. "None have received clearance to leave the docking area."

My heart beat faster at the words *nonviable constructs.* Would this be the Oracle Metatron, somehow spirited from the Element to engage us in his battle plan? Too late I wished that I had brought a weapon. I turned the last corner, blinking at the unaccustomed brilliance of the sunlamps, and saw them silhouetted in the corridor.

There were three of them. After so many weeks without human personnel on board, they looked absurdly small to me, although only one of them was actually human—a woman, slight even by human standards and wearing the crimson-and-black dress leathers of an Ascendant Aviator. She knelt before the other two and trained a protonic gun on me.

"I am not armed," I said, and stopped. "Name yourselves."

Despite my cold tone I gazed down at them fearfully. Because surely here was the Oracle and another like it, come to wrest us from Quirinus and thrust us into the genewars below.

Behind the kneeling woman stood two constructs. One was a replicant in the form of a man cast in crimson metal and plasteel, wearing an Aviator's leather uniform and upon its breast the sigils of an Ascendant Imperator—the Aviators' blighted moon and the Autocracy's malevolent Eye of HORUS. And beside this crimson figure was another, as like to the Oracle as my sisters and I are to each other.

Only this oracle was silver and cobalt where Metatron was limned in violet and black, and in the likeness of a woman. But it was far more beautiful than any human woman, or even an energumen, because of the exquisite symmetry of its form and face, the shining array of lights that coursed up and down and around its crystalline body, silver and blue and gold and green, and its eyes: the purest jadeite shot with gold.

"Who—who are you?" I said, my voice catching.

The woman of glass and steel stepped forward, and as she did so, the kneeling Aviator clicked the safety on her weapon. "Greetings, sister," the replicant called in a low, clear voice. She raised her arms slowly, a motion that had nothing human in it at all, and rippling light fell like water from her hands. From within her breast I could hear a faint whirring as of hidden and subtle engines. "I am the United Provinces Recorded History project, copyright 2109, Registered Nemosyne Unit number 45: NFRTI, the National Feminist Recorded Technical Index, or Nefertity."

She paused. Behind her the female aviator shifted slightly, and took her eyes from me long enough to look at the replicant in surprise.

The woman of glass continued, "Greetings, good child. Hello, daughter of the suffering Earth. I greet you, whoever you are."

I gasped. She spoke of the Mysteries of Lysis, the words of the Great Mother in that hymn we call the "Latria Matrix." I dropped to my knees in amazement. The Aviator started, swinging her weapon, but the glittering construct called Nefertity stopped her.

"Who are *you*?" she asked softly.

"I am the energumen called Kalamat. Are you—are you an emissary from the Asterine Alliance?"

Nefertity glanced at the ominously silent replicant behind her. She shook her head. "No. We have no formal affiliation with anyone. We disembarked from Cisneros several days ago on the elÿon *Izanagi,* in search of another nemosyne, the military unit called Metatron. We thought it might be on Quirinus."

"No, Mother," I said, relief making me unwary and perhaps overbold. "He is not here—he is with our father, Dr. Luther Burdock, awaiting us upon the Element. But if you are looking for him, are you members of the Asterine Alliance?"

I frowned. I thought this would be very strange, if Ascendant Aviators had joined with the rebels.

"No." The crimson figure behind Nefertity spoke for the first time. He had a man's voice, a commanding voice, but so cold and wretched, it might have been summoned from a corpse. "We are members of no Alliance nor do we answer to the Autocracy."

"That is good," I said, "because the Autocracy has fallen."

The figure looked at me. I shuddered a little then, for though he had been modeled after a man and was smaller than I by a foot, his eyes like his voice were deathly cold. Human eyes, which I had never known a construct to have, the palest blue I had ever seen and the cruelest, too. "I gather you have aided in its defeat, Kalamat," he said. "Are there any human survivors on Quirinus?"

"None," I replied. I returned his gaze boldly despite my fears, and added, "And no Master died here from any act of Kalamat's, nor any of my sister's. But I would know your name, and your pilot's"—I tipped my chin toward the kneeling woman, who still clutched her weapon and watched me with grim intent—"and what business you have here."

The replicant shook his head. "My nemosyne told you: we are searching for Metatron. I had reason to believe he was brought here during a previous Ascension. I have since learned I was wrong. As for who I am—"

His voice rose to a roar that sent the sunlamps blinking their warning beacon. "*I* am the Aviator Imperator Margalis Tast'annin."

"Margalis Tast'annin!" I said in amazement. Of course I had heard of him—even the Architects, the chief-ranking members of the Autocracy, had spoken of Margalis Tast'annin with fear. He was the Ascendants' greatest warrior, the most famous Aviator since Ciarin Jhabvilos, but he was rumored to be mad; at least he had done things in battle that no sane man would ever do.

"Margalis Tast'annin!" I repeated, marveling. But then I

frowned as I gazed at that chiseled metal face, the corpus of molded metal that was neither body armor nor uniform. "But what have they done to you? Because surely you are not a man?"

Tast'annin bared his metal teeth in a grimace. "No, I am not a man, Kalamat. I am a *rasa*. Do you know what that is? A regenerated corpse. But my Ascendant Masters proved to have less of a will in my creation than I myself; and so I do not answer to them any longer. If I am no longer a man, still I am not *less* than a man."

I regarded the crimson-and-black leathers that he wore over his reconstructed body, the insignia of the blighted moon that shone upon his breast. "But are you still an Aviator, then? Can you be an Aviator and not serve the Autocracy?"

At this the woman kneeling before him lowered her weapon and looked up with great interest. Tast'annin laughed harshly, swiping at the air with one hand; and I saw that was all that remained of his humanity—those bleached dead eyes and that hand, its skin a sulfurous yellow and mottled with bruises. A corpse's hand. I shuddered, thinking of the rotted shell that had gone into making him. The Aviator Imperator cried, "Not an Aviator, then! Call me something else—rebel angel, rebel corpse, traitor—or no!—

"Call me this. Call me Sky Pilot. That is a name I have answered to before."

At this outburst his aide blanched and quickly returned her attention to me. I shook my head. "No, Imperator. Kalamat will call you Tast'annin. And this one—?" I pointed at the kneeling warrior.

"She is Captain Valeska Novus, Pilot Second Class."

"Very well. Will you ask Captain Novus to retire her weapon? As I told you, I am unarmed. Though if I had wanted to, I could have summoned my sisters here minutes ago. You might have withstood them for a little while; but not long, I think. And my brothers who are arriving now—I do not think you could withstand them at all."

At that Tast'annin smiled coldly, looking up at me with those orphaned eyes. "That is why she will keep her weapon where it is. Tell me, Mistress Kalamat—your Ascendant Masters, the Architects of Quirinus—what became of them?"

"They died of a plague brought aboard by a human spy, a delator from the Asterine Alliance. We did not kill them.

We did not even know of the existence of these rebels, until after many of our Masters had died."

"Did you try to save them?"

I shrugged. "There was nothing to be done for them. The delator died as well. We performed our own rites for them and gave their bodies to the Ether—you may have seen them as you docked."

A glimmer of unease passed across Captain Novus's face. She glanced back at Tast'annin, who stared at her for a long moment before saying curtly, "Put away your gun, Captain. For now, at least."

With the weapon gone I felt emboldened. I turned to the replicant Nefertity and asked, "But you, Mother—what are *you* doing here?"

She looked at me with those lovely clear eyes. "I was commandeered by the Imperator," she said. "Against my will, to help him find my brother nemosyne Metatron. Since my awakening I have seen little to endear humanity to me—indeed, I have seen almost nothing but cruelty.

"But if what Tast'annin has told us is true, and your Alliance has declared war upon mankind and intends their destruction, I want no part of that either. I was programmed by Sister Loretta Riding, a member of the Order of Divine Compassion, a pacifist and freedom fighter before the recusants drove her into hiding hundreds of years ago. My allegiance is not to Ascendants or rebels but to womankind, and so to humanity. I will not aid in its extermination."

"What of us, then?" I asked, my voice rising. "Do you support our enslavement by human Tyrants?"

"No, but neither will I support a world ruled by energumen Tyrants," she replied coolly.

I nodded. Overhead the lights dimmed momentarily. From the voicenet came a soft but urgent announcement.

"Three ancillary craft bearing the designation Helena Aulis have entered the docking area without formal clearance."

Captain Novus looked around anxiously, her hand at her weapon.

"Those are our brothers from Helena Aulis," I said. I crossed to where a small monitor was recessed into the wall and switched it on. Blurry images of the three aviettes appeared on the screen. After a moment I switched it off again and turned to the others. "On Helena Aulis there *was* a violent rebellion. All human Masters were slain and many of them tortured. I did not support this or even know of it; I am merely informing you of what happened. The surviving energumens have contacted my sisters and told them of their union with the Asterine Alliance. Now these rebels are here. With them, we will be transported to the Element via your elÿon.

"Their leader, my brother Kalaman, says that the Oracle has told them they will breed with us. Our lives will no longer be governed by an Ascendant clock. We will be as humans; we will live and reproduce as humans do. *But*"—my voice rose angrily as I continued—"this thing called Metatron, the Oracle you call a nemosyne—it is a chary freedom he offers. He brings us to the Element only to draft us into battle. You know that our lives are short: a thousand days, less than three solar years. Mine is nearly ended, but I would not have it end in battle.

"And I am the only one of my sisters who fears this Metatron. I think he intends to betray us. At any rate, I do not believe in exchanging one form of tyranny for another."

Captain Novus stared at me dubiously. "How can you breed? None of the energumens—"

"What of the rest?" broke in Tast'annin. "The others here on Quirinus?"

I bowed my head. "They will do as Metatron bids them. They believe it is the will of our father."

"Your father?"

I nodded. "Luther Burdock."

Tast'annin gestured impatiently. "Luther Burdock was executed shortly after the Third Ascension."

"No," I said softly, "he is alive. The Alliance found his DNA master and regenerated him. I have seen him. Last night, on a 'file transmission from the Element. There is no doubt in my mind but that it was our father."

Captain Novus whistled. "They cloned Luther Burdock? But you've only seen a 'file—how can you be sure?"

"I remember him," I said, nearly in a whisper.

"Remember him?" echoed Nefertity.

"They're clones of his daughter." Rage gave Tast'annin's crimson mask a demonic aspect. "The energumens all share her memories, up until the time of the first successful cloning experiment. There have always been rumors that he had set aside his own DNA material, in case he was assassinated."

"He is alive. I saw him," I repeated.

Tast'annin turned to Nefertity. "This is how they will be able to reproduce and have normal life spans," he said. "Among his effects there were records alluding to further work he intended to do with the Kalamat strain—he thought they could be manipulated so they could breed, and the matter of extending the life spans of geneslaves is really a very simple thing. But after his death this simple thing eluded us. Eventually the Ascendants turned it to their own purposes, shortening the lives of the geneslaves to a few years."

From down the hallway came a faint noise, the sound of the doors in the docking area opening.

"They have arrived," I said. "My brothers." I looked at Captain Novus and said, "They will be armed and will kill any human on sight."

"Captain Novus," Tast'annin began; but Nefertity cut him off.

"She is under my protection," she said in a low voice, but there was a cold warning in her tone. "They will not harm her."

She turned, and Tast'annin and Captain Novus with her. We watched as the doors slid open, and the rebels entered Quirinus.

One does not become an Ascendant Imperator without developing a certain intuition regarding the minds and motives of others—even energumens. I did not believe the one who called herself Kalamat was lying to us. But she seemed unsure of herself. Despite her brave words, her girlish voice betrayed her. She seemed restive, almost frightened. She had said that she was nearing the end of her thousand days. That might have been what caused her unease, but I detected a desperation in her that I feared might endanger Valeska Novus, if not myself and Nefertity.

And what of the others on Quirinus? How many were there, and were they prepared to fight against their brothers? Certainly Kalamat would be a formidable enemy. Over seven feet tall, golden-skinned, and with the enormous opaque eyes of her kind, like those black crystals the Emirate uses to hone their telepaths.

Still, there was something bizarrely childish about her, not in her appearance but in her mannerisms and voice. The nervous manner in which she moved her great long-fingered hands, as though unsure where to put them; the way she had called Nefertity "Mother." I had seldom seen an energumen who invoked in me any sense of pity, any feeling that I was dealing with another human being, rather than a heteroclite.

But Kalamat put me in mind of that other creature I had seen so long ago, her namesake at the NASNA Academy. It was not long after we had seen *that* Kalamat in our classroom that Aidan Harrow had killed himself. I always wondered if he had glimpsed himself in that pathetic chained monster; or if in his arcane books he had read something of the tangled destiny of those demonic creatures, perhaps the Final Ascension that Jude Hwong had predicted. A destiny that it seemed might now be coming to pass; a destiny the thought of which had driven Aidan Harrow mad.

But this was no time to dwell upon such matters. I heard the sound of many large, soft feet treading upon the floor. I looked up, and faced the rebels from the Asterine Alliance.

"Greetings, Imperator Tast'annin! And greetings to you, O my sister."

The same girlish voice as Kalamat's rang through the chamber. I gazed into the same face as well, though set within a young man's frame, and with skin of a deep red hue. He was not as extravagantly scarred and tattooed as Kalamat. His teeth were filed, and he carried a curved blade like those borne by janissaries within the Archipelago. An incongruously small blade within that powerful grasp, but no less threatening. Behind him stood others, perhaps a dozen or more. All were armed with flame guns and other weapons pilfered from their Ascendant Masters' armories on Helena Aulis.

It was the creature that stood beside Kalamat that made me wish I held one of those weapons myself. He was all energumen like Kalaman's own reflection made flesh, save that he had only one eye, and that eye gleefully ablaze with a hatred he took no pains to conceal. A number of tiny gold rings dangled from his brow. When he saw me, he laughed, and the rings jingled with a fine, chilly sound. If anything, he looked more dangerous than his twin, beautiful but with the contained madness of a caged eyra or jaguarundi.

"Who are you?" I demanded of the first interloper. I did not ask how he knew my name.

"You may call me Kalaman. This is my beloved brother Ratnayaka, and my other brothers—so." He waved the curved sword at those standing behind him. "We have been sent by our illustrious general Metatron to claim you and escort you to the Element."

There were not many of them. I counted thirteen, although I feared more might still be arriving. Along with those weapons, they might have stolen their masters' deathly manner. I had never seen such raw loathing and fearlessness in the face of any geneslave. Indeed, they might have sucked away my own courage. For as my suspicions regarding this murderous rebellion grew, so did a part of me that I had thought died in the Engulfed Cathedral. That will to life, which looks into the abyss and sickens, refusing to acknowledge the notion that there can be an end to humanity as there has been to so many other things in our world. But it was this same will that empowered me to parry with the rebels.

"I answer to no one, man or energumen. You may tell General Metatron that. Leave us now."

Kalaman hissed softly between his pointed teeth. He glanced at the one beside him, the one he had named Ratnayaka, and it seemed that a faint apprehension tugged at his eyes. Then he looked at Kalamat standing in front of us. He said, "Are you trafficking with Tyrants now, sister? Is that why you would not heed me when I called you?"

"Any fool can see he is not a human," Kalamat replied coolly.

"I did not say he was a human, sister. I said he was a *Tyrant*." Kalaman's eyes flashed. I thought he would strike her, but then his brother Ratnayaka spoke.

"You will come with us, Tast'annin," he said in that sweet high voice they all shared. He smiled, shaking his head, and the little gold rings made a faraway sound, like rain pattering on a dry shore. "And my sister, and—"

He looked from Captain Novus to Nefertity, and then turned to Kalaman, puzzled. "They have a construct, my brother—did you know of this?"

Kalaman frowned, drew his sword to his face, and stroked his cheek with the flattened side of the blade. "Is that your replicant?" he asked.

I felt a sudden surge of elation. Their Oracle had told them they would find me here, but it seemed that Metatron as yet knew nothing of Nefertity.

"It is," I replied cautiously. "And this is my aide-de-camp, Captain Novus."

Kalaman continued to stare broodingly at Nefertity. I waited for him to remark on how much she looked like Metatron, but he only muttered, "Yes. Yes, the Oracle told me you were accompanied by two others. But enough!—

"Do you come willingly, or—"

He raised his hand. Several of his brothers surged forward, weapons ready. I glanced at Valeska and Nefertity. Both stared watchfully at Kalaman and his troops. If Novus felt any fear, the energumens would never see it.

But they would kill her as soon as look at her, I knew that; might well end up doing so. I would not have her die defending me, especially as it seemed we had no recourse but to surrender.

"We will go with you," I said at last, "but not as hostages. No bonds, and we stay together. Else we will *all* die here."

I waited, half-expecting Kalaman to order his brothers to turn fire upon us, but he only shrugged.

"As you wish, Imperator." Like a child, he seemed already tired of this play. He turned to Kalamat, tipping his head to one side and gazing at her with intent black eyes.

"What of us, then, O my brother Kalaman?" she asked, her head raised as she towered above me.

"What indeed?" he countered, and smiled. "It is a small envoy you have sent to greet us. I have not seen our sisters yet. Where are they?"

Kalamat regarded him coldly: like Cruelty and Spite staring at each other across the room. Finally she said, "Waiting. They are waiting. Does your Oracle intend to make soldiers of us?"

Kalaman looked at Ratnayaka. "Soldiers? Yes, I believe we will all be soldiers. The elýon is bound for Cassandra. From there I do not know where we will go, but Metatron has hinted to me of a special journey that we chosen ones will make."

"No!" Kalamat cried. "I will not go! I have only a few days left before my death finds me. I will see our father in Cassandra, or else I will remain here."

Again Kalaman only shrugged. "As you will."

But at his side Ratnayaka narrowed his single eye and gazed shrewdly at Kalamat. He said, "Metatron will decide who lives and dies, and where they will do so. You had best tell your sisters to gather their things, Kalamat. Our elýon has an adjutant who is also scheduled to die quite soon." He grinned, showing pointed white teeth, and added, "Your brothers will grow hungry if we wait too long."

Kalaman hissed something at him. Ratnayaka dipped his head in a show of obeisance, then reached out and grabbed his brother's arm, pulled Kalaman until his face was inches from Ratnayaka's own.

"Dearest brother," he murmured, and kissed Kalaman on the mouth. Without another word he pushed him away, turned, and marched back through the ranks of waiting energumens. Kalaman watched him broodingly, then darted a glance at me, frowning as he fingered the hilt of his sword. Finally he strode across the hall to follow his brothers.

"You can't mean to go with them, Imperator!" Valeska Novus cried when they were out of sight.

"We have no choice," I said. "They would have killed you and dismantled Nefertity, and destroyed me as I tried to defend you both."

I turned to Kalamat. "You will go with us? To Metatron?"

"To my father. I care nothing for this Oracle, and less than that for my brothers." She spat and lay her hand upon her scarred breast, and looked over at Nefertity. "And you, Mother? Will you walk with me? I would like to speak with you and learn how it is you know the hymn to our Mother—and other things too. I would ask you of this Oracle called Metatron, which is as like to you as I am like my sisters—"

"Of course. We will walk together now, and talk," Nefertity said, holding out her gleaming hands toward the energumen. Kalamat took them and for a moment they stood there, the smaller shimmering figure of the nemosyne in the monster's shadow.

Then, "I will get my sisters," Kalamat said. Nefertity nodded. Together they walked back down the corridor toward the center of Quirinus. Valeska Novus and I watched them go. Then we turned and strode down the long hallway that had swallowed Kalaman and his brothers, to board the *Izanagi* and join Lascar Franschii on his final voyage.

# 13

## Icarus Descending

**Some time after Dr.** Burdock and the replicant Metatron had disappeared, a young man named Edward Dean entered the chamber where Jane and I sat anxiously eyeing the energumens and aardmen. "I'll show you to your quarters," he said, beckoning us to follow him over the waterfall bridge.

"You're the first person we've seen here, except for Dr. Burdock," Jane said as we followed him through a wide, downward-leading tunnel. Edward Dean looked at her, puzzled.

"But there are people everywhere." He was small and wiry, with short curling reddish hair and the same drawling voice as Trevor and Cadence Mallory. "I saw you with them—Suniata, and those others back in Dr. Burdock's office."

Jane shook her head. "I meant people—*human* people—"

Edward stopped, his gingery eyebrows raised in surprise and, I realized, embarrassment on Jane's behalf. He lowered his voice, looking over his shoulder to make sure no one else had heard.

"Oh, but those *are* people, Jane," he said with great earnestness. "Everyone here is treated just exactly the same.

That's the whole meaning of the Alliance: no more slaves. Everyone is treated *the same,*" he ended firmly.

"Except for human prisoners like us, I expect," said Jane.

Edward shrugged, pulling at the frayed collar of his blue uniform. "I don't expect you're actually prisoners. I mean, you're members of the Alliance, aren't you?" When we said nothing, he read it as agreement. "Well, then, you're not prisoners—you're rebels," he finished, and walked on.

"Rebels, huh," Jane repeated, looking after him balefully. "Well, among your rebels, have you happened to see a chimpanzee—a *talking* chimpanzee, name of Miss Scarlet Pan? She was abducted by one of your rebels. An aardman. Fossa. He was at Seven Chimneys with us."

Edward glanced back and stroked his chin. "A talking chimpanzee? No, ma'am, I don't think I've seen *that*. I don't think I'd forget it if I had."

Jane sighed. "No, I don't think you would."

The Paradise Caverns were endless. Each passage we walked through branched off into dozens of others, some luridly lit by electrical lights or sputtering torches, others black and ominous, with ineffectual links of rusted chain strung across their entrances and little handwritten WARNING! signs. Crates and stacks of supplies were heaped on the floor. Against the walls cartons and bales of wire leaned precariously, between sacks of grain and sodden bales of alfalfa and sheaves of wheat. Where grain had spilled upon the stone floor, it remained unswept and uneaten—I had seen no evidence of rodents, except for the bats that hung like sheets of drying meat in the reaches of some of the larger caves.

Weapons were treated with equal carelessness, and again I wondered how this so-called Alliance could be so successful. I'd seen no real evidence of organization, no one acting in authority except for the nemosyne Metatron and, perhaps, Luther Burdock—though Burdock seemed more of a human puppet, albeit a mad one, than he did any kind of leader. Yet somehow the members of the Alliance had managed to sabotage Ascendant and Commonwealth targets, at least enough of them to put by great stores of weapons and liberate those geneslaves who now called themselves rebels.

I slowed my footsteps every time we passed those seemingly forgotten piles of guns and other artillery. Once, while Edward Dean deliberated between which of two passages to choose, I caught Jane staring greedily at a row of sonic guns leaning haphazardly against one wall. Cadence had taken Jane's pistol before we left Seven Chimneys. It would have been absurdly simple for her to grab a weapon now—no one seemed to be guarding any of the stores. Indeed, except for two uniformed men who greeted Edward with loud, even overstated, cheerfulness, we passed nobody at all.

But Jane left the weapons where we saw them. Perhaps she felt as I did, that we had seen enough killing since we fled the City of Trees. Or perhaps she was simply afraid.

We did see plenty of old signs. Edward ignored them, but Jane made a point of reading each aloud:

**OBERON'S PLAYROOM**

**GRAMPY'S NICHE**

**THE FAIRY BALLROOM**

**ANGEL'S ROOST**

**MARTHA'S WEDDING CAKE**

Edward's interpretation of the same places was more mundane.

"That's the secondary war room."

"Aardmen's storage rooms."

"Mess hall."

"Dr. Burdock's meditation room."

"That's some big ol' stalagmite."

There were also many little metal placards warning visitors not to touch rock formations, informing us of the temperature inside the Caverns (fifty-five degrees Fahrenheit, year-round) and the hours of the cafeteria and the Gift Shop (ten A.M. to six P.M.). More foreboding were the hand-lettered signs, inked on cardboard or warped sheets of plywood, the uneven letters spelled out painstakingly, as though by hands unaccustomed to holding pen or brush.

ICARUS IS COMING

ARE YOU PREPARED?

AD ASTRA ASPERA, VICTORY IS OURS!

CASSANDRA WELCOMES ICARUS

THE NIGHT IS HIS — SOON ALL WILL BE HIS!

Most ominous of all were placards that showed only a smudged swirl of white or gray paint, daubed with black to indicate a sort of eye; and underneath a single word.

# ICARUS

"Who *is* this Icarus?" Jane finally demanded. We had been walking for nearly an hour, following a circuitous route that seemed deliberately planned to keep us from being able to find our way out again. Now we stood at a little crossroads where two tunnels met: a wide passage where cool air flowed and the sound of distant water echoed, and a second, very narrow corridor of stone, with rippling walls covered with the crystalline formations called anthodites, glittering spines that looked as though they would rip through your clothes if you brushed against them.

"Icarus?" Edward Dean stopped and eyed us suspiciously. "What do you mean?"

"I mean these signs." Jane tapped the corner of a damp curl of cardboard, her finger sending a filigree of limestone splintering from the wall. "Icarus, Icarus, Icarus. Must be an important person."

Edward shook his head. "Not a person, really," he said uneasily, then looked as though he had admitted too much. "You'll see tomorrow."

And we walked in silence once more, until the near-darkness grew oppressive and I finally spoke, as much to hear the sound of a voice as to learn something.

"Is this where Dr. Burdock lived? Here in the Caverns? Before—well, before things happened to him?"

Our guide shook his curly head. "Oh, no. He lived up there, in Cassandra with the rest of us."

He stopped, pointing at the ceiling, then explained, "I mean, *I* wasn't alive, all those years ago; but my great-great-great-grandfather was. Ran the toll booth there at the Shenandoah Bridge. Dr. Burdock had a place outside of town. Big research facility, and a house too. It's all still there, at least the ruins are—they burnt it before the Third Ascension. You know, when the fanatics took him and his girls and killed 'em."

His wide blue eyes glinted in the shadows as he went on.

"You know, Dr. Burdock is a real important person in these parts. He was a very great man, but he was a kind man, too. Cassandra was just a poor hollow in the mountains back then, but when he started his laboratory here, he gave jobs to a lot of people. We have 'files here of his work," he said reverently, "you know, the first experiments with Cybele Burdock and Lacey—that was his dog—and all sorts of other records as well. He always took very good care of the people who worked for him. My family never did, but just about everyone else here is descended from people who worked for Luther Burdock. The survivors, I mean, those who weren't killed when the fundamentalists came into power and tried to put a stop to his work. So you have to understand, when the Doctor came back—well, it was like Elvis or Jesus or one of the other Prophets rose clear up from the dead."

I thought of the Paphians' cult of the Gaping One and tried not to grimace. "Who brought him back?"

Edward stared at his feet, moving the tip of one worn canvas shoe to trace something indecipherable on the stone floor.

"Other scientists," he said at last. He glanced furtively up the passage before continuing. "People who'd fled the Ascendants—oh, a long, long time ago, well after the Third Shining at least. They'd been carrying on Dr. Burdock's work long after his death—trying to bring him back, you know. They came here, I guess, because Cassandra has always been a place where we don't like other people telling us what to do."

I thought of Trevor hunched over the steel tables bearing his gruesome harvest. "Trevor Mallory. Have you ever heard of him?"

Edward slitted his eyes thoughtfully. "No–oo, I don't think I have," he said at last. "Is he somehow related to Cadence?"

"She's his daughter."

"Hmm. Well, I guess someone might know him, but I don't. But that doesn't mean anything. Most of those people—the scientists—they came from away. I mean, they weren't native to here originally, though they've lived here for a long time now; and they've always kept to themselves a good deal."

"They're still here?" asked Jane, incredulous.

Edward ducked his head, his blue eyes darkening. "Some of them," he ended shortly, and stared into the darkness.

Jane and I glanced at each other, but Edward said nothing more. From somewhere came the faint *plink plink* of water dripping, and a dull rustling that might have been bats. After a minute I asked, "So you live up there, then?" I crooked a thumb at the ceiling.

Edward rubbed his head. "No; not anymore. For the last year I've been down here. Oh, I get up abovegrounds sometimes, but it's funny, you get used to it down here, you forget all about there's another place, another way of living."

He sucked his lower lip thoughtfully, as though trying to figure out if he could confide in us or not. At last he said, "You know, the Doctor says this is all preparing us for what happens next."

"Oh, yes?" Jane raised an eyebrow. "How's that?"

"Well, *you* know. Living in a confined space, the darkness, getting used to the genesl—I mean, the aardmen and energumens and the rest of 'em. Once Icarus comes, it'll be different from what we're all accustomed to. I mean, not so different for me, I grew up on a farm and we always had lots of animals—not that these other, um, *people* are animals, but you understand. It does take some getting used to, especially never seeing the sun."

"I see," Jane said doubtfully. "But—well, what *does* happen next? What was that he was saying about an ark?"

Edward Dean sighed, as though he were trying to explain something to a pair of thick-witted children. "Dr. Burdock has told us there is to be a Coming."

The way he said it made my flesh creep. "A Coming? What do you mean? Like the Final Ascension the Paphians talk about?"

He shrugged and looked furtively down the passageway. "I don't know about that," he said in a low voice. "I don't know much about Paphians, although maybe they've heard of it too."

"So what is it that's coming?" broke in Jane.

"Well, I don't understand it all that well, but Dr. Burdock says it's a sort of star. He knows about these things—he remembers from before, you see, back when he was first alive. He's *seen* it. When he was a young man, he said. Once every four hundred years or so it comes. Only this time he says it will be different. He says it will be *dangerous*. That's why they're trying to gather all these starships—you know, the elÿon, the Ascendant's transport fleet. You understand?"

Jane looked at me blankly. "Not really. Wendy?"

I leaned against the wall, the chill from the stone leaching into me. Inside my head I could feel a pounding, the dull pain that had once presaged a seizure but now seemed only to bring a blankness, a darkness where once visions had held sway.

"I don't know what this means," I said slowly. Dread seeped through my body, numbing as the cavern's cold. "But it sounds like—well, what kind of star did he say it was?"

Edward shook his head. "I don't know. But you understand, don't you—the Doctor remembers things from a very long time ago, from before we lost the power to see into the sky. Up there"—he made a circling motion with his finger—"up where the Ascendant Tyrants lived, they could still *see* things, although Metatron says they didn't *understand* what they were seeing. And because they didn't understand, they didn't warn us when they should have. And now Dr. Burdock says it's too late—for everyone but us. The chosen ones; the Asterine Alliance. *Ad astra aspera*—you know what that means? To the stars through great hardship. That's where we're going. To the stars."

Jane's ruddy face went dead white. "What do you mean, *to the stars*?"

"And Icarus?" I urged. "Who's that?"

He didn't reply; only turned and walked quickly down the tunnel. Jane swore and reached for my hand.

"Damn it, what the hell does all this mean? Stars falling once every four hundred years—I've never heard anything like it. If it's such a terrible danger, why didn't Trevor or Giles warn us? They seem to have known an awful lot about this place."

I bit my lip, recalling Giles's reluctance my first morning at Seven Chimneys, when I had asked him about the symbol and strange lettering on a cigarette pack from Cassandra. "Maybe they didn't know," I said doubtfully. "Or maybe they didn't want *us* to know."

Jane said, "What's this star, then? Is it a kind of Shining?" She rubbed her forehead, her eyes dark-shadowed in her pale face. "God, I wish we knew where Scarlet was."

"I don't know. I don't know, I don't know." My head

ached horribly, and I could hardly bear the touch of her hand upon mine. I pulled away, heedless of Jane's hurt look, and hurried after Edward.

We followed him for several more minutes in near-darkness, the passage narrowing until we walked in single file with our hands groping at the walls. Ahead I could see a line of very bright lights and hear muffled voices.

"This here will be where you'll sleep." Edward's voice echoed loudly as we finally stepped out of the narrow passage. Before us a large chamber seemed to have been carved out of the ocher walls, and in it many blue-clad figures sat or stood talking in earnest groups. Aardmen, energumens, even one of the profoundly strong and somber-looking starboks, its uniform torn where its massive shoulders had strained the fabric. But there were few humans. Only two that I could see, a man and a woman seated by themselves at a makeshift table against the wall.

"I've got to get back to work," said Edward. He stopped where the tunnel opened into the chamber and rested his hand on the stone wall. "Can I answer any more questions?" he added dutifully.

"Oh no, you've done a *fine* job of that already," Jane snapped. "I guess if we want to learn anything, we'll just have to ask Dr. Burdock himself."

Edward gave a small gasp. "But we don't bother the Doctor about things like that!" he said, aghast. "Especially about Icarus, or his"—he lowered his voice, looking past us to the energumens looming above the other geneslaves—"his daughter. He's very sensitive, you see."

"I'm starting to feel a little sensitive myself," Jane said threateningly.

Edward shook his head. "You've got to be *patient*—it will all be different after tomorrow. It won't just be the Doctor anymore. There'll be others we can all talk to, enough for everybody, enough to lead us all to the stars."

He sighed, as though remembering a painful memory. "You see, it's always much easier for him in the very beginning. Before he remembers it all. After a few months it gets difficult, and by the time a year's gone by—well, that's when we have the retirement party and start all over again. Only this time it will be different—"

"*Retirement* party?" My voice cracked in disbelief.

"Well, of course," Edward said, aggrieved. "*You'll* see—

but I really have to go." He started to turn away, stopped and looked back at us one last time, his plain face creased with concern.

"You *do* understand how hard this all is for him, don't you? I mean, you understand that he's not the first one?"

I tilted my head, staring into his grave blue eyes. "You mean Luther Burdock?"

Edward Dean nodded. "That's right." But before I could ask anything else, he spun and hurried down the dank passage, the *pad-pad* of his footsteps echoing long after he was lost to sight.

"Well, of *course* he's not the first one," Jane said peevishly. "Not unless he's about five hundred years old."

I thought of Trevor Mallory and his *cerebrimus* mushrooms, and said, "Well, no. He's a clone, that's obvious. Trevor and Giles said Luther Burdock practically invented the whole clonal procedure they used with the first generation of geneslaves. He must have stored some of his own tissue, in case something happened to him."

"Why don't these people just stay dead?" Jane said darkly.

"Shh—" I looked over to where the energumens had turned to watch us. "We'd best go in."

When we entered the chamber the geneslaves stared at us, the aardmen with reserved amber eyes, the energumens with a black intensity. We skirted them nervously, and Jane said, "It doesn't look to me like they're very happy we've joined their Alliance."

I nodded. Overhead a few electric bulbs hung from twisted strands, casting a weak white glare over the shadowy figures below. A few filthy pallets of straw or old cloth were strewn across the floor, along with battered pans and spilt wooden casks. At a table by the far wall the two humans we had first glimpsed looked at us guardedly. When we stopped in the middle of the room, at a loss as to where to go, the woman raised her hand and with a curt motion beckoned us over.

"Sit down," she coughed, flapping a hand in front of her mouth. Beside her the man nodded once in greeting.

"Thanks," said Jane in relief. There were a few spindly metal folding chairs leaning against the wall, and we pulled these over to the rickety table. "We're not—well, we're not really sure what's going on here."

The woman and man exchanged a look. Now that we were sitting with them, I saw how old they were, nearly as old as Cadence. Oily gray hair lay flat against their skulls, and their dark faces were mottled with sunspots and small lesions. A sour smell hung about them, rancid oil and urine and raw fear. They might have been brother and sister, or it might have been that age alone had stripped them of whatever had once differentiated them. After we sat, the woman clutched at the table, leaning forward and whispering hoarsely, "What have you heard?"

I shrugged and glanced at Jane. "Heard? We haven't heard anything. We just got here."

"We were hoping *you* could tell *us* what's going on," Jane added.

The man gave a little yelp and slammed his hands against the edge of the table. "I told you!" he cried, and the woman frantically slapped at him until he lowered his voice. "I *told* you," he wheezed, jabbing at the air with one skeletal finger. His eyes were bloodshot, and he was unshaven and so thin that his wrists protruded from his uniform like raw bones. "More prisoners, that's all they are—nothing but prisoners!"

"What do you mean, prisoners?" I looked at the woman. She shook her head, gesturing for me to be silent, then looked pointedly over to where the energumens continued to watch us. One of them laughed when it saw me staring, then, still laughing, turned back to its work. "They're holding you prisoner here?" I whispered.

The man's head bobbled eagerly on his skinny neck, and Jane stared at him in disgust.

"It's true," the woman choked. She reached across the table to grab my hands. Hers were gnarled as from much labor, but incredibly strong for one so thin and old. "After the harvest they dragged us from our farm and brought us here. They said we're too old, said we can't work anymore. Truth is, they don't *want* us to work anymore—they've brought us down here to die. It's only the young ones they keep alive—for *breeders,*" she whispered venomously. "They need some of us, you know, they can't go on without *some* of us."

"What are you talking about?" demanded Jane. "I thought you were all part of this—"

"Only the young and stupid." The man laughed bitterly. His bleary gray eyes included us in his judgment. "Like that idiot who showed you here—he don't see what it's got planned for them. The rest of us, it don't even care if we know—we're old and dying anyway. It just takes our land and our food for provisions for the rest of them, and drags us down here to rot."

"Who does?" I demanded, then lowered my voice when I saw one of the aardmen glance at me with eager sly eyes.

"That thing—" The woman made a gesture and spat. "The construct. Metatron."

"What have they got planned?" said Jane.

The man bared his teeth, the flickering light causing his dull eyes to gleam like two blood-streaked stones. "That Coming. The same thing Burdock's been talking about all these years. Just more of his craziness, is all. More of the same trouble the scientists been planning for five hundred years. Only this time they've brought that construct to back him up, and their Alliance, so's all the young people bought into it. They've got their ships on the other side of the mountain, all packed and ready to go. Just like that! Take our children and *pfft!*"

"But he's *mad*," the woman said, pounding softly at the table. Tears slid from the corner of her eyes, but she seemed not to notice she wept. "Who can believe any of it? A star coming from the sky! It's just another part of his madness."

"Her son," the man explained, leaning toward us and whispering. "Her son's joined up with them, thinks he's going to see the stars. But let me tell you, ain't none of 'em's ever going to see no stars. Ain't none of 'em's ever going to see anything except the inside of an Ascendant prison vessel been turned into an Alliance prison vessel."

The woman let out a sob. The man leaned back, his face suddenly gone slack with defeat.

I took a deep breath. "Tell me," I said, my voice catching, "about the ships. And Dr. Burdock. About his madness—what is it? What causes it?"

"It's his daughter," the man whispered, his eyes dull. "See, it takes a while for him to figure it all out, about the energumens and all. 'Cause, of course, he's actually been *dead* for all these years, but he don't know that, at least not at first. 'Cause he's a *clone*," he hissed, and from the flicker of fear and hatred in his gaze, I knew that he would have been one of those who would have burned Burdock and his child, all those centuries ago. "But when finally he understands what's happened to his little girl, the craziness comes onto him, and he just goes screaming into the night. But then, of course, he just starts all over. The whole damn thing just happens again. It's the same every time."

"Who's his daughter?" asked Jane.

"*You* know," insisted the man. "That girl, what-you-call-her. Cybele. The first one, the one in all the pictures, all the 'files. The one he cloned, the one they used for the energumens."

Suddenly I felt as I had when that grinning livid face had grinned up at me out of the black water beneath the bridge. "The energumens," I murmured, and looked to where they lolled against the far wall of the dim chamber. "He—he really did clone his daughter to make *them*?" And I recalled those creatures outside by the river: their immensity, the ease with which they slung upon their shoulders steel beams and sacks of grain; but also their oddly childish faces, their haunted obsidian eyes. "His *daughter*?"

The man nodded. "Of course she didn't look like that in the beginning—there were a lot of, well, *improvements* that the Ascendants made to the stock. Only Burdock, of course, wasn't too happy to find out his little girl grew up to be one of *those*. But Jesus Christ, that was what, four hundred years ago? Seems like a man could get used to anything in four hundred years."

"He hasn't been *awake* for four hundred years." The woman glared at him, then turned to me. "They only found him fifty years ago," she said, and sighed. "Fifty years and I should know: I was there. One of those scientists came out to our farm, looking for anything might have belonged to Burdock's labs back then. He wanted to sift through the ruins back of our fields, but I wouldn't let him. Showed him a gun and he went off quick enough," she said, smacking her lips at the memory. "But then there were others felt differently about it, you know, a whole lot of fools here had their daddies and mamas worked for Burdock back then. Soon enough that scientist found what he wanted—"

She made a strange gesture, dipping her head and touching her head and breast with her closed fist. "God save us, he found it all right. Found *him*, found Luther Burdock, and after a few years managed to bring him back, like he was never dead at all. Poor soul," she whispered, and for a moment a shaft of pity lit her dark eyes. "He wakes up and he don't know all these years gone by. He thinks it's only yesterday he had that girl and now she's gone. Nothing left but *them*—"

And shuddering, she cocked a thumb at the energumens.

I looked at them and shivered. The man nodded eagerly. "It happens every time, the same way. He doesn't believe it's really her. He keeps thinking he'll find her the way he left her, but when he realizes she's gone—" He made claws of his hands and raked them through his thin hair, miming desperation and madness. "Happens every time."

"How many times?" My voice sounded cold and much too loud. Because all of a sudden it all began to make sense to me, with that terrible kind of logic that adheres only in dreams. "How many times has it happened?"

"Who's counting?" the man said, and cackled.

"He starts out by helping us, or wanting to," the woman whispered. "Thinks he's going to save us from his crazy star. Then he starts to look at all his old 'files and records, and the madness comes onto him, every year it's the same."

"But this time it's worse," the man broke in. "He's *obsessed* about this imaginary star of his. And that robot Metatron backs him up, tells us all that the Doctor's right, there's this star headed *right for us.* Comes by every four, five hundred years, bang-o—but now who could count all that time? I know they say the Doctor saw it, I know they say he's that old; but I don't believe it. I think this Metatron just wants a way to kill off all us old people and send the young ones to their death. That's what I think."

I remembered the unearthly malevolent green eyes that had stared at me from behind Metatron's metal mask. It was easy enough for me to believe that he would do such a thing.

"And Dr. Burdock?" I asked. "What happens to him? Tomorrow night?"

"The scientists will come," the woman began; but before she could finish, a shadow loomed across the table.

"Will you help us with this packing?" one of the energumens asked in its clear, girlish voice. "Our fingers are far too big—" And it raised its clawed hands as it gestured for us to follow.

"I guess we're just going to find out when everyone else does," Jane said darkly. Her brown eyes were wide and shot with a desperation I'd never seen before. "God, I wish I had my pistol."

I bowed my head. "I don't think it would help this time, Jane," I whispered, and turned to follow the energumen.

"You must be brave, Kalamat," my father had told me in my dream. And so I made a show of fearlessness and went with the Sky Pilot and the Light Mother into the elÿon: myself and all my sisters. I had already told them that I had no intention of leaving this place where our father was; no intention of going forth to battle as the Oracle had commanded us. Brief as it was, my entire life had been tied up with a dream of my father. If I was to die now, I would die with him. And perhaps it would be as he had said, perhaps death would not truly claim me at all.

I was a fool. I thought my sisters would stay with me. I was expecting for Hylas, at least, and Polyonyx to follow me, and I was prepared to fight our brother Kalaman if he tried to prevent them and force them to accompany our brothers into war.

But my sisters did not care. They were being sent as janissaries to a place we had never seen, to a planet we had only ever glimpsed in dreams, but this meant little to them.

"O Kalamat! It seems sad, that you will not come with us, and that we will be going so far away," said Hylas. But she did not look sad. We were on the viewing deck of the *Izanagi*, staring out at the gauzy stars, the tiny fractured wheels of the distant fallen HORUS colonies. Her eyes had a molten glow, like jet with a faint silvery sheen. "But then you would be leaving us soon, anyway . . . perhaps it is for the best."

I nodded sadly, and with disappointment. Of course: why should my death matter any more than the myriad other deaths we had witnessed during our thousand days?

But then my sister suddenly grabbed my arm. "Look there," Hylas said, her voice rising slightly. Her forehead creased and her delicate mouth bunched into a frown as she pointed at a dark celestial body, neither star nor HORUS station, that bloomed behind the thick curved glass of the viewing deck. "What is that? A comet?"

I moved closer to her and looked out the window. I could see it in the distance, an amorphous shape that stood out against the nether background like a ragged hole cut in black silk. "A comet would not be so dark," I said, though the object had a somber halo, a dusky violet haze that surrounded it and seemed to pulse as we watched. "But I do not know what it is," I went on, and added, "And really, I do not care."

Hylas's frown faded. She tilted her head, gazing at me with soft black eyes, and said gently, "At least you will see our father." She reached out to trace the foggy outline of that strange radiant object upon the glass. A note of longing crept into her voice. "Will you tell him—will you let me know if he remembers me?"

A wave of sorrow overwhelmed me. I turned and embraced her. "You will know, Hylas. You will still be able to hear me within your mind." I stroked her forehead, then leaned forward to kiss her.

"Perhaps," she said absently. She pressed her face against the glass and stared at the strange pulsing glow. "But I do not think so. I think the sounds of battle will drive you from my mind."

I nodded, then whispered, "But not your heart, sister. Do not let them drive me from your heart." For the last time I looked upon her, the darkness at her back pierced only by the gleam of that black star without a name. Before she could see the tears upon my face, I fled the viewing deck.

The energumen Ratnayaka refused to allow Valeska Novus to stay with me during the elÿon voyage.

"I do not trust humans, Imperator," he said, flashing me a grin with those pointed teeth. "Our history is one of betrayals by them."

"As is my own," I began tersely; but he waved away my protest with a frown.

"No! Had not the Oracle ordered that we bring you and your entire escort to Cassandra, she would not be alive now—" His pointed white teeth glittered like a gavial's in the elÿon's rosy light.

I had Nefertity accompany Captain Novus to her room. I would not trust my aide alone with the energumens—I had seen myself how they would cannibalize humans and each other—nor did I wish for the nemosyne to be left unattended. Ratnayaka was not happy with this arrangement, but Kalaman grew angry when he complained.

"You will answer to *me,* brother, until we set foot upon the Element. And then you may answer to whomever you please."

Ratnayaka bowed, grimacing. He had removed the crimson patch from his eye; the wound there had begun to fester and seemed to pain him. I could see a speck of blackened metal embedded in the flesh, and guessed there had been a keek there once, or some other prophylactic monitor. But his remaining eye held enough black malevolence to intimidate an entire battalion of humans. When he turned it now upon his brother Kalaman, I marveled that the other did not cringe beneath its glare.

I thought then that Kalaman had not too long to live. He sweated as though from fever, and I never saw him eat or drink—though that was not unusual; many people do not feel comfortable eating during an elÿon voyage. But Ratnayaka too seemed consumed by something—illness or desire or perhaps that madness that stalks the elÿon's rubeous hallways.

"As you will, brother," Ratnayaka hissed at him. He turned to walk a little unsteadily toward where the other energumens had gathered upon the viewing deck.

"He is ill," I said to Kalaman.

"It is his heart that eats him," Kalaman replied. Sorrow seemed to vie with pride in his voice. "He does not like it that I am master now; but he will not turn against me." He looked at me with glowing black eyes and said, "You must understand, I have only a few more days left of my thousand. But it is enough, that I will look upon our father and this Oracle before I die; although it may be that our father will not let this happen to me. The Oracle has said there is a means now for us to outlive our destinies, that there is a way for us to grow old and bear young as humans do. Perhaps I will live long enough to see Ratnayaka harrowed by my children," he ended, and his eyes glittered cold as Ratnayaka's own.

Just then a cry rang out from the viewing area.

"O my brother, but look!"

Kalaman strode to where the others pointed, and I followed slowly, my metal boots striking the floor and sending sharp echoes across the chamber. A great foreboding hung about me, a cloud of fear that made me wish I had Nefertity by my side, or even Valeska Novus. Twice before I have felt this sense of brooding horror. Once as I stood upon a high place in the Archipelago, and looked down upon my troops as they walked into a tide of liquid flame and writhed in silent agony amid the waves of gold and black, like maggots dropped in burning oil; and again when I first gained a sort of half-consciousness within the regeneration vats of Araboth and realized I had lost forever the last traces of my humanity.

But this was a different sort of fear. It encompassed not only myself, but also all those I had ever held within my heart with either love or hatred. At the window I stopped and looked to where the energumens stood in a long line, some forty-odd creatures more monstrous even than myself, each reflecting the face and manner of the one next to it so that I seemed to look upon some ancient frieze showing a more ancient race than humanity, gazing out upon the stars.

"What is that, O brother? Can you see it?"

A few feet from where I stood, Kalaman's brothers and sisters moved aside to let him press himself against the window, staring out with those obsidian eyes. A moment later his voice came to me softly, filled with wonder.

"I do not know what this is. Perhaps *he* does—" He glanced over his shoulder and gestured for me to come closer. "Imperator—?"

I joined him at the window. On the other side of the thick glass the universe loomed, a darkness so vast that even the million stars pricked upon it seemed nothing but stray motes of light, put there perhaps by nothing but the will of myriad creatures that refused to acknowledge the void. At the rim of my vision I could just see the first sweet curve of Earth showing as we approached, and I knew that somewhere out of sight the moon waited, a hole in the sky through which we might escape that endless night. And then I saw what Kalaman and all the others were pointing at.

Had I still been mortal, my heart might not have been able to bear the sight. I felt a small gratitude that Captain Novus was safely drugged within her chamber. Slowly I drew my hands up before me and rested them upon the glass, my metal hand beside my human one, and stared between them at what was there.

In the formless void there grew a point of still greater darkness. In mass and color it was like one of those bursts of neutronic power favored by the Air Corps of the Habilis Emirate, which turn the deserts to black glass where they fall. As I watched, this celestial object grew deeper in color, showing within its heart shafts of blue and violet and crimson. All around it the atmosphere *glowed*—though that is too weak a word for it; it was as though it somehow swallowed the light of all those other pallid stars, then gave it forth again a thousandfold. In all my years I had never seen anything like it. Not in the shining azure skies above the Archipelago, nor in the desert's stark and frozen nights, or even during my tenure on the great glittering weapondecks of NASNA Prime.

All around me I could hear the energumens murmuring, their clear high voices bright with amazement and childish wonder. None of them seemed to be afraid.

"Imperator?" Kalaman's voice came again at my elbow, and when I glanced up at him, I saw that his face was lit with curiosity but no fear. "My brothers say they have been watching it for some time now. Some admit they first saw it days ago, but never spoke of it to me."

I drew back from the window, but then that word *watching* stung me like a thornfly. I recalled the thing Captain Wyeth had written of in the *Astralaga:* the mysterious star traveler, the Watcher in the Skies. He had described it as an object that his entranced crew had observed for over eighteen hours before it disappeared. A freakish black aurora, most had believed; some kind of solar flare that had come and gone within a matter of hours. But now Kalaman's crew claimed to have watched it for several days.

"Who has seen this thing?" I cried out. Several of the energumens turned to me, their beautiful faces calm, their colorless eyes holding within them the reflected flare of the Watcher's gaze.

"I have," one said in his lilting voice. "Many days ago. As the orbit of Helena Aulis shifted, I glimpsed it, like a violet lumiere flickering in the darkness. It is far bigger now than it was then."

Indeed, even as I stared, I could see that it was growing larger. Whatever it was, it still must be untold miles from where the *Izanagi* made its stately passage through the Ether. But it *was* moving. And it was headed toward the Earth.

"Imperator?" Kalaman laid his great hand upon my shoulder and gently turned me to face him. "What is this thing? Can you tell us?"

"I do not know," I said, my voice sounding hollow and disgustingly weak. "But I will find out." And I left them and headed for the library.

In the skies above the dreaming Blue Ridge Mountains hung a pinkish glow, a brilliance that faded only slightly during that long afternoon. By nightfall the aurora had grown to a splendent luminous sheet, rippling and coruscating so that the stars were swallowed by it and showed as tiny puckered flaws in the fabric of the night, if they showed at all. For the last few weeks this roseate glow had been glowing slowly brighter, as each day more and more of the Alliance's captured elÿon were brought here to join the fleet that now numbered nearly forty.

Had there been anyone to glimpse that fleet billowing across the haze of the Blue Ridge, they might have imagined the mountains were afire; but in Cassandra hardly anyone remained above ground. Those few energumen sentries guarding the entrance to Paradise Caverns were inured to the wonder of the elÿon. If they had had any say in the matter, they might have wished to be with their brothers and sisters, gathered deep within the mountain's granite heart, and there await the Coming they had so long awaited.

It was an evening in late summer. The fields that a few days ago had been bright and green and golden were now stripped to a dull viridian, laced with red where the raw clay had been exposed by the passage of agricultural machines. Once there would have been much celebration in Cassandra, for it had been a good harvest; but there were no humans left to rejoice. They had all gone underground, or else had been slain when they fought to keep their lands from being given as fodder for the geneslaves. Now the fields lay barren, and the scraped earth steamed in the dying light as the sun fell behind the glowing hills and the harvest moon began to creep above the shattered plain to the east.

At the base of the nearest mountain, where the energumen guards stood watch over the black mouth of Paradise Caverns, a tiny procession unfolded. They crept from down the mountainside: twelve white-hooded figures divided into pairs, and each pair carrying between them a long silvery object, like an aviette capsule or coffin. The eerie glow of the elÿon fleet touched their bodies with lurid pink and crimson, and made the capsules they bore gleam as though they were cast in gold. They moved in a silence that was unbroken by the song of night birds or insects, or the voices of those human onlookers who might have been expected to gaze upon this autumnal ceremony with awe. Even the sound of the encircling river was muted, as from respect—or fear.

But while the flame-tinged darkness made an eerie background to their vespertine procession, those white-clad acolytes were not quite alone. A single figure observed them, hidden by the shadow of the mountain itself: watched them and then raised its head to the fiery sky beyond. The light from the elÿon fleet sent waves of lavender and rose streaming across the dark and angular planes of its body. To one looking down from the billowing craft, the figure might have seemed that of a man, save for the faint purple lightning that played about its head, as though reflecting some storm behind its deceptively calm metal face.

So in silence Metatron watches the sky: waiting, waiting in the silence. The twelve hooded figures with their silvery burdens step slowly and carefully down the last few feet of the mountain. Their tiresome descent at last completed, they pause, shifting the weight of the caskets from shoulder to shoulder, then round the final curve of the path that will bring them to the cavern entrance. Still Metatron gazes heavenward, as the pairs of cenobites bear their softly gleaming caskets beneath the steel archway and into the patient darkness; and finally he is rewarded.

Above the dreaming mountain a spark appears, a thing like a glowing coal that grows brighter and brighter in the gaudy sky. As it grows nearer, it seems to billow and swell, surging through the air like a cloud traveling at impossibly high speed, until it is close enough that Metatron can without a doubt identify it—another elÿon come to join the silent fleet tethered above the Blue Ridge.

But this is a singular vessel. As he watches it float among its brethren, nudging between their rounded pink flanks, Metatron smiles and raises one metal hand as though in greeting. Then he begins to walk toward the entrance to the caverns, to initiate the last part of the ritual that will bring about his Final Ascension.

On the eastern cusp of the world the moon is poised to rise. The *Izanagi* takes its place among those other crimson clouds above the dark-bound mountains. Untold miles above them all, Icarus has begun the weeks-long descent from its parhelion passage. The regenerated corpse of Margalis Tast'annin shrieks in impotent rage as he sees too late the cold grace and frightful elegance of Metatron's last betrayal.

From within Paradise Caverns echos faint chanting and the sound of childish voices singing. The last Long Night has begun.

•   •   •

*Do not fear the darkness, daughter,* my father had said; but the thought of my sisters embracing their own deaths with such fervor had sickened and saddened me so that I could not bear to be with them any longer. I knew it would be a very little while before I stepped upon the Element for the first (and last) time. I would seize these few minutes to compose myself, to decide how I would greet my father, how I would ready myself for the death that awaited me there.

So it was that I took myself alone and headed for a chamber where I would prepare myself for our final descent. I was walking through the endless rose-colored corridors of the *Izanagi* when I heard a terrible cry. My heart froze at that sound: as though a man looked upon his own death and shrieked to see it there before him.

But it was no man who met me in that hallway. It was the *rasa* Tast'annin, fleeing from one of the elÿon's chambers with his hands raised as though to shield his eyes from some unspeakable torment. When he looked up and saw me, I wished he had kept his gaze from meeting mine. The harsh lines of that metal face were twisted into an anguished mask, but a thousand times more agony was trapped within his eyes. They were the only human thing about him, those eyes. Now it seemed that they sought oblivion, and seized upon me with horror and no hope of escaping whatever doom they had looked upon.

"Imperator!" I cried, and tried to make my voice commanding. I feared he had succumbed to that madness which seizes humans during an elÿon passage. "We are making our descent, you should be in your chamber—"

"The Watcher!" His voice rose to a howl, and he turned to slash at the air as though someone pursued him. "Your warning came too late, Aidan, too late!—All these years and we never *knew*—"

Without looking back at me, he raced down the hall. I watched him go, my heart pounding, then hurried into the room he had left.

It was the elÿon's library. A chair had been overturned, and several books lay spilled upon the ground where they chattered and sang softly to themselves. I bent to pick them up, silencing off their soft voices, then hurried to the row of empty carrels against the wall.

The first two showed no evidence of having been used in many months, but in the next I saw what I was looking for.

A shimmering image hung in the empty air above the desk, a fist-sized ball of perversely radiant darkness with a violet aura that streamed into the empty room like a beacon. Beneath it flickering golden letters spelled out the doom that Tast'annin had fled.

SEARCH REQUEST 10254799
SUBJECT: APOLLO OBJECT **ICARUS 3**
CARBONACEOUS CHONDRITE ASTEROID DISCOV-
ERED BY NORTHEASTERN REPUBLIC ASTRONOMER
GEOFFREY CHESTER [2097–2189]. FIRST APPARITION
RECORDED IN 2172, ALTHOUGH PRIMITIVE RECORDS
SUGGEST EARLIER APPARITIONS IN 1743 AND 1320
A.C.E. (CF MICHEL DEFRIES'S **ICARUS 3: HARBINGER
OF REVOLUTIONS?** AND MARJORIE ALACOSTA'S **THE
PLAGUE YEARS: AN ACADEMIC SUMMARIA.**) NOW
KNOWN TO BE THE PARENT BODY OF THE ATOYOTAN
METEOR SHOWERS, ICARUS 3 IS BELIEVED TO HAVE A
RECURRENT PERIOD OF 423–427 YEARS. PERTURBA-
TIONS OF JUPITER MAY CAUSE ITS ECCENTRIC ORBIT
TO COME DANGEROUSLY CLOSE TO EARTH WITHIN
ITS NEXT INTERVAL, WITH POSSIBILITY OF COLLISION
RATED AT .97 ON THE DARTMOUTH SCALE. ICARUS'S
DESCENDING NODE IS ANTICIPATED CIRCA 2522 A.C.E.
AT PRESENT, A UNITED EFFORT BY U.R.P.H. AND
MIAEYAN CONFERENCE SCIENTISTS IS UNDERWAY TO
DEVELOP SOME MEANS OF AVERTING THE CATA-
STROPHIC CLIMATIC CHANGES THAT MAY BE CAUSED
BY ICARUS'S RECURRENCE. SEE ALSO **KT EXTINC-
TIONS** AND ENTRIES FOR **WINSLOW, TUNGUSKA,** AND
**MANHATTAN (KANSAS) CRATERS.**

I read the words twice, then with shaking voice commanded the scholiast to give me the date of the entry.

"Twenty-two oh four," the scholiast intoned.

More than three hundred years earlier, and well before
myriad Ascensions and Shinings had seemingly destroyed any
records of the meteor's earlier sightings.

Before that moment I had never heard of Icarus. Neither
had the Imperator, nor I was certain, anyone else now alive.
It had been discovered during that brief golden period when
technology flowed between the nineteenth and twenty-first
centuries—discovered, dutifully recorded, and forgotten. This

is what Hylas had seen and pointed out to me on the viewing deck. This is what had driven Tast'annin from the room in madness. For many minutes I sat there, silent, staring at the letters shimmering in the air before me. Finally I commanded the scholiast to retrieve them, and turned away.

I thought of the Oracle. Another remnant of those days; one that seemingly had knowledge of many things forgotten by men and science and never known to us, the twisted children of men and science. I thought of my father, of the secrets he must have brought with him from that earlier time when we first lived in the shadow of the mountains. And suddenly it seemed to me very clear why we were bound for the Element, and what the special destiny was that the Oracle had promised to us. And were it not for the thought of my father there below, innocent of this and like all his kind doomed to death, I would have run madly after Tast'annin and, shrieking, given tongue to the fear that overcame me.

But I did not run. I did not cry out, or even weep, thinking of the world below and this strange thing poised like a hammer above it. Instead I walked very slowly to a room near the docking chamber. There I strapped myself into a hammock and waited, counted the minutes and waited until the elÿon's passage halted, and I could embrace my father.

In the navigation cell I found Lascar Franschii suspended within his web of light.

"You knew!" I howled. I grabbed his leg and yanked it, heedless of the sprung wires and cables whistling as they whipped around him. "You had to know, making these trips—"

Lascar Franschii bounced and jiggled like a toy tossed into a rubber net. "Imperator—" he began. Then the voice tube slipped from his mouth and he moaned. I reached and snapped one of the tubes running into his throat. A hissing as air escaped, and his chest began to cave in like a deflated balloon.

"*You knew!* All this time shuttling back and forth for your master, while *that* waits for us! How could you? How could you doom mankind, doom an entire *world*—we might have done something, might have tried to destroy it, but now it's too late—"

Without the voice tube, Lascar Franschii's voice came out in a barely audible wheeze. I pulled more tubes and wires

from his body, each one severing a vital connection; but still
he managed to gasp, "Your kind, Imperator—doomed *me*!—
what care—take to skies—*never*!—"

The last wire uncoiled in a serpentine tangle of red and
gray. Lascar Franschii's head lolled upon his shrunken chest,
his empty eyes bleeding and his mouth ajar. I stared at him,
my fist clenching trailing strands that gave off a putrescent
stench. Abruptly the floor beneath me trembled. Lights
flashed around the perimeter of the nav chamber, and
throughout the web that had held the adjutant, glowing white
lines appeared in meaningless patterns. A calm, hushed voice
breathed from the voicenet.

"The Human-Assisted Biotic Navigational System is en-
countering communication difficulties. We are now indoctrinating unassisted alternative landing procedures. All
biological personnel, please ready yourselves for docking in
Cassandra in four minutes. We are now indoctrinating unassisted alternative landing procedures. All biological personnel,
please ready yourselves . . ."

As the voicenet continued its soft chanting, I stumbled
from the room, heading for where Valeska Novus and
Nefertity slept in the innocent wombs of their safety ham-
mocks. The elÿon's truncated landing found me crouched before the door of their room, gibbering like an adjutant myself
at the thought of what awaited us in the sky outside.

I was safely in my hammock when the voicenet began its
emergency announcements. I recall little of the last minutes of
our flight. My mind was too full of thoughts of my father, of
the images that had sent a madness upon Tast'annin and
which my own mind could still barely grasp.

I don't know for how long I lost consciousness. Perhaps
a few minutes, perhaps an hour. It was one of the Maio servers that found me, its small cold fingers probing for a pulse
in my throat until I woke, gasping as from a terrible dream.

"Icarus!" I cried, then drew a shaking hand across my
eyes as it came to me that it was *not* a dream. The server
looked at me with its tiny unblinking eyes and said, "We have
made a successful emergency landing at Cassandra, former
Free Take of Virginia. All other biological personnel have ex-
ited the craft. I will escort you to the docking area."

It waited with an idiot's patience while I extricated myself
from the hammock, which was too small for an energumen

and left cruel red markings on my thighs and arms. Then I followed it into the main corridor. All around us the elÿon's walls pulsed, their color fading from fuchsia to soft pink as its random energies discharged into the air outside. I was going to my death, I knew that; but then so was everyone else. With slow steps I crossed from the hallway into the docking area, and then walked to meet the doors slowly opening to welcome me with the sweet warm scent of the Element.

There was no sun to wake Jane and me from our exhausted sleep. We were roused by an energumen, the same one who had drafted us into helping to haul sacks of grain from one cavernous room to another. It was backbreaking, mindless work, but afterward even the foul-smelling pallets on the floor were welcome, and the two of us collapsed into dreamless sleep. When we woke, there was no light, and the room was empty save for the one who shook us with her huge clumsy hands.

"You would have slept through everything," she said accusingly. "Come on now, and hurry."

"Is there water anywhere to wash with?" Jane asked plaintively, but the energumen only shook her head.

"In the river, if you want. But hurry."

We followed her, Jane pausing, before we climbed back over the narrow rope bridge, to splash her face and drink. I joined her, cupping my hands into the water and bringing it to my lips. It had a harsh taste, like stone rasping across my tongue, and was icy cold. I shuddered and stumbled back to my feet.

It was a different path we followed now, one that we had not seen before. In some strange way I felt that we were in the oldest section of Paradise Caverns: that part which had seen little of the hands of men upon its cold, forbidding walls. In other tunnels I had watched the energumens run with an awkward stooping gait, to keep their heads from grazing against the low ceilings. But here the ceiling reared so far above us that it made me dizzy to look up. There were few electrical bulbs, and these cast a faint glow that did little to pierce the gloom. The walls were crenulated, as though made of paper that had been crumpled into endless folds of cream and dull orange, stretching up and up until the darkness swallowed them. And while I could see nothing of the farthest reaches of the ceiling, somehow I sensed that it receded as we traveled onward; that the tunnel was widening to form a chamber huge enough that it could encompass a vast building, one as large as the Engulfed Cathedral or the City's Obelisk. Our footsteps sounded weirdly in that immense space, the slapping of the energumen's bare feet echoing until it seemed an entire unseen army marched there beside us.

Far ahead lights began to show in the darkness. As we grew nearer the passage, these grew larger and brighter, and finally we walked along a wide avenue strung with solar globes and smaller electrical bulbs, all of them leading into a vast cavern. The energumen glanced back at us, then paused and waited until we caught up with her.

"This is where they will be," she said, pointing.

The room was filled with people. Humans, energumens, aardmen, starboks, the wistful argalæ and hideous salamanders; all of them standing and staring patiently at the front of the cavern. Thousands of them, all in the worn blue uniforms of the Asterine Alliance, all with the same expectant expressions. But there were only a few hundred humans, and most of these were young, my own age or a few years older.

"God—look at them all," breathed Jane. She turned to me, her face flushed. "Scarlet might be here, Wendy!"

"You're right—" I felt a sudden rush of hope and fear at the thought of her small simian face peering up from the tattered folds of one of those ill-fitting uniforms. I grabbed Jane's hand and together we started to push our way through the crowd, when our energumen guide stopped us, one huge hand clapping upon our shoulders.

"You're to stay with me," she said. "Up here, to the very front." With what must have seemed surpassing gentleness to her—but forcefully enough to leave my shoulder bruised and aching—she turned us and directed us to the front of the immense chamber.

So with her guidance, we plowed through that mob. They were very well behaved for rebels, I thought. They scarcely acknowledged Jane and me at all, though some of the waiting energumens reached to stroke their sister as she passed among them, or called to her softly by name. I craned my neck, trying to see above the heads of the energumens and other geneslaves, but all I could determine was that the chamber was even larger than I first guessed. And there must have been an opening somewhere. The air was fresh, and carried with it the warm sweetness of a late summer's night, the smell of honeysuckle and wild roses and the dusty scent of goldenrod. Beneath our feet the floor had a decided downward slant, like a steeply raked stage, so that those tall enough to stand on a level with the energumens would have been able to see quite clearly whatever was happening in the distance. The waiting crowd was quite still, the energumens and aardmen nearly silent, the argalæ sometimes calling out in their questioning owlish voices. Only the other humans spoke to each other in low tones, and turned to look at us curiously, though no one greeted us. And we never saw Miss Scarlet, though I scanned the crowd for her desperately, and stared at every aardman I passed in vain hopes that one might be Fossa.

After many minutes of jostling we finally reached the front of the cavern. The crowd thinned out, until there was only a long line of energumens standing straight and tall, their faces innocently alert in the glare of the electric lights. Their hoods were thrown back and their tunics draped in loose coils around their long legs. They resembled so many beautiful statues, save only for the weapons they held; stunners and sonic guns and even swords, all of them human-sized, and so too small for those fearsome warriors, but still intimidating. Our guide led us to the center of this line. Two of her sisters moved aside to let us stand between them.

"Metatron has asked that they be brought here," she told them. "He said it is most important that they be able to see clearly." The other energumens nodded, staring down at us with their eerie, nearly pupilless black eyes. With a slight nod of her head, our guide turned and quickly disappeared into the throng.

"It will begin soon," one of the waiting guard told us, not unkindly. She moved aside to give us a better view. "Just a little longer until the moon rises."

I looked behind us. There stood rank upon rank of blue-uniformed figures, large and small, gargoyle warriors and sun-pocked women who must have been farmers, men whose hands held their weapons uneasily and aardmen who gripped theirs in strong, gnarled paws. All gazing toward the front of the room where I stood, so that after a moment I had to turn away, frightened by the sight of all those eyes.

But what lay in front of me was no more reassuring. It reminded me of an operating theater in HEL, only larger and brighter: as though it really *were* some kind of theater, one where unspeakable rituals were played out within the looming darkness.

At the front of the great cavern was a round raised dais, brilliant white and surrounded by small spotlights set about the stone floor. Upon the platform gleamed six metal boxes, man-sized and coffin-shaped. They were set upon six broad steel tables like those I had seen in Trevor Mallory's cellar, arranged in two rows of three; and in the center was a single empty table. I caught the same unforgettable scent that had tormented me at HEL, the sharp stink of iodine and alcohol and formaldehyde, the faint organic smells of neurotransmitting fluid and the saline solution used to preserve living tissue for transplants.

"Jesus, Wendy, what are they going to do?" Jane's voice came through chattering teeth. I pulled her close to me and stroked her hand, as cold as my own.

"I don't know." The horrible thought seized me, that it was for *me* those cold chambers were intended. But before I could say anything, the already hushed space grew deadly still.

"The moon," one of the energumens whispered, and pointed at the ceiling. I looked up, and with a gasp saw that what I had taken to be the closed darkness of the cavern's roof was in fact a great hole gaping there, a ragged vent that opened onto the night sky. This was where the smell of honeysuckle came from. And now I could also hear the distant chittering of bats, and see them in a thin skirling cloud fleeing into the night sky. Faintest of all came the sound of the great river on its slow sad course about the mountain. As I stared, a faint gleam appeared on the lower lip of the cave's yawning mouth, like a row of teeth suddenly illumined there. A pearly glow that grew brighter and brighter, until in the cave's opening there appeared the curved rim of the full moon, so brilliant that I had to shade my eyes. At sight of it a great sigh ran through the cavern. Humans and half-human creatures alike raised their arms, as though they were looking upon the moon's pale face for the first time; for the first time, or the last.

Gradually the sound of all those yearning voices ebbed, and the moon slowly tracked her milky path across the sky. Other noises began to fill the cavern; rustlings as of impatience, agitated murmurs, and the questing low cries of the argalæ. Beside Jane and me our energumen guardians stared fixedly at the raised platform, and so we set our gaze there too. There was nothing else to see, really, save the blue-clad troops of the Alliance stirring restlessly beneath the harvest moon.

And then suddenly a figure appeared on the dais, his arms raised in greeting. Silhouetted against the moonlight, a tracery of violet and pale lavender like veins beneath his metal skin: Metatron. Behind him marched a row of figures, human-sized and wearing hooded white tunics. There were twelve of them. They moved in utter silence, walking slowly until they reached the center of the platform. The last two bore between them a long silver capsule, like those already resting upon the steel tables. They paced to the single remaining empty table and carefully lowered the casket there. Then the other white-robed acolytes stepped silently across the dais until they stood behind the remaining capsules, faceless hooded forms like the ghostly figures of astral navigators in the most ancient of the Ascendants' 'files. There was something about the slow, almost rehearsed precision of their movement, that made me think that they had done this many times before.

*Retirement ceremony,* that nameless old man had told Jane and me. *The whole damn thing just happens again; it's the same every time.* I shivered, but even as I tried to look away, to seek vainly for some escape from the room, for some sign of help unlooked for—Miss Scarlet or Giles or even Fossa—I felt eyes upon me, *his* eyes, and helplessly stared up once more.

He stood there, a shining icon in black and lavender, and from within the perfect curves of his replicant's face those other eyes gazed down upon me. Green as new leaves, green as poison, *Eyes I dare not meet in dreams:* the vernal gaze of the Boy in the Tree, the Gaping One, imprisoned or reborn in that hollow construct's shell. His polished body reflected the liquid darkness above, the luminous moon: a lunar deity or a man made out of night. I tried to pull away from his gaze, fought against it as though it were a serpent casting its coils tight about my chest; but I could not. And then very slowly Metatron smiled at me, and in that smile I saw the death of all that I had ever held dear.

"Welcome!" he cried, his raised arms stretched toward the moonlit sky. Behind him the waiting figures tilted their heads back, so that shadows slashed the cowls of their pristine white robes, poured from their breasts to cover the silver capsules beside them. "Welcome to all the Alliance; welcome to Icarus!"

From a thousand throats, human and animal and heteroclite, came an answering roar. Only the other figures on the platform did not to reply. They remained stiff, hands resting uneasily at their sides, their hooded faces staring at god knows what as the cries and howls of the Asterine Alliance filled the cave. Smiling, Metatron waited until the voices died, until the last echoes flew from the cavern like the bats who had fled before them. When he dropped his hands, silence fell upon the crowd, sudden and ominous as a cloud extinguishing the sun's warmth. He turned toward one of the white-robed figures, and in a low, clear voice said, "We are ready."

The figure turned to Metatron. I could see nothing of his features, but somehow it seemed to me there was a reluctance in the way it responded, reluctance or perhaps even enmity. The acolyte nodded curtly, took a step until he stood directly above the silver capsule on the center table. He seemed to hesitate, and glanced up to where Metatron stood with coldly glowing eyes. The replicant nodded, still smiling, and the acolyte turned back to his task.

He bent over the capsule, his hands sliding from beneath the long cuffs of his robe to grasp a set of heavy-looking handles set into the metal casket. As he bowed, he tossed back the hood of his robe. For a moment his face was obscured as he yanked at the cover of the steel pod.

With a soft sucking noise the lid popped open. The white-robed acolyte fell back, glancing up at the silent Metatron. Then he turned to look out upon all those assembled in the cavern. His gaze swept across the line of energumen guards. I heard Jane gasp as it rested on her, then moved to link with mine. His eyes were blue, blue as irises, and showed no recognition of me whatsoever. His face was smooth and unlined, his hair black; but there was no doubt who it was. It was Trevor Mallory.

I had thought that our arrival upon the Element would be met with some fanfare, that there would be a boarding party or some other group of rebels there to greet me. But there was no one. The Maio server gave me a cool goodbye—"Farewell, Kalamat"—and left. In front of me, the loading ramp unfolded and spiraled down into the twilight. For a moment I felt a heart-stopping terror: we were still in the frozen wastes of the Ether, and in an instant I would be dead from trying to breath in that airless place. But air filled my lungs, warm and with a sweet taste like watered honey. I breathed deeply, and were it not for the sorrow that cut the edge of my exhilaration, I might have laughed with joy.

The *Izanagi* had docked beside a great shining mist-shriven tower, wrapped about with gangways and stairs and chutes for the unloading of freight and personnel. In the air around us I glimpsed other elÿon, bobbing like slowly deflating balloons. Fougas drifted between them, their smooth sides gleaming dull gray. Some had been sloppily painted blue and stenciled with the symbol of the Asterine Alliance, a pyramid surmounted by a black star. But most still bore the insignia of their original affiliates—the white hand that was the sigil of the Balkhash Commonwealth, the Emirate's yellow stars, the Eye of HORUS and blighted moon of the Autocracy's NASNA Aviators.

Behind me I heard footsteps. I drew back until the rosy shadows cast by the elÿon fleet hid me. I watched as my sisters left the *Izanagi,* and with them the brothers I had never known. They were quiet, silenced perhaps by excitement or trepidation, though my brothers held within their eyes something of hunger or desire, a small spark of untriggered violence that I had seen before, in the fearful grinding eyes of some of our Masters. They had daubed themselves with symbols of their allegiance, tattoos and scarifications of pyramids and stars. One of them bore in his arms something as limp and shapeless as a suit of our Masters' astral vestments. As he passed me, I saw this was the desiccated corpse of the vessel's adjutant, a forlorn creature that had been half-dead before we boarded. Down the ramp he went, to be given whatever obsequies they provide such hapless things on the Element.

A few minutes later my brother Kalaman appeared, and with him the one-eyed rebel called Ratnayaka. Between them they carried a figure that fought furiously, cursing as they held him up by his arms, so that his leather boots hung a full two feet above the metal flooring.

"Let me go!" he shouted. His voice sounded thin and surprisingly fragile in the open air. He looked frail too, where he dangled between my brothers, his crimson leathers askew upon his angular metal limbs and the red mask of his face twisted into an agony of rage and despair. "I will *not* serve him—I will *not*—"

At that sight a great sadness filled me. All the fury and controlled venom of the Aviator Imperator stretched like a taut line between Kalaman and Ratnayaka until I feared he would snap, and these last traces of his command fall limp as the adjutant's own body within my brothers' arms. But Tast'annin's strength and rage, at least, did not fail him. He railed ceaselessly as they bore him away, and while from another throat his last words might have sounded peevish or frightened, to me they rang in memory like my father's own voice, proud and deathless and indomitable—

*"I will not serve him! I will not serve—"*

That was the last I saw of him; the last I saw of any of them. Within minutes they were gone, the tall loping figures of my brothers lost in the fog. Of all the passengers of the *Izanagi,* only I remained. Obviously I was not deemed important enough to require an escort, energumen or replicant, to see me from the vessel. I stood alone behind the curved metal balustrade overlooking the long gangway that wound like a silver stair through mist and clouds of tiny flying insects, until finally it disappeared beneath the tops of trees that crowded the side of what I now knew must be a mountain. From below I could hear voices, my sisters calling out to each other and the hollow booming sound of a robotic Watchman shouting orders. For some minutes I stood and listened, until abruptly the voices ceased, as sharply and suddenly as though they had come from a vocoder that had been switched off. The silence was disconcerting, until I realized that probably they had all been herded into one of the other elÿon. I strained to see through the mist, looking from one narrow spiraling stair to the next, seeking to find any of my sisters ascending to their new lives aboard the warrior vessels. I never saw them again.

At last I could wait no longer. Soon someone would board the *Izanagi,* and if I did not want to be conscripted into service upon her or some other Alliance ship, I would have to leave. I still held within me the vision of my father, and it was this that finally give me the strength to take my first step down that long narrow walkway. The air was chill, cooler than it had been aboard the elÿon, but as I descended, it grew warmer, and with this new warmth came the scents of many things: flowers, water, the stored sunny heat of trees just being released into the evening air. I had thought it would be a

strange thing, a frightening thing, to first set foot upon the Element. But when at last I stepped from the smooth metal path
onto stony ground, it was as though I had awakened to find
myself within a familiar dream.

I remembered this place. I remembered the trees and their
names—oak, aspen, stunted pines—and also the sounds that
came to me. Noises not unfamiliar because I had heard them
on 'files and in the stim chambers of Quirinus; but still it was
thrilling, almost terrifying, to hear them now—wind, water,
the faint rustling tread of an animal's footfall in the bracken—
and to see in the darkness not far from me a blurred light that
I knew was the mouth of a cave. We had come here once,
long ago, my father and I. There had been smiling men in
uniforms, and a shop where they sold rocks—I had thought
that was funny, to sell rocks when there were so many lying
about the floor of the cavern. Indeed the whole place was
nothing but stone, a castle of granite and limestone and shale
embedded in the heart of Mount Massanutten. The name
came back to me too, as surely as if it had been my own; and
now my heart was pounding and I had to clasp my hands
tightly to keep them from shaking.

Because of course he would be here. Of course he would
remember—it was the last thing we had done together, before
the operation. He had brought me here, to show me that even
in the blind core of the Earth there could be light and beauty;
that even things seemingly as cold and dead as stone could be
seen to have a life, and in stalactites and anthodites could
grow and bloom like roses.

*See, daughter? Nothing to be afraid of, nothing at all . . .*
He was here. He was waiting. *Do not fear the darkness,*
he had said. *We will always be together, somewhere, . . .*

And so I walked unafraid into the Paradise Caverns, nodding silently to my brothers and sisters who stood guard beside the main gate, and went to meet my father.

"Wendy! It's Trevor—it's *him*—" Jane's shrill voice cut
through the room as she grabbed me. "But he's dead! We saw
him, he *died*—"

I could only shake my head, my hands clutching helplessly at the air. The tall man on the platform shook back hair
that was dark and thick as a girl's, and his eyes, though beset
by a kind of despair, were blue as Cadence's had been. Once

again I saw him standing in the cool darkness of his cellar, the corpses behind him glowing faintly as he spoke.

*Of course, it has some interesting applications for clones. . . .*

And I heard Giles's grief-ridden voice choking, *He made plans. . . . I know I'll be with him again. . . .*

"It's his clone," I said hoarsely. "The scientists, the ones they told us about—they're all clones. They've been hiding here for centuries. That's where Metatron came from. That's who found Luther Burdock . . ."

I fell silent as one of the energumens looked at me warningly. I stared back up at the dais, where Trevor stood gazing into the recesses of the open capsule. His expression was absolutely desolate. Whatever he glimpsed there might have been enough to sear away his vision and leave his eyes dead and blank behind their scrim of flesh. When he looked away again, all the light was gone from them. He seemed as aged and blind as the man I had known at Seven Chimneys.

"What are you waiting for?" Metatron's voice held an undercurrent of mockery, and slivers of emerald light danced from his face as he looked at Trevor Mallory. "You have done this before. There's no time now for dalliance. Begin, else I will do it for you."

Bleakly Trevor nodded. He edged closer to the open capsule, then bent over and tugged at something inside. In all the vast space around us I heard nothing, save Jane's ragged breathing and the slower, measured breath of the energumen guards. On the dais the other hooded acolytes stood still as columns in their white robes, their blank faces turned toward the center table. Then something scrabbled at the inside of the capsule. A horrible sound, as of a corpse trying to claw its way from its coffin. Trevor frowned and leaned in more closely, then drew back, his face knit with dismay as a hand appeared above the pod's metal rim.

On the other side of the pod another hand clutched at the metal. A moment later a head emerged: a face so white it seemed incandescent, topped by a shock of thick brown hair. For an instant he flailed at the air, and I thought he would fall back inside. But then he righted himself, and slapping away Trevor's hand, he sat up.

"Luther Burdock," whispered Jane. "But—what's *wrong* with him?"

"It's his clone," I said dully.

"But the other—the one we saw last night—"

"Dead," I whispered. And somehow I knew that was the truth of it, and that we would never see *that* Luther Burdock again.

This one was naked, and so pale, it seemed he must be terribly ill, but I knew that was not the case. I knew it was that he had just been born. He pulled himself clumsily from the silver pod, swinging his legs over its edge and nearly falling, then jumping to stand shakily beside Trevor Mallory. He was naked, his skin almost translucent and gleaming as though oiled. His face had the unformed look of an infant's. There were no lines to show where experience had been etched upon him, no scars or blemishes. His skin had a soft, slack look to it, as though the muscles beneath had never been stretched or pulled. He looked around blankly, then stared down at his feet. His eyebrows knit together, and slowly he drew his hands to cover his genitals.

Trevor Mallory looked impatiently at the nearest acolyte, who pulled a faded blue robe from beneath his white one and handed it to Burdock. Burdock stared at it, his expression so transparently innocent that I felt I was looking at one of those robotic models of the human brain that the Ascendants used to train their surgical technicians. When Trevor put a hand upon his shoulder, he started, then quickly shrugged into the robe. He shook its folds from his face, squinting painfully. With a wry smile Trevor reached into a pocket and drew out a pair of spectacles. For a moment Luther Burdock only stared at them. Then he grabbed them and slid them onto his face.

With that small gesture he truly seemed to be born anew. Behind the plastic lenses his brown eyes glittered. The innocence drained from them, and he made a fist of his hand, opening and closing it as though deriving strength from the motion. He looked around, his face carefully set to show no fear, no surprise. He stared at the white-robed acolytes, the six remaining capsules with their hidden burdens; then gazed out upon the ranks of silent waiting creatures. At sight of them his composure seemed to fail him. He turned to look first at Metatron and then at Trevor Mallory.

"Where is my daughter?"

His voice was tremulous as an old man's. When there was no reply, he called out again, loudly and with such a commanding tone that far overhead the stalactites gave off faint tinging echoes.

*"Where is my daughter?"*

A nearly imperceptible shifting among the acolytes on the dais. Trevor Mallory bowed his head and stared at the floor. Metatron's emerald eyes flashed, and he started to raise his hand, as though to point out at the massed throng of geneslaves. But before he could do so, there was a sharp cry from somewhere behind the stage. The hooded acolytes looked around, alarmed. A murmur passed through the crowd, as people and geneslaves murmured and shuffled, striving to see what was happening. On the dais Luther Burdock stood with his hands clenched at his sides, and stared accusingly at Trevor Mallory. Behind him Metatron turned, slowly as though pulled by wires. His torso glowed a brilliant angry purple.

*"Daddy!"*

Up the steps leading to the dais a figure ran: taller than any human girl, but with a girl's voice and a girl's sweet smile. An energumen, identical to all the others in that place save only that she had no uniform, and her voice, if anything, was purer, more childlike than that of her cloned siblings. She wore nothing save a loose short linen skirt that hiked above her knees. Her skin was tawny brown and she wore her hair long and in loose curls. Smooth white scar tissue marked where one breast had been. Tears streamed from her huge black eyes as she ran to where Luther Burdock stood with his back to her. She towered above the cowled acolytes, pushing them aside. "Daddy, it's me!"

Luther Burdock whirled about. At first his gaze swept across the cavern, but then he stopped and looked anxiously back and forth, as though searching for someone shorter than himself. "Cybele?" he called, then cried out more desperately, *"Kalamat? Cybele?"*

"Father—"

And looking up he saw her: a grotesquely tall scarred figure, arms outstretched, her ecstatic voice ringing throughout the cavern. For an instant his expression was one of joyous disbelief. Then, like petals falling from a faded blossom his joy fell away, and there was only disbelief and horror.

*"No!"* He fell back as she lunged to embrace him.

"Daddy!"

She had nearly fallen herself as she grabbed him. For a

moment he struggled in her arms, his white face twisted with loathing; but then he stopped. I could see another expression trembling there, another kind of disbelief, but tempered with wonder and not fear. Above him the energumen looked huge, a giantess toying with a man. But her face was tender, and glowed with delight as her huge hand cupped his face and she gazed down at him with an expression of transcendent joy. And suddenly it seemed that he recognized her, recognized *something*. A soft cry escaped him, a word I couldn't understand. Slowly he opened his arms to her embrace.

"Stop her! *Save him!*"

The shriek came from Metatron. Violet lightning shimmered as his hand sliced through the air and he pushed one of the acolytes forward. The man moved slowly, as though frightened and unsure what to do. But then, as though the replicant's will moved him, he suddenly darted across the stage. I glimpsed a silvery dart at the energumen's breast, something flashing at her throat like a feeding hummingbird. Luther Burdock shouted, tried to stand and push away the other man, but the energumen held him too tightly. She seemed not to notice her attacker at all. A last stab of argent light; then she threw her head back, staring at the shadows high high above. Her great hands fell loosely from Luther Burdock. As slowly as though she lay down to sleep, she drooped back upon the floor.

Burdock stared at her, then savagely pushed the other man aside. He knelt beside her, pulling the huge head into his lap and leaning over her so that his tears fell onto her face.

"Kalamat."

His head bowed as he called to her, his hands stroking back the tangled curls from her forehead. She moved, and I could see how she smiled, how she tried to lift her hand to graze his cheek. "Oh, daughter," he moaned, and bent closer. Her eyes closed, though she still smiled, a child falling into a long, sweet sleep. Suddenly she cried out. Her back arched violently. One of her hands moved as though to grasp his, dropped with a soft thump to the floor; and the great figure was still.

For a moment all was silent. Then Metatron shouted a command. Several energumens loped up to the platform and dragged her body out of sight. Behind them Luther Burdock screamed and fought, as Trevor Mallory and another energumen restrained him. The other white-clad figures remained beside the six silver caskets, quiet as ever, though from the way they turned and looked from one to another, I imagined they were as dismayed by this turn of events as those watching them. All around us I could hear whispers and growls, and from the energumens scattered angry shouts. But then Metatron stepped forward and cried out, "It is a sacrifice, that is all—another sacrifice!" He turned to Trevor Mallory and hissed, "Now—do it *now*."

Trevor moved back, so that only the other energumen held Luther Burdock's struggling form. Burdock's glasses had come off, and his faded blue uniform was stained with blood. He kicked fiercely at his captor and spat at Trevor Mallory.

"You let them kill her! You did that, you and the others— you ruined them all—how could you, how *could* you?—"

Trevor stared at him, his eyes round and empty. Next to him stood the acolyte who had killed the energumen. His hand still held a red-slicked knife. As I watched he took a quick step forward and plunged it into Luther Burdock's breast. With one fluid motion he stepped back, as though he had performed a task he had long rehearsed.

I cried out, aghast, and Jane beside me. But all around us we heard nothing. Luther Burdock's hand slapped against his chest, gripped the handle of the knife. His fingers tried to close about it, then splayed open as he sank to the floor. Blood spread across his white shirt. His head tipped backward, so that he seemed to stare up to where the full moon hung like a huge calm face above the cavern. In a moment he was dead.

Metatron stepped across the platform. When he reached the corpse, he stared at it with impassive emerald eyes. Trevor Mallory glanced down as well, but his face was contorted with anguish. He quickly turned away, gazing at the acolytes still waiting patiently beside the remaining capsules. He made a sharp slashing motion with one hand and barked out an order.

At the signal the acolytes bowed over their silver caskets. They fumbled with unseen clasps, slowly pulled at the lids until each was open. Clear liquid streamed from the metal, pooling on the floor and staining the hems of the acolytes' robes. My stomach churned and I fought to keep from running. I did not want to see what those caskets held.

At the steel rim of first one and then another, hands appeared, fingers grabbing at the metal and clutching frantically, slipping on the wet surface. As before, they rose awkwardly from their resting places, liquid streaming from their shoulders and torsos so that they glowed in the moonlight like quicksilver.

"Jesus," breathed Jane. "It's *him* again."

It was Luther Burdock. *Six* Luther Burdocks, each one naked and shivering, all shaking their heads and looking around with the same blank infant's gaze. As they stumbled from their cells, they were helped by the acolytes, who wrapped them in stained blue tunics and wiped their faces with the hems of their own robes. When they had finished, the white figures stepped back, turning to where Metatron watched with a small smile.

"Very good," he said at last. "You may go now and ready yourselves for departure."

The twelve acolytes filed from the platform. Last of all went Trevor Mallory. When he passed Metatron, he stopped and looked at the replicant with burning eyes. Metatron met his gaze coldly.

"Well?" he asked. I waited for Trevor to say something, to shout or strike the inhuman figure standing there; to show some of the rage and brilliance I had known in Trevor Mallory. But that man, it seemed, had died at Seven Chimneys. After a moment he lowered his head and shuffled after the others.

Now only Metatron and Luther Burdock's clones remained, six pallid men blinking and abashed in the moonlight. I cannot explain to you how horrible it was to see them, how they made my flesh crawl until I wanted to do as that acolyte had done and murder each of them with my own hands. They were so alike, so new and utterly unformed, with adult faces and bodies and expressions that were not so much innocent as mindless, so many empty vessels waiting to be filled.

Metatron stepped forward. He tilted his head, regarding them coolly. For the first time in many minutes he turned his unblinking gaze upon the throng assembled in the cavern.

"We are ready now," he cried. He swept his arms out to indicate first the clones of the ancient geneticist, and then the rows of watching energumens. "We have the wisdom of Luther Burdock, the strength and numbers of his children, and enough of humanity to serve us all. Across the globe our brothers and sisters are set to join us as we harvest what remains of this poisoned earth and leave it to be burned clean.

Let the avenging star come: we are ready to flee this world and find another!"

The cavern erupted into cheering and shrieking howls. I pulled Jane to me and held her close as the floor beneath us shook and overhead the stalactites trembled.

"I will lead you," cried Metatron. "I will lead you in this last holy war, and I will have as navigator the mightiest of our Enemy's warriors—"

His voice shook as he raised his hands and turned. And that was when I saw him, borne forth by two energumens as though he were a man in flames, his face and body destroyed and encased in scarlet metal. Only his eyes remained to betray who and what he had been: the Ascendant's greatest hero, the Aviator Imperator Margalis Tast'annin.

"*No!*" His voice rang out, louder even than Metatron's. My own voice echoed his disbelief. On the platform the six men who were Luther Burdock looked around uneasily. "*Let us go!*"

Metatron only smiled at the Aviator's fury, and looked past him to where two other figures stood at the edge of the platform. One struggled within her energumen captor's grip— another Aviator, her face bruised and bleeding but her eyes aflame with hatred. But the other figure stood quite calmly, between two energumens who kept back from her as though afraid. When I saw her, I gasped, because her form was identical to that of Metatron, only encased in shining silver and blue and gold instead of violet and black. And as though she had heard me, she turned, seeming to search through the crowd until her eyes caught mine. Eyes as green and lambent as Metatron's own; but where his held malice and cunning, hers were mild, seemingly unperturbed by all the chaos around her. Foolishly, I started to speak, as though she might hear me. Indeed, from the way she tilted her head, it seemed she did. But then Metatron's voice cut through the air, and she turned away again.

"Take him to the elÿon *Izanagi* and install him as its adjutant." Metatron pointed at the energumen who held Tast'annin. "Since he was careless enough to kill its navigator, he shall act as mine, and guide us to the stars."

Tast'annin howled again, but his voice was lost amid the clamor. He fought to turn his head, looking desperately through the crowd; and then his gaze pierced mine. Jane gasped and try to pull me back, but I did not move, only stared at him.

It seemed that the roaring around me grew still. In all that vast space there was only myself and that crimson figure. Of his human visage nothing but a tormented metal mask remained. His eyes were so pale, it seemed all color had fled from them at sight of things more terrible than I could imagine. But what was most frightening was the expression in those eyes. I had seen them to hold only rage and lust to power. But now they gazed upon me pleadingly and with a desperation so awful, I nearly wept. It seemed I heard his voice again, as I had heard it in the Engulfed Cathedral, telling me, *"Even I must serve something . . ."*

It was as though he heard my thoughts. The silence was riven by a great roar as he threw his head back and shouted, *"I will not serve you, Metatron! I will not serve!"*

Metatron laughed. "You have no choice, Tast'annin. None of us have any choice. We all serve a greater master now—"

He pointed at the sky. A few bats still skimmed across the entrance to the cave, flecks of black skating across the moon's weary face. On the platform the pale blue-robed figures of Luther Burdock looked up, as did everyone around me. It seemed that the moon grew paler; that it faded until it was little more than a blurred cloud floating in endless darkness. For a moment it was as though we stared into some terrible colorless dawn. And then I saw what it was that drove the moon from her rightful place.

At the edge of the sky a radiance appeared, a brilliance that was not white but tinged with blue and red and violet and yellow, like a shattered rainbow hurled into the night. It grew brighter, and brighter still, until I shaded my eyes with my hands and gasped, my voice lost amid a thousand others.

"Behold Icarus!" cried Metatron. "My son in his glory, the burning boy! He comes, he comes. Within weeks he will be here, and the mutilated Earth at last will be freed from its suffering!"

Within the blinding light that filled the sky a point of black appeared, a small ragged core of darkness like an eye or mouth. It did not move or grow larger; only seemed to pulse slightly, like a heart beating within the void of heaven.

"This is *crazy!*" Jane yelled. Fear and anger tore at her face; anger won, and she pounded her thigh with her fist. "I thought the Aviator was mad, but this—" She grabbed me and began to pull me through the crowd. No one stopped us now; no one noticed us at all. "Come *on*, Wendy, this is—"

I yanked back from her. "We can't go," I said numbly. My eyes remained fixed on the deathly radiance above us. "Don't you see what that is? Metatron is right—it's some kind of falling star—where can we go?"

And in answer I felt huge hands close around my arms, and saw Jane fall back into the grip of another energumen.

"You're to come with us," it said. I did not fight, and after a moment I saw Jane grow limp as well. She shot me a last desperate glance as they led us from the shouting throng, up the steps to where Metatron stood surrounded by his cloned aides. I tried to shake off my captor's hands, and looked to see Tast'annin and his two companions being led out through the cave's entrance. Then the energumen pulled me, until I faced Metatron upon the dais. He looked at me and smiled, his eyes throwing off shafts of jade and emerald where they caught the reflection of Icarus's brilliance. His voice was mocking as he greeted me.

*"Come with me, ladies and gentlemen who are in any wise weary of London: come with me: and those that tire at all of the world we know: for we have new worlds here."*

Another wave of shouts and snarling cheers rose from the cavern. Metatron stretched out his glowing hand to touch my chin.

"You are very fortunate, Wendy Wanders, to see the new world that awaits us."

For a long moment he held my gaze, then pushed me away. "Bring them to the *Izanagi* with Imperator Tast'annin," he commanded the energumens, and stalked from the platform.

Behind me in the darkness Luther Burdock's corpse lay cold and still. Above it the empty-eyed forms of his cloned brethren stared impassively into the sky. I turned to where the corpse of the creature who had called herself his daughter was sprawled upon the floor. As I stared, it seemed to move slightly. Then it *did* move, and with pity and horror I watched as it struggled to turn its head. At my side, Jane's brown eyes grew wide with rage and compassion.

"It's not dead yet!—" She looked around for help. "They can't just leave it, it's not—"

But then our guards tugged gently at us. Jane's hand groped for mine as we were led away. A warm wind poured through the cave's opening, and a rosy light that came from the elÿon fleet.

All about us the air echoed with cries of wonder and terror, as the geneslaves and people of Cassandra gazed into the sky. I walked slowly before my captors, as though I were being taken to see a marvelous surprise and wanted to delay the pleasure. I could see my own shadow in the brilliance cast off by Icarus, faint as though drawn in water. I continued slowly until someone pulled Jane's hand from mine. Then I was borne by arms larger and stronger than my own, up the rocky slope to the billowing crimson cloud that had swallowed the Aviator Tast'annin. I did not look back, though I heard Jane calling for me, her voice faint as a swallow's thrown into the throat of a storm: not then, nor when the energumen carried me into the waiting elÿon.

With surprising gentleness, it bore me through twisting passages, until we reached a tiny room where it placed me in a sling. Carefully it bound me against the rigors of the journey, then showed me where soon tiny needles would prick my wrists and throat and lead me into dark sleep. Only after it left did I turn to gaze out the tiny window opening onto the world.

It was all there: trees, rocks, mountains, river: all of it, and people besides, weeping and pointing at the sky; and aardmen and energumens and the other geneslaves, rushing to herd their charges into the waiting elÿon. For many minutes I stared out, never lifting my gaze to the sky. Not until the walls surrounding me quivered, and I knew the elÿon was beginning to take flight. Then I looked up.

There it was. Icarus, the falling boy, the black eye of fate gazing down upon us with that deceptively calm and brilliant stare. I could imagine his laughter, a sound that would rock worlds, and see his hand reaching for me, reaching for all of us: vast and implacable and terrifying. Soon he would be upon us; soon there would be no escape. But then like a cold kiss I felt the prick of unseen needles upon my flesh. Warmth surged into my veins. I saw the eye recede, saw the imagined retreat of the asteroid into the void; and in darkness fell into my final voyage.

In the darkness something warm and wet streams from Kalamat's breast. Behind her closed eyelids she can sense a brightness, a warmth; the promise of something wonderful, something more marvelous than she has ever known. She can feel her father's hands upon her forehead, so small and light they might be leaves blowing across her skin, and though the raging pain does not subside, her body relaxes, her hands unclench, and her jaw, and she tries to speak.

"Daddy," she chokes. "Daddy—"

Even as she winces from the effort, she smiles; because this time she knows he hears her.

"Do not fear the dark, daughter," he whispers. His voice catches, and something falls upon her face. "The night can never harm you, and anyhow soon it will be time for us to wake."

"Yes," she wants to say. "Yes, I know." But already death has drawn a noose tight around her, yanking words and finally thought from her mind.

And then in the darkness Kalamat smiles, knowing her father is there amid all those small struggling figures, knowing that even death is a small thing now. Because she has found him, she has found him at last.

## ABOUT THE AUTHOR

ELIZABETH HAND is the author of the novels WINTER-LONG and ÆSTIVAL TIDE. Her short fiction has appeared in numerous magazines and anthologies, her articles and book reviews in the *Washington Post, Detroit Metro Times, Penthouse, Science Fiction Eye* and *Reflex Magazine*. She lives on the Maine coast with novelist Richard Grant and their two children, where she is working on a supernatural novel called WAKING THE MOON.

# 6 DECADES FREE

By subscribing to **Analog Science Fiction & Fact** you'll receive a **FREE** copy of 6 **Decades–The Best of Analog** with your paid subscription. Analog readers have enjoyed over 60 years of penetrating, absorbing science fiction and science fact. From the earliest and continuing visions of cybernetics to our ultimate growth in space–Analog is the forum of the future. Let the pages of Analog expand the realm of your imagination...as today's fiction turns to tomorrow's fact.